Diary
of an
ALASKAN MADAM

Lorina Ewing

www. alaskanmadam. com

Lorina's Touch Publishing
Durango, Colorado 81301

Published November 4, 2010 by Lorina's Touch Publishing

ISBN: 978-0-692-01189-8

Library of Congress Control Number: 20109388407

Printed in the United States of America
Ashland, Ohio

Dedicated to Bob and Amy Ewing.
Thanks for all your love and support.

ACKNOWLEDGEMENTS

Through the Lens (Durango, Colorado)
The Strater Hotel (Durango, Colorado)
The Carrie M. McLain Memorial Museum (Nome, Alaska)
Lisa Marie Jacobs, Copper Graphics, Durango, Colorado

Special thanks to my daughter, Athena (Athi) Andrews, for gracing the cover of this book with her beauty. Athena was born at home in Nome, Alaska.

Prologue

During the eight years I lived in Nome, Alaska (1978 – 1986), I often found myself wondering what life must have been like during the gold rush days. One afternoon a friend described a vision he had while flying in a small plane. A tale of guns, gold, and a frozen river intrigued me. Wondering if it could be true, I set out to find evidence of such an event in Nome's history. I pored over historic documents, read books on prostitution and mining, and sifted through old photos from the Nome museum. *Diary of an Alaskan Madam* is the culmination of my love of Alaska, my love of story telling, and my love of history, which has shaped this story like water shapes the earth. Mandy and her alliance are fictional, as are their interactions with historic figures in turn-of-the-century Nome.

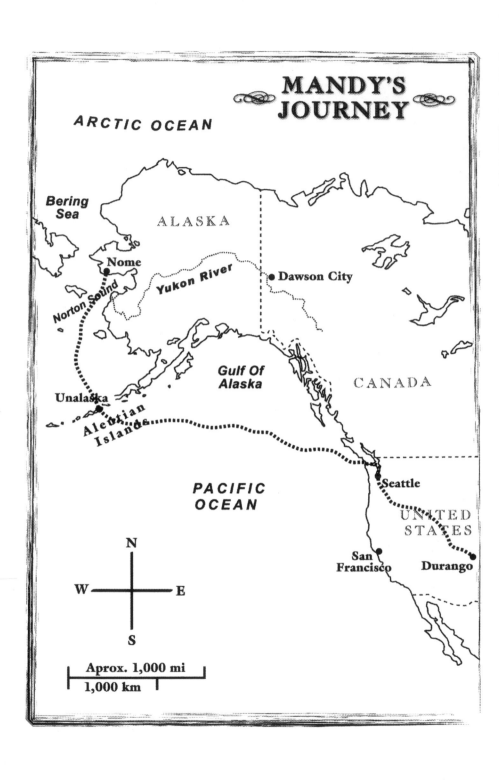

June 1899

June 10, 1899   **8:00 p.m.**

At the precise moment the massive ship started moving away
from the port of Seattle, Washington, it began to rain quite heavily.
All the birds in the harbor took flight and all the women in the
crowd—about one to every 50 men—opened their brightly colored
umbrellas. The sight of the flock flying in unison and the brilliant
colors dispersed throughout a crowd of brown and black attire
heightened the excitement brewing inside of me.

Between all the people on the ship and all the people in
the port, I had never see so many humans in one eyeful. The
disappointment of being left behind was apparent on the frustrated
faces of the people slowly waving their pitiful farewells. In
contrast, the people aboard were all radiating confidence. We feel
very fortunate to have the foresight and resources to arrange such
timely passage to Cape Nome. We believe it's a sign of prosperity
that the gold rush is beginning just as a new century is dawning.
When I say we, I am referring to the people who make up my
business alliance. I am the soon-to-be Madam.

I predict meeting all the new people aboard will be a very exciting aspect of our journey. The way I see it, all the people who paid to board this ship are gamblers. We are all taking risks with no idea of the consequences. Everyone has an expectation of wealth simply awaiting discovery. I wonder which of those among us will leave Alaska Territory as millionaires and which of us will never leave? From all the stories I heard from my grandparents who were a part of the '49 gold rush and living in Durango, Colorado, during its boom time, I guess I have gold fever in my blood. I find it incredibly reassuring to meet others who have a common spirit for life.

The *S.S. Roanoke* is a 500-passenger steamship, but from the looks of things there are far more souls aboard. Yet no complaining could be heard this evening among the laughter and joking about what an adventure we have begun, especially among the members of our business alliance. We are all very lucky to be traveling with Jeremy James "J.J." Cotty, the sole investor of the future Belmont Saloon and the Bantam Belmont.

Ryan is J.J.'s personal mixologist. Dorothy and Jime are the couple that will ensure we have all the food and hot water we need for our business. Alex, Natalie, and Ria are the ladies in my bevy. Between J.J.'s smooth talking and his tidy sum of money, he always gets what he wants. He has already secured all involved in our business a berth for the duration of the trip. Thanks to J.J.'s abilities, he has been able to keep his promise to make me feel as comfortable as possible. He knows how much I love to write, so I have the luxury of a foldout desk attached to the wall in the berth I share with Alex.

It has stopped raining and the crowds sound louder than ever. I hear them celebrating their illusive upcoming fortunes, but sleep would be very welcome right now. I plan on waking early so I can start conversing with the passengers sharing this voyage. I hear Alex softly breathing as she sleeps. She must be as tired as I am. I think I will curl up next to her warm body before falling asleep myself.

June 11, 1899   **2:30 p.m.**

Yesterday I felt so lucky and today I feel cursed. I am seasick.
I hate it already and the voyage has just begun. The atmosphere in
the lower decks was musty and I was desperate for some fresh air
blowing in my face so I went upstairs. Most of the people aboard,
including myself, have never been at sea and therefore, never
experienced seasickness. The results of people on all sides of the
ship coughing, heaving, and vomiting could be seen, smelled,
heard, and even felt, as the wind blew mists of others' misery
everywhere. Every sense a person has is sucked into this vile cycle
of torment.

With all the seasickness surrounding me, my time on the deck
was more appalling than enjoyable. When walking I had to balance
my weight in an unusual way, to keep from falling. My legs felt
like they could give out on me. Looking at the horizon helped but
as soon as I turned to face the ship the windows, the furniture, and
people would look like they were slowly moving. When I tried to
find the horizon again I would notice how quickly the ship was
moving. My blurred vision and my stomach hurting like it could
explode would start me being nauseous all over again. Already, I
heard many cures for this condition, such as moving to the center
of the ship. Covering your ear with one finger. Looking directly
into the water while standing at the bow. Closing your eyes while
lying down. By far the most popular is drinking to dull the senses.
I don't understand the logic of it but sitting at my desk and writing
seems to take my mind off of the suffering.

This last month has been the most demanding time of my
life. I have not had much time for writing. I am exhausted, yet I
am more alive than ever. Jeremy and I have strived to bring with
us everything we'll need to get both businesses up and running. I
hope we've thought of every detail.

Jeremy James, my cousin, is putting up all the money to
get things started and then it will be my responsibility to run
the establishment. In the business we call such establishments
boarding houses because the ladies really are required to pay
for their room and their two meals a day. The going rate is 50

3

percent of their earnings. The ladies will be expected to dress in a tantalizing manner and will be encouraged to charge their new clothing at one of J.J.'s soon-to-be stores. Before leaving Seattle, each lady in my bevy had to have eight unsnap working dresses, two formal dresses, and one street dress. Of course, with me being the madam my wardrobe is far more extensive. I hate getting other women trapped in this lifestyle, but truthfully, I'm glad I'm going to be making legal tender off them instead of someone making it off me. Being a madam is not exactly what I thought I would grow up to be, but I can already see that it will be an excellent opportunity to put all the knowledge that I acquired in the past two years about men and the business to some profitable use.

J.J. was just at my door. He was checking to see if I felt any better. He left me with some beef jerky and dried fruit from his private cache, hoping that it would settle my stomach. J.J. is having a grand time aboard the ship. He doesn't get seasick. He has met several of the men who will be our competitors in Cape Nome and has already shown them his skills at playing keno and poker. He reminded me that the currency he is gaining from those men is a percentage of resourses they were planning on using once we reached Alaska Territory. That makes him one step ahead, and he is ecstatic.

He tried to talk me into starting up the business on the ship like much of the competition has already done. I talked him out of it, saying the ladies and I are too nauseous to work. I also suggested that since he was already gaining so much wealth gambling, he could afford to give us a rest. He agreed because he's in such high spirits due to his winning streak. It really is thrilling to be with Jeremy again. I miss the memorable times we had growing up together in Durango. When he was five years old, my mother's sister, Geneva, found him walking by the Animas River. No one ever knew for sure where he came from, how he got there, or how long he had been surviving on his own. My aunt couldn't have children so she felt very blessed to raise him as her own. Even though he isn't truly my blood, he's been more like family to me than anyone else.

Jeremy is one of the handsomest men I've ever seen—tall, lean, and muscular. He towers over other men and has a way of making them look very small. J.J.'s dark brown skin, full lips, big brown eyes, and black hair create a mysterious, undeniable attraction, despite his large, oddly shaped nose. I've noticed that women can't help but stare at him. He seems to have the best of both worlds: knowledge of his intuitive self and knowledge of the progressive business world. I remember that it was very easy for him to learn how to read. I wonder if that is what influences the fact that he is successful in every venture he takes on. I never dreamed that J.J. and I would someday be in business together. I take this as good sign that riches await us in Cape Nome.

In J.J.'s opinion, another good sign of wealth is that Ryan is among us. Jeremy met Ryan in Dawson and I have heard him brag, "Ryan knows how to make more drinks than any other mixologist this far north." It's been rumored that ice is his secret ingredient. In my opinion, Ryan is rather shy and quiet. J.J. says another quality that makes him an excellent mixologist is that he is a great listener, and in this business it pays to listen. Ryan is a bit taller than J.J., but when the two stand next to each other, a person can't help but notice my handsome cousin. From what I know so far, I must admit that I do like Ryan and can see why J.J. thinks so highly of him.

June 12, 1899   8:25 a.m.

Last night, I dreamed a massive iceberg trapped the ship. Not wanting to wait until the ice melted several people aboard jumped off. Within seconds of hitting the frigid water their bodies started floating. Next I found myself in the water. I tried to swim away but my father grabbed me from behind and began forcing his swollen manhood in me. He is so rough; he's hurting me and he doesn't even care. The whole time he is having his way with me he is whispering something in my ear. I can't quite make out what he is saying, something about how this is his responsibility. I become so outraged that when he has reached his ecstasy I push him off of me. I see him slowly falling to the ocean floor, gasping for his life, every muscle becoming weaker by the moment. His life is ending and he knows it.

June 13, 1899   4:10 p.m.

Truthfully, I'm not going to miss Seattle. It was always so rainy and I barely ever got the chance to explore the city. I don't know what the weather is like in Cape Nome. I hope that it won't be as gloomy as Seattle, but more like Durango's weather: always changing and inspiring to the senses. Even though I only spent two years in Seattle, the constant rain bothered me, keeping me indoors like a prisoner. When the rare chance came for me to explore the city, I really enjoyed discovering the abundant variety of plants. The growth flourished from the rain and was exceptionally lush and green.

Of course, the weather wasn't the only reason I rarely got out. Being a naive prostitute, I was forced to work whenever my company was desired. Rosa's boarding house was open 20 hours a day so personal time was a great luxury.

I hated not having an opportunity at the beginning or end of the day to relax. As a madam, I hope to run a high-class brothel. We will be open from four o'clock in the afternoon until two o'clock in the morning. Our slogan will be, "We're worth the wait." This way the ladies and I will be able to recuperate and enjoy some personal time. On the other hand, J.J. and Ryan will share the responsibilities of The Belmont between two p.m. and two a.m. We're anticipating that business will sometimes demand more hours. The same applies for The Bantam Belmont, which is what we're calling the tent establishment the ladies and I will be working out of.

June 14, 1899   7:15 p.m.

I awoke early this morning just so I could hopefully walk around the ship on my new sea legs. I wanted to enjoy the calm water and the lush islands within our view. I was anticipating seasickness to be a problem, but this time pollution is the bigger problem. I was on the port bow of the ship and there was a strong wind blowing from the north. I was consumed by the ship's coal smoke. I could feel the gritty soot cover every inch of my body, even though I was thoroughly clothed. It reminded me of Durango. It seemed that no matter where I walked on that section of the ship, I couldn't escape. I just couldn't endure the filth for one more minute. Thank goodness I have my diary to keep me occupied; writing really helps to pass the time and keeps my mind off my stomach.

I know I'm going to miss Rosa more than anyone I left behind in Seattle. She became like a mother to me. She was much older and to my knowledge only had a loving relationship with the oldest lady in her bevy, but she sure knew how to make each bird in her flock feel loved and appreciated. She figured if she treated us with respect we would work hard for her. I know her philosophy worked on me.

When I asked Rosa for some advice, she said, "Successful madams are truly a remarkable breed." She talked about how they must have a keen sense of business, with the ability to purchase and manage extremely well. They must know how to be discreet in handling both customers and the law. Madams who want to be known to their girls as "a mother" must be very patient and understanding with their doves, especially when they are going through their runty times. I remember her saying that in the many years of being in business she has known some madams who beat their ladies to get them to do what they want, but in her opinion, that wasn't a productive way to get "the doves under your wings."

Last night Ria came to my bed. She was scared by the vastness of the water and just wanted me to hold her. What an emotional experience! Now I know what Rosa was talking about concerning a prosperous madam having strong maternal instincts. In a matter of days I will be living as a madam and seeing if I possess the qualities Rosa spoke of. I hope I am capable of the task ahead.

My first challenge as a madam was to select ladies I felt would be diverse enough to entice the many men in Cape Nome. I look at each of my ladies as a unique creature in my masterpiece for success. Before we reach our destination, I will strive to paint

7

a picture of each lady. I will start with Alexandra because I've known her longest.

I met Alex my first day at Rosa's. She, too, was new and I could tell by the way she was playing with her fingers so near her mouth that she was just as nervous as me. We were like mirrors to each other—not in our looks, but in our emotions. We became close friends right away. She is the one person who always understands what I am talking about and how I am feeling. I enjoy the way she is such a sensitive lover.

Alex is one of the most alluring women I have ever seen. She plays cards and gambles with a keenness that frightens most men. We have talked several times about her leaving this business and trying her luck at gambling for a while. Each time she has the same answer: "I just can't give up the covered money." I think the reason is that she loves her profession. I doubt she would be as content in any other line of work. I remember hearing Rosa say that only one girl in a hundred really enjoys this occupation. I believe Alex must be that rare one percent. She is definitely one-of-a-kind. That's one reason I love her as much as I do.

Alex and I are the same age: 27. She has curly long blond hair with bright, cobalt eyes that sparkle when she laughs. Alex possesses a rare quality of having such a pretty face that men look at it before fixating on her firm bosom, thin waist, and proportional hips. She loves to dance and has a natural rhythm about her. Whenever she hears music, she automatically begins moving to the beat and she even walks with a bounce. Because she enjoys moving her body in such a rhythmic style, she is mesmerizing to watch. Both men and women find her provocative.

Not too many people know how well read Alex is. She perceives the world like no one I have ever met before. I enjoy talking to her because every time I learn something intriguing. She has a great interest in Greek and Roman structures. Sometimes when she's talking about the history of that area I get an intense chill down my spine, like we both lived in that place and time before. I don't know how that could have happened, but I feel that it did.

Alex has a smell about her that touches my senses deeply. It reminds me of what a young, healthy man who starts out clean smells like after he has been poking hard for several minutes and is dripping wet with sweat. For Alex, that smell just comes naturally, and whenever I smell her, it makes me winsome.

June 15, 1899   1:00 p.m.

The seasickness is taking a toll on me. I am more grateful than ever that I have my writing to keep me sane. My next dove to introduce is Natalie. It's a good thing that I worked with her for the last two years at Rosa's and saw her money making potential. Before getting in the business, I never would have believed that men would find her appealing. At 35, she is the oldest of my ladies. She is a large Italian woman with long black hair. Her dark eyebrows are set just perfectly above her brown, oval eyes as if they were painted on. Men seem to be intrigued by the "darkness" that surrounds her as she basks in the light reflected by her olive skin.

Most of the time she's extremely kind to everyone, but I will really have to watch her. It happens about once a month, now that I think about it – an instantaneous switch from a kindhearted person to an animal in a furious rage. She either has a real mental unbalance or an outstanding, devious plan for releasing her frustrations.

In Seattle, she had a reputation for being violent and that appeared to be what the men were attracted to. The only thing I can figure is they believed that if they didn't get assaulted, they had somehow conquered her wild spirit. I have learned to live with her and to let her finish beating up whichever small man she has chosen for her monthly wicked game. It's eerie; the next day she is euphoric. During the two years we worked together at Rosa's, I learned to deeply love both sides of her.

Her enormous bosoms were a gift from the good Lord, but in return she was cursed with crooked, stained teeth that are quite noticeable when she smiles. She swears that she was born with the crookedness, and over the years, the cigar smoke has stained

9

them permanently. She loves to smoke cigars and when she does, her facial features look more like a man than a woman. It is only her hair, bosom, and her eyebrows that remind a person she is a woman.

The older men find Natalie very desirable. I have noticed that in this business, men not only pay for a screw but for female companionship as well. When she isn't in her monthly moods, Natalie picks up the clientele looking for conversation, motherly love, and the comfort of large bosoms. She also attracts customers because she is the only lady I know in the business that will take several men at a time. She told me that she likes to serve more than one client at a time because she can make twice the money. I have learned from offers made to me in the past that some men are willing to pay whatever price to have the pleasure of more than one man to a woman.

Most people find that talking with Natalie is an ordeal. She has an excellent understanding of the natural sciences and when she believes she is correct with her information, she will argue until her logic is justified. I would bet that nine out of ten times she is correct. We have learned not to ask her a question unless we have time to listen and uncover the answer.

I'm fortunate that Natalie decided to come to Cape Nome and bring her crystallized ginger with her. I have discovered that sucking on a piece helps decrease the vomiting. At first she wasn't going to join us because she felt that she owed Rosa her loyalty. Rosa knew that only a select few people ever have an aspiration to come to Alaska Territory, and she made it clear to all the ladies in her bevy that they were free to follow their passion. When Natalie realized that Rosa was sincere, she knew that she couldn't pass up this opportunity.

I'm thankful that Rosa is not a possessive person and that she let three of her bevy, including myself, free to seek our dreams. This whole situation has been prosperous for everyone involved. Just because Rosa isn't possessive, doesn't mean she's not a businesswoman. J.J. paid her 100 ounces of gold for our freedom. I know that between what she has made selling booze in her brothel for the last 20 years and now all of her gold, she will soon be on a South Sea island living out her dreams.

Natalie is the only lady in my bevy who has children. Her daughter is ten years old and her son is seven. She sends them most of her hard earned money. They are being raised at a baby farm in Seattle. A baby farm is a place where fallen women can have their children raised if they don't have any family to help them. She keeps a picture of both of them in her room and every time I see them it makes me think of my family. I like to have a picture of my mother, my sister, and Galen close to my side when I am writing.

June 16, 1899   **3:20 p.m.**

We are now about 1,700 miles northwest of Seattle. We made our first stop today at Unalaska, a village near Dutch Harbor. We stopped to get fresh water, coal, and to make sure that the passage to Cape Nome was free of ice so we could continue. I really enjoyed being on land even though my legs felt like I was still on the ship. It's amazing how welcome the reassuring ground is after days of bouncing up and down. We also had the pleasure of warming ourselves in the first sunshine we've felt in three days. In the distance, to the northwest, I could see the gorgeous peaks of what must be the Alaska Range. Unalaska is breathtaking. Its rolling fields are abundant with four-foot high violets and little patches of pink, blue, and yellow wildflowers. I have never seen such intense colors in nature before: the bright blue sky above, the deep blue-green sparkling ocean on the horizon, and the huge brilliant purple flowers covering most of the land. Not only was the view intoxicating, but the smell was as well. The strangely warm breeze slid under the hair on my arms and I felt as one with the land.

Everyone was overjoyed that a passage free of ice was spotted and within hours we continued sailing north. For me it was hard to get back on the ship. I wanted so much for the journey to be concluded so the dreadful seasickness would be over and my feet could once again be planted on the solid earth. I must admit that the tea we purchased from some older native ladies has already helped quell my blurred vision. I can now look at the horizon without getting dizzy and the fresh air seems to smell better than ever.

I keep hearing that because Cape Nome is on the coast, this gold rush will be easier to get to than any preceding gold rush in history. I guess that means I shouldn't complain and instead be grateful that I am aboard this ship heading toward the greatest adventure of my life.

June 17, 1899   **11:35 a.m.**

I woke up this morning to a horrifying sound. It was as if a gigantic animal was screaming for its life. In a panic, I ran up to the top deck not even properly dressed. When I saw the huge white ice floes and patches of blue sea surrounding the ship, I was instantly relieved. Natalie assured me that the sound I heard was the ice slowly breaking up by the force of the ship. I am grateful that the ship was not crushing against a solid mass of ice that could sink us or force us to travel hundreds of miles out of our way looking for a free channel. Before leaving Seattle, J. J. said that it would be necessary to travel through splitting ice packs. Even though it is risky navigating through the ice, it must be done. Otherwise a vessel might not arrive in Cape Nome until mid summer.

Along with the ice came the opportunity to witness herds of walrus basking in the sun. There were so many lying around on the ice I thought it might be driftwood, but as I looked closer I noticed their magnificent ivory tusks. At first they didn't seem to be aware or afraid of the massive ship slowly passing them. Then something spooked the herds and all at once they started diving into the water to escape the vessel next to them. Seeing the huge velvety brown animals rushing for protection stirred emotions in every witness. For several hours after people rambled on and on about what they thought they knew about the walrus. I heard so much I wondered what was true. Are polar bears and killer whales their only enemies? Do they use their tusks for fighting or for digging clams? Do they really use their bristly whiskers to feel the clams? When a walrus dives does its blood really leave the skin and move to the organs deep inside the body? How do people know these facts? I wonder if they even are true. I guess just because I have never seen this type of creature before I am naturally surprised that other people have so much information.

Instead of going to sleep right away last night, I had to go break up a fight Ria was involved in. She had met a photographer who wanted to take pictures of her and was physically fighting with him over how much he would pay her for the photos. The girls are allowed to keep 100 percent of any money made on photographs. Ria doesn't have very good speaking skills so I guess it was just easier to fight with her fists instead of her words. The only way I could stop her screaming and slapping was to punch her in the face and knock her out before the photographer did. I hope I made the right choice including Ria in my bevy.

Two days before departing Seattle, I found Ria in a brothel about a block away from Rosa's. I was touring the neighborhood and happened to come across this tiny Spanish woman. She seemed to have an adventurous spirit but also some personal problems. Ria is the smallest of my ladies, and at 22, she is the youngest. Her figure is very petite and she barely reaches my shoulders. Segments of her curly brown hair hang sweetly around her face, which has a fair complexion. Her radiant brown eyes may be small, but there is a hypnotic quality about them.

Another piece of advice Rosa had concerning my bevy was that I definitely needed a woman who comes across to men as totally helpless. Ria is that woman. Although she may appear to be weak as a kitten, she fights like a tiger. Just two nights ago Alex and I had to break up a fight between her and another chippie. She reacts to situations in a wild manner.

To my good fortune, I was able to talk to Ria's former madam before we departed. She said, "Whatever it is about Ria's act, the men really enjoy her company." Her former madam told me that Ria is well known for her days of gloominess in which she doesn't talk to anyone. She also told me Ria likes to indulge in laudanum, which is an opium tincture. Of course, I have brought up a good supply for all the ladies of my bevy, and I will distribute it to prevent pregnancies and to induce numbing as needed. I will have to keep a good eye on Ria to make sure she doesn't find another way to get the laudanum. I don't want her escaping so much that she isn't profitable.

I have already noticed that she requires constant reassurance. She has even asked me if I will keep her working no matter how old she gets, if by some chance she doesn't get married. I told her yes. But honestly, I will just have to see how good her money making potential is. I hope bringing Ria turns out to be a good decision. I guess only time will tell.

I had made arrangements for two other ladies to join our alliance, but hours before departure they both changed their minds. J.J reassured me we would be fine, and as he pointed out, "It is better they change their minds now than when we reach Cape Nome." I know that he is correct but I just worry a little about finding sporting girls where we are going who are willing to work hard and will fit comfortably into the new family.

June 18, 1899   9:25 a.m.

On the day we began our journey, the masses were packed tightly together clutching their possessions, be it suitcases, trunks, or even rocking chairs. I hold my diaries to be one of the most sacred things I possess. Thanks to my mother, who was a teacher and a great lover of history, I began the ritual of recording events and daily reflections early in life.

Maybe someday, my diary will provide a glimpse of what the past was like through the eyes of a woman. I need to be very careful where I keep my diary once we arrive and my new life begins. I will need to get into the habit of learning to protect my clients. I will hide it in a different place for each day of the week.

Whenever I think about my mother, I think about my childhood. I grew up on a farm in Durango. My father didn't get the boys he wanted so he made my younger sister, Lizzy, and me do all the hard labor. Due to my upbringing, I am a strong, assertive woman who can speak her mind. I can do farm chores and shoot a gun better than a lot of men, and I can do arithmetic and read better than most people.

When I think back, I remember my mother's great devotion to reading. As a family, we used to read the newspaper and Mark Twain aloud every evening. I also remember that each year on my birthday or my sister's, our mother would elaborate on all the main events that had happened during that year of our life. She would go on and on talking about Charles Darwin and how knowledge makes a person fit for survival. She would say she was preparing us for the future by increasing our knowledge of all the changes that were taking place. That was my mother's way of educating us. My father had different ideas.

My father was a miner and a marksman whose brother, Ike, was no stranger to the law. The Stockton gang had a reign of terror in southwest Colorado for years. Each night after the family reading, as soon as the light went out, our father would come and force himself on either my sister or me. The comments my father made as he thrust away made me believe that he really thought it was his God given right to "educate" his daughters.

I never really knew my sister Lizzy. She was always so quiet when we were growing up. Between the education she got from our mother, "There are many changes taking place in this world; be prepared for them," and the education she got from our father, "Women are only good for one thing," I guess it caused her to become a lunatic. I must be a little crazy also, but I am a survivor. Instead of going to an asylum, I became a prostitute.

Thanks to my father's educating, prostitution was an easy path for me to follow because I had already learned to numb myself. When I got old enough to understand what my father was doing to us at night, I began to make my mind escape the pain my body endured. I knew that what he did made me feel so disgusted that it couldn't be right. I didn't want to be in my body when he was touching me. So, in my mind I would pretend that I was about five years old and I was swinging on a rope down by the river. As I went back and forth on the swing, I became mesmerized watching the rushing water. I would just stay right in that thought until my father was done. Soon I learned to go there when he was educating my sister, too. I couldn't stand the sound of his grunts knowing that his pleasure was our pain.

I wondered if my mother had us read more and more as we got older for our own education, or to keep my father from having more time to educate us in his own way.

June 18, 1899   3:05 p.m.

I got married when I was 17 years old and if Galen, my husband of eight years, had not died in a mining accident, I never would have met Rosa at his funeral. Rosa is Galen's sister. She runs the brothel above the Merchant Café in Seattle, and she asked me after the funeral if I wanted to work for her. I didn't really have many choices available to me; my father had disappeared several years earlier. Everyone figured he ran off with his brother's gang. My mother had died of pneumonia the month before Galen died. Not having any family to turn to, what else could I do?

I rode the stagecoach back to Seattle with Rosa. When I wasn't captivated by stories of Galen's childhood, my mind raced with thoughts of what I had gotten myself into. My only option if I were to remain in Durango was housekeeping. I felt that it would help me deal with my grieving if I was in a new location. Somehow selling my body seemed a better option than allowing the man of the house free access to my body whenever he desired. I had this illusion that somehow I would have more leverage in my life if I made money for providing that service instead of someone taking it for free. I soon learned that as a prostitute, the only levers I had were my choice of clothes and how I made up my face. Now, thanks to J.J., I will hopefully gain more control of my life.

June 19, 1899   11:30 p.m.

Earlier this spring, J.J. wrote me a letter from Dawson, Canada, where he was experiencing the riches of the gold rush selling whiskey to the miners. There he met Mattie Silks, a successful businesswoman. She played a large part in encouraging J.J. to expand his investments. He was impressed by the fact she got in the business at the ripe age of 19. The letter he wrote asked me to become a madam and run a boarding house in Cape Nome. My first thought was to decline the offer. It was a gamble to venture north, but I was already taking all the risks that come with this profession: disease, disrespect and mistreatment. Why would I not allow myself the opportunity for larger profits? I believe he is presenting me with a golden opportunity.

The talk on the ship is that we should arrive at Cape Nome within days if we don't get caught in any ice packs. Thanks to the constant drizzle that has been with us for three days, there is a melancholy mood about everyone aboard the ship even though we should all be counting our blessings for the short trip the calm winds have allowed us. From the discord that can be heard among the passengers, I think that all will be happy to be on land again. All, that is, except J.J. I ran into him this evening and he started rambling. "Mandy," he said, "This voyage has been a highlight in my life. Never before have I won so much money in such a short time. I'm afraid that once my feet are on the sandy beaches, this magic spell cast over me will disappear and I will go back to my old streak. Mind you, it wasn't a bad streak of luck, but nothing compared to the one I have had on this ship." He smiled as he said, "I had better get back to the game while we're still floating." He walked away without even asking how I was. Oh well, his luck is my luck and I am delighted for him. I hope he's wrong and this streak does continue when we reach Cape Nome.

With each passing day, we get closer to the Arctic Circle and to the longest day of the year. The sky has remained about the same darkish gray for three days now. It has been raining lightly so there is no way to see the midnight sun through the swell of clouds. With the light always remaining about the same shade of gray, the water remains the same pale blue and at times it becomes hard to tell the difference between the two. When this visual effect happens I get the feeling that we might be dropping off of the face of the earth.

The sky never gets completely dark and we all find it hard to sleep. My ladies and I passed the time last night sharing childhood memories. I've come to find out each one of us has had our share of education whether it was a father, uncle, brother or grandfather. Sharing our experiences with each other has created a bond that is almost as powerful as love. I'm overjoyed that we can all find comfort with each other.

June 20, 1899   3:30 p.m.

It was a good thing I was on the deck before retiring last night and saw for myself the massive storm surrounding us. It made the ship seem small in comparison. This information helped me deduct why Alex and I were thrown from our berth, otherwise I would have thought it was a bad dream coming true. We both wanted to witness the waves crashing against the ship, but we knew from the constant water at our porthole that it wasn't safe to leave our enclosed space. Instead, we curled next to each other and held on tight. I don't think either one of us got much sleep. We both were scared that we might not live to see the shores of Cape Nome. By the time the storm receded it was late morning. As soon as the rain let up, people started gathering on the decks to converse about how they had survived the night. The main topic was how enduring the storm, the only rough water we have encountered on our journey, was another sign of the riches waiting for us in Cape Nome.

The storm has really churned up the sea and along with it, my seasickness. I'm so tired of being on the ship. The only thing that seems to change is the weather and the vendors taking up shop on the decks. They are already beginning to sell the supplies needed in Cape Nome to highly anxious individuals. The vendors who get the most attention are those pedaling a cure-all for everything that could harm you. Of course, they never have any cures for seasickness.

My whole body is anticipating being on land again. My seasickness seems worse than ever. The tea that helped earlier seems to offer no relief now. As strange as it may sound, I feel drunk. I lose my balance when I walk and I'm constantly bumping into the corridors. To make matters worse, it has been drizzling all day. I felt like running around the ship screaming out of pure frustration, "Let me off the ship – Now!" Instead I kept my composure and used the opportunity to sit down and visit with Dorothy and Jime, the couple we brought up to take care of the daily chores. It was the first chance I had to visit with them since we left Seattle. Once we arrive, Dorothy's main jobs will be cooking and cleaning. She will wash both the clothes and the clients.

To run a high-class brothel, I must be aware of hygiene. Hence, all customers will be required to have either a bath or a genital wash before they can touch one of my ladies. If a client chooses the wash, Dorothy will tightly grab his privates and squeeze while washing him. If the client chooses the bath, whichever lady he has chosen will check him once they are alone. If the potential customer is extremely sensitive to that touch, then we don't want his money or his disease.

Thanks to what J.J. learned from Mattie Silks about protecting his investments from disease and pregnancy, and thanks to his wealth, we have brought with us a large assortment of condoms. He believes that if a man has some choices concerning which type of condom to wear he will be more inclined to use one with the lady who is about to service him. The skin condoms are cheaper and offer more sensitivity. Rubber condoms are more expensive but since they are re-useable the clients with a healthy vigor might prefer those. I wonder if the ancient Chinese and Egyptian prostitutes had as much trouble getting their clients to wear them as we did at Rosa's. To help that situation, the ladies have been instructed to give them free of charge, even though they are an expensive item.

When we are on land, Jime will first set up the tents. Then he will gather wood and water. We hope to open up business within hours after landing on shore, therefore Jime will be extremely busy. He will be responsible for heating the water for the customers' baths and keeping things moving in the bathing tent. As soon as he can, Jime will begin supervising the building of The Belmont Saloon. Once it's built, Ryan and J.J. will sleep in the saloon, that way J.J.'s investment is always protected. We only brought up enough lumber to build the saloon. J.J. says that until The Belmont is paid off in full, hopefully by next spring, the Bantom Belmont will have to operate out of tents. He keeps assuring me that this is only happening because it is good business not to over-invest and that he will change the situation as soon as profit permits.

While visiting with Dorothy and Jime, I discovered why I hadn't seen much of them since we got on the ship. They told me that they have spent most of the journey in their berth making love, talking, and reading to each other. I have never before seen two people so much in love. Dorothy is a large Irish woman with long red hair that she wears in braids. Jime is a large Irishman with no hair on his head. They appear to be in their middle thirties, but I have never asked. Given the warm grin upon both of their faces, they look like they were made for each other. They have been married ten years and have never had any children. Both of them seem to be very tenderhearted people, the kind who would help anyone in need. I met them on the same day I met Ria. J.J. loved the idea of bringing a couple with us to do the chores so that we could concentrate on making money right away.

June 21, 1899   11:59 p.m.

Happy summer solstice! The ship is wild tonight. It finally stopped raining and most everyone is on deck celebrating the midnight sun and the warm westerly wind speeding up our journey. Natalie is sharing with all who will listen that she calculates we are getting over 21 hours of direct sunlight. As I write, I am on deck with the other passengers. Looking at them, I see mostly unshaven white males wearing coonskin coats and hats with their chests puffed out and their heads held high. Some are staring off into space but most are engaged in loud conversations about what supplies will be needed once they arrive. Every once in a while, I see a lady with small children who, I have learned, is the wife of a soon-to-be store keeper, doctor, lawyer, or banker. Since it's obvious there are not a lot of women in our upcoming community, it would be nice to get to know these women better. Of course, a lady would never lower herself to talk to a public girl. When I

entered this profession I left humanity. I miss looking people in
the eye and smiling.

It is always very easy to tell a lady from a public girl. One
breed of woman must paint on artificial beauty and the other gets
to live with, and hopefully enjoy, her natural beauty. I miss not
wearing makeup and being able to converse with women outside
of our kinship. Speaking of the kinship, most of the other chippies
aboard are down below working on their backs. Thanks to J.J.'s
winning streak, my ladies and I have continued resting throughout
the journey, which I must admit is the one thing that has made the
seasickness bearable. My eyes reveal to me, as I watch a young
chippie in the corner enduring some manly muscle one minute and
throwing up the next, that not all sporting ladies are as lucky as us.

As I continue to write about what I see, I must make note about
what has entertained the masses on board. Cards! Most passengers
are either playing cards or watching a group of men play. It seems
that cards are a savior for some and a demon for others. I have
seen people enjoy playing cards when there is nothing else to
do and I have seen others who will do nothing but play cards.
Watching the players, I sense the lack of emotion coming from the
men seated around tables and on empty whiskey barrels. I know
that a good card player never reveals his hand by revealing his
emotions. Consequently, each man I see holding cards is definitely
wearing the so-called poker face. Very serious scowls are void of
any passion and oblivious to everything but the cards. Thankfully
the engulfed audience makes up for what is lacking among the
players. They seem to be experiencing a range of emotions, from
melancholy to zealous enthusiasm. It is as if they were the ones
losing or winning. I personally like table games like Faro, which
must be played on a stable area. Of course, where there are cards,
there is gambling, drinking, laughing, shouting, and fighting. They
all go hand in hand with each other whether on land or water.

Beyond the freshly painted walls of the ship, my eyes are
drawn to the dazzling blue water. When the spell of the rhythmic
water is finally broken, I notice countless greenish-brown hills
rising up from the earth. Next, my eyes fixate on the snow-capped

rugged mountains that create the northern horizon. Directly behind the peaks sticking up like fingers, I see the most incredible scene of my life. The perpetual sun, which has been shining all day, is now behind those peaks and is displaying an intense array of amethyst and burgundy. Above the jagged peaks are some wispy clouds, which illuminate lighter shades of purple and pink. Being witness to this magical display has stirred emotions similar to those I felt when I was in Unalaska. It is as if the earth and I have blended together as one. If nothing good comes from our trip to Alaska Territory, I think it will have been worth it to come all this way just to behold this magnificent sight.

I can see just a few others who are captivated by this unbelievable light show. Everyone else seems to be absorbed by a whirlwind of illusive thoughts. I can feel it in the air. At first I thought it was the happiness of being so close to land that was making everyone excited, but as I listen to the conversations, I hear and feel an atmosphere of pure greed anticipating release. I need to get used to hearing talk of large amounts of gold waiting to be discovered, as well as the high flowing emotions of excitement surrounding people as they speak of their upcoming wealth. I will stop writing for today and go enjoy some of this gold fever for myself. I love conversing with people when they are so optimistic.

June 22, 1899   5:55 p.m.

I am watching the first passengers leave. It is total chaos as people push and shove to get off the ship. I can't believe the remaining water that needs to be crossed to reach the sandy shores. Men too anxious with gold fever to worry about their clothes getting wet are wading the last few yards to the beach, hoping to discover gold before others. Their prospecting is already impeded since the first ship arrived two days ago. No one told me there wasn't a harbor here, but then what did I expect? There has never been a need for one until this gold rush. For each person who comes in search of golden riches on the shores of Cape Nome, there will be a greater reason to construct a harbor. I sense history is being made with each footprint.

The grayish blue water with its tiny waves is so shallow that to get to the shore, we will have to climb into a small barge that will take us within 30 feet of the land, then the men will carry the women and supplies ashore on their backs. I have already asked J.J. if he would carry me. I know that he would never drop me in the water. I have a real trust in him, unlike most men. I guess because we are family. J.J. pointed out that our luck continues because there is no wind blowing right now. It is difficult enough to reach the shore without having to struggle with the coastal winds.

Each one of the ladies, including myself, has made a money arrangement with Jime to carry ashore all of our belongings. Our trunks possess everything we own and without our clothes, jewelry, perfume, and makeup, we couldn't work – or at least not charge as much.

While I watch everyone hustling around, I wonder if I really have what it takes to be a madam. I have to believe that I do, or I wouldn't have come this far. As soon as I get off the ship I will begin to have more responsibilities than I have ever had in my life. I'm nervous about remembering every detail required to ensure that the operation runs smoothly. Will Jime have enough wood gathered for heating all the water we might need in one evening? Has Dorothy really learned how to check thoroughly for diseases? Do all the ladies have enough butter for the night ahead? How quickly will we need other ladies, and how will I find them? Does Ria know the proper way to test condoms for holes? How much laudanum do I need to give Ria to keep her from getting in some kind of trouble? I just had to console her when she found out that we would be carried across the water. Everyone could hear her fearful, angry screams. Once I finally found my way through her swinging punches so that I could comfort her, she told me through sobs how afraid she is of being dropped in the cold water, and that she can't trust anyone to bring her safely to shore. As I was contemplating how to solve this problem, Ryan volunteered to take her and she accepted with a wet smile.

It's silly, but my biggest fear is using the gold scales accurately. I guess I'm really nervous about having the customer watch me. With so much to think about, I am bound to make a mistake or two. I guess that's all part of learning something new. I'm thankful that I have J.J. to turn to for advice and Alex to turn to for comfort. Within hours it is all going to start and I know that my existence will never be the same.

June 27, 1899   3:10 a.m.

Life has been unusual since we arrived. All my life I've gone to bed when it's dark and awakened when it's light. I feel like it's just been one long day since we got here. Having light all the time is strange. Sometimes I wish it would just get dark for a little while so I could see the twinkling stars again. With the abundant light, my body feels full of energy, which is helpful since there has been a lot of work involved in getting both businesses running. I don't think anyone in the alliance has gotten much sleep lately.

Sometimes I wonder why I traveled this far to be in such a desolate place. From what I've seen, the Bering Sea coast is greenish-brown, flat and monotonous. There are no trees, only green bushes of varying sizes. The land has no contours and no outstanding features, except for the snow capped mountains to the north. From what I can see the tundra, which I know now means treeless land, is covered with thick mosses scattered among sections of grass. Maybe once I spend some more time here, I will learn to appreciate this strange land. As bleak as this place appears, it is obvious that the prospects of exchanging our services for gold are very high, even if we do have to live and work out of a tent and put up with the clouds of mosquitoes that surround you the minute the wind dies down.

With all the gray, dim light in the sky, and the many hammers J.J. has hired, The Belmont is quickly becoming a reality. It already has four walls and a roof. The windows aren't in yet, and the big open space looks bare with just a plank for the bar and a few barrels for sitting on. All that can be heard is hammering, but that hasn't stopped booze from selling within the structure.

The first evening we arrived was spent organizing and getting our bodies used to being on land again. The next day was the most savage working day of my life. We were in such a big hurry to feed our fever that all of the ladies worked in one large tent, while J.J. and Ryan served drinks out of another tent. Three partners engaged in the act with no privacy. It truly heightened the randiness in the air. The men's venereal appetite was already potent after being on the ship for 12 days. The dozen or so working chippies on the ship couldn't satisfy the hundreds of men on board. It's one thing to hear what's happening in the room next to you, but quite another thing to see human lust at its peak. The men being served were lustful creatures depositing their seeds, the ladies passive receptors. It makes me think about what a Roman orgy must have been like. One big difference was the lack of music and exotic dancing. All that could be heard was the abusive remarks the men made toward the women as they grunted and groaned their way to pleasure. The men waiting to be served watched this event unfold before their eyes and were an example of perverted voyeurism at the highest end of the spectrum. The majority of them were so aroused they couldn't wait any longer for a woman and allowed Mary's five to pleasure themselves right in the tent for all to see.

Later that evening, all of the ladies and I talked about what it was like working out of one tent. Even if I wasn't working on my back, I was still working. I made sure the clients were clean, the gold was weighed out correctly, and new customers served as quickly as possible. Within minutes, we all confessed that the events of that day had been extremely arousing. Smelling the musky sweat, hearing the moans of pleasure, observing the large array of sizes as the men in the audience abused themselves, and watching the faces of men reaching satisfaction each to his own unique rhythm was very invigorating. Even if all the ladies were completely dressed and just using the convenient snaps built into their working dresses, it was a sight to behold.

After the confession the doves in my bevy and myself slowly started caressing each other and before we knew it we were tangled up and engaged in the most erotic uniting of our lives.

25

What we experienced that day was a unique situation in our alliance's history that should never be repeated. The heightened arousal, which made the men overly aggressive, couldn't be healthy for the ladies or society. I think I could have avoided the whole situation. I felt so much compassion for the customers standing outside in the pouring rain, that I gave some of them something they didn't pay for. I will never again let my emotions get the better of me. Of course J.J.'s little talk, "Our sole purpose is to make money, not lose it," and "Don't ever give people something they haven't paid for," helped me understand.

I am no longer just selling my lust like I did when I was only a prostitute; I now arrange and profit from other screwing. I'm hoping it will have some benefits along with all of its many duties. One advantage that comes to mind is the pleasure to choose whom to serve. As for the ladies in my bevy, they have no choice but to take whoever will pay. Somehow being able to pick and choose makes the thought of the job a little easier.

June 28, 1899   2:50 a.m.

I went for a walk around the growing gold rush city before work this evening. I can't believe all of the changes I've seen since we arrived almost a week ago. It's truly amazing to see a town being built so fast. Everywhere I look I see tents and more tents surrounded by trails of mud. Durango didn't have an influx of population at such a fast rate, and Seattle was well established when I arrived. Rumor has it that the town site covers 40 acres, extending from the beach to the land on both sides of the Snake River. They say the city boundaries were staked out last month when there were only about 250 individuals here.

I can see with my own eyes that the daily arrival of new people has made lot jumping as prevalent as claim jumping. New tents are put up wherever space can be found on the beach, if the owner is fortunate enough to have a tent. With each passing day I see more and more new faces, mostly extremely greedy men. That feeling of greed on the ship was nothing compared to what I see now. Instead of men prospecting for gold, they are searching for shelter.

Wood planks are very scarce, since the closest tree is a hundred miles away. If people didn't bring up their own timber, then they're out of luck because they can't expect to find an adequate supply here. Some prospectors have built their cabins with logs they have scavenged from the small piles of driftwood on the shore. Everywhere I looked today on the coast I saw people without provisions. It is heartbreaking to see so many without a warm place to sleep. I forget not everyone could afford to come to Cape Nome as well prepared as J.J. and me.

Front Street is the only street that has already been laid out for a town site and several buildings have been framed. One is a bank, two are assay offices, two are general stores, and all the others are saloons. A sure sign that J.J.'s lucky streak continues is that his saloon, The Belmont, is now one of the finest saloons in Cape Nome. It consists of a 30-foot long rosewood bar with a brass foot rail. Behind the bar is a large nude painting. On the east wall there is a Cassidy Adam's "Custer's Last Stand" painting that's distributed by Budweiser to advertise their beer. Hanging on the west wall is an array of mining equipment and glittering fossils, crystals, and ore samples. Kerosene lamps hang from the ceiling and produce a dim light. In the middle of the room is an iron stove with six tables surrounding it. Several spittoons are placed throughout the saloon. I can already see that cleaning around them will be almost as tedious as actually cleaning the spittoons. Most of the men don't make their spit into the provided disposal area, which makes Dorothy's job even more sordid.

I find it hard to believe that we have only been here seven days and so much has happened. The constant sunlight has a lot to do with advancing the progress of this tent city. J.J. can be thanked for his foresight in bringing everything he wanted and needed for his enterprises. His profits can be thanked for powering the man-hours that have transformed this relatively small spot of sand on the coast of northern Alaska Territory into one classy drinking establishment.

Since we learned so much from our first day of business, the ladies and myself now run things a little differently. I make

arrangements with the clients in The Belmont. Once I know if
a gentleman is interested, I will show him a photograph and tell
a little story about each lady to add to the enticement. After a
gentleman has made his selection and I weigh the gold dust or take
his coins. I escort him in back of The Belmont and signal to Jime
with my fingers indicating which lady is being requested and how
the gentleman wishes to clean up. The client then goes to the bath
tent, which is the big tent used the first day and now serves as Jime
and Dorothy's sleeping quarters as well. At last he is ready to enjoy
the lady of his choice in a tent large enough for a double bed and
the trunks. For now, that is the best we can do.

Late this evening as I traversed around the ladies' tent, getting
a bit of fresh air before retiring into my own, I heard the moans of
Alex and Ria engaged in some serious pleasuring of one another. I
would like to think when you know your companion is selling her
body as you sell yours, it stirs the passions. I wouldn't like to think
that Alex and Ria are getting involved emotionally. Alex feels so
good to touch; I can see why Ria would desire her. To survive,
ladies of the evening may have to let men who have no intent to
pleasure them lust their bodies, but that doesn't mean that they
aren't capable of enjoying pleasures themselves. I sure hope Ria
doesn't fall in love with Alex. I don't mind if they make each other
feel good, so long as that's all it is.

June 29, 1899   4:45 a.m.

It has been overcast since we arrived and today for the first
time we saw the cloudless, brilliant sky. I have never in my life
seen the sun shine for so long in one day. As I write, the sun is in
the northeastern sky, already creating as much darkness as it will
all day. Today while walking on the sponge tundra all the beautiful
flowers captured my attention. I counted more than 20 varieties.
My favorite flowers were the tiny light purple ones growing in
clusters. It's amazing these delicate plants can survive in this
climate. I guess their key to survival is their smallness, as they
are close to the ground and protected from the harsh wind. The
flapping tents are a constant reminder of the wind, which at times

seems like it's talking to me. I have already learned that this far north, you have two choices when it comes to being outside: wind or huge mosquitoes. I prefer the wonderful, wonderful wind.

I walked about two miles north this evening, away from the tents and all the people. As I looked back over the speck of civilization, I saw tents spread from the shoreline to the tundra along the water for what seems like miles. It is as if the people are trying to see how close they can exist next to each other. Of course, the real reason is that no one wants to be very far from the establishments. That's why The Belmont and The Bantam are right in the middle of the town. Fewer steps for the fatigued miners to travel, and both businesses are always buzzing with excitement. It's so peaceful and quiet on the tundra. When I'm out there, I am reminded of how I felt when I was a child in the mountains of Colorado. Not aware of anything but the present moment, taking in all nature has to offer with each and every sense. That feeling makes me content to be in Alaska Territory even if I can't see any stars at night.

June 30, 1899   4:30 a.m.

I just returned from another quick stroll and it was magnificent. I wanted to spend some more time outdoors before it started to rain again. The swelling dark blue clouds in the south sky revealed that the moisture would soon be released. I love walking on the peaceful tundra. Already I can see that being afoot is a great luxury. With the rain that seems to be ever present in this country, I know that I won't be able to escape as much as I would like. While I enjoy my walks on the beach, I like traversing the tundra even more, though it is a greater challenge. Neither is as complicated as walking the winding streets and muddy trails, holding up a skirt to avoid tripping.

The tundra is unlike anything I have ever seen. At first glance, it appears dead and unchanging, but as I look at it more, I can see the tiny flowers and mosses everywhere. The tundra is made up of many types of tiny bushes. Some resemble sponges in both their appearance and texture, while others are brittle and break

easily, creating a crunchy sound. I am learning slowly what areas
to walk on and which ones to stay away from. It is a very unstable
foundation to travel and can be dangerous to someone's ankle
if they are not watching where they are going. Consequently, I
look down when I walk and I observe the tundra. When I walked
toward the north last night after work, I saw some gorgeous long-
stemmed yellow flowers, brown toadstools, and bright red berries.
Tonight I walked toward the northwest and saw another display of
equally beautiful flowers. These were tiny dark purple blooms that
resembled lilacs, without the bush. I have seen so many different
kinds of wildflowers, I can't wait to walk in another direction and
find new ones.

J.J. understands my need to walk, but since he is a man and
a family member, he is concerned for my safety. He insists that I
tell him the direction that I plan on walking and how long I will be
gone. He also requires that I carry one of his guns with me when
I leave. He's afraid I may encounter a bear and he wants me to be
prepared to kill it if I need to. The last thing J.J. demands is that I
always have water. He makes sure that I have an adequate supply
because he knows that my walks can last up to three hours.

July 1899

July 1, 1899   3:40 a.m.

I hear from my clients that most of the men are staking claims in the names of their friends and relatives for whom they have the power of attorney, instead of actually working them. Optimism is so high that the masses believe gold can be found in every stream and each and every one wants to be the first to claim ownership. The greed is driving them hard now. They look more like hastily moving ants than intelligent creatures of God. The law requires that a mineral discovery be made before a claim is staked, but nobody has time to verify the presence of wealth. As a result not much mining is happening and the town's economy is beginning to feel the effects of that.

J.J. believes that the long-term optimism is excellent for business. He often says, "Given time, this gold rush camp is going to be a first rate city." He aspires to every challenge set before him. It amazes me day after day how well prepared J.J. was for this adventure. How could he really have known how fast the populace would consume the supplies that he ordered? We have already had our reserves restocked. He loves to be prepared for the future.

I was faced with several challenges last night. Ria was fighting again. I had to run and get J.J. to break it up. No matter what I did, Ria and the chippie who works out of the tent next door wouldn't stop. This time Ria insisted that the other lady had made some comments about her perfume not smelling good. My heart went out for the other working gal. She was beaten up pretty badly. All she could say was, "I didn't say anything to her. I swear on the Bible." I am beginning to think that Ria has a real problem. Lately when I talk to her she appears to be a totally different person. I do remember back in Seattle seeing several other working ladies who acted the same way. I think it must be a way to deal with the guilt that can weigh heavily on a soiled dove.

The grand finale for the evening was Natalie beating up a man so badly that there is talk he may not live. Now that I am the madam, I'm expected to solve most of the problems. All of a sudden I am supposed to know all of the answers. All I know this morning as I write is that I'm sure glad J.J. restocked us with about four times more laudanum than I thought we would need all summer. He is such a wise planner. He made an excellent decision by bringing up more of the brown liquid that numbs our very souls.

July 2, 1899   3:00 a.m.

I had a much better day. Everything went smoothly and for the first time, it feels splendid to be in charge. What a difference 24 hours can make. Yesterday I felt overwhelmed; today I feel empowered. After weighing out the profits last night and seeing how much gold I have made in this short time, there is no way I could give up this profession.

Our profits were high today as the patrons paid tribute to Captain W. E. Geiger, for he has solved the problem of getting from the sand spit to the opposite side of the Snake River. This has become a real dilemma because of all the activity on the sand spit. Captain Geiger has built a wagon bridge across the Snake River that cost him $19,000. He is charging $.25 per man for the use of his bridge. He is real proud of the fact that women and children

are allowed to cross free of charge. I overheard him say that once
the bridge has paid for itself, he will turn it over to the city. I also
heard him say that he will probably lower his prices if he ever gets
any competition. Either way, the bridge is good for all business in
this thriving community.

J.J.'s winning streak is still going strong. Last night he said to
me, "Looking back, it really started in Seattle those last two weeks
before we departed. During the day I would barter with merchants
for needed supplies and then make arrangements for its shipment.
By night I would enjoy the finest gourmet cooking to be found in
Seattle, then spend the late evenings playing poker. Since that first
day in Seattle I have either broken even or gained a large profit
in every hand of cards I have played." I love the way I feel after
talking with J.J. His life always seems exciting and he's always
grinning.

When I think about the profits his Faro tables are making at
The Belmont, I guess that is good enough reason for anyone to be
happy. Faro is a very prestigious game that is most popular because
it offers an exciting spectacle to the onlookers and gives the player
an almost even chance. It is believed to be a straight game because
it is hard to manipulate the cards. This game got its name from the
Pharaoh because the image of an Egyptian king is on the back of
the cards. The cards are dealt from a box that has a tiger painted on
the lid. When a man wants to bet against the Faro bank he says he
wants to "buck the tiger." Cards are drawn from a slit in the side of
the box in pairs face up; each pair drawn is a turn. Every card from
ace to king is painted on a wax cloth draped on a table. Players
place their chips, dollars, or gold nuggets on the layout. If the
card a man bets on is drawn first, he loses. If it comes up second,
he wins. And if neither happens then he can bet again. The dealer
rakes in the profits after paying off successful turns. There are 25
turns from soda to hoc, after which the game begins anew. I love
observing this game and its spectators. I must be aware so I don't
get too involved watching and forget I am working.

J.J. has several gambling tables operating at the same point
in time; therefore his profits are increasing by the hour. I'm

dumbfounded to see so many people throwing away their hard earned gold to the hands of destiny. I prefer to hold on to my earnings a little tighter.

I didn't have a chance to go on a walk tonight because of the rain. I've tried to get out of the town every day, or at least write in my diary, whether it's after work or before. I was hoping that it wouldn't rain as much here as it did in Seattle, but from what I've seen, there hasn't been much difference. I can't figure out why, but the rain doesn't seem to bother me as much here. Maybe the constant light outside has something to do with it. Or maybe it's because the periods of perpetual rain aren't as long. I guess I shouldn't complain because when the clouds do cease, the ocean and mountains create a splendid scene and make the predestined rain bearable.

July 3, 1899   3:15 a.m.

Today I met Jafet Lindeberg, who was one of the first people to discover gold in this area. He's a tall man with light brown hair, bright blue eyes, tiny ears, and an enchanting smile. He has a great sense of humor and laughs often. He paid for an overnight and we spent most of our time talking. I could tell that he respected me as an intelligent person. I find myself extremely attracted to him. When I look into his eyes, I see a spirit that is tender hearted, yet extremely strong. What an excellent combination! He is the first man since Galen who actually listens to what I am really saying and feeling. I would be a fool to start thinking that we could ever be together as man and wife. Once a woman chooses this profession, it's usually for life. I have seen only a few ladies escape through marriage.

It was so exciting listening to Jafet tell me about how he and his partners, Erik Lindblom and John Brynteson, started staking their claims on Anvil Creek on September 22, 1898. Now they are referred to as the "Lucky Swedes" because of their Scandinavian backgrounds. Even though everyone is getting used to calling this tent city "Nome," Jafet insists it is called Anvil City. He says the property belonging to his partners and him is called the Cape

Nome Mining District. Between the three of them, they now hold 90 claims, many of which just lay idle.

With the Lucky Swedes having already staked the best ground out at Anvil Creek, there has been a lot of resentment and anger among American miners who feel that only citizens of the United States should be able to stake mining claims here in Alaska Territory. The situation is getting so bad that men are using guns to protect their claims. With no civil authority in the Cape Nome Mining District, I have a feeling that it won't be long before all hell breaks loose here in the rainy, cold north. I hadn't anticipated the ever-changing atmosphere. I had the illusion that a gold rush city would always be full of elated emotions.

July 4, 1899   3:25 a.m.

Today I heard from customers that there must be over 3,000 people here and a great many of them are destitute. These are the men from the Klondike stampede who bet everything on striking it rich, and have lost it all. The predominant talk is that the real cause of the stampede is the 1893 depression. Whatever the cause of their situation, they are now stranded in Anvil City with no money, no supplies, and no hope of staking a claim. There are so many speculators and claim jumpers in the district that there is no real mining work being done. These penniless miners have no chance of finding a job to earn enough money to pay for a passage back to the States. It appears that the flood of disappointed and impoverished miners has wiped out any order that the early miners' meeting provided. Between the general mood of the busted miners, the constant drizzle that makes the mud-covered streets impassable, and the abundant claim jumping, I'm afraid trouble is brewing.

The more time I spend in The Belmont, the more I get to know and admire Ryan, the mixologist. I can see he is a hard worker. Customers regard him as a solid, trustworthy citizen. I have noticed he smoothly avoids conversations dealing with religion or politics, and instead encourages talks about lust and sports. I guess that's just being clever when he has to deal with drunks day and night.

Ryan has a rather sweet, innocent-looking face, despite his large framed body. He is always sticking up for injustices he witnesses, from animals to humans, no matter if it is a male or a female. I think the reddish tint in his hair and beard and his cheerful personality draws people to him.

July 5, 1899   12:30 p.m.

Independence Day was sensational! The sun was shining throughout the whole day and night of celebration, except for about four hours when it went behind the mountains to the north. As the sun returned to sight again in the northeast during the early morning hours, the sky began to lose its paleness and regain its bright color. The thick fog that emerged from the river created a map of its path as far back as one could see. A layer of light pink was on the bottom of the fog and the further away the moisture got from the river, the brighter the layers became. As the fog grew thicker, creamy shades of red, orange, and yellow were visible in perfect proportion, changing lighter in color with the passage of time. The blue hues in the puffy white clouds increased the visual appeal of the sky. Adding to the beauty of this enchanting land was the full moon directly above. The air had a crisp smell about it that made my nose hair tickle and I couldn't help but laugh aloud. I had never witnessed any scene in nature to compare it to. That was the beauty surrounding Nome.

As for Nome itself, it was the wildest place I have ever seen on any Fourth of July, or any other day for that matter. With all the talk about who was and who wasn't a true-blue American citizen, there was a lot of shouting and fighting. There were so many guns going off that a person didn't know if they were fired in hatred or happiness. I was grateful for the silence when the last of the merry-makers passed out. I know that between The Bantam and The Belmont, J.J. made a sizeable profit. The ladies served an average of 30 clients each, which easily made it our most profitable day in Nome.

To help the ladies and me unwind last evening, everyone was treated to extra laudanum. For the first time, I really enjoyed the feeling I got. Within seconds, my head was light and my body incredibly relaxed. Every aspect of work completely vanished from my mind. All I could do was sit at the bar and feel the deepness within myself. It was as if I was floating directly above my body. After hours of everyone floating around, Alex and I went back to my tent. We fell asleep in each other's arms as soon as we were on the bed. I miss sharing a room with her. I guess I just need to explain our physical relationship to J.J., how I love her and need to have her near me. I don't care what it will look like for the alliance. If I am working so hard to meet others' needs, I need someone to fulfill mine.

July 8, 1899   2:15 p.m.

After the large amount of business that we did on the Fourth, I have to make sure to order twice the butter as I had originally planned. Ever since that wild evening, the ladies have been complaining of soreness. I can't imagine how they would feel if we ran out of butter. Because it's the perfect lubricator, I must have plenty available. Using butter instead of lard is another sign of a first class house of joy.

We will also need more butter and syrup than expected for a reason I never would have imagined. Already the brunch that is served in the large tent at noon is becoming a ritual for all of the members of the business. It's as if we're all one large family and sharing a meal together gives us a chance to visit. If we're not talking about personal hardships, we're talking about how many new people we see each day.

Yesterday Ria commented how many sourdough griddle cakes Ryan can eat once he gets started. She noted it's hard to get any to eat for yourself when he's around. Alex suggested we should celebrate Natalie's birthday by letting her have as many warm griddle cakes soaked in steaming hot syrup and melting butter as she could eat before any of us could even sit down. It was enjoyable to watch each and every delicious bite disappear as she consumed her gift. Everyone enjoyed the moment and as a result, we will start a tradition of all-you-can-eat griddle cakes for your birthday. I remember Rosa saying it was important to find ways to keep your ladies feeling loved. I think this will help all members of the alliance know they are part of a family that will take time for a little celebration just for them.

Today a Public Safety Committee was formed to try and bring some order to the development of the town. The men held their meeting in the Straver's Saloon and five men were elected to serve on the Anvil Town Committee. I hope at least one of the men on this committee will have the foresight to look at the negative aspects mining has had on other communities in the past, and learn from their mistakes. I will never forget what the smelter did to Durango. When I was a child, the air was so clean. I didn't even realize air could get dirty until I saw the filth with my own eyes in my teenage years. Some evenings there would be so much smoke in the air, it was best just to stay indoors. Those evenings really stand out in my mind because we always had to go to bed sooner. I hated the waiting, wondering who my father would be taking out of bed for the evening. As I got older, I began to see a pattern in his nightly pleasure. If his plan were to take my sister out of bed, he would ask me questions about my day. If he conversed with my sister I knew he had plans for me. He treated the daughter who would be his toy for the evening as if she was an object, and not a live human being. I wonder if that was how he prepared himself for the event: striving to forget that we were alive and had feelings. I think that men who abuse females and men who make decisions for the public have a resemblance. Both think only of the gratification they receive immediately, not of the future or the consequences of their actions. If only they knew the damage they have done to both women and the earth. I learned a lot from J.J. about respecting our earth and the cycles of life. I wish everyone shared the same wisdom.

July 10, 1899   **3:50 a.m.**

Now that I'm beginning to feel confident running the business, I have slowly started serving more customers myself. When I'm with a client, Dorothy steps in to make arrangements for the ladies and collect fees.

Each night we serve over 50 men, most of whom we have never seen before. Truly, I couldn't name the ladies' frequent clients. I don't even know if we have any. That is definitely the next step I need to work on, getting to know the men by name. Rosa always said it was very important to make a man feel welcome in your brothel. With so many new clients showing up at The Belmont every day, I'm delighted I can weigh out the gold with ease and speed. The going price for one of the ladies today was 1/6 an ounce of gold for a quick encounter, where the ladies simply undo the snaps in their working dresses, or 1/4 an ounce to have one of my girls naked for an hour. If by rare chance a man wants one of the ladies for an overnight it is 3/4 of an ounce. If they want me it is one ounce for the whole evening. The cost changes daily as does the price of gold.

All my ladies are elated with their profit margin and that has kept me from looking for others. Everyone agrees that we shouldn't hire anyone else until one of us physically can't take the high demand put on our bodies and we begin to tire. Only then will the ladies welcome more competition in the bevy.

Jafet has visited me the last five evenings and his frequent visits are making him my favorite overnight client. During each of the visits we make merry bout right away. There was nothing exciting about our body chemistry. It was about the same as the usual man paying for a prostitute. The man is always on top. He pumps ten to twenty times; you hear his heavy breathing and a sigh of release. Done in about three minutes from beginning to end. No emotional or spiritual connections of any kind—just simple depositing of his seed. I was anticipating more from Jafet since he was paying for a madam.

We stayed awake for hours talking. I listened and laughed as he told me story after story. I noticed that whenever I spoke he gave me his undivided attention and never asked me any questions. I felt really comfortable with that. I also felt extremely secure in his arms. He is truly a kind and gentle man. His humor comes from his heart and is very sincere. I've never enjoyed the company of a client so much before.

Because Jafet has been so consistent in his visits, I started getting worried when I hadn't seen him by early evening. Before the shift was over, I received a letter from him. Last night after returning back to Anvil, about four miles north of town, someone tried to shoot him. He said he wasn't hurt but he couldn't see me again until the greed and hatred had died down. The situation was so heated that it wasn't safe for him to leave his claims unguarded. A part of me was sad to hear that I wouldn't be seeing him soon, but another part of me was happy. Business is going good and I don't need any complications. I have to admit though, last night when I laid in his arms and laughed, I knew that I could break the number one rule in the business and get involved with a client. It will be good to have some time apart from Jafet.

July 12, 1899   11:10 a.m.

This was the most exciting evening that I've spent in Anvil City. About five or six hundred men gathered in The Northern, the biggest saloon in town. Tex Rickard owns it. J.J. asked if the ladies and I would like to close up shop and go listen. I said that I would love to witness the event. Jime told the other ladies to take a break and to come watch the excitement if they wanted to. They all took the opportunity to walk around our growing town and to spend some of their hard earned gold dust on trinkets. I was too interested in what was unfolding to join them, so J.J. and I walked over to The Northern together.

Once we were inside, it only took a few minutes to figure out what all the excitement was about. The miners who had not gotten lucky yet wanted to declare all of the existing mining claims in the Cape Nome district void and illegal, which would open all the creeks for re-staking. A young man in the crowd spoke up to say that United States mining law does indeed hold that only citizens or aliens expressing the intent to become citizens can make valid mineral claims. Another outspoken member of the crowd went on to say that a group of men were waiting out at Anvil Creek to see a bonfire from Anvil City. That would be their signal that they were to race to relocate for themselves and their partners all of the best claims in the district.

That may have worked as planned if it hadn't been for Lieutenant Spaulding, who had been sent to Anvil City last month to maintain some type of order. I watched Spaulding and his six soldiers standing in the back of The Northern as the anger mounted. I always notice tall men in uniforms. From my experience, most men in the military have very muscular bodies from the rugged exercises they endure. I always indulge my eyes when I see fitness at its peak.

With confidence that only a man in command can project, Lieutenant Spaulding listened until right before the men were ready to agree on the plan. With bayonet-toting soldiers at his side, he ordered the resolution withdrawn and the meeting adjourned. Despite loud curses and threats to Spaulding, order was maintained and the crowd dispersed. Men who still didn't have claims were outraged. They shouted as loud as they could, "This unwarranted decision interferes with the American right of free speech!" The three men leading the meeting were told that they would be arrested immediately if there was further trouble. After the meeting settled down and Spaulding left The Northern, J.J. offered to treat the three men to a drink at The Belmont. To turn down a drink is a great insult and one not taken lightly, so they gladly joined J.J. and myself.

As soon as we engaged in conversation, I found myself extremely attracted to all three of these men, each in a different way. First there is Milroy. He has the same dark handsome appearance about him that J.J. does. A woman can't help but stare when she sees such a work of art. Both Milroy and J.J. have bodies like those of Greek statues, but their faces are very different from one another. J.J. has warm compassionate eyes and a strength driven by a white light that surrounds him and all he touches. I guess that when a man's intentions are pure like J.J.'s, he just naturally commands respect. In Milroy I see a person who demands you respect him or risk his huge fist in your mouth. His strength appears to come from a malicious nature. My first impression of him is that he is dangerous and quite capable of taking a life to get what he demands. Yet, I felt a desire to get close to him.

As soon as I looked into Rawslin's eyes, he introduced himself as a journalist for the Nome newspaper. He said the only reason he piped up tonight was because he had recently written an article on mining law and he knew for a fact what was true and what wasn't. My first impression was, here is a man who likes himself because he likes what he does for a living. I found myself enthralled by Rawslin's baby blue eyes. Then Clark introduced himself and instantly broke the spell between Rawslin and me. Just as one bond was broken, another one was created.

I took one look into Clark's big brown eyes and was overwhelmed with visions of another time and place. I had no control over my mind. I wasn't in The Belmont. I was a mother outside calling loudly for my child. My heart was alive with a mysterious love for the human being that had grown in my body. I knew without reservation I would give my life for his. I saw my young blond-haired boy laying face down in a field of wheat. In my final vision, I was holding the child's cold body as I rocked back and forth crying deeply. I found this experience so moving that I was just about to ask the gentlemen to excuse me while I got some fresh air, but Milroy insisted on having my company for the evening. I think J.J. wanted me to leave so that he could have the full attention of the two other men to answer his many questions concerning successful ventures. I have observed that a secret to J.J.'s success is he believes there is something to learn from everyone, and he doesn't hesitate to inquire.

Against my better judgment, I agreed to go with Milroy. A part of me wanted to run away from him, to physically flee as fast as I could in the opposite direction. I had a quick vision of a tunnel with only darkness. A voice within gave me warning. If I entered the tunnel, it could only end in despair. But I couldn't stop myself from the raw attraction that was burning inside me. It was as if a force beyond my control had entered my body the moment I first saw him. There was something about him that made me think he could instantly give me pleasure, and I couldn't resist.

Intercourse with Milroy was like nothing I had ever experienced. He was extremely aggressive. As he enjoyed the pleasures of my body, I lost all track of time. I became more and more intrigued by the venereal prowess of this man. I reached an explosive satisfaction and Milroy knew it. I remember Rosa encouraged her ladies to stimulate themselves to pleasure before starting work for the evening, that way we didn't give the customer the satisfaction of knowing he gave us pleasure. I guess I need to start practicing her sound advice. It just wouldn't do for Milroy to become more than a mere client.

July 13, 1899   3:40 a.m.

I'm quickly learning to enjoy all the privileges that bestow a madam. For example, I like living in the tent closest to Front Street. I know that when our cabins are built, mine will be first and will proudly display the number one and my working name on the door. My favorite reward so far is being the first one each day to take a bath. The order after me is rotated daily. That way, one lady doesn't constantly get stuck using the dirtiest water.

Routinely after brunch, while Dorothy cleans up the meal, the ladies and I clean ourselves. It is up to us to heat the water Jime has hauled. If we didn't heat the water, it wouldn't get done. Jime and Dorothy already do more than we ever expected. While we wait for the water to heat up, we take turns brushing cornmeal through each other's hair. This helps to keep our hair looking cleaner longer. Everyone in the bevy gets the luxury of shampooing her hair once a week.

Being in Dorothy and Jime's tent is such a contrast to our tiny canvas structures. Their tent is four times the size of the tents where the ladies and I work. With no calendar pictures on the wall, the space looks very large. All that is within eyesight are the

43

necessities of life: a ready food supply, one large table and the required chairs for feeding the crew, one bed in the corner, one large stove and the pots, pans, and utensils needed for cooking food and heating the water. I cherish my tiny, cozy space I have made home.

The ladies and I look forward to our daily cleansing ritual. It gives us time to share our latest experiences. I find it amusing that we all have had similar encounters. For instance, we all agree that when a man requests to put his manhood in your mouth, that is a sure sign he has a little wife tucked away, whether it is in Anvil City or back down in the States. The general consensus among the ladies is that if married women ever started performing the evil deed on their husbands, they could put us lewd women out of business. I think they refuse that task in order to keep feeling superior to us. If the truth were known, most public women don't allow a man's genital in her mouth. An old wives tale says that doing so will make your teeth fall out. It is believed that is why you see some real old women of the trade without teeth. I am not sure what the truth is, but my ladies and I aren't going to find out. To keep the clients who have an interest in that sort of activity content, we encourage them to talk about their desires. It seems to work!

July 14, 1899   1:30 a.m.

It's been raining since the night of the meeting. When the clouds hang down close to the earth and leak their tiny droplets for days in a row, it gets quite dismal and the ladies and I start to crave the sight of clear skies. Since the night of the meeting at The Northern, the tension in this town has grown and conflict between rival claim owners has become more frequent. To prevent bloodshed, the Army has forbidden anyone from carrying firearms in hopes of stopping the violence before it starts. I figure that if something is not done within a few days, there will be an all out war between the desperate miners in town and the miners at Anvil.

Today before work, the ladies and I went exploring on the thriving tundra. It was lightly raining. The further we walked away from town, the quieter it got. At one point during our walk, we all stood still and just listened to the silence. I'm not sure what the other ladies were looking at. The water that had been captured in the lowest depths of the tundra fascinated me. I could see six separate little ponds, all crystal clear. The only movement I witnessed was the rings created by raindrops gently touching the surface.

On previous hikes, all I could hear was the loud chirps of the tiny creatures but today the lack of singing birds added to the tranquility. It was so very peaceful that I forgot about the tension brewing back in town. We all walked slowly back to our tents, not one of us wanting to return to the boiling pot of Anvil City. Natalie thinks it is impossible for this town to go another week without something drastic happening. For the first time, everyone agreed with her. I never would have imagined gold fever could create such tension between people.

July 17, 1899   **3:05 a.m.**

There was so much excitement today that I never heard who actually discovered the gold on the beach. Yesterday the mood in the town was one of pure desperation and now everyone feels euphoric. I have never seen so many people on the beach at one time. As far as I could see both east and west, there were men, women, and children with various mining equipment scattered around them. There was no logical path to travel and no space available to make one. Everyone seemed to be moving quicker than usual. It was comical. Many with fancy mining equipment tried desperately to work efficiently. Others simply used a shovel. I even saw young children alongside their parents digging with spoons. After minutes of observation, it was plain that the individual miners thought they were making paths to endless wealth.

Most everyone in town can be found on the beach. Only a few saloonkeepers remain in their buildings; no lawyers are in their offices, no bankers are in their banks. Even J.J. and Alex are on the beach trying their luck, while Ryan keeps The Belmont open for the thirsty miners.

Rumor has it the men working the creeks are coming back into town to get a piece of the action. The feeling is one of pure bliss. Everyone thinks they have found the paradise. It's incredibly exhilarating! I was on the beach today for a short time and I witnessed the gold in the sand. People are starting to call Anvil City just plain Nome, as well as the "poor man's paradise." Hurrah! We are back in the large profit margin!

I have become more efficient with the gold scales, so J.J. has me weigh out more and more of our profits. I had never touched so much gold in my life even before the big discovery. I wonder what it will be like now! Maybe I will have to start looking for more ladies. Perhaps I can find some among the new arrivals. Tomorrow we will have to raise our prices to fit the supply and demand.

As my gold collection grows I'm beginning to have a passion for this gold fever. With the prospect of higher prices for our services, I don't think I'll even need to try my luck panning. My business is my beach. I just need to work it carefully each day to gain my wealth.

July 19, 1899   4:00 a m.

The only thing we heard today from the customers was about the rich beaches extending 40 miles in both directions. Everyone was talking about how a miner needs a shovel, and if he doesn't have that, a bucket or a large tin can with a handle on it to carry water will do. He also needs a cheap wooden rocker. Three or more men are needed to operate a rocker: one to shovel in the sand, one to pour water over the sand, and one to rock the "cradle" back and forth. The lighter sand is washed down while the heavier flakes of gold are caught on screens or wooden rifles in the bottom of the rocker. The finer gold is trapped by a copper plate at the bottom of the cradle, which is covered with mercury. The gold sticks to the mercury and prevents it from being washed away. I have heard from some miners that rocking can be very slow and it is only worth it if you are working rich black sand.

Mercury reminds me of Galen. I miss him most in the morning when I am just waking up. I remember how I used to lay in his arms and talk to him until he was almost late for work. Those memories I keep close to my heart. When he worked at the smelter, he used to bring home mercury. It was fun to watch him roll it around in his hands. The magical silver substance couldn't decide if it was a liquid or a solid. I always liked it when two globs would come together as one. It made me think of how I wanted to be as one with Galen, more with each passing day. I miss his loving touch. We had a good life together. What would my life have been like had Galen lived? I probably would have become a teacher in Durango after Mrs. Put retired. My life didn't go as planned, but I have to admit I am pleased to be a madam in Alaska Territory during this gold rush.

July 20, 1899   **2:50 p.m.**

This morning Jime cooked breakfast instead of Dorothy. She caught a cold a couple of days ago and finally decided to stay in bed today. With everything going around, it's hard to believe that only one of us has gotten sick. Our whole alliance has been lucky ever since this journey began. I have to stop myself every once in a while to thank God for all our good fortune. For now, we are happy and looking forward to what the next day will bring us. Even Ria seems at ease. We talk about the endless possibilities and predict the future will bring something new and exciting. As usual, J.J. is more joyous than anyone else, thanks to his continued winning streak. Each day at brunch he brags, "If business keeps up at this pace, I will own The Belmont free and clear by winter. I wonder how many other proprietors in Anvil City can say the same."

Although J.J. and the rest of the business alliance have not changed much, the town sure has. This desolate seashore was barely a speck on the map a month ago and now it is a bustling gold rush town. I'm overjoyed that I have this opportunity to be part of all that's going on. It's so exciting to see the changes. I see more and more tents, and framed structures are being built with the many tons of lumber that arrive daily. The most noticeable sound is the pounding hammers. This constant noise can be heard in every direction. It is like a music all its own, each hammer creating its own tones and following its own beat. Since so much has happened here in one month, I wonder what this town will be like a year from now.

July 22, 1899   **4:20 a.m.**

The constant light of the midnight sun allows miners to search for gold on the beach all night long. Everyone is full of energy and no one is getting much sleep. I am told that beach miners are making from $20 to $100 a day. Their gold is assaying out from $16 to $17 an ounce, depending on the impurities. I also heard that gold from the creeks is worth more, but to recover that type of gold one must have more equipment, which means more money. It's easier to just stick with the poor man's diggings. Rumor has it a sick old man named John Hummel was the first person to discover the gold on the beach. He was getting some sunshine on the sand to help cure his scurvy when he started panning to pass the time. That's when he figured out the sand was so rich. Another rumor I heard is there was a group of miners camping on the beach and as they were putting on their shoes one morning, they found gold dust on their feet. The third rumor is two of Lieutenant Spaulding's men prospected on the beach and found as high as $.70 to a pan over a week ago. So much excitement and confusion surrounds this town, I don't think we'll ever know for sure who really discovered the golden beaches of Nome.

July 24, 1899   **3:10 p.m.**

Ria's strange personality came out today. Just this morning at brunch she was telling us how much she enjoyed this "beautiful land where the sun shines forever." Then about a half an hour ago when she and I were in Ames Mercantile Company searching for new perfume, she completely lost her reasoning. A couple of proper ladies were standing together in an aisle full of fruit crates. They whispered secretly to each other. I thought nothing of it and walked past. Ria on the other hand lost her composure and began yelling at the top of her lungs, "I didn't steal anything. Don't talk about me that way, you little bitches! Don't ever say I took something when I didn't!"

Ria was just about to throw a punch at one of them, when the storekeeper intervened and asked what the problem was. One of the respected ladies spoke up. "We were just standing here talking about these apples when this public person came up to us and started yelling for no reason. I think you should never allow them to come in here again." I knew I had to do something so I stepped up to the keeper and told him that I was sorry about the scene my lady had caused and that it would never happen again. Before we left the storekeeper insisted on making sure Ria didn't have any stolen goods tucked into her clothes. That only made her more outraged. As I led a sobbing Ria out of the store, the customers stared at us until we were on the mud-covered front street. Ria continued to cry until we reached our tents. I didn't try to console her. What she did was wrong; she can't just go around yelling at everyone because she thinks they said something about her. I don't know what to tell her. I love her as if she were my own chick, but if she keeps up this unpredictable behavior, I don't know how we can keep her. I thought it had something to do with the weather, but now I'm not so sure. I guess I'll have to talk to her about this. In a way I wish she had been caught stealing—at least that would explain why she had such a breakdown so quickly.

July 25, 1899   **3:15 a.m.**

The time J.J. and Alex have been spending on the beach during the day is paying off for them. Now, all Alex can talk about is the dark ruby colored sand that can be found anywhere from one to four feet below the surface. She said, "The two biggest 'pay streaks' where gold can be found in paying quantities are right on the edge of the water, and further back near the edge of the tundra." J.J. and Alex, along with 2,000 other men, women, and children, are elated because the sand is not frozen, and doesn't have to be thawed as the stream gravel does. Alex said, "The best part of beach mining is the fact that no one can stake a claim on the beach, which leaves it open to everyone. I can hold my space, the length of my shovel, as long as I work that section of the beach."

Of course, everyone has his or her own theory about how all of this gold got here. Some believe it's a result of glaciers, while some think it's because of meteors or volcanoes. Others argue that the ocean floor is full of gold and each storm replenishes the beach. A lot of people just like to think it is a miracle. I tend to believe J.J.'s idea the most and it rings in my mind, "My instincts tell me the mother lode can be found several miles inland of this tent city and that this is only the beginning of the riches that await all of us." I love keeping that thought in my mind. How exciting to think that there is an abundance of gold, enough for everyone to share, waiting to be uncovered.

July 26, 1899   3:30 p.m.

I just returned from a hike along the beach. It was quite a challenging task with all the tents and equipment dispersed throughout the area from the shore to the tundra. Before entering my own quarters, I stopped in each of the ladies' tents. Alex was reading a book, and Natalie was knitting a scarf for her daughter. Ria wasn't doing anything really, just sitting on her bed "contemplating life," as she put it. I've noticed that Alex, Natalie, and I have hobbies. Natalie is always knitting scarves, sweaters, and blankets. The scarf she was working on included all seven colors of the rainbow. The red, orange, yellow, green, blue, indigo, and violet were the prettiest colors I have ever seen in yarn. With all the rain we have been having, I wonder if the rainbows we have seen inspired Natalie. If Alex isn't reading she can be found playing cards, even when she's by herself. When she does read, she enjoys a variety of books, anything from history to romance.

I don't really know what Ria has a passion for. She tends to sit around and think a lot, which isn't always a good thing in this profession. Ladies begin thinking about how much they hate their lives, which could lead to drastic situations. I hope Ria finds something that she loves to do, and soon, too. We can't have her thinking too much.

July 29, 1899   **2:40 p.m.**

There has been such a beautiful feeling of harmony here in town that I knew it was too good to last forever. Someone had to make trouble and who better than the rich mining company. They say their mining claims extend to the normal high tide level. The beach miners are coming back with the argument that according to the U.S. law, a 60-foot roadway must be reserved above the high tide line for the public, and that individual claims on that strip of ground along the coast are not valid. I hear tell that no one really knows for sure where the normal tide line is and the situation is very uncertain. People are starting to fear that their "poor man's paradise" will be turned into a rich man's paradise. I wonder where the greed will lead this time?

July 30, 1899   **2:55 p m.**

Once again it is drizzling outside. The weather brings on discontentment. Today I was really missing the hot July days that I spent in Durango. I thought of those days as a gift from heaven. I remember loving to lie on an old blanket under a large cottonwood tree. I especially treasured the clear days, that way I could look up and see millions of pieces of white cotton floating in the brilliant sky. It was almost like it was snowing except the trees were alive and displaying their many shades of green. If there were huge puffy clouds in the background of my perfect picture, it wouldn't make the contrast seem as brilliant. Just thinking about Colorado made me cry. I miss the feeling of the sun rejuvenating my body and soul. If the wet weather continues I'm afraid I will go into winter without the strength to take on the worst that Mother Nature can present.

July 31, 1899   **3:50 a.m.**

Natalie's second beating occurred tonight. The man looked helpless, laying on the floor with blood streaming out of his nose. He was speechless as Jime pulled him from the floor and handed him a wet cloth. His gaze was fixed on the floor and I could tell he was humiliated to the extreme. This could be bad for our business because I seriously doubt that he will be returning soon. Yet in an awkward way, it's good for business. Natalie was fresh and revived after the man left and much happier than she has been lately, which is always good. Plus, I don't think the man will tell his friends what happened because he's too mortified to admit he was beat up by a woman. As long as Natalie's beating doesn't affect the profit margin, her need to hurt men could have its benefits.

August 1899

August 1, 1899   **1:30 p.m.**

During brunch today I found myself looking at Alex and thinking about her firm bosoms, knowing that last night I had the pleasure of her lush nipples in my mouth. I became highly aroused just thinking about how I love to hold her bosoms in my hands, while I gently use my tongue to flick back and forth the very tip of her nipples. If I'm positioned just right, rubbing my little hill on her warm leg, I can easily reach satisfaction. I love the way we get so moist when we are lovers. Does she respond to everyone's touch the way she does mine, or is it a special connection that we share?

I have a feeling it isn't something unique to just her and me. With all the time J.J. and Alex have been spending together, in and out of her tent, they both must be enjoying themselves. All a person has to do is watch them for a little bit and before too long they make eye contact. Anybody who knows anything about people can tell they are starting to fall in love with each other. Oh, what will I do without Alex to hold and smell?

August 3, 1899   **4:15 a.m.**

Dorothy's birthday was actually on the second of August,
but she didn't want to celebrate it with griddlecakes. Instead she
cooked a magnificent baked salmon feast with a dill sauce for our
evening meal. Although that meal is served after work at about
2:15 a.m. and everyone is usually exhausted, we all perked up
tonight. Everyone in this alliance is very thankful to have Dorothy
and we wanted to make her birthday special. It was evident in our
gift giving we were all concerned about Dorothy's hands since she
does all the washing. Each of us got her a different type of cream
or balm. A tear came to her eye that showed all how appreciative
she was that we knew just what she needed. Jime told us that he
offered to cook for her so that she could relax, but she enjoys it so
much she wouldn't let him. She was so happy to share this birthday
with everyone she insisted on cooking a splendid meal. We all
thanked her and wished her and Jime a wonderful evening before
slipping away into our own tents. They are such a cheerful couple.
I wonder if they know how lucky they are to have a relationship
where each person is respected and cherished. I would like to think
that my love with Galen was comparable to theirs. I know Galen
and I loved each other greatly. We probably didn't show it as often
as Jime and Dorothy. The love they share is evident to all.

August 4, 1899   **3:30 p.m.**

I just returned from a fast paced walk on the beach. Out about
a quarter mile in the calm water of the Bering Sea was a wide
canoe-like craft holding a dozen dark-featured men. Each one was
holding an oar in his hands. Those not wearing hats revealed an
odd bowl shaped haircut.

I wonder what they think of the image of the tent city before
their eyes? How strange it must be to see so many humans,
especially fair skinned ones, all at once. I wonder if they are
frightened and that is why they stay away from the shore.

August 5, 1899   **3:00 p.m.**

Yesterday the largest holder of beach claims, the Nome
Mining and Development Company (which is made up of several
of the original locators in the district including Jafet) decided to
stop fighting the hordes of beach miners. Instead they will try to
make some money from the situation. They are now going to start
charging $.50 per day per person for a permit to work the beach.
They say that anyone found working on the company's ground
after August 6, 1899, without a permit will be prosecuted for
trespass and larceny.

It saddens me to discover that Jafet, my favorite client, is just
as greedy as everyone else. What could I expect? He believes in
Darwinism. He is just trying to be one of the fittest. I have not seen
Jafet since the evening he was shot at. I miss him.

August 6, 1899   **11:00 a.m.**

Today at breakfast Natalie said Kama was the Hindu god of
love in India around AD 400. In those days, the acquisition of love
and sensual pleasure was of great importance. Men made love
like it was an art form. The act was more about the union of the
body and the mind. It was a connection that centered on feelings.
Everybody was quiet until Alex asked why she was telling us
about this while eating. Natalie quickly replied, "Oh, I am sorry. I
dreamed about that last night and it was just on my mind." That is
all it took for everyone to start talking about the dreams they have
at night. Everyone, that is, but Ria. She said that she has never
had a dream she remembers. That could be a blessing or a curse
depending on what you dream. I wonder if Natalie really does get
some of her knowledge from her dreams? Maybe we all could if
we would just be open to the possibility of it.

August 7, 1899   **3:15 p.m.**

It stopped drizzling about 11:00 this morning and I was able
to go on a saunter for the first time in days. Walking out on the
tundra, I noticed the abundance of blueberries growing in little
patches. I stopped to pick a few and had hoped to bring some back

for breakfast tomorrow, but I made the mistake of eating one. They were so ripe and delicious that by the time I got back, they were all gone and my mouth and my fingers were strained dark blue. Maybe next time I can bring a container and any of the ladies who want to can join me. I'd love to share this delicacy that Mother Nature has given us.

August 9, 1899   2:15 p.m.

Alex just left my tent after coming to ask if she could borrow a pair of boots. She has been so busy working the beach during the days that she has broken the heel on her one and only pair. She has plenty of gold to buy a new pair but not enough time to go shopping. Of course I said yes, and then joked that I got to keep any gold dust in them when they are returned. When Alex first arrived I was writing in my dairy and she asked if she could please read it. I answered, "Yes, someday I would love very much for you to read what I have written. For now I write for future readers." She accepted that answer the way she does life—very content with new knowledge, never overbearing for more. Alex is the most pleasant person I have ever shared time with. She never seems sad or depressed; I guess it's because she knows how to ensure her own happiness. She loves herself more than any one I have ever known. Maybe being that rare one percent that enjoys this profession contributes to her constant bliss.

I feel content knowing that I never have to question Alex's love for me. Being a woman, she knows how important it is to have a lover truly acknowledge her feelings. When Alex and I are alone she openly speaks of her love, always letting me know what she admires about me as well as how I could improve difficult situations in my life. I don't know what I would have done if Alex wouldn't have joined our alliance. I know I wouldn't be as strong if Alex wasn't a part of my life. I love her with all my heart and soul.

August 11, 1899   **2:45 a.m.**

Since so much news is either made or talked about in saloons, Rawslin said he gets a drinking allowance so he can afford to spend his time there. Since I am a madam, my drinks are free, but of course I let men spend their hard earned gold to buy drinks for me that Ryan waters down. It wouldn't do for a madam to lose her composure.

I really enjoyed my conversation with Rawslin while in The Belmont today. Somehow we got to talking about authors we like. We discovered that we share very common interests in literature. For example, we both enjoy Emily Dickinson, Steven Crane, and Sister Carrie. It was funny because we both admitted at the same time that Mark Twain was by far our favorite author. Then we went on to talk about some of our preferences such as *The Innocents Abroad, The Tramp Abroad,* and *Roughing It*. He was astonished to find out that a fallen lady could read. I told him that not many women in the kinship were readers, but there are a few. He asked if I would like to borrow a book from his collection. He assured me that he had plenty; he wouldn't think of being without books. I told him that I would love that very much, having only brought Lew Wallace's *Ben Hur*, one of my favorite pieces of literature.

I have lifted my tent flap and am watching the rain pour down. I'm thankful that I lived in Seattle. It helped me get acquainted with rainy weather. Having no experience other than Durango with its hot summer days and warm summer evenings, I would have gone zany living in Alaska Territory. Of course there were rainy times in Durango, but they never lasted more than a couple of days. I haven't seen the sun since my walk a few days ago. If this is what summer is like, I'm not looking forward to winter. This storm blew in from the south, bringing bitter cold gusts that earlier today were ripping apart tents.

Once again, I'm thankful for being in business with J.J. He is a smart man who pays for the best. Our tents are made of very strong canvas. I have no concerns about suddenly being exposed to the elements like the many who possess lower quality tents. My heart goes out for the countless people in this gold rush town who endure the nights without a canvas shelter of any type to protect them from the harsh weather.

August 13, 1899   4:30 a.m.

This evening my thoughts are on J.J. I find myself admiring him more each day. I love to listen to his many past adventures, for he is a great storyteller. Once he knows you're interested, he can take a person on quite a mindful journey. I also love the way he handles each situation with confidence. His calm demeanor seems to diffuse the most intense events. For example, tonight a drunk miner pulled a large hunting knife out from his long coat and said that the next person who moved would be the first killed. Instead of rushing toward the fool, J.J. remained seated at the poker table and just used his voice to convince the ass to put it away and have a drink on the house. I think the man felt very foolish but that didn't stop him from enjoying his free drink.

I have noticed when J.J. is dealing with males he is always very assertive, yet when he is dealing with females he is just the opposite. He becomes very reserved and rather shy. I have heard talk in the mercantile that women are calling him a gentle giant. At times he can come across as real giving, but I know what his real motive is—self-preservation. I know because he is the one who taught me. He is always saying, "You can't save someone's life if you have to risk your own to do so." At first I thought that was selfish, but now I understand the logic in it.

It truly is wonderful to be in J.J.'s company again. In the years we were apart I missed his big bear hugs and his musky smell. Most of all I missed hearing him laugh. Alex and I were just talking the other night about its unique sincerity.

August 14, 1899   5:15 a.m.

Today before our evening work started, Ria lost the key to her trunk and became a crazed lunatic. She accused Natalie of taking it. Natalie said she hadn't ever touched any of Ria's belongings. Ria was so hysterical I had to get J.J. to help me settle her down. His idea of a sedative was a quick punch in the face to knock her out. He suggested I stay by her and give her a huge dose of laudanum as soon as she started waking up. I did just that and hopefully she is sleeping as I write. I am beginning to regret selecting Ria for my flock. Everyone else is working out perfectly but there just seems to be one problem after another with her. I'm not sure what to do in this situation. I'll give her some more time to adjust. Maybe the weather really does affect her personality. I'm beginning to feel it affects mine.

August 16, 1899   3:30 p.m.

Yesterday was one of those rare occasions when I was able to persuade my flock to walk with me. The breezy, warm day probably influenced them more than I did. We stopped to rest before heading back to the gold rush city, when we all noticed a brown nest woven into the tundra. In the nest were four turquoise eggs. Before any of us had time to protest, Ria picked up an egg. Our laments at this act made her nervous and she dropped the egg, exposing the creature within. She started crying hysterically, realizing what she had done. The whole way back to town was spent convincing her that it was just a mistake. She didn't mean to end an innocent life. Alex repeatedly voiced, "At least there's three left!" Natalie stressed the fact that robins are the only bird that can be found in the Arctic and in New York City. As a species, they are great survivors. One fallen egg cannot harm their existence. My input was, "How could the mother expect her eggs to be there when she returned? They have no protection!" I don't know if anything we said helped, but suddenly that strangeness came over her and she stopped crying. We remained silent the rest of the walk.

At bathing time today, we each reflected on our own mothers— what they did well and what we would do different if we ever got the chance. A tear fell from Natalie. "I have children that I don't even get to be with or raise myself. I miss them, and I wonder if they miss me. At least they have food and shelter and they are safe."

Last night I dreamed about an egg that dropped to the ground. Out came a baby that had Jafet's eyes and my smile. I remember wanting deeply to care for the new life, but I can't remember anything else.

August 17, 1899   3:35 p.m.

History was made here in Nome today once more. The Nome Mining and Development Company requested Lieutenant Craigie to guard their beach claims against jumpers. As the Lieutenant and six of his men walked onto the beach, they were greeted by almost 300 angry miners who kept saying that the mining company had no right to claim that part of the beach. To show that they were serious, the men said that they would not stop working the beach as requested. To stop them the Lieutenant would have to arrest them all. So Craigie was given no other alternative but to do just that. Rumor has it that 286 miners were arrested for trespassing on the mining company's beach property and then marched off to a military camp.

There is always power in numbers, so none of the men arrested would post bond for his release. All of them demanded a separate trial by jury. There are no facilities in Nome to house that many prisoners and the Army didn't have enough money to pay the $1,000 a day that it would take to feed that many prisoners. Naturally, the mining company refused to post a bond to cover the expenses. Lieutenant Craigie's only choice was to release the accused within hours after they were arrested. Hopefully there will be no more trouble on the beach now that it must stay open to everyone.

August 19, 1899   6:00 a.m.

Now I'm sure that bringing Ria here was a mistake. Last night while serving a soldier, she took his gun and started firing in all directions. I don't know how she got his gun but whatever happened he sure looked embarrassed. Lucky for the young man the bullet that hit him only skimmed his arm. J.J. risked his life to get the gun away from her. As soon as he got close to her, he planted his fist onto her face and she went out cold. He quickly said, "I really don't like to hit women but this one just keeps asking for it."

As soon as I bent down to see if she was still breathing, I could smell booze on her. She must have gotten it from another saloon. I know that Ryan would never give or sell her any. He is too much of a businessman and he knows how that could interfere with the profits. I guess tomorrow I will have to talk to her and let her know I will not put up with her drinking while working. I will have to start keeping a better eye on her during the day. I also will have to begin checking on her several times in the evening. I know now that I can't trust her. I wonder if the fact that Ria shot a soldier will be bad for the business? Although if it did have an impact, I don't think we could tell. There are so many men here, I'm sure the military clientele won't be missed.

I have heard that the long, hard winter can be devastating to a person's mind, body, and soul. I am fearful that Ria may not make it through. Next time she just might shoot herself. I have a feeling that's what she was trying to do.

August 20, 1899   **4:05 a.m.**
The wild merry-making I witnessed on the Fourth of July was nothing compared to the celebration that has been taking place in the last 48 hours. The Belmont rose to the occasion of this joyous conquest by serving drinks for two days straight. Alex added to the excitement by drawing a continuous crowd of men who were hypnotized by her expressive dancing. I had forgotten how mesmerizing she really is, so I watched for a while. Two gentlemen from the audience instigated the dancing by playing their harmonicas with a cheerful rhythm. I could tell that she was bringing in more money for The Belmont by dancing than by exercising her other talents, so I didn't ask her to work in The Bantam Belmont that evening.

The miners feel a real accomplishment having won their case against the wealthy mining company. This seems to have boosted the way each man feels about himself. Days ago the miners had a drastic outlook on life; now the majority of them are spending their money as fast as they make it. They seem to feel a need to buy themselves a luxury that has been long denied, be it a chocolate Hershey bar, a pack of Juicy Fruit gum, a Life magazine, a bath, a hair cut, or a few minutes with a fallen woman. This new frame of mind is excellent for our profits.

Speaking of profits, my gold collection is really starting to grow. Because I don't have to pay for my room and board, I am able to save a large portion of the money I make, unlike the other ladies. With that money, I am slowly paying back J.J. for the investment that got us started. Last month I placed an order from Sears, Roebuck and Co. Consumer's Guide, which should be arriving by October. I bought a fur muff, a beautiful blue silk dress, and some jewelry for myself. I bought a comb and brush set for each of the ladies including Dorothy for Christmas, and for each of the men a mirror and shaving mug. I have never had enough money to buy myself gifts, let alone others. Each day I find more and more advantages to being a madam.

August 21, 1899   11:00 p.m.

I had a truly disturbing dream last night. It wasn't about my father; it was about my mother, my sister Lizzy, and myself in our cabin in Durango. We were all working together to drag a very heavy object across the floor. What I remember the most is the intense silence. There was not one word spoken. Just diligent teamwork. I remember the smell in the air. I think it was the smell of freedom.

Why do people dream? Does everyone have dreams they just don't remember? Why do some dreams seem so real and others so far from reality? Why do we have visions of some dreams several times the next day and others leave our memory as soon as we sit up in bed? Are we supposed to learn something from them, or are they simply reminding us of our fears?

That dream made me think about my mother. I don't think I have any fears of my mother. In fact, I have many wonderful memories of her. Her favorite book was Mark Twain's *Prince and the Pauper*. Truthfully I had some trouble understanding that book but I loved hearing my mother's voice as she read it aloud. It had a hypnotic quality about it that I found very comforting. I think the stories I remember the most are the ones from the nights my father didn't use me as his toy later that evening. I suppose I was able to think about the story more instead of going to the swing over the river that allowed me to escape my body.

When I was growing up, we lived in a one-room cabin. My mother knew that my father was harming us girls but there was nothing she could do. I heard her one night say something to him about what he was doing with his daughters and he replied, "Woman! This is my house and I'll do anything I want!" Those words ring in my mind whenever I remember my mother, and so does the sound of my father's hand slapping her face so hard that she fell to the ground. I don't remember her ever bringing up that subject again. Right before my mother died, she shared with me her deepest, darkest secret. Her friend, a Spanish folk healer known as a curandera, would give her the herb yellow dock each time she was pregnant so she would miscarry. She told me that she couldn't stop what he was doing to her daughters, but she could make sure he never had another daughter to educate. I was elated when she confided in me. It made me proud of her. I needed to be proud of at least one of my parents.

August 23, 1899   **3:00 p.m.**

I just returned from another stroll in the drizzling rain. With summer coming to an end, I must question why we've never experienced thunder and lightning. Is it because we're right next to the coast or is it because we're so far north? The constant gray light has a way of draining my energy. I'll try to take a quick nap before work starts.

August 25, 1899   **11:30 a.m.**

Last night after work Alex came to my tent. We didn't get much sleep, but who needs sleep when you have love? I am aroused whenever I'm around Alex. I love everything about her. Most of all I enjoy playing with her large, dark nipples and watching her get aroused. There are so many qualities I love about Alex, it would be hard to say there is only one favorite. Her creamy skin is as white as the snow in winter. Her eyes are like the flowers in spring when they first appear, full of life and ready for the next adventure. Her hair reminds me of the summer wind blowing the golden wheat fields. Her innate card skills make me think of autumn, the time to think ahead and plan accordingly. Her laughter is like the seasons, always changing yet predictable.

Since we spend a good portion of our day engaged in impure acts, sometimes it can be difficult to get aroused. I guess that's the price we pay for knowing how to numb ourselves as we work. To aid that situation, Alex and I share with each other the randiest tales we have about customers. Her latest tale was one of horror. This guy wanted her to tie barbwire around his hard manhood. He said he would pay her double if she would then mount him. She declined that offer.

I told her about a client I saw last week. He had the largest piece of male equipment I have ever seen or touched. He looked more like a horse than a man. I almost declined his offer, but my curiosity was stronger than my fear. I asked him if I could please get on top of him. He said that's where all his ladies ride. Once I was in position, not too far but in far enough to feel my vessel tightly wrapped around his rod, I started slowly moving up and down his shaft. Suddenly he put his hands on my waist and started forcing himself farther and farther into me. I thought I was going to split wide open from the pain of having this huge organ penetrating me forcefully. Next time I will pass up the opportunity.

When I was finished sharing my tale, Alex and I focused on watching each other twisting our hard nipples and softly fingering our own little hill. Watching each other touch ourselves is one of our favorite activities. We have done this so often that we can reach satisfaction together whenever we want. After the feeling of bliss, we curl up in each other's arms and fall asleep.

August 28, 1899   **4:25 a.m.**

Just like anyone could have predicted, the flood of gold from
the beaches has sent profits soaring and that makes all business
people elated. By day the miners earn their money and by night
they spend it on gambling, liquor, and soiled doves. The going
price for one of my ladies has increased; it now takes a miner
a half-ounce of his hard earned dust to bed down. My rate has
ascended to one whole ounce for a quick unsnap. I love this gold
rush city!

We have been so busy that it's hard to find the time to sit and
write. As I write now, I am falling asleep. This work is really
strenuous. I am thankful that we brought up Dorothy and Jime. I
don't know what we would do without them. As we have found
out, Dorothy is an exceptional cook. Her cooking is what helps us
endure these hurly-burly times. They both admitted to me tonight
that being surrounded by all this wanton energy has added greatly
to their busy activities. Deep down inside I'm jealous of their glee,
but at the same time happy for them.

August 31, 1899   **3:55 a.m.**

I serviced Clark today, one of the three miners I met at The
Northern last month after the miner's meeting. As we partook in
the act my mind was once again in a trance, locked into images
of a mother and son bonding. It was as if our spirits were in other
bodies. I was the mother and Clark was the little boy. We were
engaged in suckling. I was giving him the essence of life, my milk.
He was giving me the pleasing sensation of his tiny feet kicking
my bosoms while his tiny hands grabbed at them. It felt as if we
were making love because so much loving energy was being
exchanged. The image ended as I looked down and saw my child
so content with life that I began to cry with happiness of my own.
As soon as Clark got off me, the images were gone. It was the
oddest experience my mind has ever had. I don't have any control
over the visions when I'm in close proximity to Clark. I really hate
not having power over my own thoughts. I suppose there's always
the fear that I might go insane like my sister.

Clark informed me that another reason he came to see me was to say good-bye from Milroy, Rawslin, and himself. Since the night in The Northern, they have become partners in their own mining company. They all believe that if the beaches are so rich, the gold must be coming from somewhere and they want to find the source. They are going to try prospecting as many areas in the Seward Peninsula as they can before the ice sets in. He said they hoped to at least reach Council, Solomon, Candle, Kougarok, and Teller. Clark thinks they make a great team. He is the one with the money to invest thanks to his wife back in Seattle. Milroy is the mining expert with his years of mining in California. Rawslin is the one with the knowledge of mining law due to his recent assignments.

Clark went on to say when they returned, Milroy would be the first to visit me, then Rawslin, and finally it would be his turn again. He said that it was an arrangement they had already worked out in a poker game. Since they all met me at the same time, they felt they needed to share me fairly amongst themselves. That's the sweetest thing I've heard in a long time.

Oh, I almost forgot! Clark gave me a map he had drawn earlier. He said he wanted me to have a better understanding of this area so it will make more sense to me when they return with their stories. I am already looking forward to hearing their adventures.

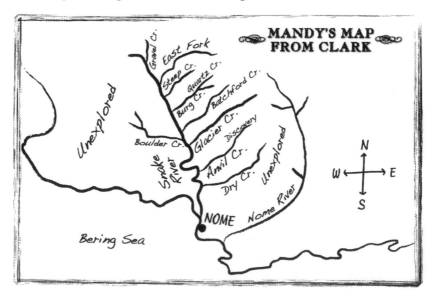

September 1899

September 1, 1899   **3:30 a.m.**

This afternoon before work I went on a long walk and for the
first time I got frightened. I saw something moving really fast on
the horizon. At first I had no idea what it could be. Then it dawned
on me—it was a bear. I had never thought about how fast a bear
could come after me if he so desired. With that fear I walked
back to town as quickly as I could, looking back often. I hope this
experience doesn't hinder me from other outings.

September 3, 1899   **3:50 a.m.**

Tonight Natalie chose a rather large man for her monthly
beating. When Alex came to tell me of the trouble, I was in the
middle of serving a client. I told him I had to leave because my
ladies always come first but I would be happy to refund his money
or he could wait till I returned. Lucky for me he was an easygoing
older man and he said, "I will just go drink in The Belmont for
free until you are ready for me." When I arrived at Natalie's tent,
she was sitting on her cot just watching Dorothy and Jime help the

poor fellow up. Once standing, the dejected man refused any more help from Dorothy and Jime and said he could find his way out.

Although this is the third time she has attacked someone since we arrived, I still don't know what to say to her after all the excitement is over. I told her to take the rest of the evening off and she did.

It would have been nice to take the rest of the evening off myself and spend it in Alex's tent, but I knew that wasn't going to happen. I took comfort in the thought that later we could lay in each other arms. I was anticipating her scent. Before I could talk to her about my idea, I heard J.J. and Alex making arrangements to spend the evening together. My heart sank deep within my body. I love Alex. Not just her beautiful body, but everything about her. I would wager at present J.J. is only falling in love with her physically. I am afraid the more time they spend with each other, the more he will admire her other qualities. I might be losing the love of my life and there is nothing I can do about it.

September 4, 1899   2:25 p.m.

At brunch this morning J.J. told us about losing some money to a fellow named Wyatt Earp, the owner of The Dexter Saloon. J.J. said he was a playing cards at The Dexter last night and he suspected that there could have been some cheating going on. Even though Wyatt is a good friend of Tex Rickard and comes highly recommended, J.J. seemed stuck on the idea that Wyatt had cheated him.

To help even the profit margin, J.J. has invited Wyatt to The Belmont this evening for some honest card playing. J.J. is too virtuous of a businessman and too admirable as a person to even think of cheating, and he doesn't take kindly to people cheating him. He is a true believer in the Golden Rule.

I wonder if J.J. is right about this guy Wyatt? Is he really running a dishonest house, or was J.J. just having a bad night at cards and can't admit it?

September 6, 1899   **2:40 p.m.**

I finally got up the courage to ask J.J. if Alex and I could get a bigger tent and share it. I was very surprised by his reaction. I tried to explain how much I love her. He said, "I understand how you can have loving feelings for her, but I don't understand how you can be intimate with her." He told me there was no way he would ever let us share a tent, unless it's a necessity. Then he stated, "A madam must always present herself as an object of desire to men. It wouldn't be sound business for the men to know about your personal affairs with Alex. With this position come some requirements. A successful madam is never allowed to make public her weaknesses." The last thing he said was that he never wanted to talk about the subject again. That was the first time he has ever been so cold and abrupt with me. I wonder if he's jealous of Alex and me?

Last night Wyatt took up J.J.'s offer to play cards in his establishment. To the dismay of the audience, the two of them battled for hours with the upper hand switching constantly. It became apparent to all that J.J. had met his match in gambling. I guess he is so accustomed to winning that he doesn't take to losing very well.

September 8, 1899   **4:45 a.m.**

I'm sitting in my tent listening to the rain trickle upon the canvas. I have three candles that are providing the light I'm writing by, as well as the heat that keeps me warm. My bed is in the northwest corner of the tent. My three trunks are placed throughout to serve as either a dresser or a stand. On each wall is one of my favorite calendar pictures. When I feel a need for a change, I put up a new picture. Hard packed sand makes up my floor and a large braided oval rug covers most of it.

I'm sure it is the laudanum that makes me notice the pattern of the weave on my tent. The candles make a flickering reflection on the walls that I find mesmerizing. The rhythmic rain has a peaceful essence as it washes away the filth.

September 9, 1899   **2:15 p.m.**

I just returned from a tramp on the tundra, a luxury I haven't had in a while. The sun was shining, but clouds hung heavy in the southern sky. My desire for sunshine was greater than my fear of a bear encounter. Already the few colors of green that are present in the tundra are starting to change to many shades of brown. I can't believe the land is already preparing for its winter nap.

I remember growing up in Durango. Autumn was my favorite season. I loved going on long walks with J.J. and Lizzy, watching the leaves flutter leisurely out of the trees on warm Indian summer afternoons. We used to gather as many leaves as we could and then jump into our piles and bury each other in them. When I think back to the days in Durango, I reminisce of our innocence before time forced us to grow up.

I miss the trees far more than anything else I left behind. I must admit, I'm starting to like it when I go walking and can see everything unobstructed in all directions. That's the only good thing that comes from not having trees around.

This time of year, the light from the sun is more of what I'm used to: sunshine throughout the day and a star-filled sky in the evening. I do miss seeing the stars. There is a comfort in their return. I hope we are ready for the coming winter. Our next barge order should arrive soon, and then we will feel more prepared for the predicted extreme cold.

September 11, 1899   **2:30 p.m.**

Once again my father was present in my dreams. This time it was a reminder that as I got older, my father found new ways to torture me. In my dream I was about 13 and my father was hurting my body in a new and very painful way. While his body slammed against mine he sucked on my ear muttering what seemed to be the same sentence over and over again. The only word I could understand was "ass." His muffled tone got louder and louder until finally I exploded. I took a gun I had hidden under the bed and shot myself.

As I laid awake in bed this morning thinking about this bizarre dream, I knew I could never shoot myself. It would go against everything Jeremy James has taught me — "Only the strongest survive."

September 13, 1899   3:45 a.m.

Last week when Judge Charles Johnson was here, he urged the community leaders of Nome to organize a consent government because of the large growth in population. I hear from clients that Nome has no right to create a municipal government because Congress has not passed any legislation permitting the establishment of a local government. Thank goodness we have some men in town that can think for themselves and can see the urgency to create a local government now instead of next summer, when it could be too late.

Because of the quick action in creating a consent government, everyone was given the honor of voting in the city election today, including myself and the other women here. I heard several men in The Belmont bragging they had voted more than once. It was easy since no one had to be a registered voter. Nome's first mayor is Thomas Cashel, an outspoken defender of the open beach. The city attorney is Key Pittman, a clever lawyer who also played a role in the fight to keep the beach open. Key says that it was his idea for miners to submit to being arrested on August 10th and to eat the Army garrison out of its provisions. He also claims that he went through the saloons looking for volunteers to be arrested, just to make the burden on the military post even greater. The chief of police is William Eddy and he was also one of the leaders of the beach miners.

I'm glad solutions are being found to help the sanitation problems in this community. We are all quickly learning that the tundra has very poor drainage. All of its moisture mixes with the human liquids, for which no drainage system is in place. In the lame excuse for a street, one sees pools of stagnant water, urine, and feces. As a way to help make the paths passable, straw, paper, and other packing materials have been thrown on the ground to be

71

trampled on. I can only see this situation getting worse before it gets better.

September 14, 1899   3:10 a.m.

The idea afloat this afternoon was that the new consent government will not last very long because they have no real power to force anyone to pay local taxes. By evening over $1,800 poured into the city treasury through public donations, which helped to ease the general tension. Throughout the evening, the main topic of conversation was that no matter how bad the consent government is, it's better than a vigilante committee or martial law, which were the only other alternatives. Not knowing what to expect from day to day is kind of exciting and a constant reminder this is a gold rush community where change is inevitable.

September 16, 1899   12:15 a.m.

The consent government ordered all the prostitutes in town to pay $10 a month as a fine for performing an illegal activity. I went to talk to Key Pittman myself to investigate the logic for this new fine. He replied, "We have to start collecting from everyone in this town who makes money. That's just the way the city has to operate to survive." I then asked him, "Is it true that you and your newly appointed committee members will be helping yourselves to a share of the money before it goes into the treasury?" He said, "Of course we will, dear madam, where else do you think we could get money for doing this job?"

By the time I left, I was so angry I had to go for a long walk on the beach to calm down. Once I sped past the hoards of people (which must have taken an hour or so), I did find walking on the beach very relaxing. I enjoyed hearing the small waves crash against the shore and seeing the starfish lingering around the tiny smooth rocks. I had to search to find seashells. They were very small and lacked any bright colors. The seagulls were full of energy and their constant caws were rhythmic with the waves.

I had walked so far and so fast out of anger, that by the time I got back to The Belmont, the evening shift had started. J.J. had sent Jime out looking for me and he had put Alex in my place for the evening. Instead of taking over for Alex, J.J. insisted I have the evening off and have dinner with him. During dinner we talked about some changes he wanted to make in The Belmont, but mostly we talked about Alex. He kept questioning me about her.

J.J. is falling in love with Alex. I can't blame him, but I can't encourage him either. He just doesn't understand how much I love her. I met her first so she should be mine. I know I can't keep Alex in a cage. I love her so much, I would do anything for her. I know if she has feelings for J.J., there's nothing I can do but give them my blessing. Why does she have to be attractive in so many ways?

September 18, 1899   3:20 a.m.

Tonight I met an inebriated dimwit. He came up to me in The Belmont and got right in my face. "Hey, gold dust bitch! Why should I pay more for you when I can have two of your doves for less? Tell me what it is you do that's so fucking special." I tried to ignore him by walking away but he followed and whirled me around so I was very close to him. He yelled, "Don't walk away from me, bitch!" He was ready to slap my face when J.J. intervened. He told J.J. he just wanted to find out if what he heard was correct.

I wished J.J. would have told him to leave then, but instead he invited the boozer to share his scuttlebutt. As everyone in The Belmont stopped talking so they too could hear, the drunk continued with his speech, as he looked right at me. "The talk is that after paying the going rate, a man can stick anything he wants up inside of you. We're not just talking about a hard cock. We're talking about fists, bottles, pieces of wood, rocks of all sizes, food." About then I stepped in and said, "I think everyone here has heard enough of your vulgar mouth. Thanks to your lack of manners, you, sir, will never know first hand what I do and don't allow inside myself. You and your money are not welcome at The Belmont. So get the hell out!" J.J. stepped in, "You heard the lady." In return the soaker answered, "She's not a lady, she's a wild fowl." I strode up to him once more and said confidently, "That's madam wild fowl to you."

By then Ryan and J.J. were both at my side and the worthless swill pot left without a fight. After he walked out the door, I turned around and saw everyone's faces staring straight at me. It was dead quiet until I smiled and said, "I wonder how this damn gossip gets started." That seemed to make everyone laugh as they all returned to their own little conversations. I got this feeling they were all talking about what I really do allow inside myself. I hate to say it, but this kind of attention will probably be good for business.

Most women work for years learning a specialty, which helps them become an exceptional prostitute. The money made from performing their specialty helps them move up to being a madam. My situation is different. J.J. offered me the position and I've just looked at it from a business point of view. Until today, I've always thought the clients were just buying the title. I need to think about something I can develop as my specialty. The overnights are very profitable because you have time to make a man feel like a king and in return you get bigger tips. I will have to put some more thought into it.

September 20, 1899   3:30 a.m.

While I was in The Belmont today, I heard one of the sweetest comments. I was talking to Erik Lindblom, one of Jafet's partners, and he said, "Jafet sends his warmest regards to his lady Mandy." Erik told me that Jafet's health is fine but he doesn't feel safe coming into town. He went on to say that Jafet was wondering if I would come out to Anvil one night after work and pay him a visit. I told Erik I would be looking forward to that event. He said he would let me know when the arrangements had been made and then he left. Erik was like a true messenger; he brought the words without the emotions. Now I'm wondering if Jafet wants to see me because he misses me or if he just wants a body to release his lust. He is a man, Mandy. You are a scarlet woman. What do you think he wants?

September 21, 1899   **12:30 a.m.**

Today was my 28th birthday. It often falls on equinox. With
us being so far north, I have a feeling the days will quickly grow
darker.

We began the day by celebrating with the griddle cakes. It does
indeed make one feel good knowing she has family who cares. J.J.
had two surprises for me. The first was a brand new beautiful oak
desk and chair that will arrive on the barge in a few days. He said,
"As a madam you will enjoy this place to weigh out gold and keep
your books. As a writer you will now have a comfortable place to
record. When I saw the picture, I thought it was perfect for you." I
agree it is perfect for me. I love him and my new desk.

His second surprise was letting me have the evening off.
Dorothy had some food and water packed in a cloth bag ready for
me so I wasted no time escaping onto the tundra. I headed toward
Anvil, not hoping to find Jafet, but just to enjoy the beautiful
scenery. Before I left town, I indulged in some laudanum. When
my ladies and I took the large doses on the Fourth of July, it was
the ultimate escape. We enjoyed just sitting on the chairs and
watching our bodies as our minds hovered above. Ever since then
I've wanted to experiment with the laudanum in a natural setting.
I spent a good portion of my day walking. The one thing I will
always remember about this birthday is the fog that hung from the
sky and covered the tops of the small brown bushes. It filled me
with a tranquility I have never known. The muffling fog created an
intense silence. This combined with the laudanum for pleasure and
not having to work created the best birthday of my life.

September 25, 1899   **3:45 a.m.**

Tonight while I was servicing Arthur Wine, the census agent,
I learned that three weeks ago he counted 500 tents, 17 building
frames, and about a dozen log cabins. Today he counted 200
frame structures, either under construction or already finished.
He reminded me that there was no way to get an accurate count
because of the irregular way in which the tents and buildings
are located. Someday I'd like to find out for myself how many

facilities are actually here. I bet I could get an accurate count if I tried.

I heard from another patron this evening, who is actually a doctor, one of the most nauseating things I have ever heard. He stated that the Snake River, which is a large source of the community's drinking water, is the site where most of the sewage and garbage in town is dumped. He reasoned that this problem is why typhoid fever, bloody dysentery, and pneumonia are already so common here. He also said that dysentery was common among newcomers and hard drinkers, and if you looked you could see blood in every public convenience. I wonder how these diseases are spread. I must speak with Jeremy James to find out how our alliance can protect itself from them.

September 26, 1899   **2:30 a.m.**

Hurrah! The long-awaited barge arrived yesterday. We had to close both operations for 24 hours while we all worked together putting away the new provisions. Seeing the crates filled with an abundance of supplies created a sense of security. We now have provisions to make it through the long winter ahead. The brightly colored packaging on the new supplies made me want to walk outside of The Belmont and purposely observe the vividness of nature that surrounds this budding community. For the first time I was able to define what is so unique about this strange land. Unless it is a clear day, and we haven't seen many since we arrived, all the colors have a very light hue to them. All of the buildings and even nature itself look as if they have been painted with watercolors and are rather washed out. Colorado was quite different. The bright sun, which we saw a lot of no matter what the season, had a way of making everything look dazzling. I've been deprived of colors.

J.J. must have paid a fine price to have all of our supplies delivered this far north. What I find most amazing about this barge order is that J.J. had the foresight to predict what was needed and how much. Once again I must say I love being in business with that brilliant man.

I feel a need to write about what has arrived; I'm that excited about it. The items taking up the most weight would be the two tons of coal and the four new coal stoves. J.J. has already had to hire someone to guard the coal. It's too precious to be left unguarded. He would love for Jime to be able to do this duty, but Jime is already overwhelmed with the responsibilities he has.

The next category of items that took up a tremendous amount of bulk is all the new building material that J.J. ordered so that he can make changes in The Belmont. He ordered two large pane windows that will be put on the south side of The Belmont so we can see the ocean. A real sign of a saloon's prosperity is its windows, even though no one wants to be seen inside drinking. He has also ordered some swinging doors that have panels of stained glass. J.J. was not pleased with the bar that he brought up in June, so he ordered a new 60-foot mahogany hand-sculpted bar. It's in four separate pieces that we must assemble. J.J. reminded me that with all the new saloons opening, he should have no trouble whatsoever getting rid of his old bar.

The four large mirrors that arrived unbroken are J.J.'s prize possessions. He's planning on putting two behind the bar and one on each side. Beautiful new chandeliers will replace the kerosene lamps once we get electricity. Jeremy James believes that a saloon is all things to all men, and he wants to make every man who walks into The Belmont feel comfortable. As part of his plan to make The Belmont the most exquisite saloon this far north, he hopes someday to attach a restaurant and a hotel. For now he will be satisfied with the new improvements being a barbershop, an ice cream parlor, and what J.J. refers to as his theater. We've had so much fun tonight playing with the flamboyant kinetoscope. To make it work, you look into the scope and crank the handle as you watch the jerky movements of the can-can dancers. We've also enjoyed playing in the new barbershop chair. We took turns spinning around like little children while eating the first batch of ice cream ever made in The Belmont. Ryan confessed he has a passion for ice cream, and there aren't too many things he wouldn't do just for the simple pleasure of eating the frozen dessert. It was fun to see Ryan show such emotions over this delicacy.

J.J. feels it's important to have other things offered in a saloon besides alcohol, that way people who publicly oppose drinking can feel comfortable coming into the saloon. I have witnessed firsthand that indeed the saloon is more than just a drinking establishment. At times I've seen it become a courtroom where legal battles are settled. I've also seen this be a dueling ground where people resolve their conflicts. I've heard undertakers do their business in here, while others seek employment. From the looks of this place, it does resemble a museum and it serves as a trading post when J.J. can find someone to barter with. I've learned from Rawslin that saloons are places where news is made as well as history. Saloons are the places where states are named, candidates are announced, and elections are held. Rawslin says that saloons are as American as apple pie. I guess that's why J.J. puts so much time and energy into making The Belmont the best. I'm looking forward to all the changes that J.J. has planned.

Of course you've got to have booze if you're going to have a saloon. The immense quantity took up a large amount of space on the barge. J.J. ordered 300 cases each of rye and bourbon, along with 500 barrels of beer. This far north, not too many people have an educated thirst. In case an educated drinker does care to spend his money on fancy mixed drinks, J.J. has ordered two bottles of every available liqueur. This doesn't include the many cases in J.J.'s private stock. Even though J.J. is striving to have one of the best saloons in the north, he will still dilute his booze to ensure it lasts throughout the winter. This is done to increase profits but also to increase the life of the drinkers. If the miners drank this rotgut booze full-strength, their insides would be eaten up before spring arrived. I'm shocked to discover how much alcohol men can consume, drinking morning, noon, and night. When I was a little girl, I used to think my dad was the only one who drank that much. After working out of a saloon, I can see most men like to drink. They seem to pursue alcohol more than they do mining, gambling, and even women. I personally believe if men had more food to eat, they wouldn't be drinking so much booze.

Speaking of food, J.J. ordered twice the amount we brought

up in June. He also bought one winter coat and a set of boots for each of us. I received the fur muffs, jewelry, and blue silk dress I ordered. I was happy to see that the gifts I purchased looked far more elegant in real life than they did in the consumer guide pictures. I'm not sure what items other people received. There was so much secrecy, with everyone striving to hide presents they had ordered for others. I sense we are all looking forward to the holidays so we can express our gratitude to one another by giving gifts. I am now able to sit at the beautiful desk J.J. gave me for my birthday!

The very last item was the laudanum. Even though it took up the least amount of space, it was one of the most important items that arrived. I don't know what we'd do without the laudanum. It keeps the ladies in a sedated state of mind. They don't seem to question too much about the profession, they just passively do what is needed for survival. As we all hustled about, putting away the new provisions, we all indulged in some extra doses of laudanum. It just seemed to be a day to celebrate. When I say all, I mean the ladies, J.J., Ryan, and myself. Dorothy and Jime don't want anything to do with the laudanum. Everyone can clearly see their marriage fulfills all their needs.

I really do look forward to the blissful feeling that encompasses my body when I allow myself the indulgence. It takes my body and my mind away. I can't focus on the responsibilities of the past working day. Instead my senses are heightened to their fullest. I'm aware of details in The Belmont that didn't seem to exist previously. I hadn't noticed how unevenly spaced the lines in the wooden planks on the wall are. I hope I never start to love this feeling too much.

September 30, 1899   3:30 p.m.

Last night I had a customer complain that the sheets Natalie and he were using over the new squeaky bed weren't clean. Today at brunch, Dorothy told a hilarious story about running to recover her sheets after they were thrown to the sand by a strong gust. I remember at Rosa's, we used to change the sheets after every customer, but then Rosa's had been established for a long time. We're not quite there yet. The best we're doing is to change them after each shift. Already it's obvious the washing is too much for Dorothy to accomplish with all her other tasks. I should look into paying one of the laundries in town to take care of that responsibility for us, that way Dorothy could spend more time cooking.

October 1899

October 2, 1899   **8:10 p.m.**

    The first thing I noticed this morning when I went outside was that the usual puddles of urine in the streets contained ice crystals. I could feel the lowered temperature and the effect it had on everyone. The moment I stepped into The Belmont, I was caught in a trap of tension. A storm was brewing. When I stepped outside and looked at the ocean I knew my predictions were precise. Huge bluish-gray clouds looked as though they had been released from a vat and were tumbling toward this little town with intent to crush it. The wind was picking up and the waves along the beach became louder and louder. The ocean was looking darker by the minute. Rain began falling, slowly at first, but soon huge drops fell faster from the sky. Few people left The Belmont once the storm set in, for fear of getting drenched and possibly carried away by the violent waves that were crashing into the streets.

    My ladies and I were extremely busy today servicing all the patrons who didn't want to go far from shelter. We usually don't start work so early in the day, but the demand was there and we had to be the suppliers. It was a wild day and J.J. allowed my ladies and me to take off early this evening since we worked so hard.

Seeing the wicked storm this morning, I felt compelled to write about it. I like being able to write in the evening when I'm not so tired, but instead of writing more, I think I'll begin reading the book Rawslin dropped off for me, Mark Twain's *Joan of Arc*. My mother read the book aloud to us when I was young but I have never read it myself.

October 4, 1899   **4:20 a.m.**

It was that time of month again for Natalie. This time her victim was a short, chubby man who was one of her regular customers. He was actually very lucky; Natalie went easy on him. His nose was the only bone in his body that looked broken. I have never seen a man leave after being beat up by Natalie cussing or trying to redeem himself. They all look like sad dogs walking out with their tails between their legs. I guess being beaten up by a woman really destroys their confidence.

I offered Natalie the evening off again, but this time she rejected the suggestion, saying that she wanted to finish working so she could make money to pay for her Christmas gifts. Although I feel bad for the men when this happens, I'm really happy for Natalie. She lets out all her anger on the man and she is much more pleasant because of it. It's a good thing she picks the weak men to fight with. I don't know what would happen if one of her monthly victims tried to fight back.

October 5, 1899   **3:05 p.m.**

The Seward Peninsula this morning was blanketed in white. The rain changed to snow during the night. The tundra seemed asleep under the thin blanket and the mountains had nightcaps on the top of their heads. Their dark blue bodies spotted with white snow were barely noticeable through the mass of clouds. The wind had stopped and the snow was gently descending, covering the tops of buildings and structures. It was a beautiful sight, but at the same time it was sad. The snow reminded me of Durango. I used to love shaking the tree branches while standing underneath, enjoying the snow as it gently fell and tickled my nose.

We're very pleased the snow arrived after the barge. Without the coal-fueled stoves we each have in our tents, my ladies and I would be extremely cold. The thin walls of our tents aren't much insulation. With temperatures below freezing and quickly dropping, I know we will be even more grateful for the radiant heat as time passes by.

October 7, 1899   3:15 p.m.

I went walking this afternoon for the first time since the snow arrived. I can't believe how different this place looks. I walked toward the Cape of Nome, one of my favorite places, and was amazed to find everything completely covered. In Durango this time of year, the snow would have melted during the day. Here, with the days getting shorter and colder the snow has no chance to melt.

Despite the cold, my walk was very enjoyable. The wind wasn't blowing very much and I could see the mountains behind Nome. Everything looked pristine. Not a single thing stood out because it was all camouflaged. That's what made it gorgeous: just a huge, white quilt with white bumps in the background. I can't wait until the snow hardens so I can walk on the covered tundra without sinking in.

October 9, 1899   2:50 p.m.

I just read an article in the newspaper about the town's development. Nome now has six bakeries, twenty saloons, five laundries, twelve general merchandise stores, three second-hand stores, four real estate offices, three fruit and cigar stores, two tin shops, four drugstores, two photographers, one brewery, three watchmakers, two meat markets, two sign painters, one boot and shoe store, one book and stationary store, three packers and forwarders, two dentists, eleven physicians, sixteen lawyers, one mining engineer, two surveyors, one massage artist, four bath houses, one bank and safe deposit, two printing offices, one blacksmith, one assay office, two contractors and builders, two hospitals, four barber shops, two clubs, and my favorite, one confectionery store. This is pretty impressive for a place that didn't even exist a year ago.

October 11, 1899   1:45 p.m.

Ria complained of being cold last night. Dorothy got her an extra blanket, but if she's getting cold this early into winter, I'm not sure how she'll react to the predicted below-freezing temperatures.

Natalie joked at brunch this morning about how she's been really warm, and that she's got a lot more natural insulation than Ria. We all laughed along, but I think Natalie was right. Ria is tiny and doesn't have much fat to keep her warm. Sometimes I wish the ladies and I could share tents so we would have someone to cuddle with and keep warm at night, but because we are striving to create a first class establishment, we provide privacy for our clients. They enjoy the discrete arrangements, but I sense all the ladies are missing the closeness gained by sharing living quarters.

October 14, 1899   2:50 p.m.

I enjoy reading the newspaper because it's much more factual than all the information we hear from the men we serve. I read there is a real concern for the sickness throughout town at the present time and it is feared that the situation will get worse as we head into winter. Another matter of concern is as the close of navigation nears, the crime rate increases. Because there's no timber for miles around and such a small coal supply, people are beginning to either stockpile driftwood or steal coal from others to get their winter fuel supply. J.J. has hired two down-and-out miners to rotate 12-hour shifts to guard our coal. In return, Hank and Preston are paid $5 a day plus the opportunity to poke one of the doves each evening.

I heard a story yesterday about a woman who awoke in the night when she heard some thieves cutting right through her tent.

Everywhere I go, there is talk about something being stolen.
People are beginning to fear for the safety of their person and their
property.

October 15, 1899   **3:40 p.m.**

In the last week, all the members of the alliance have been
feeling ill. I'm not sure if this is caused from actually drinking the
contaminated water, or just knowing that it is contaminated. I have
had a bad feeling about the water. It tastes so dreadful. But there
is no time to think about that small problem. To solve that worry,
J.J. has instructed Jime to go at least half a mile up the mouth of
the Snake River before he gets our drinking water. Not that anyone
drinks that much water, but the ladies and myself do enjoy drinking
coffee and tea throughout the day and evening.

October 16, 1899   **3:35 p.m.**

I had another wicked dream of my father last night. I remember
it real well. I'm laying in bed alone and I can hear my father
mounting my mother. I can hear my mother moaning and groaning
and I believe that she is actually enjoying herself. After my mother
falls asleep, my father gets up and crawls into my sister's bed.
Within seconds he has entered her and is pumping away to his
pleasure.

In the dream he continues to have his way with Lizzy for what
seems like hours. As I lay in my bed stiff with fear I can hear
my mother in the background softly snoozing while my father's
moaning is in rhythm with his motions. It is strange! I never hear
my sister make a sound. I'm afraid that I might be next and if I fall
asleep, I won't have time to numb myself. The anticipation drained
me of my energy and I woke up feeling tired.

Now it is time to wear the mask of a madam and I'm still tired.
It makes me angry that a dream of that man can exhaust me. I
wonder how I will make it through the day?

October 18, 1899   **2:55 a.m.**

Alex turned 28 today. I could not believe how many griddlecakes she managed to stuff in her mouth at once. All she could talk about was how good they taste when they're so hot that you can watch the butter melting and how she'd been looking forward to this day since the first hotcake celebration.

It became obvious to all that J.J. and Alex are developing feelings for each other. Jeremy James displayed constant affection toward Alex throughout the day. He presented her with a beautiful sapphire necklace and some exquisite French perfume at brunch. Before the shift began, they went on a long walk even though it was quite chilly out. As the evening ended, I heard them conversing in low voices. Then J.J. approached me and asked what it would cost to have Alex for the entire night. J.J. may have started the business, but I've already repaid him and now he only gets a quarter of the profits and I get the rest. I replied, "For you there's no charge tonight or any night," yet secretly I had hoped to have her to myself after closing.

Although I am a bit jealous that Alex has affection for J.J., I am pleased for her because I love her with all of my heart. As long as she's happy, I'm happy. It was hard letting her go with J.J. and not having the opportunity to give her my real present. Of course I did take advantage of the only confectionery store in town and bought many of Alex's favorite candies to give to her at brunch, but I was planning on giving her another, more personal present tonight.

On this day, I don't feel any resentment toward Alex or J.J. I really am just grateful that they are both alive and that I am blessed to be in their presence.

October 19, 1899   **11:15a.m.**

My dream last night was frightening. I was on the beach, but it wasn't full of people and mining equipment. It was drizzling and I felt a tickle when the moisture gently landed on my body. The light fog surrounded me as I walked. Ahead of me I could see Alex and J.J. walking and holding hands. I called out their names but no sound came from me. I attempted several times to make myself heard. As the fog began to lift I noticed that I was surrounded by a flock of large black birds, getting closer to me with each passing second. Gathering all my strength I strived to make my voice be heard. A loud scream came out but J.J. and Alex were not available to hear my anguish. Without warning the winged creatures began attacking. I started fighting them off with my arms. It only made the situation worse. Feeling like I had no choice, I peacefully surrendered, letting the birds consume my body and soul.

October 21, 1899   **2:20 p.m.**

I hear reports that about two or three thousand of the estimated 5,000 people in Nome have left or are planning on going south for the winter. I think that as the days get shorter, the fear of running out of food, the threat of typhoid, and the scarcity of adequate shelter has convinced many people that it would be in their best interest to spend winter in a warmer climate. One good thing about the miners leaving is that they won't have many hard luck stories to tell about Nome when they get to Seattle. I've heard that most miners have anywhere from $500 to $15,000 in gold to show for their summer's work. I can imagine this will create even more of a desire for people to come to Nome next summer. I'm anxious for all the novices to come with new hopes and new ambitions. All the optimism makes everyone desire to be a part of the gold rush. I'm especially enthusiastic about the many naive gents willing to spend their hard earned money on my enterprise.

The main topic of conversation these days is speculating what the world must be thinking of Nome. Today the headline in the *Nome News* read, "We will be it next summer. Let's plan wisely." I sure hope somebody does. It is very exciting to be a part of something grandiose!

October 22, 1899   **5:10 a.m.**

I thought the long talk I had with Ria was starting to pay off, but then she up and surprises me. Since she shot the soldier, she has been different. Instead of talking about how she is going to find a husband soon, she has been asking the other ladies questions about their personal lives and really paying attention to their answers. But for the last five days no one has heard her say a word. She walks around like she isn't even aware of her surroundings. I wonder if she has her own source of laudanum or if this is just the gloominess her old madam talked about. This can't be good for business. Not too many men want to pay to have a merry bout with a melancholy lady. I'm sure that is exactly how she is responding in bed. What am I going to do with her?

October 24, 1899   2:15 p.m.

Just when I'm so frustrated with Ria and all my responsibilities as a madam, Natalie got in a fight with J.J.'s friend, Wyatt. Her monthly outrages were no longer shocking me—I was actually beginning to anticipate them—but this was totally off her cycle. Natalie may have the upper hand when she attacks a small gent, but she was no match for Wyatt. I heard screaming and the breaking of furnishings. I ran as quickly as my legs allowed. Once in Natalie's tent I wailed for Jime's help. He tried to break it up but got slammed on the ground as a result. After realizing the seriousness of Wyatt's intent, I ran to get Jeremy James. Wyatt had almost beaten Natalie to death by the time J.J. could pull him off of her. It was a terribly bloody sight. All the ladies and their clients stood terrified, watching the life rush out of Natalie's body. J.J. reminded Wyatt that this was part of his merchandise he was destroying. Wyatt bellowed, "She fucking started it and there's no whore who's going to hit me and live to tell about it."

Because I had Dr. Miller as a client, I called upon him to help us. Dorothy went to get him and he came right away. He said Natalie was in horrendous shape and he didn't know for sure whether she would live or die, but the next couple days would tell us. He went on to say that it really all depended on what her spirit wanted to do. If she sincerely had the desire to live, she would.

Since this happened one of the ladies or I have stayed by Natalie's side at all times. The only good thing to come of this is that Ria snapped out of her depression. We try to talk to Natalie but

Dr. Miller says she is in a deep coma. We all believe she knows we are there because of the loyal bond we share.

Women who work the sheets like to think that we have a closeness that isn't possible for proper ladies. They have knowledge of how to care for a home and children. We have carnal knowledge. We see men and share the tales of them in their most unruly state. They appear more like animals than humans, thinking only of satisfying their lusty appetite. Knowing that we profit by allowing our bodies to be the receivers of such raw emotion makes us feel like we are sewn tightly together with a common thread. Our life together is like a nest, each experience like a twig woven into the others. The more we collect, the more we have to make a safe, secure home for ourselves.

From this unfortunate incident, I understand now why J.J. bought me that belt in Seattle that's specially designed for a madam to carry a small weapon or gold. He anticipated something like this would happen. I don't like to carry a gun because they remind me of my father, but I will protect my ladies. I will begin to carry a small pistol with me so I can be prepared at all times. I will not wait for J.J. to solve the problem. I will shoot any son-of-a-bitch harming one of my girls right between his eyes without hesitation. I don't have a choice. It's either him or my ladies. I feel like a mother to all of my doves and I will protect them.

October 25, 1899   **2:20 p.m.**

Alex never ceases to surprise me. She had this idea today at brunch that we should all take our plates into Natalie's tent just so she could feel our presence. We were there about ten minutes and just as we were finishing up, Natalie started moving. Alex jumped up and went to her side. Touching her gently, she said, "Honey, we are all here for you." Slowly and very sluggishly, Natalie awakened from her deep sleep. Her bewilderment was replaced by a smile as she became aware that all the members of her kindred family surrounded her with love.

Looking at her today, I can see that it'll be awhile before she can work again. Truthfully, it'll be quite awhile until she can even chew again since she's missing so many teeth. Her jaw is badly damaged. This sure can't do anything to help her repulsive smile. I'm not sure what we're going to do with her now. But she's a family member so we have to take care of her.

J.J. made it very clear to Wyatt today that if something like this were ever to happen again, he wouldn't live to tell about it.

October 28, 1899   3:25 a.m.

Today there was a roundup of all known or suspected criminals. They were placed aboard the *Bear,* the only U.S. ship left on shore. Captain D.H. Javis has been asked to carry ten known crooks and several other people who have no means of support to Seattle. There was no court decision that prompted this event because there was no time before the sea froze. I feel safer having these criminals off of our streets. So many people are leaving Nome for the winter. I hope we are prepared for the coming months and I pray everyone makes it through. There is no turning back now.

October 29, 1899   3:00 p.m.

It's been a week since Natalie's incident and, aside from her awakening from the coma, I have seen no signs of recovery. Her condition hasn't gotten any worse, but I'm still worried. Work has been hard this week with only two doves and myself. I can't imagine what life would be like without Natalie. Her presence makes all of the ladies comfortable because they know if they were being harmed, Natalie would rescue them.

I talked about finding another lady to join my bevy when we first arrived, but now I really need to find one. If Natalie doesn't make it, I don't think The Bantam Belmont could survive through the winter without another lady. I will start my search tomorrow.

October 31, 1899   3:40 a.m.

There still hasn't been a decline in J.J.'s winning streak, except for the encounters with Wyatt that remain a constant adventure for both of them. Today a man who used to call San Francisco his home walked into The Belmont thinking he was an outstanding gambler. He made it clear he had lots of money to spend, so J.J. opened up the house to him. The man said Faro was his favorite so J.J. set a "no limit" on the game. Within two hours, that man had lost all the money he came to Nome with. He walked out of The Belmont a very somber, dejected man. I hate to see gambling do that to a person, but I love to see the effect it has on J.J. When he wins lots of money, he is very generous. He treated everyone to drinks on the house tonight. He also made a point of telling Dorothy not only could he afford to pay someone else to wash the clothes, he was thinking of using this money to invest in his own laundry house. "Everyone needs their clothes washed sooner or later. It would be a great long term investment," and he returned to the spending of his most recent fortune. I love the way he thinks!

November 1899

November 1, 1899   **3:45 p.m.**

Every afternoon before work begins, one of the ladies or I stay in Natalie's tent and talk to her. She doesn't say much back, but she can talk a little. Her jaw still needs to heal. I am overjoyed that we have all created such a strong bond and that we will be there for each other no matter what.

November 3, 1899   **2:35 p.m.**

This afternoon while drinking some tea in my tent I envisioned myself in a large house painted white on the inside and the out. Everything looked so bright and clean. The rooms were filled with useless objects of various shapes, sizes, and colors. I guess one could call it art.

A part of me might enjoy being around fine art in my future. For now, I'm quite content living among the art that nature displays. I'm learning to love the beauty of this land even as the temperature drops daily. Thanks to Natalie, I'm learning the source of the beauty. About a month ago, I learned that we are living in an

Arctic desert, where the cold temperatures evaporate the water just like the heat does in a desert. As a result, there are no longer any puddles; instead they have been replaced by intricate ice designs. I find myself looking at them for minutes at a time. I just can't help it. They are breathtaking!

November 4, 1899   2:55 p.m.

Now that things are beginning to settle down in Nome, I have heard a lot of talk about just how much gold was recovered from the beach and creeks this mining season. I hear most of the tents were gathered over the richest ground. This is the area just in front of town and on the stretch from the sand spit on the Snake River to Cripple Creek, ten miles east of town. The general opinion among miners is anywhere from $1 million to $2 million was taken from the beach. From the few dozen creek claims that were being developed, they say nearly $1.5 million worth of gold was discovered. Of course, those miners never tell anyone how much they really recover.

Natalie still can't walk around by herself so she has a little bell by her bedside that she rings and either Dorothy or I attend to her. Her body may not be functioning properly, but her mind is stable. Natalie and I stayed up last night in her tent talking. I held her in my arms and played with her hair while she cried. She told me how depressed she is because Christmas is less than two months away. She was planning on knitting everyone sweaters, but her hands are too weak now to even finish the one she had started. I can tell how much it hurts her not to be able to knit. She has a passion for it. I would hate it if I couldn't take walks or write.

November 5, 1899   2:30 p.m.

Alex and I had another opportunity last night to enjoy each other in the flesh. I say that because even when Alex can't be next to me in her body, she is always with me in my heart.

Alex's latest tale was a sad one. It was about an older man who tied her up with his torn shirt. Then he forced her to take his manhood in her mouth. He became so aroused that he ejaculated in her throat, which caused Alex to vomit. Since she was tied up she couldn't do anything to prevent throwing up on herself. The client got so disgusted that he left her tent as fast as he could. He was kind enough to tell Ryan that one of the whores needed some help.

Ryan told Alex later he had wanted to hurt that man and if the opportunity ever presented itself, he would. He knew if he had started a fight it would have prevented J.J. from getting to Alex quickly. Alex broke into tears. "You should have seen J.J. when he saw me laying naked on my bed with my hands and feet tied up and soaking in my own vomit," she said. "I saw the hurt in his eyes. For the very first time he understood this woman he is falling in love with sells her body to survive." Through more tears, Alex told me how J.J. helped untie her and clean her up. Then he silently helped her get dressed. "He didn't have to say a word; all the disappointment was in his eyes."

As Alex cried herself to sleep in my arms, I whispered gently into her ear, "Baby, I love you, and I will never condemn. Never be ashamed of what you do. Everything will be alright. I will make sure of that."

Now that J.J. has seen Alex for what she is, maybe he will no longer be a threat to our love.

November 6, 1899   3:50 a.m.

I may have found another working lady. Her name is Margerie and she is a beautiful red haired woman. She is smaller than me but much bigger than Ria. Her bright hair is so long and incredibly curly it almost hides her face. The scarlet hair gives her a fiery look that could definitely attract men. Her eyes and lips are tiny but her smile is big. Her face is round and almost childish, yet the cigarette in her hand told me she definitely wasn't a child. She is really lanky. The fingers surrounding her cigarette were incredibly thin. I wonder if she is naturally that tenuous or if she is sick.

Margerie accompanied her wealthy brother, Edwin, to Nome in hopes of finding a rich man to marry. Edwin planned on becoming even richer, but gambling and booze got the best of him. She told me that he made a wager and lost. He didn't have enough money to pay it off, and one night he just vanished. Now Margerie needs to find a job and is leaning toward prostitution. I talked to her in The Belmont this afternoon and have been thinking about her all evening. Teaching her everything about the profession would be hard and I'm not sure I'm ready for that added responsibility. Also, I don't know much about her. She could have underlying problems that might be harshly uncovered by the nature of this trade. I don't know how well I could cope with extra problems.

November 7, 1899   3:30 a.m.

I'm back to being worried about J.J. taking my Alex away. I guess seeing her that night working, with all the disgust it entails, has only intensified the love he has for her. Alex says he still has not mentioned that experience, but has gone out of his way to be nice to her several times since then. Once again I'm afraid I'm losing her and there is nothing I can do.

November 8, 1899   3:15 a.m.

I was delighted to hear that the Botton's Circulating Library opened today. Now that we have a literary selection available, Alex, Natalie, Ria, Margerie (if she joins us), and I will begin reading aloud to each other to pass the time in the afternoon. I'm putting up the $1 it costs to rent a book for two weeks so the ladies can work on improving their literacy. It's the least I can do in return for all the money the ladies are making for me. All the ladies read at different levels and this will ensure their skills increase. Ria may be embarrassed at first because she doesn't read much, but with practice I'm sure she'll feel more comfortable. Natalie's jaw has healed enough so that she can speak pretty well. Hopefully reading will help Natalie recover. Literature can be an excellent escape from pain. I wish that intelligent women had more opportunities in this populace. But all one has to do is look around to know that this is a man's world, particularly here in Nome.

November 10, 1899   3:20 a.m.

Natalie got up on her own today! When Ria, Alex, and I went

into her tent this afternoon and found her dressed and putting coal in her stove, we were astonished. It was crazy because we had just finished brunch in her tent about 30 minutes before. After the hugs and the soft laughing we all sat down and took turns reading. I'm happy that Natalie is recuperating. I was really afraid that she wouldn't make it. I think I might still hire Margerie, though. It would be nice to have another worker on board, but it could also create an odd situation between her and the ladies. Margerie would have to learn a lot in a little bit of time and I don't know if she could handle it. Truthfully, I don't know if I could handle it. Everything is going O.K. as it is and when Natalie starts working again, we'll be even better. If we were to hire Margerie we'd have to get another tent, another bed, and another stove. I don't know what to do. I'll have to think about it more.

November 11, 1899   1:45 a.m.

The Snake River is beginning to freeze and it takes Jime longer to collect water now. He has already talked about how important it will be to keep his hole through the ice open. If it freezes over, getting water will be a much harder task. It's a good thing we ordered so much coal for the winter because it would be impossible to find what little wood is available now that we're well into winter. I've noticed it doesn't really snow much here, but the problem is the snow never has a chance to melt because we're losing sunlight every day. Right now the sun stays up for about six and a half hours and it's dark the rest of the time. It's odd eating brunch when the sun has just risen. I'm already looking forward to the summer when the sun radiates light throughout the day.

When it has been cold for so many days in a row I find a melancholy growing from within. I hate to admit this, but I feel jealous toward Dorothy and Jime. I ask myself what do I have to be jealous about? I have power, responsibilities, and money. All they have is each other.

I guess that is what I'm jealous about. They have a true love for one another. Deep down inside, I too would love to have someone to love and someone to love me. I don't want to be a madam forever. Someday I might find a man who can really love me for what I am, or was. I'm beginning to give up the idea of Alex and I being together after we leave Nome. Everyone can see that J.J. is in love with her, maybe even more since the night he had to untie and clean her up.

November 13, 1899   8:30 a.m.

I just awoke from a dream that still has my heart pounding with fear. I was a teenager living in Durango. My father had fallen asleep without performing his educating ritual. I lay in bed motionless, my body paralyzed. My eyes were wide open. I took in every sound and movement in the cabin, waiting for my father to awake and begin his routine. All I could think about was not reaching my swing before he climbed on top of me. If I didn't see myself going effortlessly back and forth across the glistening water, then I would have to endure the poison that man put in my body. In the dream it seemed like hours I went without sleep. It was more like a nightmare—the longest nightmare I ever had.

Did I have nights like that growing up? I must have. The more I learn about men, the more I know there is only that rare one percent of men who crave vigor night after night. Maybe there were nights my father just slept, the way my girlfriends implied their dads did. If that is true and my dad didn't get his pleasure every night, did I lay awake on those nights filled with apprehension and unease? That could explain why at times my life seemed like a nightmare.

November 14, 1899   2:40 p.m.

Each day more and more people arrive from Dawson City. I didn't understand why anyone would want to come to such a desolate place this time of year, but Natalie explained. Dawson is in the middle of Canada, so people can't come here by sea and they can't travel over the tundra. Instead they travel down the frozen Yukon River, then follow the coast until they reach Nome. These Canadian arrivals say that once winter sets in, there will be

97

thousands more joining them, using dog sleds as their mode of transportation.

Even though the temperature is rapidly dropping this month, and the obvious criminals are gone, there has been no relief from crime. Today I read the following quote in the *Nome Chronicle*, "The organized gang of crooks which is preying on this community has reached the limit." Thieves dashed into a cabin the other night, grabbed a stove that contained a burning fire, and threw it on a dog sled all in less than 60 seconds. Thanks to Hank and Preston, this establishment has been fortunate enough to have all our belongings still safely in our care.

November 17, 1899   3:20 a.m.

Today when I went outside, I noticed something very different about the town's atmosphere. I couldn't hear the waves crashing against the shore. I walked down to the beach to see what was going on. To my dismay, I discovered a sea completely covered with ice. It's incredible; I've never seen anything like this. It was as if I was in another world. It's like the entire ocean changed colors overnight. I could barely see the horizon where the light blue ocean ended and the gray, cloudy sky began. It was so quiet without the tiny waves slowly washing out the beach. Maybe someday I'll gather enough courage to walk on the ice. It's rather frightening to think the only way out of this place is across thousands of miles of either frozen tundra or ice.

November 18, 1899   3:05 a.m.

Seeing the frozen Bering Sea was enchanting for some, and eerie for others. For Ria, it was a different story. She was terrified of the ice. She said yesterday she just tried to pretend that it wasn't there. Today she said she could no longer block it out of her mind. Ria said it was too quiet and she missed hearing the ocean surf. When she went outside and saw the frozen body of water, it made her want to scream. "I feel like a captive," she said.

As the day went on, it got worse. She was obsessed with the thought of being in a frozen prison with no way out. By evening she wasn't able to work because she was crying hysterically. Through her sobs, I gathered the reason for her horrendous fear was that her brother used to force her into a shed and leave her there for days. Ria said the most terrifying part was that when he finally let her out, no one would inquire where she had been. Ria knew her brother had complete control over the family, and that locking her in the shed was one of the many things he did to abuse her. She repeated, "I've been a prisoner before and I can't be one again!" Then she would continue crying out of control.

I felt so helpless. I've never dealt with a situation like this before. I asked if she wanted more laudanum and she said no. That was the first time she's ever turned it down.

I never should have left her alone. She was incapacitated by the thought of being in this frozen land. I should have had one of the girls watching her at all times. After servicing a client, I returned to see how Ria was doing and to my dismay, she had vanished. I noticed right away all of her winter clothes and supplies were missing as well, yet a bottle of perfume was lying on her bed. I alerted J.J. to the problem, but he didn't seem to be too concerned. He said, "Oh that's just like that woman! Getting hysterical and running off. Give her some time. She'll come back. Where do you think she's going to go?" I hope J.J. is right. We all pray she returns quickly and safely.

November 20, 1899   3:20 a.m.

No one has seen Ria for two days. Jime and Dorothy have spent a great portion of their time asking others about her location and we have no leads. We're beginning to fear she is dead. I fear her desire to leave was so strong, that instead of being a prisoner, she chose to try to walk out of here. I know there are no people outside of this area and by now she's probably frozen to death. I read in today's newspaper there must be 4,000 to 6,000 people who have decided to remain in Nome for the winter. The following is a quote: "We are prisoners in a jail of ice and snow, a little group of adventurers acting as outposts for a civilization."

I guess Ria really felt like a prisoner and she didn't want to be a part of this frozen wasteland. Please forgive me, Ria.

November 21, 1899   2:50 a.m.

As I was servicing a client this evening, a familiar-looking man barged into my tent rambling about how he found Ria out on the ice and I needed to come with him to get her. Jime and J.J. followed him in soon after, wondering why he was interrupting me. When things finally settled down, the man said he had been a client of Ria a few times. He explained that he was walking on the frozen ocean this afternoon when he came across a lifeless body that he recognized as Ria's. Being a small man he knew he couldn't carry her all the way back to town by himself, so he came to get help. J.J. made the point that we couldn't do anything with her body if we brought her back and Jime agreed. I replied angrily, "She was like a daughter to me. There's no way I'm going to leave her corpse out there to be eaten by anything that comes along. The least we can do is bring her back and give her a proper burial." No one disputed me. I wanted to go with J.J. and the man, but I'm still afraid of the ice. I don't trust it.

After about an hour and a half, the men returned empty handed. I guess the frozen ocean was too vast and uniform for the man to remember where Ria was. I was devastated. I had wanted so much for them to find her so we could bury her properly. At least now we know that she's moved on from this world and we don't have to worry about her anymore.

November 22, 1899   3:30 p.m.

I cried myself to sleep last night feeling guilty that I didn't do more for Ria. At times I regretted hiring her. Now that she's gone, I'm not sure that we can keep up with the demand, especially with Natalie still being a couple weeks away from recovery. Our clientele has decreased due to the many who have left for the winter and the cold weather that's hampering the mining activity. I feel bad for Alex having to pick up the excess deposits. She's working incredibly hard, but also making more commission as a result. I'm fortunate to have already met Margerie and have a possible replacement.

November 23, 1899   **2:50 p.m.**
        The entire country surrounding Nome is camouflaged. The ocean, the mountains, the tundra, and even the sky are the same shade of dull white and they all blend into each other. As I walked further away from town today, I noticed the tiny tents along the beach looked like little snow piles and not like tents at all. The eternal wind and snow have created giant structures especially out on the ocean. I try not to think about the ocean too much; it reminds me of Ria. I hate thinking about her tiny little body freezing to death in the bitter cold with the wind blowing hard against her.
        J.J. came into my tent this afternoon when I was crying over Ria. He reassured me that even if we had found her body, there's nothing we could have done. There's nowhere to bury her because the land is frozen. We would have had to store the body and bury it in the spring when the ground thaws. That calmed me a little because having Ria's corpse around would have been a constant reminder of my failure.

November 25, 1899   **4:20 a.m.**
        Today was Thanksgiving and there was a lot of celebrating. People told what they were thankful for. It was a regular working shift for the ladies and throughout the night, I kept hoping Jafet would appear, anticipating maybe he came into town to enjoy the festivities. I couldn't stop thinking about him as I serviced my clients. I kept recalling the stories he told me and how they had made me laugh. Rumor has it that none of the Lucky Swedes have been seen in town. Everybody says they've got so much gold out there at Anvil it isn't worth the risk of losing it just to come into town.
        Instead of sharing Thanksgiving Day with Jafet, the day was made special for me by the arrival of my three miner friends. It was wonderful to see Milroy, Clark, and Rawslin again. Since they

let me know I was special to them, they became special to me. We spent hours talking about all the prospecting they had done throughout the Seward Peninsula.

When I made merry bout with Milroy, he was even more aggressive and arousing than the previous time. He forcefully manipulated my body into his desired positions as he spoke of the various acts he wanted me to perform. I became more lustful as he had his way with me. It was like the horned animal in me had been released. After what my father did to me, I always thought coitus was something dirty. Then being forced to sell it to survive, I thought I was numb to a man's touch.

But with Milroy, I couldn't help but feel a healthy vigor awakening. I've never encountered a man who is so creative and has so much energy when it comes to making merry bout. Just as I started to get comfortable in one of the positions, he would switch to another scenario, totally different. I definitely saw a pattern in his moods. He would be very tender one moment and then extremely aggressive.

During his overnight, I lost all track of time, floating in and out of reality. It reminded me of how I feel when I take the large amounts of laudanum. They're both definitely an escape. The more responsibility I inherit with this position, the more I long for an escape. I know I said I couldn't let Milroy see that I reach satisfaction with him, but it is out of my hands. I had at least two releases and he commented on each one. He knows what he does to me and that scares me. I'll have to work on being stronger when I'm joining with him.

November 26, 1899   3:05 a.m.

Last night I learned that Alex is suffering from the losses of Natalie and Ria. She is working harder than I ever expected and I feel terrible. I told Alex about meeting Margerie. We talked for hours about all the reasons we liked the idea and all the complications of bringing her into the business with no experience. Finally we decided to incorporate Margerie in our kinship.

Before work, I went searching for her around town and finally found her serving food in the St. Nicholas Restaurant. I waited for her to get off work then we walked to my tent to discuss business. I explained she could make much more money as a bird of the night and that she would be lovingly embraced into our family. I told her we already have a tent, bed, and stove for her and the ladies and I would lend her dresses until she could buy her own.

She was hesitant at first but I could tell after I spoke with her, she was much more convinced. She said she still needed time to think about it. I hope she decides to join. We could benefit from a new set of wings in the nest.

November 27, 1899   2:30 p.m.

With the temperature dropping each day, I am very thankful the business alliance has such a large food cache. I'm already beginning to see evidence of an inadequate food supply for the winter throughout the town. For example: the only place to get eggs is at the Nome Café. A plate of ham and eggs costs $2.50, beans are $1 a bowl, coffee is $.25 a cup, and evaporated spuds are $.50 an order. Just last month, a person could buy that same breakfast for half the price.

I'm beginning to hear a little bit about the Natives. They are called Inuits. There are only about a dozen Native families in Nome. The rest are out at King Island and will return here to fish in the summer. They all seem to have rust colored skin, high cheekbones, and dark black hair. The women wear long braids, while the men wear their hair short in a bowl-shaped cut. Both men and women wear coats of fur that are pulled over their heads. The outsides of the coats are decorated with pieces of fur and intricate beadwork. I admire the way the women carry their babies on their backs inside their coats. It must be comforting to the child. I find some of the women to be incredibly beautiful, while other Natives are rather homely, but I guess that's the same in any race.

Jime has been spending as much time as he can with an Inuit acquaintance, Kuduk. He's learning the best hunting and fishing spots. Jime hasn't learned much of Kuduk's language yet, but the natives are rapidly learning English so they can trade with the miners here. Even though they may not speak the same language, Kuduk and Jime seem to communicate easily since they have a similar interest: obtaining nourishment. The majority of Inuits who are here sell fresh fish they have acquired by ice fishing in the ocean. They also sell ptarmigan that they've killed on the tundra. I sure hope Jime is a fast learner and we will have free fish and ptarmigan to eat soon.

November 29, 1899   2:50 p.m.

Margerie said she was ready to unite with our alliance. I was overjoyed! I know I was scared to take on the added responsibility, but I can't possibly expect Alex to work this hard any longer.

I introduced Margerie to Alex and Natalie. I think Margerie was a bit surprised at Natalie's size; she has put on more weight since the accident. Margerie seemed pleased with her new family and the ladies appeared eager to help her. I learned Alex and Margerie had met previously at the St. Nicholas Restaurant. Hopefully knowing someone here will make Margerie a little more comfortable. She'll start working in a couple days, but first she's going to take the time to learn some of the secrets of the trade. Seeing everyone get along was such a relief for me. I don't know how this organization would work if we didn't all respect each other and work as a team.

November 30, 1899   3:05 p.m.

This was the second time I have had to turn back on a walk. I noticed that the sun softened the snow a bit. What used to be hard and could easily carry my weight was sinking with every footstep. I had not even gone 15 steps and I was exhausted. The snow was up to my knees in some places and I wasn't even enjoying it, so I decided to come back on a colder day.

December 1899

December 1, 1899   **4:10 a.m.**

J.J. and I had an agreement that he would try out any woman before we hired her. He tested Margerie and came back with a smile on his face. He said, "She has a little bit to learn, but she'll please our clients just fine." He had been satisfied with all our ladies and he had been more than pleased with Alex. J.J. didn't have to "try me out" since he already had carnal knowledge of me from our teenage years in the barn. I remember during those playful times, my stomach never hurt the way it did when my father touched my body.

Now that Margerie is officially a part of the bevy, we will begin training this evening. Our bathing time will be the perfect opportunity for us to share all our experiences with Margerie, and what we have learned in our years of being involved in this business.

December 2, 1899   12:40 p.m.

I had a dream about my father again last night. I remembered every detail about our one room cabin and how my mother and sister passively endured my pain. I hate being reminded of that man and all the rage he created inside of me. I haven't dreamed about him in a while. After each dream I pray never again. The dreams remind me he was my father, otherwise I do very well at forgetting that fact. The day after I have a dream, I don't like the way I feel about myself. I am reminded with clarity what that man did to the very fabric of my being.

December 4, 1899   2:30 p.m.

Life without Ria is getting better. It is strange to say, but this frozen land is helping me heal my pain. The snow has covered up a large portion of the human waste on the ground. Everything sounds rather muffled. I didn't notice the constant sound of the hammers until the cold ceased their noise. It is the first time I have slowed down enough to notice. I am enjoying the quiet town.

All members of the alliance have mentioned that although there is plenty to go around, they just can't seem to get enough to eat lately. That must be one way nature gets us ready for the long winter ahead.

December 5, 1899   2:35 p.m.

Margerie worked for the first time last night and she did extremely well. Only one of the clients verbally abused her, something the ladies and I tried to caution her about. I tried to talk to the clients about how her performance was when they were finished. The ones I asked seemed pleased. I don't want to be optimistic about this situation too soon. I would love for everything to be ideal for Margerie, but this isn't a pleasant livelihood and things rarely turn out perfect. A part of me is hoping for the best, like I always do, and another part of me is feeling wicked for having anything to do with getting this young lady involved in a lifestyle that has such risks associated with it.

December 7, 1899   **8:15 a.m.**

Last night I had a dream unlike any other. I don't know if it is
the lack of sunlight or the lack of warmth but this dream seemed
to have the most brilliant colors. The dream began with a dark-
skinned young girl wearing several animal skins. She was walking
toward me. The furs looked lush and rich. She seemed warm and
comfortable. She told me to follow her and not be afraid; she was
here to teach me. I don't know how long the dream lasted but it
seemed like days as this young girl showed me the cycle of the
animals living in this land. As we encountered each animal, it was
as if we became that creature. We saw, smelled, heard, touched,
and tasted the world through the senses of each animal we visited.
First I was a brown bear running with great speed. Once I reached
the river I moved through it as if I was still on land. With my
senses alert I searched for the next substance I needed to survive. I
used my nose and eyes to locate the squirming fish and I captured
it with my large paws. The instant I ate I felt nourished. Just as
magically as I became the bear, I was transformed into a fish. After
the fish, I became a seal. The dream ended with me as a polar bear,
the biggest, most terrifying mammal in the arctic. I swam in the
icy water with no awareness of the cold on a quest for the seals
I smelled miles away. After waiting patiently, a seal came up for
air. I quickly killed and consumed the bloody meal, leaving some
reminders of my feast to the arctic fox that had been watching me.
The warmth of the sun began to make me sleepy and I curled up
and fell asleep. When I awoke in my dream I was Mandy again.
The girl dressed in furs asked me, "Now do you understand? One
creature must always prey upon another to survive."

December 8, 1899   **4:15 a.m.**

It's been almost three weeks since Ria disappeared. My mind
clearly sees her tiny Spanish face and the way she laid in my arms
when she needed comforting. I think about her often and wish I
could have done something to stop her terrible destiny. I've always
believed everything happens for a reason, but I can't seem to figure

out the reason behind Ria's death. Maybe she just wasn't fit to be in this frozen world. I hope she is content wherever she is now.

December 9, 1899   10:30 a.m.

Last night I heard soft crying that woke me from my sleep. When I rose up from my bed I noticed that my hand was wet. I felt the actual water droplets on my skin. Then a very warm sensation came over me and I had a feeling that Ria was in the tent. After several minutes the feeling grew cold and her presence was gone. It scared me, but I'm more curious than frightened. What happened? What was that warmth?

December 10, 1899   3:45 a.m.

Today I had an extremely pleasant visit with Rawslin. Instead of sitting in the tent visiting, we decided to go on a walk. I was worried I would miss work, but Rawslin assured me not to worry and that he would pay for however much work I missed. He encouraged me to bundle up so we could spend as much time outside as possible. The sunset was spectacular over the frozen Bering Sea. It filled the sky with an array of different shades of purples, reds, and pinks. With each day's beginning and end we see less and less sun, but more and more beautiful colors in the sky. Natalie says since nature doesn't give us much sunlight this time of year, she makes up for it by giving us lots of color.

Tonight before leaving The Belmont, Ryan brought the lights in the sky to everyone's attention. It was our first experience with what is called the Northern Lights. I'm not sure what's more beautiful, the Northern Lights or the winter sunsets. When I first saw the lights, I thought my imagination was playing tricks on me. Green and red patches of light danced in the sky, like bright, colorful sheets blowing in the wind against a dark background. Then as quickly as they had arrived, they were gone. I'm grateful all the members of the alliance were together to witness that amazing sight.

December 13, 1899   **2:10 p.m.**

Today Dr. Miller was here and gave Natalie permission to return to work. It will take time for all her scars to heal, and I'm not sure she will ever look the same. That doesn't really matter, though. We're all so glad to have her back. It will ease the load for almost everyone. Dorothy is going to miss her, though. Natalie has been helping to heat the water, cook, and clean, while she has been slowly recovering.

Before Dr. Miller left, he asked to speak with me in private. He said he was alarmed at the rate that venereal diseases were growing through Nome. He wanted to ensure my ladies were properly protected. I reminded him that the men were washed up before ever seeing the ladies. He said, "Well, that's about all you can do. I'm glad you're taking those precautions." He also informed me that the arrangement of trading exams for the act was working quite nicely but he was not interested in mounting anyone but Alex. He said he is growing quite fond of his visits and he would like to be a steady customer of Alex's. I told him, "The choice is yours, Dr. Miller. Whatever you want to do is fine." He replied, "Thank you, Mandy. It has been a pleasure doing business with you."

December 14, 1899   **11:30 a.m.**

With the colder temperatures come more of nature's beauties. Last night after work when I was having the usual nightcap with the alliance, Natalie mentioned the intricate patterns of frost on the windows. She said, "If you watch you can see how the hoarfrost changes daily as the temperature and the slight vibration of the earth changes." With laudanum to enhance the moment, I spent several minutes just staring at the tiny crystal structures that had grown on the window. It was fascinating!

December 15, 1899   **2:45 p.m.**

I can't say enough about Jime and Dorothy. They are extremely hard workers and a great asset to our business. Already J.J. is paying them double what their wages were in June. He comments over and over that he's never seen two people get so much done in such a short amount of time. He is thrilled they joined us on this adventure. J.J. said he got a real bonus with Jime because he never knew what a skilled hunter he is. Each day Jime acquires more knowledge from his Eskimo friend and we reap the benefits of his new found knowledge.

Dorothy prepares exquisite meals with the meat Jime brings home. This week we have enjoyed reindeer stew and moose roast. I really enjoy working with Dorothy and Jime. Dorothy's laugh reminds me of my mother's in a way. Whenever I hear her laugh, I can't help but smile.

December 17, 1899   1:25 p.m.

My father paid me another visit last night. Instead of remembering all the details of the room and my mother and sister suffering in private, I remember every detail about that repulsive man. I taste his sweat as it drips into my mouth. I feel his rough whiskers on my skin. I smell the stale whiskey on his breath. I hear his disgusting groans and I see the ecstasy on his face. Once again I become outraged. I want to kill him. I wish I could, but I always wake up before I get the chance. It would feel rewarding to put an end to my misery. The dreams of my father seem to paralyze me and I can't concentrate very well the day after. I hate it that even in the present he can influence my mood.

December 18, 1899   3:10 p.m.

As we get less sunlight each day it becomes obvious the sun is the creator of the earth. Without the heat and light it gives us, we would be frozen. There would be no life. Natalie told us, "We'll start to notice a change in a few days, 'cause we'll start getting the sun light back—a couple more minutes each day." I sure hope she is correct.

December 19, 1899   4:10 a.m.

I forget sometimes Margerie is new to this business. She's grown up with money and respect from many people. Suddenly she's at the bottom of the social ladder and doesn't understand how to deal with it. We took a walk tonight after work and she had many questions. She wanted to know why the men always degraded her and called her ugly names. She wanted to know why they regarded her as a piece of flesh and nothing else. She couldn't understand why any man would get pleasure out of pulling her bright red hair and calling her a flaming bitch.

All the other ladies have grown up understanding they are weak and worthless. They have gotten used to the fact men can be bastards and we just need to give them what they want in order to keep them content. Margerie, on the other hand, never had to do farm chores and rarely even did housework. Her father loved her until the day he died last year. None of my other women have had the experience of a man loving them. I have at least had a husband and can fathom what it is like for a man to have respect for me.

I explained to Margerie this is a man's world and in order to survive in it, we must sink below them and allow them to do almost whatever they want to us. Margerie explained she doesn't like it when men call her a bitch. She didn't know what she had done to deserve that title. I told her I was sorry and assured her someone from the alliance would always be there for her.

I hope I made a good decision hiring Margerie. She's an excellent moneymaker, the men love her tiny body and gorgeous hair, but I don't know how mentally fit she is to handle this job. I suppose I should just stop worrying and pray for the best.

December 21, 1899   11:45 a.m.
While talking among some other madams and chippies today I heard about a man, Barth McCoy. Rumor has it he is a stud, a natural born wolf. It appears he enjoys pleasing a woman and he takes great pride in his work. All the females I talked to agree time spent with him is indeed a lesson. From what I hear he is getting lots of practice. I wonder why he is sharing his wisdom with the sporting class. Maybe he figures we will appreciate the knowledge.

December 23, 1899   4:40 a.m.

I was awakened just minutes ago with a strange sensation that Ria was in the room. I heard her crying softly. I could hear her tiny voice but I couldn't make out the words. I felt the moisture but this time it was on my face. The warm sensation lingered for awhile and faded away slowly. There is no logical explanation for this. I wonder if this is what happened to Lizzy. Did she start feeling as if there were spirits around her? Am I going insane? I had better not tell anyone about this.

December 24, 1899   11:30 p.m.

This day will be embedded into my mind for two reasons. The first was the incredible sunrise and sunset I had the honor of observing. We only got about four hours of light as the sun rose just a tiny bit above the horizon. The yellow ball of light was hidden behind a dismal gray mass. What light did escape cast vivid shades of magenta directly above the clouds, the brilliance of the light reflected off of the white snow to create a pastel pink that encompassed the sky in every direction. What a strange and beautiful land this Alaska Territory is.

The second memorable aspect of the day was brunch. Jeremy James announced that nobody would have a usual working day. He reminded everyone his good friend Tex Rickard, who owned The Northern Saloon, was having a huge feast on Christmas to celebrate. We were all invited. Tex had specifically asked if Jime and Dorothy would help him prepare the food for the feast. Since Jime and Dorothy would be helping Tex all day, they would not be available to do their regular chores such as gathering and heating water. The Bantam Belmont depends so much on all the services Dorothy and Jime provide that without the two of them, we can't work.

The ladies and I spent the rest of the day taking long baths, curling our hair, and making sure our formal dresses were looking their best. We all felt like little children anxiously anticipating Christmas.

Margerie had trouble deciding whose dress to wear. She tried on Alex's dress but it was too big throughout the whole dress. My dress was too big also, and there was no need for her to try Natalie's dress. We had no alternative but to open Ria's trunk to look at her dresses. Margerie tried on both of Ria's formal dresses and both of them were a bit too short, although they fit perfect everywhere else. Margerie doesn't know yet, but I took Ria's green dress to a seamstress and she's going to do some work tonight and hopefully lengthen it. I can't wait to see the look on Margerie's face when she sees the dress. It was sad for all the ladies thinking about Ria. I still remember that terrible day when she disappeared five weeks ago. I think of her often and hope she is resting in peace.

December 26, 1899   **12:25 a.m.**

What a grand affair! Over 400 people were served a hot meal in The Northern. For the first time I really enjoyed being in this distinct community with its unique people. So many guests were asking Tex Rickard why he was having such a big party he finally stood on a table and yelled to all, "I value Christmas the most of all Christian holidays. As a child, it was always an exceptional time every year. My mother continually went out of her way to ensure that. Since I can no longer celebrate with my mother, I choose to share that special day with my friends and business associates. Giving a warm meal to others is my way of thanking my mother for all she gave me." The loud cheers gave the impression that everybody was satisfied with that answer.

The highlight of my evening was Jafet showing up as we started serving the food. Just seeing his face created a magical, warm feeling within me. It was wonderful to see him again. He made sure he sat next to me as we ate. When the music began, he asked if we could dance. Jafet apologized for not coming to see me or not arranging for me to come see him. He said that the tension had never waned and instead increased daily. He said, "I've done my best to try to talk to them, but no one will listen." He told me not only did he fear for his life, but for mine as well. He didn't want anyone to know he had feelings for me. As he spoke those words, my heart melted inside my body. For a Christmas present Jafet brought me a leather pouch with a red ribbon tied on it. Inside were seven large nuggets. I was overwhelmed by his generosity.

Everyone in the alliance seemed to be more than pleased with their gifts. Everyone knows how much I like to write so each of them bought me a new journal. J.J. also gave me some feathers and ink. It makes me happy that they know me so well. Then I handed out the shaving sets and the comb and brush sets to the crew. I gave Ria's set to Margerie and she cried with happiness, being so surprised I had gotten her a present. I was overjoyed that Ria's green dress fit her so well, even if I did think of Ria's dreamtime appearance every time I looked at her. She was delighted I had taken the time to get the dress lengthened. I think she actually felt like a part of the family for the first time.

So many wonderful things happened today, I couldn't possibly decide which one was my favorite. I danced several songs with Jafet and a few other gents. I sampled foods I had never even heard of before: rabbit braised with cream sauce, fillet of grouse with truffles, and roasted cinnamon black bear. Along with the food came new knowledge. Jime told us that eating the liver of a bear can kill a person instantly because of all the iron in it.

Having a day as a leisure woman was a welcome change. Unfortunately, the finest day of my life was also the worst. Tex Rickard's saloon looked elegant with all its decorations and beautiful mirrors on each of the walls. The candles on the Christmas tree reflecting off the mirrors were fascinating. What I didn't like stopped me in my tracks. A gold rush can't help but change a person. This one has changed me. I just hadn't taken the time to notice. When I saw my reflection in the mirror, I no longer had a choice but to observe. On the outside, I saw an attractive woman with a warm smile, about 5'9", 150 pounds, with brown curly hair and a dark blue silk dress covering her muscular, big boned body. On the inside, the vile, filthy smut I saw standing before my eyes appalled me. I had never seen anything so evil looking in my life. Every time I walk past a mirror, I will be reminded of what I really am. I can't run away from it. I arrange for an abundance of men to have intercourse with my ladies. In return I profit. I am as disgusting as the animals I cater to.

For the first time in my life I am making money and acquiring something for myself and in return, I've lost my pride. I guess we pay a price for everything.

December 27, 1899   3:45 a.m.

Tonight after work, during our nightcap ritual, Ryan recounted that J.J. had run into the ass that left Alex tied up in her own vomit. Ryan made the story sound gallant. J.J. didn't lay a hand on the man but instead gave him one verbal insult after another. Ryan told us the last thing J.J. said was, "Have some respect for yourself, man. Then it will be easier to respect others."

Hearing that story brought tears to Alex. She said, "No one has ever stood up for me before." When J.J. came to the bar to join us for another drink we all pretended to be talking about the snowstorm. It wouldn't do to let J.J. know we are aware of his softer side.

Seeing Alex radiate with joy when she heard about J.J. made me radiant as well. I'm delighted she has another who loves her as much as I do.

December 29, 1899   2:50 a.m.

I was hoping since Jafet had come to town on Christmas, I would be seeing him again on a regular basis. But since he left that night without any physical contact except when we were dancing and no mention of when he would return, I don't know when I'll see him again. Every time we touched at Christmas, I could feel the electricity flowing between us. When I looked in his eyes I could see it too. I want to think he has feelings for me like I'm developing for him. It's crazy, Mandy. A man like that wouldn't want a woman like you. Get it out of your mind. Concentrate on your work.

Speaking of work, things have been running very smoothly. Nothing unusual with any of the customers, no exciting stories to share, just the same old men who can't get enough love or lust. Natalie was telling me last night about a man whose hands were so rough that he actually scratched her body. Margerie said she had a man who could not get hard unless he peed on her first. All of us agreed that it is one thing you don't have to get used to. Just refuse! We agreed that men are strange creatures. What amazes me the most about men is when paying for a quick unsnap with one of my girls, they will always take their hats off but taking their boots off is out of the question. There is no time for that ritual.

It feels good to have the enterprise running with such ease. I have to admit without Ria, the family flows together quite well, even with Margerie. Ria really was the one having problems, and in return she caused others in the bevy problems. I hate admitting it, but we are much better off without her. God bless your soul Ria. I hope writing about her doesn't cause me to dream about her, if that is what it was.

January 1900

January 1, 1900   **5:15 a.m.**

New Years Eve was not what I had expected. With all the rowdy people here, I thought there would be lots of merry-making. Instead the town was deserted as the miners prepared for the race that began at midnight. As the New Year began, each of the claims was opened up and the claim-jumping stampede was back on. It's way below zero, but the temperature didn't stop anyone from running out to the creeks to stake claims and then rushing back to the recorder's office. I hear from my customers that U.S. mining law states a claim owner must do at least $100 worth of assessments on their claim each year if they want to keep it. No one knows for sure if that law applies to Nome so everyone is taking advantage of the chaos.

Business has been slow. Slow. Meaning the girls average ten customers an evening instead of their usual twenty. I figure within the next few days the men will start coming back into town looking for a little warmth and affection.

This evening while in The Belmont, that same inebriated simpleton who was harassing me in September walked in with a large icicle in his hand. Immediately he started shouting, "Madam wild fowl, madam wild fowl, look what I brought for you! Let's see how fast you can melt this in your hot hole." Thankfully this time J.J. didn't see any humor in the situation. Within a minute after that man walked into The Belmont, he was escorted out by a group of gentlemen who surrounded J.J. and Ryan.

I didn't understand why all those men jumped up to help. Alex told me it was because they respect me. "They see how hard you work everyday." Then she said, "Do you know how much I respect you? I also envy you." I told Alex I envied her because she enjoys mounting so much. It made her laugh and she replied, "I don't cherish joining with anyone as much as I do you." That was all it took for me to fall helplessly into her arms. We made merry bout for several hours tonight. I wanted to ask her about her feelings for Jeremy James and if he ever asks about us being lovers, but I couldn't bring myself to do it. What's between them is between them. I won't interfere with him if he does not interfere with me. I must admit with each passing day I find myself falling more in love with Alex. The more Alex is loved the more she radiates love.

January 3, 1900   4:50 a.m.

Although it is the budding of a new year and a new century, I don't feel any newer. I thought maybe with the new beginning, I could start my life over and would be a different person. But I'm not. I'm still Mandy, a madam. I still sell myself and others for merry bout and nothing is going to change that. Margerie is a constant reminder of that fact. She was innocent and so oblivious to what this society is really made of and I turned her into a whore. I wonder how our lives would be different if we had never met. Once Natalie was back in business, I was thinking that we probably could have made it through the winter with just two girls and myself, yet with new miners arriving each day from the Yukon Valley, the Kobuk River, and the Kotzebue Sound, we would have had to get someone sooner or later.

I'm sure Margerie could have supported herself working as a waitress. I hear those ladies make about $5 to $7 a day. Sometimes I wish I could tell her to leave for her own good, but I couldn't do that. I'm the one who convinced her to join us in this business, and now I have to show her it's really not that bad. There are people who enjoy it; take Alex as an example. I should have known I couldn't bring a girl into this profession who didn't know anything about it. I ruined her. I am detestable.

January 4, 1900   **10:10 a.m.**

I'm sorry I let my emotions get out of hand last night. Margerie came to me when work was over and cried. She expressed in great length how she loves this family, but she is quickly learning to despise the men who use her body. Now that she is one of the daughters of sin, she understands what it's like. She understands no one ever chooses to be treated inhumanely and money really does go hand in hand with power. Now she knows what it's like on the other end of the spectrum. I'm just sorry I was the one to introduce her to this reality. It would have happened sooner or later.

January 6, 1900   **4:40 a.m.**

The moon was full and it was a cloudless, starry night. That in itself outweighed the 30-below temperature. After spending what seemed like an hour dressing, I finished putting on my last layer of clothes. Once I was past the influence of the city, I emerged into a winter dreamland. The bright object in the sky reflected off the perfectly white ground. This created so much light I could actually see the bead work on my seal skin mittens. I had taken some laudanum before leaving town. I know now I can't indulge and then venture out in the cold. My mind became so engrossed taking in the view of the magical reflection I forgot about my body. After standing and staring for I don't know how long, my stinging feet and nose brought me back to reality.

I am back in my tent and I still feel the pain. This must be the frostbite J.J. warned me about. How foolish to put myself in such a dangerous situation. I'm lucky I didn't get hurt badly and I must take this as a warning not to be so desperate for escape that I bring harm to myself.

January 7, 1900   1:15 p.m.

The main topic of conversation at brunch this morning was my red nose. There was nothing I could do to hide it so I had to admit to everyone what a foolish thing I did last night. Of course they all took the opportunity to ridicule me. J.J. even suggested he be the one to dispense the laudanum. I was thankful Kuduk, Jime's Eskimo friend, was in the tent and reminded everyone frostbite is nothing to laugh about and that it can happen to anyone, regardless of their state of mind. Kuduk told me if I was able to walk today, I had nothing to worry about and that my feet would be just fine.

January 8, 1900   3:35 a.m.

We had another batch of snow today. I thought it would snow a lot here because we're so far north and it's just supposed to snow all the time. I've noticed the snow doesn't fall from the clouds much and instead the wind blows it around and piles it in certain places, making the area look like it has been snowing for days. I've also noticed after a snowstorm, the pile of snow down Front Street seems to have grown massively. It's because a small section on both sides of the street, in front of the stores and saloons, is kept free from snow. In order for this to happen, men shovel the snow on the ground onto the pile in the middle. This, combined with the wind, leads people to believe that it has snowed a lot. In all actuality, if people look out on the tundra, they will see it hasn't snowed much and Mother Nature, along with humans, has been playing tricks on them.

January 10, 1900   3:05 p.m.

I had to return from my walk quite a bit earlier than I had hoped. I hadn't been out in a few days due to the harsh weather, and I was getting annoyed just sitting here in my tent. The wind wasn't as bad as it has been so I decided to try my luck. I had walked about ten minutes toward the north when the wind picked

up speed so fast it almost knocked me over. Snow was blowing in
my eyes and I couldn't see any landmarks. I started thinking about
getting lost out here in this frozen wilderness and I got scared. I
was also getting cold, so I decided to find my way back to town
before I walked further and became thoroughly confused of my
whereabouts.

January 12, 1900   **3:15 p.m.**
    Instead of waiting around to have brunch with everyone today,
I put on all my winter clothing and went outside. The sun was
shining in the cloudless sky and reflecting its brilliance. I had this
overwhelming desire to walk on the glistening ice. Since the day
the Bering Sea froze, Natalie has been explaining to everybody
that the ice is definitely safe to walk on. "You don't have to worry
about it cracking and you falling in. The ice is too thick. It just
won't happen." She added it would not be wise to go out on the
ice when the wind is blowing from the north, especially when it's
a strong wind. The bright sunshine and lack of a breeze fueled my
curiosity and I finally got brave enough to try that adventure for
myself. As soon as I started walking on the ice, I realized it was
very strong and my fears were unnecessary.
    As I relaxed, I began to enjoy the beauty of the frozen ocean.
Natalie says the ice floes piled on the frozen sea come from
the clean water of rivers. The clean water doesn't mix with the
salt water so instead the river water freezes on top of the ocean,
creating beautiful sculptures. Natalie explained if the ice sculptures
were made from salt water, they would not have any color to them
and we wouldn't see the magnificent shades of blues and greens
that reflect from the designs. I'm thankful the river water has made
its way upon the Bering Sea coast to be trapped inside by freezing
temperatures, just so I can dwell upon the magnitude of its beauty.
    Looking into the numerous frozen shapes that surrounded
me, I was mesmerized by the variety of astonishing colors I saw
entrapped within the ice. I stared as deep into them as I could. I
wondered if I wasn't here admiring this beauty, would it still exist?
I remember my father saying that if no one is in a forest and a tree

falls, there is no sound. If that's true, does it mean that when I walk away all this beauty disappears? I can't grasp that. I used to argue over the subject with my father all the time.

When I was a little girl I would lay outside on summer evenings and watch the stars. I would try to speculate what life was like on another planet. I always envisioned it would be deathly cold, with the sun being so far away. Today walking out on the ice reminded me of being on another planet. It was so quiet I could hear my own footsteps. The depth of the silence and the sparkling, geometric ice was incredible. I have seen many outstanding natural phenomena here in this Alaska Territory, but walking on the ice had the most emotional effect on me. Journeying in such peacefulness was the most relaxing activity I have ever had. I would have stayed and enjoyed the beauty of this strange, beautiful land longer but my feet and my nose began to get numb. I knew that wasn't a good sign. Even though my heart and soul didn't want to leave, my body and my mind knew it was time to return to the warmth of The Belmont. I'm already looking forward to my next adventure out on the ice.

January 15, 1900   10:10 a.m.

Today I was awakened in a most unusual manner. The first thing that caught my attention was the howling wind as it swept across Nome. The second thing I noticed was I had no heat in my tent. I quickly got out of bed and put my coat and boots on. I attempted to look outside through the tent flap, but to my dismay, I couldn't even open the flap because there was so much snow against my tent. I knew at once this must be what is known as a whiteout. Natalie had warned everyone these blizzards would be coming but I had no idea what to expect. In Colorado the snow usually came down gently out of the sky and in Seattle we didn't get much at all. I have never experienced anything like this.

January 15, 1900   12:15 p.m.

I had fallen back to sleep so I wasn't sure how long it was before I heard J.J. calling out my name. He was at my entrance. I got out of bed and walked toward his voice, hoping he was there to help me. Over the storm he yelled "Mandy, stay right where you are. Whatever you do, don't get out of your tent." I said, "J.J., I have no heat." He replied, "Nobody does, Mandy. The wind is blowing so hard that it's creating a negative pressure. Just stay in there and when things settle down, I'll come get you. You'll be fine, Mandy," I heard his voice fade away. I almost started to cry, but that wouldn't help so I got back into bed, put my head under the covers and went to sleep again. I woke up minutes ago and as I write, I am in candlelight. It was pitch dark inside my tent even though it is early afternoon. I hope nothing has happened to J.J. and he will return to get me soon.

January 15, 1900   **3:25 p.m.**

I'm thankful I had *Huck Finn* to keep me company. I read for about two hours but my body began to numb and I knew I had to get up and move. I started jumping around just to get the blood flowing. After a few minutes of running in place, my heart jumped for joy as I heard J.J. calling my name again. He said, "Mandy, in 30 seconds I'm going to open up your flap and you better be ready to come with me. This wind is not going to give anybody mercy. It will start ripping right through your tent so be prepared to grab onto a rope I will hand you. Ryan is holding onto the other end and if you follow the rope it will get you to The Belmont. Whatever you do Mandy, don't let go."

Now that J.J. and Ryan have rescued all us ladies from our cold, separate spaces we are very grateful to be sitting in The Belmont surrounded by the heat of the stove and the warmth of our family. The stove in The Belmont is enormous and is not affected by the strong winds. The highlight of our conversations this evening has been J.J.'s details of each lady's rescue. He said he about had to push Natalie through the snow in order to get her into The Belmont. At Alex's tent he said he spent what seemed like hours moving snow before he could even find the structure, but he knew it was there so he just kept digging. J.J. apologized for waiting so long before coming to get anyone. He thought the winds would die down and it would be easier to get to everybody but as the afternoon wore on, the temperatures grew colder and the winds grew stronger. The storm wasn't going to wane so he made his move before somebody froze to death. To show our gratitude, we smothered him with hugs and kisses. I think he was actually blushing at one point. Jeremy James reminded us Ryan had helped but then Ryan reminded us J.J. was the one who went out in the blizzard while he stayed in the secure building. J.J. really was the true hero.

Just as we were all settling in and trying to go to sleep on the floor of The Belmont, we heard horrendous screaming outside. Jime predicted that it was probably the Horton family that lived a couple tents down. The wind must have blown apart their shelter. They had some young children and Jime wanted to go outside to see what he could do to help. J.J. forcefully kept him indoors. He declared, "Jime, at a time like this there is nothing you can do for those people. Going out that door will just endanger your life and I cannot let you do that. There are times when you have to take care of yourself and this is one of them. You are not going outside Jime, now sit down." J.J. wasn't trying to be mean or controlling. He was a survivalist and he was just trying to teach us his ways. I am finishing up this entry as I see my comrades falling asleep on the floor of The Belmont. Once again I must comment on how lucky we are to be in business with Jeremy James Dean Cotty. I'm not sure how other people are enduring the blizzard, I only know we are here in a warm shelter thanks to J.J.

January 16, 1900   11:45 p.m.

Late this evening the blizzard let up and even though it was dark, people still scurried outside to try to find the remains of what was left of their belongings, the ladies and myself included. All I could see inside my tent was my bed frame turned upside down. Since none of us took time to close our flaps as we clung for life onto the rope, our tents are now filled completely with snow. I'm grateful I was able to grab my diary quickly when J.J. told me to prepare for our evacuation. I would be devastated to think that all the events I recorded could never be shared with another person. Of course, I would have to start a new journal right away because writing is such a part of my survival.

We spent the rest of the night shoveling snow out of our tents. None of the ladies could work because we couldn't find a bed to lay on. As bad as it is to have to spend the night shoveling snow out of our tents, it is better than not having a tent at all. It's freezing cold outside. I'm thankful the canvases we brought are extremely strong, and have endured the worst blizzard we've had so far. Unfortunately, other people were not that lucky. Outside I could hear people sobbing. What little they had is now gone.

January 18, 1900   3:30 p.m.

I'm hearing from my customers that gold is no longer the commodity it was when the sun was shining upon the Seward Peninsula. Now people are using guns to guard their woodpiles, food caches, as well as their tents. It's fascinating to live in a community where the priorities change with the seasons. There is never a moment of lull. People have to be on guard at all times to keep what they rightfully own. Once again my heart goes out to all the poor souls that are this far north without the proper provisions needed to survive in this frozen land.

January 19, 1900   2:40 p.m.

Margerie reminded me of a young child today. It was her birthday and she was bursting with contagious excitement. We spent an unusually long time at brunch today. I'm really not sure if it was the pleasant company that kept us sitting so long or if it was the howling wind that delayed our departure. Whatever it was, I'm grateful we all could take the extra moments to celebrate Margerie's special day. I know she appreciated the spotlight. One could see it in her smiling eyes and hear it in her cheerful voice. She even stood up and announced, "Thank you all for taking me in and treating me as a part of your family. I love each of you so much. This has been the most heart-warming birthday I've ever had." I think her straightforwardness was appreciated by all.

January 20, 1900   **3:30 a.m.**

Last night Milroy paid for an overnight. As soon as the act was over he started telling me one story after another about killing animals when he and his brother were growing up in Deadwood, South Dakota. He spoke of the many different contests they would have to see who could kill an animal the fastest and then the slowest. He said that it didn't matter what type of animal it was as long as they could catch it. He stressed that his adventure had nothing to do with hurting and everything to do with the joy of watching a living creature die. That seems perverse to me. I wish he wouldn't share those stories.

January 22, 1900   **1:20 p.m.**

Two nights ago four other predominate madams and I met to discuss the $17.50 a month we are being fined by the municipal court for selling what men can't seem to go without. We all agreed if we didn't pay there was nothing they could do about it. As a result of our decision, we were all arrested yesterday and taken to a make shift jail on the second floor of the city hall. To make the best out of a bad situation we began singing songs in French and English. I can't sing in French but the three other ladies knew the songs quite well so I picked up the choruses quickly. We were making so much noise the dogs in town started howling, which encouraged us to sing even louder.

When Thomas Cashel, the Mayor, and Key Pittman, the city attorney, decided they were not getting anywhere using that method, they decided to let us go and try talking instead. After listening to what they had to say, the madams all agreed we could pay a percentage of our income each month. That would depend on how much income we were bringing in, but it could not be a fixed amount.

Speaking of income, I must remember to complete two important tasks that will increase profits. For one, I need to create a Belmont page for the town directory. This is a way of advertising in hotels and restaurants the available ladies at The Bantam Belmont. Second, I need to get wooden disks made with each of the girls' names on them so that J.J. can pass them out as complimentary try-outs to his business associates or friends.

Here I am thinking of how to make more money for myself and the town, when a part of me is so frustrated for what we get in return. It is acceptable for men to visit prostitutes, but prostitutes themselves are considered immoral and are condemned. Society doesn't respect our profession, yet they expect us to donate generously to their worthy causes. Without the money we working girls are forced to donate, I wonder where the town would get the money to pay the rumored $2,500 a year each for the Mayor and the city attorney.

January 23, 1900   2:40 p.m.

Today as soon as I walked outside to go to The Belmont, I knew the temperature was colder than my body had ever experienced before. There were two strong indicators. The first was my face. Instantly it felt like a thousand needles were being pressed into my skin. The second was my lungs. I could only take short shallow breaths. I guess my body knew if I consumed too much of this air, it could freeze my lungs within seconds. I had never thought of the distance between The Bantam Belmont and The Belmont as a long journey, but today in the bitter wind, a few steps took forever.

The freezing temperatures have not affected me the way I thought they would. It's always frigid here and my body just seemed to acclimate. I remember being cold at night in the wintertime in Colorado. I guess because it got warm during the day, it seemed so chilly at night. This far north there is no temperature fluctuation; it's either cold, or really cold.

January 25, 1900   2:45 p.m.

During my visit with Alex last night, she told me about an outrageous client she had that evening. She said when he grunted he sounded like a pig and it took everything she had to keep from laughing. As she relayed the story amidst laughter, I couldn't help drifting back to my time with Galen before he died. Alex's laugh reminds me so much of Galen's. It's hard to believe two people I love so much can have identical laughs. That is just another sign showing Alex and I are meant for each other.

After we talked for a while, Alex suggested we take turns kissing every inch of each other's bodies. It must have taken each one of us over an hour to please the other. As she was slowly traveling over my body with her loving touch, I was anticipating my tongue deep within her juicy wetness. Every part of Alex's body smells of heaven to me. I find myself craving it. It is always so sweet, never an unpleasant odor. I wonder if it's her scent that makes me love her so much, or if it's that I love her so much, I find her smell arousing.

I also wonder if Jime ever says anything to J.J. about Alex sleeping over in my tent. After all, it is so obvious. Whenever she is going to stay, I always request Jime to leave some heated water in my tent. The water is to wipe off the filth of the day so we can enjoy each other's fresh bodies. I have a feeling that J.J.'s love for Alex is so great all he wants is for her to be fulfilled. He knows we bring each other much happiness so I guess that is why he doesn't say anything about the nights we spend with each other. I'm grateful J.J. can share her. Some days I'm not sure what I would do without her.

January 27, 1900   1:10 p.m.

Natalie and I took a walk together after brunch today and we both saw two proper ladies wearing long, thin wooden feet and holding on to slender poles. They were laughing and having fun. We had never seen such a thing. We were both a little jealous of their joy and the winter toys on their feet. There never seems to be enough time to enjoy the simple activities in life.

As we walked through town Natalie couldn't stop talking about how wonderful Nome is. She loves the atmosphere of its constant growth. The people fascinate her and she wishes she could talk to more of them. She stated, "I really don't mind working the sheets. The only part I don't like is how we are looked down upon.

Everyone likes assembling. Why are we appalling just 'cause we cater to that desire?"

I guess this town does grow on people. Natalie loves it. I notice she rarely goes on walks away from Nome, but instead roams around the town always looking for the new things and people that arrive everyday. I would rather get away from all the people, but everyone's different. I'm just happy Natalie is content.

January 31, 1900   **3:20 a.m.**

Brunch was not served and will never be the same after this day. The business alliance has suffered a great loss, one I'm not sure we can ever recover from. At ten o'clock, when Jime had not returned from his eight o'clock routine of gathering water, Dorothy went up the Snake River to his favorite watering hole to check on him. The usually small hole was greatly enlarged and the jagged ice revealed signs of a struggle. Dorothy ran back to The Belmont to get J.J. and he confirmed Jime did in fact drown in the freezing water when the ice broke. I can't believe last week it was unbearably cold and this week it's warmed up enough to weaken the ice for human sacrifice.

I don't know what we'll do to replace Jime. He was such a hard worker. Right now my main concern is Dorothy. It's been hours since we learned of the tragedy, and she has not shed a tear. Instead she has had a private conversation with each person in the family. She expressed how grateful she was that the sunrise was so stunning this morning and what a gift Jime received on his last day on earth. Although she appeared to be calm and collected at this grievous time, I could see her not quite so hidden sorrow. It was written in her face, the lines tight with restrained emotion. I noticed her hands were clenched, opening only as others reached out and touched her. When I held her tightly I could feel her pain in my own heart.

All of the other members in the alliance were showing their grief. We all gathered around each other and cried without abandon. I was impressed by Jeremy's lack of hesitation to put a sign up on the door saying we were closed for the day. For hours,

The Belmont was silent. The eerie stillness resonated through all of us. We were consumed by our grief. Ryan was the first to talk about what an outstanding man Jime was. Dorothy acted almost as if nothing happened, and demanded to start cooking before we all starved. J.J. refused to let her, and Marjorie quickly prepared food for us all. I am perplexed. I know she is a strong woman, but holding that pain inside cannot be healthy. I would offer her some time off, but I don't think she would accept.

I wonder in our moments of silence—was everyone thinking the same as me? We had already lost two members. Which egg will be next to fall to the earth, smashed and broken upon the ground? Will any of us soar to the heights of our dreams?

February 1900

February 1, 1900   **2:40 p.m.**

Both good and bad news seems to travel fast in this frozen
tent city. As soon as Jime's Inuit friend, Kuduk, heard about the
fatal accident, he actively sought out J.J. At brunch this morning,
J.J. told everyone Kuduk had offered to take over Jime's chores.
Kuduk confessed to knowing much about this alliance because
Jime was always talking about us when they went hunting and
fishing. J.J. said he wanted everyone's opinion. Was it too early
to think about replacing Jime? Could we all work extra hours to
help Dorothy with the heavy labor? With everyone feeling they
were carrying as much weight as they could, it was unanimous
to hire Kuduk starting today. J.J. relayed that Kuduk was pleased
we decided so quickly and took it as a sign he was welcome. He
stated, "I will work for you as long as I have time to hunt and fish
for my family." He left J.J. with our first Inuit word, "quiana,"
which means thank you.

February 2, 1900   10:15 a.m.

Last night I was awakened by two crying voices. One sounded like Ria and the other like Jime. When I got up from my bed my feet touched a small puddle of water in the middle of my rug. If I leave a container of water by my bed at night it is frozen when I wake because the fire has burned down. So how can I wake up to a liquid on my floor when it should be a solid? How did it get there? There wasn't water any place else. This time I never felt any warm sensations although I kept expecting them.

I wondered if I was losing my wits, but my mind works just fine in every other area. I'm beginning to think maybe, just maybe, it was Ria and Jime visiting me. I can never tell another soul what I think. They might lock me up like they did Lizzy.

Having another experience with what must be Ria's soul made me think about the first time Ria came to me and wanted me to hold her when we were still on the ship. That was the first time I had really felt like a mother, as if these women were my own children and I had to love and defend them. I thank Ria for the many bonding experiences she allowed me. Perhaps I should consider these visits to be bonding experiences of another sort. I feel like there must be some reason for them.

February 4, 1900   3:30 a.m.

Yesterday was Jeremy James' birthday. Although we are all still very sorrowful, Dorothy insisted we go on about our routine. She said, "Jime would have wanted us to go on living." Once we got past that awkward stage, J.J. consumed more pancakes than three of the ladies combined. He took his time eating and commented that watching all of us grow hungry was the best part. When we made our barge orders, I should have been thinking ahead and ordered a birthday present for J.J. Next year I'll know better. Lucky for me, I ran into Rawslin yesterday and asked if I could borrow one of his Mark Twain books to lend to J.J. He thought it was an excellent idea and went right away to get the book for me. J.J. liked the idea as well. In return he gave me a great big hug, picked me off the ground and said, "I love you,

Mandy." I was overjoyed to hear those words from him.

After everyone left the brunch tent J.J. took me aside in a secretive way and said, "Mandy, I need to talk to you." I had never heard him use that tone of voice, so right away my curiosity was aroused. As he led me into The Belmont, he said, "I want to show you where I hide some of my gold." Once we were there he removed the picture of "Custer's Last Stand," exposing a vault built into the wall.

He said, "I have been making a huge profit since we arrived and here is what I have to show for it." He then took out several bags of gold nuggets and poured their contents onto the bar. He said, "Go ahead Mandy, touch it. I think gold is good for the soul." As I played with the nuggets of various sizes and shapes, he said, "I wanted you to know about the safe in case something should ever happened to Ryan and me." He concluded by saying, "I always keep a little money behind the bar. That way if someone ever broke in and robbed us, they would think they won, but I don't ever plan on being beaten."

I believe by the time the day was over, J.J. had an excellent twenty-ninth birthday and his increased profits had a lot to do with it. Last summer, saloonkeepers could buy a barrel of beer for $30, but due to the shortage of grains, a barrel of beer now costs $60. J.J. still has a large inventory, therefore he is controlling the beer market. Beer today began selling for $1 a glass making J.J. happier with each glass sold. I can see why he wants to be involved in the booze market. It's apparent in this gold rush community that he who controls the liquor, controls the town. I'm just thankful there is still plenty of whiskey around to keep the miners sedated.

February 5, 1900   2:50 p.m.

I just returned from the mercantile where I saw a couple customers I served last night. Neither one of them acted like they even knew I was in the store. I made a point to get in their path after I saw their behavior, but they just turned around and walked the other way. I am infuriated thinking of how well they knew my body last night, yet in public they won't even make eye contact with me. Maybe they think if they don't acknowledge my presence, the savage act they performed last night will be forgotten. They're wrong. The only thing they're doing is making the situation worse. If they would just give me a simple "hello", it would be fine. I will never understand men. It aggravates me to no end that the men I entertain have a way of making me feel worthless, just as my father did.

February 7, 1900   **3:00 a.m.**

It has been a week since Jime's shocking accident and Dorothy still hasn't shown any signs of mourning for him. She has been working harder than ever and no one can persuade her to slow down. I talked to her a little bit today and asked why she hasn't cried for her husband whom she loved so deeply. Her reply was, "What good would it do? Crying won't bring him back." "But doesn't it hurt you to think about him?" I asked. She responded, "I miss his companionship, but I love having this family to keep me busy. Working shelters my mind from thoughts of him."

I hope she is okay. Although she says she is, I know she must be hurting inside but wants to stay strong. I'm glad she's such a stable person, for the sake of this alliance. We would be devastated if we lost both of them. I just hope that she doesn't bottle everything up and let it all out one day. Maybe we can all take a day off, that way she wouldn't feel like she was letting down the family by not working.

February 8, 1900   **10:40 p.m.**

I decided to give The Bantam Belmont the evening off in order to relieve Dorothy from her duties. Everyone was grateful for the break and they took the opportunity to travel around town and see all the developments that have been made lately, mostly more saloons and tents to house the new arriving miners. Alex took Margerie around to give her a tour of the town since she doesn't get out much. I'm elated Margerie has found her place within the family. We all love her sense of humor and her way of enlightening a situation. I'm really the only one she approaches to talk about her problems, though. I think that she is really a happy person, but sometimes she just needs to cry. I understand. I've always believed crying is the best way to free my emotions. I wish Dorothy felt the same way. This day was supposed to be a break for her, but all evening she changed sheets and cleaned the tents. She even baked exquisite salmon she caught ice fishing this morning, as well as several loaves of her delicious bread. While the bread was baking, I did my best to get her to sit down and relax for a moment.

She said, "I have so many memories of my mama and me making bread together. Sometimes I wish I could be a child again helping my mama. Her bread always smelled so good." She confessed she and Jime had been making merry bout between the sheets since she was fourteen years old. She continued, "He is the only man my body has ever known or will know. I wish I could have one more hug from him. Just one more last embrace that could be saved in my mind forever." What a beautiful thought! I almost asked her if Jime ever comes to visit, but either way I was too afraid of her answer.

Dorothy only sat down until the bread was ready to be taken from the oven, but it didn't take her long till she lost herself in her next chore. She went about setting the table just like usual — smiling and singing softly to herself. How can she talk about the loss of her love in one minute and in the next appear to be her joyful self? That woman amazes me. It's just not in her blood to cry. Her mother must have been a strong woman and she is living up to those standards.

February 9, 1900   **10:30 a.m.**

Last night Alex and I were talking about our childhoods. She asked me what my earliest memory was. Without hesitation I told her I remembered when I was four years old, lying outside on a blanket on a warm summer day looking at the clouds. I clearly heard a voice in my head say, "Don't be afraid to die. You will live again." I also told her that as a child I remember thinking it was a strange thought for a little girl. In a real loud and excited voice Alex said, "Oh Mandy, that explains a lot. Now I know you were

born with that inner wisdom you have about our spirits needing
nature to renew, and spirits that pass needing to communicate
in some way. Having past lives to explore and future lives to
anticipate. It is your inner beliefs that make you such a strong,
remarkable woman."

Before Alex could share any of her stories we made our own
kind of merry bout and fell asleep in each other arms for awhile.
Oh, how I wish she were free to sleep with me all night long so I
could wake up smelling like her.

February 10, 1900   **3:45 p.m.**

This town is getting more repulsive every day. If something
isn't done soon about the sanitation problem, we are going to reach
a level where nothing can be done. The alleyways between the
saloons on Front Street are filled with frozen urine and dead dogs.
The center of town is like an open sewage pit. The stench about
this place is everyone's waste decaying before our eyes and noses.

February 11, 1900   **2:45 a.m.**

This evening in The Belmont a man I had never seen before
approached me from across the room and quickly said, "I love
my wonderful piece of meat." He placed my hand on his large
manhood with a grin on his face. He tried to convince me I
couldn't pass up this impressive display of a man. Before I had
time to comment, a working girl from down the street ran naked
into The Belmont and I had to take her back to her madam. I never
got a chance to tell that man I have never met anyone so proud
of his manhood. I did notice he walked with a slight limp. Is it
because his manhood gets in the way? Maybe someday I will get
the chance to ask him.

February 12, 1900   **1:10 p.m.**

Last night I had a client who was an extremely aggressive
kisser. It wouldn't have been that bad, but he hadn't shaved in a
while and his whiskers were coarse and scratchy. I would have
told him to stop, but I could tell he wasn't going to last long, and

it would have been more of a hassle to get him to stop. I have the right to tell any man I don't want him to kiss me, but I find a lot of men come to me just for that purpose. The other ladies usually don't kiss men, unless they have the desire.

Most of the time men don't want to kiss a fallen woman and I found out why at Rosa's. She said Chinese daughters of joy used to take small amounts of poison so they would become immune to it. As they got older, they would store poison in their mouths and would transfer it into a man's mouth when they kissed, as a way to end his life. Of course the doves and I don't do that, but the myth stays in people's minds.

February 14, 1900   **10:00 a.m.**

Once again The Belmont and The Bantam Belmont were closed for business. It wasn't our choice. It was nature's. The weather warmed up enough for a few hours of heavy rains. As soon as the rain stopped, the water began to freeze. From my bed I watched my hard packed dirt floor transform from its usual solid state to a rushing stream of mud, then freeze into a sheet of ice several inches thick. There was no getting out of my bed, let lone my tent. I tried and slipped right away causing quite a bump on the back of my head. I knew everyone in this frozen community was held prisoner in their structures. You could hear lots of conversation going on as people talked through the canvas to others who were close enough to participate.

I took advantage of the time by wrapping up in my rabbit fur blanket and going back to the very beginning of my diary and reading. What an adventure we have had. If I didn't see the excitment of this entrapment, I could easily lose my mind. After all, in the big picture of this gold rush town, every soul is trapped by the ice and snow that surrounds us. If we think too much about it, we might all lose our minds. Maybe I'm thinking about it right now because the majority of people trapped on their beds, if they are lucky enough to have one, are also thinking the same way. An abundance of time without distraction allows a person time to explore their thoughts. One must learn to enjoy that experience.

For the first time since arriving I let my mind really wander into the future. I imagined what my new brothel would look like once I leave. I love to think Alex would join me. We could buy a large two-story saloon and work upstairs, knowing each night that the other one is safe. The best part would be when the day was over Alex and I could curl up next to each other and sleep in the same clean bed. We could even have a bright white bedspread. Everything around here gets dirty so very quickly. It is wonderful to think about living in a place that you might be able to keep clean. Oh, how entertaining to daydream of the future!

February 16, 1900   3:30 a.m.

What a strange land. It is as if yesterday's weather didn't even happen. We are back to treading carefully on the mushy snow now falling from the sky. I didn't think I would ever say I am happy it is snowing, but I'm quickly learning snow is better than rain any February day this far north. I don't think my sanity could endure too many weather days like yesterday. From what I gathered walking through The Belmont, everyone else feels the same way. Everyone spoke of feeling trapped by the ice that allowed no movement.

February 18, 1900   11:15 a.m.

I was overjoyed by a visit from Jafet last night. When we were alone, he revealed how much he had anticipated holding and touching me since he left last fall. Once again the intimacy between us was nothing exhilarating, but laying in his arms listening to his stories was magical. I learned Jafet came to the United States from northwest Scandinavia as a reindeer herder. In Saint Michael, the reindeer project was abandoned and he thought he'd try his luck prospecting. He met Erik and John in Council City. The three of them came to Snake River in September of 1898 and panned $50 worth of gold out of Anvil Creek their first day. After returning with more supplies, they continued panning in the deepening cold for a few days and accumulated $1,800 worth. By discovering the precious metal, they had made the necessary requirements for ownership. The three organized a mining district, then staked forty-three claims for themselves. They staked seven other claims using power of attorney for business associates. They returned to their camp in Golovin Bay for the winter, swearing to secrecy their discovery, but of course the secret got out. Jafet spent the entire evening with me, but only released one load of lust into my body. Most of our time was spent enjoying each other's company and sleeping.

February 19, 1900   3:45 a.m.

Yesterday was Ryan's birthday. He emerged a hero. Not because of the amount of griddle cakes he could eat, but because of his fortitude in bringing a new life into this world. A frail young pregnant woman and her crocked husband were in The Belmont when the woman's water broke and she started having strong contractions. Being the saloon mixologist carries with it many responsibilities. The couple instantly turned to Ryan for support and comfort. Lucky for Ryan, he had witnessed the births of his nine younger siblings. While gathering up the needed equipment, he stayed as composed as if he was mixing cocktails. He barked orders to the fidgety bystanders to arrange the tables so he would have a place to work. Soon, a healthy boy breathed his first breath in the smoky Belmont. Since the couple didn't have much money they named their first-born Ryan to show their gratitude.

February 20, 1900   1:55 a.m.

This evening I could no longer pass up the opportunity of being paid for by two men at the same time. They were young, handsome, very randy brothers. The encounter was all very confusing, too much for my senses to take in at one time. I cannot even remember many details. What I do remember is vile!

February 21, 1900   3:20 a.m.

The main topic of conversation this evening was the polar bear that tore apart several tents on the west side of town. I even heard gruesome details of how the bear had dragged a man south to

Sludge Island, leaving a trail of blood as a symbol of his strength and dominance. To take everyone's minds off the horror, I asked J.J. if Alex could dance. Several men had been encouraging me to have her dance nightly. Alex thought it was an excellent idea and wondered why we hadn't brought it up earlier. Alex made her first formal appearance this evening. In her shimmering, dark purple dress she danced more gracefully than I had ever seen her. I think she was excited about all the people watching and wanting her to perform.

I originally thought we would be losing money in the hour she danced; I had no idea what a stint she would do in arousing the customers. I noticed most men could only handle watching her for about fifteen minutes before they were ready to explode with lust. J.J. couldn't help but get just as aroused as the other males. I have never seen him look so weak as when he watched her. Alex just has that way about her. This was definitely a wise business move. Starting this week, Alex will dance for an hour twice a week. This seems to be an arrangement that makes everyone happy.

Hopefully, I will sleep a little better tonight knowing The Bantam Belmont is in the middle of town, not on the outskirts where the polar bears like to roam.

February 22, 1900   3:30 a.m.

The highlight of my evening was a merry bout with a young man who was not big, strong, or handsome. He was rather lanky and odd looking except for his perfectly shaped lips. He makes the seventh client in my career, other than Milroy, who has taken my body on a flight of pleasure. Lusty men belong in three categories. First there is the type who enjoys pounding hard and grunting loudly. The next type grinds into your body as if they are trying to see how close they can get their manhood up inside of you, the whole time moaning and groaning. The third, and my favorite, is the stud. He has a natural rhythm as he moves up and down on my body. His consistent movement and constant soft sighs of relief create a pleasure that I can't ignore. Of course, Milroy is in a category all of his own. That man has such a hold on my healthy, animal vigor.

February 23, 1900   **4:10 a.m.**

Before going to sleep I either write in my journal, read, or play with my growing gold nugget collection, unless Alex sleeps over. A gold nugget is like nothing I have ever felt before. It is heavy for its size. It feels warm as I glide my fingers across its smooth surface. I love to hold several in my hand at one time. I rearrange them to make different designs in my palm. Then I give each design its own name. For example: The Tree, Animal Fights, The Train, and The Balancing Dog. It is kind of silly. But it makes me feel happy. I really love my gold!

February 25, 1900   **10:20 p.m.**

We have had several whiteouts since January 15th. We've learned from Kuduk that it's in the cycle of the earth for this to be a harsh winter. He said last summer he had seen an abundance of owls. His elders believe it is a sign of a harsh winter and we should be prepared. We have adapted for the blizzards. We no longer risk our lives traveling to The Belmont by rope. Instead we all sleep on the floor of the saloon if it's snowing hard. We almost lost Margerie the last time we tried the transferring maneuver. She could no longer hold onto the rope and the wind literally blew her away. J.J. acted quickly and searched the circumference of that area while struggling to keep his grip on the rope. Within seconds Margerie grabbed onto his foot and J.J. pulled her into his arms. After that J.J. insisted that we never take chances with the rope again.

Since then we just enjoy each other's company in The Belmont when there is a blizzard. I know everyone sleeps much better than if we were in our ailing tents. We know we have a family and it warms our hearts and our souls. Each time we gather during a blizzard's rage, we get started on one topic that dominates the conversation throughout the night. Tonight the topic was funny things. Dorothy told us the real call of the wild in this frozen wasteland was not the sound of any animal. It is the nauseating belch of a miner with a twisted stomach. We all laughed hard when we heard this because it's so true. Most miners live on baking powder bread, beans, and fat pork. They have indigestion quite often. I'm not sure which is more disgusting: their rank farts, their bad breath, or their lack of manners.

February 27, 1900   3:15 p.m.

The storm that started two nights ago is still raging strong forty-eight hours later. During that time there have been seven adventurous souls that have wandered our way in search of liquor. We were enjoying our time together so much we were reluctant to answer the pounding on the door, but we could not turn anyone away in a blizzard like this.

We were all sitting quietly, hypnotized by the raging wind outside our walls, when Natalie jumped up screaming, "My tent, my tent! I know it got blown away, I can feel it. There goes all my stuff. I'll never see the pictures of my children again. Alex put her arms around Natalie and said, "It will be O.K., baby. We'll take care of you. When I was just starting out in this business, a fire destroyed my clothes. The sisters in my bevy took care of me and we'll do the same for you, Natalie. We will. Don't worry." I was proud of Alex for stepping right in and letting Natalie know we all cared for her.

Alex's memory gave J.J. an idea for a game. The object of the game was to identify the year an event took place. He said in order to make the game a little more challenging, he would give the person that was speaking a gold nugget if another person in the room could validate with a thumbs up signal the year the event took place. Everyone became excited and began to search their memories for dates. J.J. announced the oldest person in the room should go first with their recollections. John Hummel, the old miner who was rumored to have discovered the gold on Nome's beach, started by recalling the forty-nine gold rush and how the civil war was just beginning. He spoke of President Lincoln's third son Willie dying in 1863 and three years later the war ended. He

reminded us all in 1867 the United States purchased this great
Alaskan Territory for two cents an acre, the grand total being
$7 million. In 1869 those golden spike rails joined the east and
the west. In 1870 women in Wyoming were given the right to
vote. In 1874 there was gold discovered in the Black Hills, and
Philadelphia was blessed with its first zoo. 1876 was Custer's
Last Stand as he pointed to the great picture on our wall. John
said it saddened his heart to speak of 1877, the year Chief Joseph
surrendered, but on the bright side in 1879 Edison succeeded with
electric lights. In 1881 the honorable President Garfield was shot.

Before the old man could go on J.J. piped in with, "I know
what happened in 1881. The Grand Canyon was surveyed.
Ever since I heard of that river, I have imagined riding down
it in a homemade craft. That's one thing I really want to do in
my lifetime." It was unnecessary for anyone to validate John
Hummel's historical recollection. It was obvious he knew it
well. The whole room benefited from his years of experience.
J.J. walked over with a handful of nuggets, not even bothering to
count, and put them in John's hand. He said, "Impressive, thanks."

John had done such an outstanding job of presenting his
memories, it started the game off in a real heightened manner.
Everybody wanted to do their best and get some gold nuggets for
themselves. I started the next go around sharing that in 1882 Billie
the Kid was shot. Alex chimed in that the first electric company
was started in New York that year. Margerie added that in 1882 her
favorite poet, Ralph Waldo Emerson, had passed away. Ryan said,
"Don't ask me how I know, but I remember hearing that in 1884 a
man invented a container with ink so you could have your own pen
with you at all times." Natalie added that in 1884 Edison patented
a phonograph. Margerie said she was in New York in 1886 when
the Statue of Liberty arrived from France. Dorothy stated in 1886
she remembered sharing one of the first bottles of Coca-Cola with
her family, and in 1887 she got to see Annie Oakley's Wild West
Show. Ryan chuckled and said in 1889 the coin-operated telephone
was invented, and then laughing even louder he said in 1891 was
the invention of the zipper. They had hoped it would replace those

time consuming buttons. Alex said in 1892 Ellis Island opened and was predicted to have a profound impact on America.

Dorothy commented, "I remember in 1892 Coca-Cola had to admit their product had cocaine in it and it was causing addictions. I know because my mother became addicted to the intellectual beverage, or temperance drink, as it was being called." From the back of the room, one of the seven men that had joined us added that in 1892 the Sierra Club was organized to prevent the total annihilation of the wilderness. Dorothy joined in again by saying in 1894 Isabel Beecher Hooker, Elizabeth Katy Stand, and Susan B. Anthony argued before a Senate committee on behalf of women's suffrage.

Another man from the back of the saloon spoke about the devastating effects of the 1894 railroad strike in Chicago. He said it had such an effect on America that President Cleveland created the first Labor Day holiday to help the morale of the nation. Alex continued the game by saying in 1895 there were reports of over 300 motorcars on the road in the United States and she had gotten to ride in one of the first. J.J. made a comment about McKinley defeating Bryan in 1896 and how in those four years of office he hadn't done much for the country. Natalie knew in 1898 the war ship *Marina* blew up in Havana, and the U.S. began war with Spain. Dorothy added in the same year the reluctant Hawaiian Islands became a territory of the United States.

Using his famous loud voice, J.J. offered three nuggets for the last question. "How many of you guys know what year Nome got its name?" Everyone's face revealed they didn't have the answer, so he continued, "It was just last year, 1899. Nome was named a thousand miles from here when a British cartographer heard there was a strike where Anvil was located. He didn't know the name of the city so he wrote 'Name' with a question mark as a reminder to find out the name of the new frontier. He sent the map off to be printed but forgot to find the answer. The printer mistook 'Name' for 'Nome' and the question mark as a 'C'. When he put them together, he came up with 'C Nome', or 'Cape Nome'."

Several of us tried to pick an event that had happened this year that someone else could validate, but we are so far away from any other civilization we don't know what is happening outside of this frozen world. We have no news to share except what's happening in Nome. Before the game ended I tried to bluff everyone into thinking I knew what year Samuel Clemens began using his pen name Mark Twain. I was just sure someone would pipe up with the answer, with lots of excitement in their voice, and I would just agree. Well, it didn't turn out that way and everyone knew that I didn't know the correct answer. It was a little embarrassing. I guess I should have Alex teach me the art of bluffing when playing a game that involves a profit.

Throughout the game, I wished Kuduk could have joined us, but the game we played was about our history, not his.

Tonight was the most stimulating night I have had in Nome. Thanks to my mother's passion for history, I knew of several events named this evening. I wish every night could be as intellectually challenging. It was like we had traveled back through time. Thanks to my journal writing, I have endured the longest storm of the year with my sanity still intact. I've had a wonderful opportunity to record the happenings of our history game. I hope I remembered everything correctly.

March 1900

March 1, 1900   **2:10 p.m.**

It turns out Natalie was correct in her premonition. Her tent was indeed destroyed by the fierce winds. For whatever reason, all the other tents remained unmarred. Now Natalie and Margerie have to share a tent until we get our own cribs. It comes from being the "bottom bitch." It's the code of the doves for the last one hired to always take up the slack.

Everyone joined in a search to find Natalie's possessions, but without any luck. I can already see I will have to lend Natalie money to replace her wardrobe. Natalie is so large, there's no way she can borrow dresses. I'm not sure whether I should lend her money, or restore her wardrobe, since it really wasn't her fault the wind took her items. I'll wait and see how she approaches the situation.

March 2, 1900   **3:20 a.m.**

Perhaps Natalie was frustrated her possessions were stolen by the blizzard, or maybe she's recovered enough from the damage

Wyatt did to her, but she was ready to begin her monthly beatings again. Near the end of the evening, a hysterical Margerie came running into The Belmont to inform me Natalie was beating up one of her clients. I rushed over to the tent they're sharing only to find Natalie sitting on her bed. The man must have had enough strength to walk out before I got there. Natalie seemed pleased to see me but was confused to find Margerie standing nervously in the corner. She asked her what was wrong and Margerie replied, "That scared me. What just happened?" "Oh, Margie," Natalie responded, "I'd never hurt you. I'm so sorry I scared you." Natalie informed me that she would like to take a short break before returning to work. I told her of course and she grabbed her coat—one of the few possessions she had left—and headed outside.

Margerie slowly moved from the corner to her bed and sat down. I sat next to her and tried to explain that before Wyatt beat her, Natalie would choose a man once a month to release her anger. I reported she has been doing this ever since I met her at Rosa's and in the entire time I've known her, she has never once laid a hurtful hand on another lady. That seemed to calm Margerie down a little and I left her with a hug. I bet that must have been terrifying to see Natalie attack that man. I always seem to get to the tent after the action has already happened. I'm sorry Margerie had to witness that.

I must admit to myself I'm starting to enjoy that Margerie comes to me when she is in need of comfort. I love listening to her talk about her life. I'm a good listener. I know if there is anyway I can help her, I will. I love it that she needs me. I want to be there for her.

March 3, 1900   3:35 p.m.

Two days ago the town government declared it has run out of money. They have no way to deal with the present sanitation problems or the expected sanitation crisis that is sure to happen once the summer visitors start arriving. Today a total of 884 people signed a petition to Lieutenant Craig asking him to declare marshal law and take over the city. I'm glad it has finally come to this. Something needs to be done before we all die in our own filth.

March 4, 1900   2:40 p.m.

As sad as I am for the loss of Jime, I have to admit the situation with Kuduk is working splendidly. Being about ten years younger, he is able to accomplish more in a shorter time. I think all would agree he has added to our alliance and not subtracted one bit. Lately Dorothy even stops what she is doing as Kuduk captivates us with fascinating tales of Alaska during brunch. We are learning so much from him about this land, his family, and the ways of the native people.

Since before their written language, the Inuit, which means "people," have used the mouth of the Snake River for a fishing camp. The closest settlement was directly on top of the Cape of Nome. Before listening to Kuduk, I believed the first exposure to white people the Inuit had was with the present day miners. Now I know their first contact with Europeans was about 250 years earlier. That explains their obvious addiction to tobacco. Every male Inuit I've seen has been smoking. Kuduk explained the use of tobacco among his people demonstrates a high status. The elders figure if a man can enjoy the luxury of smoking instead of spending every waking moment subsisting, he must hold wealth to afford the time and deserves a little respect.

I am fascinated most by the simple tools the Inuit have created to help them survive this harsh land. Their fishing nets are made from seal skin strips tied together. Three dangling ropes with a bone tied at the end of each are used as a bird catcher. A carved wooden instrument is used to attract seals by tapping it on the ice, raising their curiosity and allowing the hunter an even battleground.

As much as I love Kuduk's stories, I love the dried salmon he brings daily even more. I hope he enjoys being in our company as much as we do his. It's hard to tell because so far all he's talked about is what he knows and not what he feels.

March 5, 1900   **11:30 a.m.**

The lucky streak continues for the alliance and last night's poker game was proof. Having both Margerie and Natalie working and living out of one small tent wasn't working for the gentlemen or the ladies. We were in real need of a new tent. A young man who had just lost everything he had at the table believed the hand he was holding could change it all. He bet his large canvas tent and J.J. was more than happy to accommodate him. Lucky for us, he lost and we won. I say we because when Natalie is cheerful, everyone around her feels the same.

March 6, 1900   **10:30 a.m.**

Now I'm sure that I'm losing my mind. Last night, I was awakened again by soft crying; this time I only heard Ria's faint voice. I sat up in bed and saw her dripping wet body standing on my rug. My first instinct was to shoot an intruder, but it is impossible to shoot someone who is already dead. She stood for what seemed several minutes looking at me and crying. When I went to get out of my bed to offer comfort, she disappeared, leaving behind another puddle of water.

Why does she keep visiting me? Next time I will get up the courage to ask her what she wants. Does she visit anyone else? I'm so afraid that if I do say something about my encounters and no one knows what I'm talking about, my family will think that I'm incompetent.

March 8, 1900   **3:50 a.m.**

As a result of the petition, a series of meetings are being held in town to determine what should be done about the city government. I asked J.J. what he thought about me attending some of the meetings. He said he thought it was a good idea because they needed insight from a woman's perspective. That's all I needed to encourage me to attend with confidence. I went to three different meetings today and learned the men are only concerned about their personal gain in solving the problem. Nobody seemed to consider the health of the general population. At the first and second meetings, I didn't speak up, but at the third one I couldn't hold my opinion back any longer. I stood up and spoke in a loud enough voice to be heard by all. "Gentlemen, we need to start looking into the future. The decisions we make today are going to affect us tomorrow. We need to stop thinking about what is in it for us. We need to think about the physical health of everyone, not the health and wealth of our pocket book. If we all had to pay a tax, just like the madams have to pay a tax, we could come up with money to dig ditches so this sewage could drain from the places we live and work." No one seemed real impressed by my words. As I somberly departed, Key Pittman, the city attorney, asked if he could buy me a drink. He was impressed a woman could see the solution so simply, when all the greedy men he talked to made it more complex than it need be. At least one person appreciated my opinion.

March 9, 1900   11:15 a.m.

Milroy paid for another overnight. As soon as he walked out of my tent my body longed for his return. I wanted his body on mine. I wanted to smell his skin again. I wanted to hear his voice more. I didn't know it was possible to be filled with so many emotions during the exchange of bodies. I have never had feelings for a man like this before. Why do I find myself attracted to him? Then I had to ask myself, "What am I doing thinking about that man?" In the last week he has stayed over all but one night. Each night after our merry bout Milroy shares with me more stories of peril. With each story he reveals how treacherous he really is. I get the feeling that not only could he be dangerous to me, but to everyone he is around. Maybe I am attracted to him because I am wicked just like him.

March 10, 1900   3:25 a.m.

We were honored with more than eleven hours of uninterrupted sunshine. I skipped brunch and packed some food so I wouldn't miss a minute of the hint of warmth. The dormant wind allowed me to choose which direction I wanted to journey. I usually try to walk into the wind so the return trip is easier. I headed north because I was drawn to the snow-covered peaks. They were captivating as they glistened beneath the brazen sun. Sauntering on the tundra was easy because of the hard packed snow. I ate leisurely and I enjoyed the breathtaking view. The sun reflecting off the endless snow was so bright I felt a headache coming on. My mind insisted I seek shelter from the immense brightness, but my rejuvenating spirit didn't want to leave. The walk home was a continuing dispute between the two.

I returned to my tent for a short nap. When I awoke my eyes were still burning. They hadn't adjusted to the dim light of the tent. I began to worry and went to find J.J. Right away he knew I was snow blind, something he had learned from Kuduk. He said the best thing I could do was rest and not strain my eyes. He insisted I take the night off to help them recover. I crave the sun so much; I never believed it could be harmful.

March 12, 1900   **4:05 a.m.**

Every night while weighing out the profits, I think how this gold is the key to my prosperous future. I have so many plans for a truly high-class brothel. I figure I will leave Nome in maybe five years. I came this far; I might as well stay where money is to be made. I think I would like to move to California. I heard it is warm there most of the time.

My first priority will be to have good ventilation, unlike most other brothels I've heard about. I wish my house to be lavished with decor that surpasses other homes in the neighborhood. I hope to have servants, a bouncer, and a piano player known as a "professor." I will hire a different one each week to play music for the ladies and guests to enjoy. Of course like all notorious madams, I will have a soft, cuddly poodle. I don't really care for that type of dog, but by then I will have an image to uphold.

I think of the future frequently, especially when dealing with clients who have "different" requests. Tonight I had a man who wanted me to pour hot wax on his chest as I rode up and down on his manhood. The pain he endured seemed to give

him much pleasure. It was rather fascinating to watch. He kept
getting real excited but right before I thought he would explode,
he would request a fresh dripping that would take his mind from
the pleasure. This client stayed like a horn for the whole hour.
I have never seen anything like it. His ejaculation was a first
time experience as well. It lasted for what seemed like several
minutes—fluids pumping from his body, leaving his seed to die in
me.

March 13, 1900   5:30 a.m.

Alex won a great deal of money today playing poker in The
Belmont. The heavyset miner who lost wasn't pleased. He kicked
the chair Alex was sitting in and knocked her to the floor before
J.J. was aware of the situation. Ryan and J.J. arrived seconds later,
tossing the patron through the closest window. Large and small
pieces of glass were scattered both inside and out. Jeremy James
remarked, "That just cost me a pretty penny, but it was worth it.
No man is going to harm my ladies and feel welcome within these
walls." He personally took care of Alex. They went into her tent
and didn't reappear for hours. We all thought that was the end of
the situation, but no such luck.

I just returned from helping Alex clean up the blood that froze
and dried upon her lovely skin. The man who lost his money
earlier came back late this evening for revenge. When Alex
was walking from her tent toward The Belmont for our evening
nightcap, the man and several of his friends knocked her out by
breaking a whiskey bottle over her head, and then they carried
her away. They ripped every inch of clothes from her body and
repeatedly raped her. With their resources depleted and the chill
setting in, they left her to die.

When Alex didn't show up in The Belmont after about a half
hour, the alliance knew we had a problem. The bit of luck we did
possess tonight was Natalie telling us she felt Alex wasn't far from
us. With that in mind, we all set out on separate paths surrounding
The Belmont. Ryan found her naked, freezing body several steps
east of her tent. I guess the savage creatures who did this to Alex

were so excited by the power of their wicked plot, they couldn't wait long for their so-called just rewards and they didn't take her very far. A few more minutes of freezing temperature against her naked, helpless body would have surely killed her.

Once Ryan found her, he started yelling and we all headed back to The Belmont. As soon as J.J. saw her in Ryan's arms, he ran toward them and gently took Alex. Instead of shouting orders for blankets and a doctor to be summoned, he used a soothing voice of request that comforted all. He quickly stripped off his clothes and held Alex's naked body next to his in the barber chair until the doctor arrived. It was apparent how deep J.J.'s love for Alex is. He was just as concerned for her life as I was. How can I be jealous?

March 14, 1900   3:10 p.m.

Alex awoke this morning as if nothing life threatening had occurred. Perhaps she just doesn't remember. When I did try to explain what we thought had happened to her, she joked about it saying, "Well too bad I wasn't awake to enjoy it." I can't believe the way she reacts by laughing instead of crying. She wears an armored suit that no pain can penetrate.

J.J. was ready for justice. First thing in the morning, he went to The Northern to see Tex Rickard. Together they talked to every saloonkeeper in Nome telling them of the harm that came to Alex. They were able to convince each saloon owner to ban the rapist from their property. That way if there are no watering holes for the man, he will be forced to leave our community. What an excellent idea! I love the way J.J. gets even without physically harming a soul.

J.J. also proclaimed, "From now on, Alex will not be available for over nights." He went on for a while talking about how he needs to spend more time with her to ensure her safety. I think he is not only looking out for Alex's well being, but his as well. Each day he is falling more in love with her.

March 15, 1900   3:25 p.m.

I was overjoyed when Kuduk stopped by my tent just a little while ago. He began telling me that I need to take care of my eyes and when I go walking in the snow, I need to wear protection over them. Then he handed me a pair of carved wooden glasses and told me to wear them whenever I walk on sunny winter days. I thanked him greatly and gave him a kiss on the cheek. It was so thoughtful of him to make me a pair of glasses. Kuduk is a unique man and a pleasure to be around. I'm proud he's a part of this alliance.

March 16, 1900   2:30 p.m.

The ladies and I just finished bathing and more than anything I want to go outside for an escape into nature, but she will not let me. Her below-freezing temperatures and her howling winds force everyone to stay indoors. I'm learning when the sun does peek out from behind the prevailing clouds, a sound person drops whatever they are doing in their shelter and steps out to bask in the sun. On the frozen Bering Sea coast, the sun may just stay for a few minutes at a time, and to our disappointment appearing only shortly again in a couple weeks. At times like this, the sun seems to be the most precious commodity.

March 17, 1900   3:45 a.m.

It really grows old having to deal constantly with bad-mouthing, foul-smelling men. The majority have a mean disposition and are rude. I wonder if that has anything to do with the fact they spending more money on booze than food. I think the lack of nourishment affects their overall attitude. Maybe if we fed the men something as they gathered in The Belmont, I could tolerate them better. I would almost be willing to pay for it myself just to keep the atmosphere more pleasant.

March 20, 1900   3:10 p.m.

The highlight of this week was the first school in Nome opened for twenty children. Just as the children were walking to school, the sun was coming up and several people, including the ladies and me went into the streets to wish the children a good first day. Seeing the children walk off to school reminded me of the days J.J., Lizzy, and I walked to school. It seemed on some days I learned more from J.J. than I learned in the classroom. He was always sharing his knowledge about the earth. I discovered first hand the cycle of butterflies and how water always takes the path of least resistance.

March 22, 1900   2:50 p.m.

To enhance our pleasure last night after work, Alex and I indulged in a large dose of laudanum. As much as I wanted to step outside to enjoy the Northern Lights, I was forced by the extreme cold to stay inside. It was not a hardship because I had Alex by my side all night. We pleased each other several times. Instead of falling asleep right away, we stayed awake talking. I was hoping she would bring up the subject of J.J., but she never did. I'm so curious, but I have enough respect not to meddle in her business. When she feels comfortable enough to tell me about their relationship, I'm sure she will.

March 23, 1900   2:35 p.m.

Last night before the end of the shift, Milroy showed up unexpectedly. He requested my company for the evening. Part of me wanted to refuse, but part of me missed having my body entangled with his and engulfed in his scent. I couldn't stop myself from asking where he had been lately. He said, "Honey, I was just checking out the other madams' equipment in this town. I have concluded there is none as fine as yours and I am back for good."

Our merry bout was entirely different than the other times. On this particular visit he never penetrated me, instead he touched himself until he exploded on my bosoms. As he rubbed his hot liquid on me he kept saying, "You are mine, Mandy, you are mine." I was thrilled, but I was afraid to speak—afraid of losing what control I had over my body. When he left me this morning, I was sad to see him go. I was already craving his lips upon my body.

March 24, 1900   3:10 p.m.

This afternoon I'm being entertained by something I wasn't
even aware of before coming to Alaska Territory. There's a strong
wind from the north, which allows me to sit next to my open flap
and watch the snow racing south. I thought it would be easy to
sit here and write about the beauty, but it isn't. I can't keep from
watching the quickly passing view. There is something about the
hard snow blowing a few inches from the ground that makes it
easy to see there isn't any moisture in the air. It is clear to me this
is indeed an Arctic desert.

In Colorado, I was used to big, fluffy snowflakes falling
straight from the sky. They were so moist they began to melt as
soon as they landed on your tongue. In this freezing climate it
is best to keep one's tongue inside where it belongs. Exposing it
could result in serious injury and is not a pleasant thought.

March 26, 1900   2:45 a m.

Today one of my customers, the proud owner of a mercantile
in town, was commenting on how he can tell so much about his
customers by the supplies they buy. The story that intrigued me
the most was about a man that came in with two of his partners
wanting to buy some gun powder. He said the three of them were
starting a new mining company and would need lots of explosives.
The storekeeper, Steve, said one of the men really stood out in his
mind because he knew so much about explosives. Steve said he
could tell by the look in his eyes he was evil and meant to initiate
havoc with the gun powder. Steve said he didn't want to sell the
gunpowder to the man, but he felt his life would be in danger if
he refused. I was starting to lose interest in the storekeeper's story
when he mentioned the man buying the powder was named Milroy.
I repeated, "Milroy?" He replies, "Yeah, I won't forget that name
or that man's face. No town is safe with a man like that in it." He
must be talking about the same man with whom I am becoming
more and more obsessed. I should take this as a warning. If it's
obvious to other people how evil Milroy is, I should stay away
from him.

March 28, 1900   **4:20 a.m.**

I saw Clark today in The Belmont and I asked him why he
hasn't come to see me lately. Secretly, I've been longing to explore
the loving sensations of the mother/son vision. Clark told me
Milroy has now made it clear to everyone that I am his woman
and he doesn't want any of his partners touching me. Clark said,
"No offense. I like excitement as much as the next man, but there
are plenty of other turned out women in this town. I don't have
to get in a fight with Milroy, a fight I know I would lose, just to
have intercourse. If you don't mind, I'd like to just stay friends
and enjoy each others company from time to time." I reassured
him I would enjoy that as much as he would, but in my heart I was
disappointed.

March 29, 1900   **3:20 p.m.**

Today a man named Ed Jenson arrived in Nome after riding
his bicycle more than a thousand miles across the frozen Alaskan
Territory. He said after being on the trail for five weeks, his
"wheel" is in better shape than he is. Ed was so snow blinded
when he reached Nome he did not recognize his old friend, J.J
who greeted him on the street. Jeremy was extremely proud of his
old buddy and his two-wheeled journey that he offered him any
of the ladies for the evening. Ed said, "I hate to turn down such
an offer, but for tonight all I need is sleep." Then J.J. offered him
his own bed and boasted he has other beds he can occupy for the
evening. Ed graciously accepted and within minutes was nowhere
to be seen. I knew J.J. was referring to sleeping in Alex's bed and
a part of me burned with jealousy that I couldn't make the same
announcement.

March 31, 1900   **3:35 a.m.**

Everyone in Nome was in high spirits, anticipating the
disclosure of Ed's adventurous journey. Once Ed was rested, and
had taken J.J. up on his offer, he revealed he was a miner by trade
and the only way he could think to get to Nome was to ride his
$150 wheels across the ice and snow. He said he spent eight days

157

practicing to keep the tires in sled tracks. It took him five weeks to go 1,000 miles, which was far better timing than others who attempted this journey with dog sleds. The only real problem Ed encountered was when he broke his handlebars and they had to be replaced by a spruce bough. He then reminded every listener the mushers, on the other hand, had to constantly deal with meals and bleeding dog paws, which left a bloody trail.

People were thrilled the most by what Ed used to keep warm on his long journey—newspaper. They are a significant commodity this time of year. The people here have not seen a newspaper since October ninth, 1899, except for the Nome newspaper. Even though the newspapers Ed wore were outdated, it gave our isolated community a reason to celebrate. All night long volunteers have been standing up in The Belmont and every other saloon in Nome and taking turns reading aloud from the *Seattle Post-Intelligencer, the Examiner,* and the *Oregon.* People seemed to be most excited that McKinley had been nominated by the Republicans for reelection and thousands of people were gathering in Seattle, preparing to come to Nome as soon as the ice was gone from the Bering Sea. In all my life, I never thought I would see adults so excited over newspapers. I guess you just can't tell what a day in the frozen Arctic will bring.

While the people were inside being enticed with all the news of the past winter, the northern lights were dancing in the clear starry sky. I stepped out to watch their show and wished I had a copy of their music so I could follow with the symphony they were creating. In front of me were amethyst lights. To the left the lights were gold, and to the right the lights were rose. Kuduk says the northern lights have been seen often this winter thanks to the many cold evenings where temperatures reach way below freezing. Even though the northern lights have become a common sight, their spellbinding beauty was different tonight. It was as if they, too, were celebrating the arrival of the newcomer.

Natalie tried to explain to me about the Northern Lights and how the exact same color of light is being displayed at the exact time in the southern part of the world called Antarctica. I told her

I understood, but truthfully I don't. My mind must be too simple. I can't comprehend what the other side of the world looks like.

I can tell Natalie is more than pleased with the new library. She reads more than she knits lately. I admire her love of literature. I wish I had more time for reading.

April 1900

April 4, 1900   3:05 p.m.

I love the way Alex is always thinking ahead. Because we are so close to each other, there is never a fear of criticism, which allows us to totally express ourselves at any time. Today Alex asked me, "When are we going to start the exercise classes?" I looked at Alex in shock. I couldn't believe I had forgotten. Keeping the ladies' equipment fine-tuned and tight is a very important aspect of running a first class sporting house. I can't believe I've neglected such a needed requirement for the profession. Thank goodness Alex brought it up. Beginning tomorrow, we will start squatting together after bathing and seeing how long we can keep objects up inside of us. I must collect things today we can practice with. I'm so grateful I have Alex with me. What would I do without her? She said she knew I would think of it sooner or later, but I'm not so sure.

April 5, 1900   **2:35 p.m.**

Once again tension is growing in this frozen community. This time it's not from the mining company holding land the miners want; it's from saloonkeepers raising prices of the precious alcohol they still possess. This has created a booze famine and it is threatening Nome. A long thirsty winter has nearly dried up the reserves of rye and bourbon in the twenty saloons, including The Belmont. Instead of rationing or stretching the goods with a water, Tabasco, and molasses mixture, the bartenders have voted to raise the prices to four bits a shot. Needless to say, this has created quite an upheaval among the poor thirsty patrons. Ryan is not happy with this predicament because he is the one that has to deal with the unhappy customers. Yesterday at brunch when he approached J.J. with this growing problem, J.J. replied, "The Belmont could not exist without you. Whatever it is you need let me know. How about half of the profits during this famine?" Ryan blushed at his embarrassment. I don't think he expected J.J. to be so cordial. He was ready to defend himself, but there was no need. It makes me feel good to see how J.J. and Ryan dealt with their conflict. Anyone can clearly see those two have a mutual respect for each other, and therefore a very tight bond.

April 7, 1900   **3:45 a.m.**

Milroy is fully aware of the lustful power he possesses over my body. Today while servicing his desires, it seemed he was playing a game with me to ultimately demonstrate who was in control. Instead of him being the one telling me what to do, he switched the roles and he demanded I beg him to mount me. If I hesitated or ran out of words to say, he slowly talked to me and told me things like, "Mandy, just keep talking to me. It's alright, you know what you want. Tell me how you like it. Tell me all the things you want me to do to your body. Tell me how bad you want me. I love to hear you talk to me. You can tell me anything. I won't judge you."

As usual, Milroy took me to depths of wanton stirring I had never imagined. I felt like a snake shedding her skin, and with each shedding, a new person with new desires replacing the old. While I asked him to stay perfectly still as I moved up and down, I felt free of any guilt and more alive than my body has ever known. I don't think I have ever been so obsessed with anything before. I have given up self-control when I'm around Milroy. I can't get enough of him.

April 9, 1900   4:00 a.m.

Natalie came into my tent before work began this afternoon and said she desperately needed to talk to me. "I can't believe I've kept this in so long and I really need to tell someone." As Natalie crossed the room to sit beside me on the bed, she began to cry. I had never seen Natalie cry in the three years I've known her. "I didn't start the fight with Wyatt. I swear to you I did not do anything to provoke him. I was just doing my job when he started hitting me. By the first two punches, he had taken so much life out of me I couldn't speak to tell the truth. I feel so terrible. Everyone believed that I started it because I beat up guys all the time. But I would never hurt guys the way Wyatt hurt me. You believe me, right? Please say you believe me, Mandy."

I didn't know what to do. I want to believe her, but I don't think anyone else will. Besides, what good will it do to tell J.J.? He's developed quite a bond with Wyatt despite the injuries he caused Natalie. Jeremy admires Tex Rickard so much and he figures if Tex can trust Wyatt, then he can as well. Tex and Wyatt met each other in Dawson and he was the one who invited Wyatt up here from St. Michaels. I just don't know how he'd react to the news. I'm confused where my loyalties should lie.

Natalie went on to say that she won't be beating up men anymore. She saw what a beating does to someone's spirit. After her last one in March, she saw how much she scared Margerie. She doesn't want to hurt anyone. "I didn't even feel better after I walloped that last man. I just don't feel like it anymore." I told her how proud of her I am and how much I appreciate her coming to talk to me.

Natalie has healed quickly. The scars on her face are barely noticeable and her bruises are beginning to look like healthy flesh.

She brags to everyone it is her vigorous Italian blood that has helped her to mend so fast.

From this whole situation, I have gained a lot of confidence when it comes to carrying my weapon. I know at anytime if someone harms one of my ladies, I could shoot them without hesitation. I know I could take care of most situations.

April 13, 1900   9:40 p.m.

Although it's April, there are no signs of spring. For the past three days, we have endured the worst blizzard I have ever seen and as we go into the third evening spending the night on the floor of The Belmont, everyone is rather quiet. I think everyone is anticipating summer and all the sunshine we will be receiving. The howling wind reminded me of what Colorado looked like this time of year. Some years we would have ten feet of snow and could not even get around. Other years all the snow would be gone and we would already have flowers. That's one thing I miss about Colorado—the unpredictable weather patterns. In Seattle the weather was always predictable—rain. Of course, with the rain came the flowers and that was nice, but I grew tired of the dismal environment quickly. The weather in Alaska Territory is also predictable. One can assume it's going to be cold, it's going to storm, and the wind is going to blow. I'm ready for winter to be over. One thing I will miss about the winter is these storms that terminate our work, and allow the entire alliance a chance to relax and become closer. I will never forget the night we played the history game. I think of it often.

The main talk in The Belmont tonight is a military post named Fort Davis that has been established on the coast a little more than three miles east of town. It was named after Jefferson C. Davis, a general of the union troops stationed in Alaska Territory when it was transferred from Russia to the United States in 1867. The populace is euphoric knowing there will be an army in Nome this summer to help with the predicted chaos. Many of the old Klondike miners say there has never before in mining history been an "Eldorado" so easy to reach as Nome. The miners attest they and the forty-niners in California had to face great obstacles before arriving in their promised land. This results in the weaker souls dropping out, and only the strongest surviving. For people heading north, the only two hardships they will face is sea sickness and the danger of getting to shore once they are a mile from it. The miners say this lack of challenge will lead to hoards of people arriving who have no bond with each other, their only common motive being greed. This will only lead to trouble. One can merely imagine what the summer will bring.

I have already seen many changes in this community. From a warm sandy beach with a few hundred tents to a first class town with thousands of structures, be it made from driftwood and pieces of frozen tundra or lumber and premade fronts. I have also heard many names for this area: Cape Nome, Anvil City, and Nome. Today as I look around everything within my sight is covered with snow, waiting patiently for the thaw. I wonder what is ahead for this gold rush. I'm eager for summer and all the potential fortunes to be made, but I am also weary of the masses that will descend upon us. I think it would be wise for each of the ladies to learn to use a gun and to carry one with them at all times. Starting tomorrow, the ladies and I will alternate days of doing exercises and learning to shoot. We will walk down to the river and practice shooting into wooden crates we place in the sand.

My emotions are split this evening. In all the horrible education I received from my father, I have to admit his teaching me to shoot was a valuable lesson. How could my father be so concerned about teaching me to protect my life when he was the one who was slowly destroying it?

April 15, 1900   10:30 a.m.

I dreamed last night about my father, but it wasn't the same terrifying dream as the others. In fact, it was just the opposite. The dream covered a three-day period. In that time my sister and I spent one night camping in the lush, green forest. The second night was spent next to the ruins above Mancos, Colorado, in the dry air. The third night we slept in an open, grassy meadow as we journeyed back to Durango. One of my dad's brothers was with us, but not my mother. I was scared thinking about what the nights would bring since the four of us were sharing a tent. My fears were alleviated as the two men drank themselves into oblivion and passed out each night.

The day we spent exploring the Indian ruins and picking up relics was splendid because my father treated both my sister and me like humans. The whole trip was exciting with varied and beautiful scenery. Was this a dream or did it really happen? I seem to remember my mother and her good friend Carolyn, the editor of the town newspaper, were really against people helping themselves to the past. Maybe that's why she didn't go on that trip with us.

Now that I think more, I believe the trip really did happen. That's one of the last things I remember doing with my father before he disappeared. Thinking about the shooting lessons the other day ignited the idea that perhaps I did gain some strengths from my father. I understand now that my love of nature came from him as well as Jeremy. If I'm truthful to myself, I would have to admit a lot of my strengths came from my father. He was not all bad, but I can't forgive him for what he did to my body and soul. I will carry hate for him in my heart until I die.

April 16, 1900   **9:45 a.m.**

I had the same dream last night as I did the night before, except the ending was different. We return home and I am putting the horses away. My father comes into the barn and rapes me. His ramble this time consists of, "I've wanted your body so bad for the last three days, but there's no way I was going to share you with anyone. You're mine, Mandy, and I can never let you marry. It would drive me crazy thinking of a husband having his way with your body the way I do." By the time his words are depleted, so is his body. He gets up and leaves me laying in the straw without ever looking back.

As I lay there with straw scattered in my hair and clothes, and his sperm dripping from my body, I become so infuriated I shake uncontrollably. I hold onto the thought that someday I will escape my father's torture by finding a husband. My father thinks he can stop that.

Suddenly, I sat up in bed, my long hair clinging to beads of sweat. I wonder if that was a new dream, or if through a dream I revisited an old memory.

April 18, 1900   3:05 p.m.

I just returned from getting ice cream at the parlor and was stunned to find so many people in there, despite the cold weather. It was a wise business idea to rent out the barbershop and the ice cream parlor. This way, we reap the benefits while the men renting the business do all the work. It takes money to make money.

April 22, 1900   2:50 a.m.

I saw it happen twice at Rosa's and I was just praying it wouldn't happen here, but we can't fight the odds forever. After all, the ladies and I spend so much time together it was inevitable. We have all gotten on the same menstrual cycle. Three days ago we all got a visit from Aunt Flow. The laudanum is supposed to suppress our menstrual cycles, but it's not always effective. There wasn't anything we could do but shut The Bantam Belmont down. J.J. wasn't real happy about the idea of closing but after whining about the lost profit he realized there was nothing he could do to fight a situation like this. Natalie suggested that we could all dance like Alex. J.J.'s reply was, "Can you dance like Alex? Not too many people can dance the way she does." To involve all the ladies in something they could do Alex came up with the idea of putting on a little skit for the miners. J.J. declared he liked the idea because it was something different and something different will always make money for a few days. Alex offered to organize everything and in a few hours she would let everyone know what they would do in the play. As she joyously bounced out of The Belmont, J.J. and I just looked at each other. He said, "That woman is incredible." It made my heart sing to know Jeremy James does indeed love Alex the way I love her.

Within minutes, Alex was back in The Belmont, saying she had come up with an idea for a play inspired by the new schoolhouse in Nome. She said, "Mandy, you could be the teacher." I declined the offer and suggested we draw cards and whoever got the highest one would be the teacher. Everyone seemed to like that idea. As it turned out, Alex drew the Ace and became the teacher. Alex presented herself as a very strict teacher and the ladies and myself took turns being the class clown, the dunce or the teacher's pet. The past three nights we have performed and The Belmont has been packed. J.J. was pleased with the results. He said he hadn't heard that much laughter in years. Ryan swore the more the miners laughed, the more they drank.

Now J.J. thinks this is a great idea and if Aunt Flow ever interferes with business again, he would love to see the ladies put on another play with a different theme. In between the performances, we were encouraged to sit with the men and let them buy us drinks. The time we spent visiting with the gentlemen was quite refreshing. Because all the men knew we were not working, there was no unruly energy in the air and we could enjoy heart-warming conversations with one another. I think this was the needed change we were all looking for.

April 23, 1900   **3:45 p.m.**

Today we are back up and running. Already we can feel the influx of soldiers in town because of the new Fort Davis military post established on the coast three miles east of town. They were very randy, not having seen ladies in months. I remember Rosa saying soldiers were dirty and had to count their change to afford a lady, but they would be religious in their visits.

April 24, 1900   **2:30 p.m.**

Today was one of those rare days when I felt like a child again. The wind was blowing extremely hard from the south and that heightened J.J.'s curiosity about skating using the wind for momentum. He encouraged everyone at brunch to go play with him. Natalie, Alex, Margerie, and I became giddy as we helped each other put on all our outdoor snow clothes. The five of us headed northeast to a small pond covered with ice. It took a while to clear a skating path through the snow. At last we were ready for the amusement. We would stand at one end of the path, put our arms up in the air, arch our backs, and let the wind blow us across. It was hilarious as we strived to stay drifting and not fall on our fannies. We looked like birds learning to fly. I laughed more today than I have since I was a youngster.

April 26, 1900   3:50 a.m.

Milroy visits so often that if I was to write about each one, I fear I would not get much done. I'm not quite sure why I choose to write about the encounters that I do when I have so many to choose from. I no longer spend time trying to figure ways to keep that man away from me. I anxiously anticipate every moment that we can share with one another. He has done something to my body and I can't get enough of his horn. It seems there should almost be another name for what Milroy and I share. I know when a man and woman have feelings for each other, it's called making love. When a man needs to release his lust, that's called fornication. But when two human beings can free their vigor and play with one another, that is the ultimate in human encounters and there must be another name for it.

April 28, 1900   4:45 a.m.

Natalie was not her usual cheerful self today. No smile could be found upon her brown face or in her brown eyes. So tonight after our evening meal I inquired about her melancholy. She told me without hesitation, "I just know something happened to my daughter today. I don't know what it was, but I can feel that it destroyed her innocent soul. I just wish I could have been there to help her instead of in this frozen, God forsaken place making money to send to her." Natalie's next words I hadn't anticipated, "I'm thinking about getting out of the business. I want to spend some time with my children before they grow up. I really miss them."

I have never heard Natalie talk like that before. I hope it really is the freezing temperature that is causing her to be somber. What would I do without her? What would the alliance do without her?

I just read some previous journal entries. That can be so insightful. Of all my ladies, I write the most about Alex. I know it is because I have such a deep love for her, but I must make note I have a love and admiration for Natalie, as well. I guess it is because I have known and worked with her since Rosa's. She really does have a gentle and motherly side to her, given the right opportunities. Like Alex, I love Natalie enough to be happy for her if returning to her children is what she needs to do. I don't want to even think about how much I will miss her.

April 30, 1900   2:40 p.m.

Now that we are beginning to get more and more sunshine everyday, hopefully the weather will be getting warmer. Before the big crowds arrive, the city officials have decided to create a red light district between Lanes Way and Division Street, behind the saloons north of Front Street. The planning process has started for us all to have a wood structure to live in which has to be warmer than living out of a canvas. We also like the idea of being closer to each other and all the other turned-out women in this town. There is value in being close enough to other madams to learn about their operations. Yesterday, I heard from Lillian that the reason her sign reads, "We aim to please" is because each morning during her flock's cleanup time they play a game to see which dove comes closest to hitting the target with her pee. Lillian believes it is the best way to keep her flock's equipment fit.

Each of my doves will get her own little cabin, which we prefer to call cribs. Rumor has it that all the ladies of the evening think we should paint the cribs green. This seems strange to me. I think we should paint them red like the red lights we use to advertise our profession.

J.J. never ceases to amaze me. He had an abundance of wood shipped on the last barge order before winter. It will arrive in early summer. His ability to plan ahead is one of the reasons he's so successful. They're already starting to build a high wooden fence that will separate the prostitutes from the residential section of town. The fence is a perfect example of how Nome is growing. It is no longer just a gold rush town. It is wishing to be a first class city, and in order for that to happen, it needs to separate its soiled doves from the rest of the community. Living within the boundaries of this fence will be a constant reminder to everyone that we are nothing but receptacles of men's lust. We are wild fowl and we deserve to be put in cages so we can be controlled. I think the real reason for the fence is to hide us away so the men can't be seen visiting us. Their secret must be kept at all costs.

The more I think about it, the more frustrated I become. If the men are the ones with all the power, why are they the ones paying for intimacy? Who really has power over whom? I need to try to be more optimistic. At least all the ladies and I will be close to each other. I've decided to put our names above our doors. There's no telling when the cribs will actually be ready to move into. I hope it's not too long. I desperately need some muffling from the goddamn wind.

May 1900

May 1, 1900   **11:00 a.m.**

I have been praying that whatever was happening with the crying and the water wouldn't happen again, but I'm not that lucky. I had another visit from Ria last night and as crazy as it sounds, I got up enough courage to inquire why she was visiting me. I was shocked when I received an answer. Through her tears she told me how she had promised her mother, the last time she saw her, that she would write when she got settled. Ria, or should I say the ghost of Ria, said she had never written and couldn't move on until that was arranged. I agreed to write her mother a letter explaining Ria's life and death in Nome. She even said she wanted me to be truthful about everything. Before her misty presence faded away, she said I had her mother's address if I would just think about it. The last thing I heard was the faint sound of a "thank you."

As bizarre as it is, I'm searching my mind for where I could have her mother's address. If I do find it, I will have to write her mother a letter. She made me promise.

May 3, 1900   **5:50 a.m.**

This evening Milroy made a point of assuring he was my last
customer. That made me rather suspicious of his intentions. Within
minutes after he had me in my tent, his plan was revealed. He had
me naked and tied to my bed so fast, I didn't have time to protest.
There he left me for hours as he tortured my body. I say it was
torture because he gave me so much pleasure, but just about as I
was about to reach my satisfaction, he would stop what he was
doing and move away from me. After watching me squirm for
several minutes, he would then return and once again bring my
body to its boiling point, stopping just before it simmered over. He
did this numerous times. When I asked him what kind of games
he was playing his reply was, "I'm only playing the games you
love me to play." He was absolutely right. I did love it. The whole
time I was tied up I never once thought about my responsibilities.
I didn't have to wonder if the patrons were happy, if all the ladies
had everything they needed, or what's causing Cupid's disease to
spread. There's always so much going on in my mind, but when
I'm in the clutches of Milroy's power, my mind is free. He creates
a healthy vigor in my body, my mind, and my soul that I have
never known before.

May 4, 1900   **2:05 p.m.**

I can't believe it's still snowing. I've heard it said that Alaska
Territory has long winter nights, and now I see why they say that.
Winter seems like one long night that goes on for an eternity.
I know the weather is getting to everyone. I don't hear much
laughter. Instead I hear lots of arguing. It's not just the ones
who usually argue and bicker, but lately everyone seems to have
a dispute to share. I'm really not sure how many days we can
tolerate being cooped up inside before someone explodes. I worry
about the girls getting hurt, but I know with the shooting lessons,
if something gets too serious, they can take care of themselves. I
have heard from some other madams that their worst problem is
their own girls fighting amongst each other. I guess the more ladies

you make a profit from the more conflicts you have to deal with. I am thankful that we have a harmonious bevy.

I've seen Jafet seven times since Christmas and I cherish each visit tremendously because I learn much more about him and the two other Lucky Swedes. He confided in me each of them have backgrounds in mining engineering. It's just easier for them to act stupid instead of trying to explain to everyone that they didn't just get lucky—they really knew what they were looking for and where to find it. To keep up the dunce act, whenever they're talking about mining around other people, they speak in Norwegian so as to reserve their knowledge.

We have much fun together and I laugh more with him than with anybody else. Well, maybe not as much as Alex. When he is gone in the morning, I feel sadder than when anyone else leaves me. With Alex and J.J.'s love more apparent each day, I'm starting to fantasize about being with Jafet, like a man and a wife. I know that can never happen. Just because we can't be together doesn't mean I can't care for him.

It's ironic being around people all day, yet having moments when I feel so lonely inside. I wish J.J. would let Alex share a tent with me. Sometimes I just can't sleep at night. I crave her arms holding me. I'm so frustrated: I can't be with Alex because J.J. won't allow that. I can't be with Jafet because society won't allow it. He hinted tonight that there would be several conflicts involved in marrying a madam.

A madam is one of the few women in this society with any kind of power. There aren't too many other businesses women are allowed to run. It just makes me so angry. Here I am successful in my own right as a madam, yet I am still put down in society. I cater to men and they are the ones who degrade me. Men degrade all women, don't they? It's not just hard being a madam, it's hard being a woman. I find myself sometimes looking at a woman in the store and wondering what her life is like. I imagine a lot of drudgery, cooking and cleaning, a husband imposing his ideas and bringing home venereal diseases. Dr. Miller insists that Cupid's disease could be controlled, except proper women won't allow that. It's the one true way to know if their husbands are committing adultery.

It's a curse to be born a woman. I remember my mother telling me this, but in return we get to bear children and have a nurturing bond with them. Men don't ever have that opportunity; they have no idea how it feels to be so close to another human. I'm sure I will never have the opportunity to know. I don't believe I can have children. With the many times my father planted seed into me, if I could get pregnant I'm sure I would have.

I'm twisted with so many emotions inside me: frustration, anger, and depression. Maybe I should try to write a letter. I haven't written to my Aunt Geneva, J.J.'s mom, since I arrived. I really should try and stay in touch with her since she is the only living relative I have left. She always loved Durango. Yes, I'll write to her. Hopefully, that will get me out of this wicked stupor I'm in.

May 5, 1900   **2:55 a.m.**

Today I said good-bye to Milroy, Clark, and Rawslin. With two wagons full of supplies and four mules to pull them up the frozen Snake River, they shouldn't have any problems getting there or surviving the summer. From the ore samples gathered last fall, they think the mother lode that's supplying the golden beaches of Nome must be somewhere in that area. I hate to see all three of them leave at the same time. I enjoy each one's company and I will miss each of them in their unique way. I will miss Milroy's deep, sultry voice that has a way of penetrating my soul. It's odd; I have intercourse with ten or more different men a day, but I don't find any of them arousing. With Milroy I become so aroused that I beg for more. I am obsessed with his vigor. I love it and I hate it. I love what he does to me, the way he can bring such pleasure to my body and diversion to my mind, but I hate the way he has control over me. I'm not sure if it will be good that he's gone. I think I will love and hate that as well.

With Clark, I'll miss the endless conversations we have in which he tells me more than I ever need to know about mining, making it all sound so thrilling. Although I don't understand half of it, his enthusiasm for mining and his wonderful storytelling make it very enjoyable to listen to him. I think more than anything he just likes to talk so I let him have that pleasure. I must admit I spend time with him not only to satisfy his need to talk, but to satisfy my visions more. I'm learning that when I am with Clark, I can just look deep into his dark brown eyes and rest my hand on his arm for those visions to flood my mind. In the visions, I'm always taking care of my little boy. I feel an abundance of love for that being. I wonder where the father is, but it doesn't matter because we have each other. I believe with all my heart that these are images from another lifetime. I have tried to ask Clark some questions to see if he has visions of another life, but he has no idea what I am talking about. Maybe because as the adult in the visions, I am the one with all the memories, and as a child all he has are the feelings.

I suspect early afternoon is when I will miss Rawslin the most. That seems to be the time we just naturally run into each other. Whether it's in the general store, the library, the beach, or even the tundra, we always seem to find each other. Every time we meet up, within minutes we are deep into conversation about the latest book Rawslin is reading. He does an excellent job of summarizing and after an hour, I feel like I have read the book myself. I love the way Rawslin is so observant and such an insightful thinker.

Yesterday afternoon as we were having tea in my tent and sharing our love of literature, he noticed I didn't have a mirror. Being the very honest person he is, he piped up right away with a comment, "How can a woman of your beauty not possess a mirror?" I told him I don't like mirrors. "I understand," he said. "You probably don't like looking at yourself because you don't like what you see. You are a strong woman. I admire you. Not every woman could carry the guilt of all those ladies and your own. When you look into a mirror it only reflects part of the truth of what you are." I was so touched by his insight I broke down into tears. He put his arms around me and let me lay my head on his chest. I cried harder than I ever remember crying. He let me cry while he rubbed his hands through my hair and he kept saying,

"It's alright Mandy, let it out, let out your pain." I'm not sure how long I cried. I do know that once I stopped crying, I felt better than I had since I got on that ship to come to Nome. I got rid of so much guilt when I cried. I sensed a rebirth within myself.

After I composed myself, I asked Rawslin why he has never wanted to touch me. He said, "Mandy, I could pay to perform the act with anyone of the chippies in this town, but I don't particularly enjoy the act. I find reading more stimulating. I guess it's just because I'm not used to being around people. Women especially make me uncomfortable, except for you. I love being around you and I'm afraid that if we join together, it wouldn't feel the same. So if it's O.K. with you, I'd just like to keep it this way." I reassured him I was his friend under any condition, and I got a huge hug from him before he left. When we were hugging, I felt closer to him than ever before. It was overwhelming to have a man understand my feelings. I didn't know that was possible.

As I watched the three leaving, I was already anticipating their return visits, yet I have no idea when I will see them again. They made it clear when they were in town again, they would definitely come and see me because there isn't anyone else here that cares about them. Of course it will go in the same order of Milroy, then Clark, and finally Rawslin. Even though Milroy won't allow his partners to mount me, I guess he thinks it's O.K. for them to at least visit so we can talk. I feel good knowing I'm their friend. I can't wait to hear all their stories when they return. I can live vicariously through them and become even more a part of the gold rush.

May 6, 1900   **2:30 p.m.**
It has been nine days since Natalie mentioned her children and leaving Nome and she hasn't said anything since. I'm surely not going to bring up the subject—it will be hard to replace her as a working lady and a friend. I'm not looking forward to that. I guess it was just the weather getting her down.

May 7, 1900   **3:25 p.m.**

Hurrah! Finally some signs of spring. Before I came to Alaska Territory, a sign of spring to me meant a few flowers or a little bit of green grass. But up here in the cold north, a sign of spring is that the price of beer has dropped from $60 to $35 a barrel because the saloonkeepers know new beer will be arriving with the first barge. The only thing people are talking about is that the ice will begin to break up soon. When that happens, I know I will feel invigorated because we will no longer be trapped here.

May 8, 1900   **3:30 p.m.**

I found Ria's mother's address in my smallest trunk. She must have remembered that I asked her to write down how her family could be reached if ever needed.

I'm sure those visits from Ria were the guilt reminding me that I had not finished my responsibilities. I still can't explain where the water came from. Maybe I'm not losing my mind. I was beginning to think maybe that was how Lizzy felt.

May 9, 1900   **4:10 a.m.**

In this business one learns that selling lust means different things to different men. Tonight, once we were in my tent, a younger gentleman said, "The first time I saw you, I knew you were the one." At first I was a little frightened, but as he explained I saw he was harmless. I was the "one" because we were about the same size. He didn't want to touch me or have me touch him. Instead, he wanted to wear my dresses. He was so disappointed I didn't have a mirror for him to admire himself in. He gave me a hand full of nuggets and requested that I "please" have a mirror available next time he visits. "What makes you think I would ever want to service you again, if that is what you call this," as I pointed to him in my favorite blue dress. He responded quickly, "You can call my desire to dress in women's clothes whatever you want, but I'm sure this bag of nuggets speaks of profit in any language."

This strange man went on to tell me he would come to see me on a weekly basis and he would pay double my asking price to wear my clothes and double that price for my silence. As he handed me a month of payment in advance I shook his hand and said, "You are 100% correct. We do speak the same language. You have a deal and my silence." How could I say no? I guess I will have to purchase a mirror and keep clothes draped on it.

May 11, 1900   3:20 a.m.

Tonight will be imprinted in my mind for a long time. I've seen J.J. lose at poker before, but what makes it so memorable is he was losing to Alex. He has avoided playing cards with her since this journey began, although she has constantly offered him the challenge. I think J.J. was a little intimidated by her eagerness. I calculate he avoided playing with her for so long because as long as he didn't play, he couldn't lose. I don't know what prompted the game after so much delay. Maybe it was her constant invitations. Maybe it was the countless days without any sight of clear skies. Or maybe it was that old bottle of whiskey he had been saving for so long. Perhaps it was all the above.

If Alex and J.J. hadn't stopped after four hours, I believe Alex would now be the proud owner of The Belmont. It was exciting to watch those two outwit each other. The sad thing about tonight was Jeremy was truly humiliated. I think he has believed all these years that men are so superior to women that it just wasn't possible for a woman to beat him at poker. As he walked out of The Belmont, he looked like a little puppy that had just been kicked out of his home. He said he was going on a walk and with that he stood up and quickly shuffled through the people. I wanted to run and hug him, but I knew that was the last thing he needed.

The Belmont was dead quiet for several minutes after J.J. left. The only thing I could figure is that folks were afraid to congratulate Alex, for fear of looking like they were taking her side. Then in the next second my heart went out to Alex. She had just played several exquisite games of cards and nobody would even acknowledge her. Once again I was furious. Here we are living in this man's world and they have control of so many things right down to recognition of our accomplishments.

I walked over to Alex and put my hands on her shoulders and slowly started rubbing her neck. I softly told her how proud I was of her and that I thought she played one hell of a game. I also told her I wished there was something I could do to make the world a more equitable place to live in. I reminded her that they are just intimidated by her skills as well as J.J.'s power. I asked her if she would like the night off to celebrate. Her reply was, "There are two things I really enjoy—gambling and being mounted. I've already been gambling so I might as well go to work and make some money enjoying my other favorite past time. But Mandy, thanks for being there for me. I love you. I wish I could openly show my affection."

May 12, 1900   3:10 p.m.

Natalie and I walked along the Snake River after brunch to see the ice flowing through the water. Throughout the walk, we spoke of how wonderful it was to be coming upon spring. Natalie is anxious to begin collecting wild flowers. I told her how I was anticipating looking at the elaborate designs of the flowers and counting all the varieties. As we were talking about how much this area has changed since we arrived 11 months ago, something in the river caught my eye. I looked at the side of the ice, right next to where the ice had parted to let the water through, and saw lines of intense blues, some with hints of green. It was as if someone had taken a paintbrush and ever so lightly painted the ice. I was stunned at how the colors got there, and as usual Natalie tried to explain the science of it. She said the ice had different layers from the different temperatures it had frozen in. She went on to explain that when the sun hits the ice in a certain way, it creates these marvelous colors, just like when raindrops act as prisms to create rainbows. The entire walk back to town was spent arguing over how the colors got into the ice and I have to confess she had me convinced by the time we got back. I'd love to be able to go back sometime to see if the colors are still there, but Natalie says that the ice will be gone soon and also that the colors only appear when the sun is giving off a dim light. I must go back and check on the colors, or I'll be curious until next spring.

May 14, 1900   3:05 p.m.

Today while returning from a short jaunt on the tundra, I followed the Snake River back to town. It was fascinating to see and hear the chunks of ice as they rapidly made their way to the ocean. The ice floes varied in shapes and sizes, but the one similarity they possessed was the long, slender ice crystals that formed together to create each one. The ice floes bobbed up and down, racing to reach their destinations, their high-pitched tones chiming like elegant glass chandeliers breaking against each other. It created enchanting music for my ears. I would have loved to stay and enjoy the melody longer, but I needed to get back so I could write before starting work.

Natalie was correct again. The sun was shining brightly today and I didn't see any colors in the ice still locked to the riverbanks. I think I'll keep that a secret since Natalie would remind me of her victory constantly.

May 15, 1900   1:05 p.m.

As soon as I awoke I could feel something different in the air. Once I got outside of my tent I realized it was warmth. It had been so long since my body had felt such uplifting weather. As fast as I could, I got dressed and ran down to the beach, hoping the ice would be gone. To the south below the horizon, I saw a thin strip of sparkling blue water, but ice still covered the rest of the ocean. The structures were no longer the giant masses as in mid-winter because they had been worn down by wind. The fresh ocean air had broken the spell created by the frozen grip of the ice.

I was entranced by the view and I could hear my own heart beating with excitement. I was startled by the strangest sound I had ever heard, which made my heart beat even faster. At first I imagined it must be some walrus fighting in the open water. After listening to that bizarre sound for about ten minutes, I recognized it as massive chunks of ice breaking off the parent and crashing against each other. It was hypnotizing. The only image it evoked was giant monsters tangling with one another. I guess the sound of ice jamming against itself is also a sign of spring this far north.

May 17, 1900   3:15 p.m.

On my walk today, I saw pussy willows starting to bloom. Kuduk said this is a sign of spring. He hinted at me to keep my eyes open for dandelions because they're always the first to bloom and the first to die. It bewilders me to think this is an early spring like Kuduk claims. He also said, "Enjoy the sun while it shines upon us. I've seen ice still locked to the land when the sun is at its longest day. I have also seen the ice return to the shore after only being gone four round moons." His wisdom taught me I must enjoy each moment in nature to its fullest.

I love this feeling of being alive again! The sun is retuning more each day and it is quickly awakening the earth from its long slumber. From my tent, the tundra looks brown and dead, but once I'm standing on it looking down, there's plenty of evidence of its liveliness. It's astonishing that the tiny flowers can grow among the patches of snow that still remain. I am elated to have witnessed such an event as breakup, which literally means the ice on the once-frozen ocean is starting to break apart.

May 20, 1900   3:50 a.m.

Today at brunch Kuduk said that Nome's only cow died. The girls were disappointed because we all love milk so much. J.J. stated that it is a luxury for us, yet for the typhoid patients, milk is believed to help with their recovery. There wasn't much grieving for the cow because everyone was too excited over something else. During the night, there was a very strong northerly wind that helped push the ice south and opened up the ocean, leaving behind only a few chunks that are still frozen to the land. What a beautiful sight it was to see the open blue water. Smelling the fresh ocean air awakened all my senses, creating a feeling of being more alive than I had felt all winter long. The miners call a person who has survived the winter a "sourdough." I officially declare myself a sourdough. I love it! I made it through my first winter and now I have summer to look forward to.

May 20, 1900   **3:20 p.m.**

After brunch, most of us went down to the beach. Several adventurous souls, including Alex and J.J tried "ice hopping." The object is to hop from one piece of land-locked ice to another without breaking it. The challenge increases with the wave action and the wind. Of course, not everyone succeeded and it was quite humorous to watch people take a dip in the icy Bering Sea. Alex was one of the unfortunate ones and Dorothy was the first to come running with a blanket for her. Dorothy is a breath of sanity for the alliance. She is more of a mother to everyone than I will ever be, but I don't feel jealousy toward her. I just feel love. She has never shown any grief for Jime. Maybe it's something she does in private. I'm just grateful she is here helping all of us endure the strenuous and the enjoyable times.

May 21, 1900   **3:30 p.m.**

It was a fine day for the first steam whaler to arrive in Nome. That set off a chain reaction of celebration from one saloon to another. The only topic of conversation was that if the ice packs are breaking up, then thousands of people will be arriving in Nome shortly. The business-minded people, such as myself, are excited to think about all the new wealth that will be arriving, but the miners are fearful they will once again have to defend their claims. The councilmen are already claiming that they are worried about the sanitation problem, but nothing has been done to correct it. I sure hope Nome is ready for what the future has in store.

May 22, 1900   **3:10 p.m.**

It is invigorating to see how quickly the dead brown tundra has turned green and alive. I find it fascinating to see the animals that depend on the plant growth for survival and can now feast on the tundra. Today I saw three heavy set, shaggy creatures. I had no idea what they were. They looked like a buffalo, an oxen, and a wise oriental man combined. They didn't seem to be bothered by my presence as I stood about 150 feet away, so I wasn't afraid of them.

As soon as I retuned to town, I rushed to find Kuduk. My desire to know the name of the animal burned inside. After I described the animal, Kuduk knew instantly what I was talking about. He said they were called musk oxen and to his knowledge, they had all died out years ago. He said, "I can't believe you haven't seen any reindeer on your many outings, yet you witness an animal that is only known in our legends." He insisted I tell him exactly where I had seen them, then he quickly departed saying he had to see one of these woolly creatures for himself. I should consider myself privileged that I got to lay my eyes on such magnificent beasts.

May 24, 1900   **3:40 a.m.**

Today the steam schooner *Jeanie* of the Pacific Whaling Company arrived. Once again, the people of Nome can enjoy fresh vegetables, fruits, beef, ham, and eggs. I hope everyone appreciates the new nourishment as much as I do. My first taste of the bright orange carrots evoked memories of vegetables picked fresh from the garden. My favorite was always the snow peas. I loved the way they filled my mouth with the fresh taste of the earth's flavor.

For a special treat, Dorothy methodically arranged the new edibles on a platter for sampling as our evening meal. It was exciting taking bites of all the varieties of fresh foods. I could tell by the "ooh"s and "ahh"s that I wasn't the only one bombarded by awakening taste buds.

May 25, 1900   **2:25 p.m.**

We are now getting about sixteen hours of sunlight. Although I'm grateful for the thaw, it has created numerous streams through town, rushing to meet the ocean. It makes no difference if a tent is in the way. The water just goes right under it, resulting in soggy floors.

Walking through town is another ordeal in itself. The only possible way to travel is to wear gumboots. We are very thankful J.J. had the foresight to buy each of us a pair way back last summer when we made our barge order. If we didn't have boots we would literally be prisoners in our damp tents.

May 27, 1900   **3:05 p.m.**

Everyone is talking about how easy the railroad companies are making it to get to Seattle and how easy the steamship companies are making it to get to Nome. They're saying it's as easy as child's play to reach. I have heard a second-class ticket from Seattle to Nome costs $60 to $70, down $30 from what we paid last year. At that price I can see why so many dreamers and fortune hunters are coming to the first gold rush of the century.

Rumor has it the hotels in Seattle are so overcrowded the only place to sleep is on cots in the staff rooms. I've also heard San Francisco, Portland, Victoria, and Vancouver are all in competition for the Nome business. However, Seattle has been established since the Klondike rush, and is better equipped to handle the large volume of passengers and freight that must get to Nome. I'm sure the Seattle merchants are enjoying Nome's gold fever. This easy access is spreading our fame throughout the world.

May 29, 1900   **3:00 p.m.**

While bathing today, I told the ladies of an outrageous experience with a client last night. It was almost closing time when in walked a man with a sheep under his arms. At first I thought that it was very cute because it had been so long since I had seen an animal. Right away he inquired about my prices and without a blink of the eye he placed two one-ounce vials of gold dust in my hand.

Once we were alone I understood why he was willing to pay double the going rate. He had the most unusual request of my career. All he wanted me to do was watch him have intercourse with his sheep he called Mabel. I was a little surprised that he would pay so much for my sense of sight. Before leaving he said,

"Now my love for Mabel has been recognized because I made love to her in front of another human."

Well, at least he called me a human. I'm slowly learning in this business there is no room for judgment, only room for profit.

May 30, 1900   3:40 a.m.

This evening I enjoyed the company of one of my favorite older clients, Lucky Baldwin, owner of The Baldwin Hotel. It's one of Nome's finest. Rumor has it he has the longest bar not only in Alaska Territory, but the whole U.S. He personally told me that he made his first million in Comstock, Nevada, during its boom. He is also very proud of the fact he had the first piano in Nome, one thing he never lets Jeremy forget. I appreciate servicing him because he always smells so good. He wears high-dollar cologne because he can afford it. Most men aren't even aware of how they smell.

After having reached satisfaction, he began talking about his cousin, Veronica, who is a prostitute in Denver. He said, "That bitch shot me once when her blackmailing scheme didn't work out, but that didn't stop me from enjoying her talented body. Together we performed just about every act I can think of. Now I'm looking for something new and exciting. What do you have to offer?"

I was shocked by the question and, not having a prepared answer, I responded truthfully. "I've been so busy living the reality of a madam, I haven't even had time to think about developing a specialty. As good as business is, I've come to the conclusion that I don't need a specialty. Being a woman is special enough, especially this far north where there are at least 50 men for every one woman." He wasn't satisfied and said, "Might I offer some suggestions? Don't rush a man and always give him quality attention. Ask him questions about himself and do the best you can to listen to his response. Tell funny stories about your line of work without even using a real name. One of my favorite ways for a madam to entertain me is to have her roll a cigar for me and rub my horn while I smoke it. Of course, a woman with a mind is a specialty in itself and quite challenging."

June 1900

June 1, 1900   2:45 p.m.

Already the beach is starting to fill up with what everybody is
calling "jackass machinery." If I thought it was bad last summer,
it will be tenfold this summer. Everywhere I look I see people and
their creative gold recovering devices. Dredges of all shapes and
sizes cover the beach. Some have strange-looking pedals that men
use to help transport water and others are three to four times taller
than a man.

Editor Strom of the *Nome News* has predicted that most of
this machinery will be left on the beach to rot away when people
have recovered from their gold fever. I must admit I like it when
someone has foresight, but right now all I can see is the immediate
future and all the loot summer promises. I can't begin to see the
end of the gold rush. For me it's just the beginning of enormous
wealth that's heading our way as the masses descend upon Nome.

June 2, 1900   **3:35 p.m.**

While exploring on the beach today, I was intrigued by an Inuit woman and her four children. She was bent down cooking with a large tin can and stick over a small fire. I could smell seal oil. The woman had dark copper colored skin and puffy cheekbones and was wearing her heavy parka, even though it was a very warm day. On her back was a baby, its head sticking out from her coat. Her two older daughters were also wearing their parkas and standing right by her side. Her young son was standing opposite of her, wearing a long sleeved shirt. The children watched their mother with such intent in their eyes, as if they were in school. Watching their mother cook was a very important lesson in survival—how to make do with what one has.

I must say that the whole family looked very dirty. After living in a tent now for almost a year, I know first hand how hard it is to stay clean when a person lives directly upon the earth. I wonder where they get clean. Is it only in the summer, when it is warm? I wonder if they have any other clothes besides what they are wearing? Do they have a shelter to sleep in? Where is the children's father?

In the last several months I have spent so much time caring for my ladies, it must be second nature for me to want to care for a female in need. If I see her again, I will give her some gold dust. I'm sure she could use it with children to feed.

June 3, 1900   **4:20 a.m.**

It was a splendid cloudless night, if that's the right word for it. The sky never gets dark; I saw no harm in taking a little laudanum. I had walked for about an hour when I saw a moose and her calf in the open tundra, much farther away than the musk oxen had been. At about the same time the mother saw me and quickly went to work protecting her offspring. She nudged her calf behind nearby bushes, and it vanished from my sight. I became a little concerned of what she might do to me in order to alleviate any harm to her young, but she disappeared into some taller bushes. For moments I stood there staring, beginning to think that maybe I had just imagined their presence. As I was about to title myself insane, I saw enough of the mother's head sticking out from the top of the bushes to confirm my eyesight. Their natural camouflage defense works extremely well.

June 4, 1900   3:00 p.m.

Today after Dr. Miller's weekly check with each one of the ladies, he asked if he could speak to me in private. He said he hated to be the bearer of bad news, but Margerie is two months pregnant. He assured me he could perform the same procedure on Margerie that he routinely performs on other chippies to terminate the pregnancy. I asked Dr. Miller if he had informed Margerie of his discovery. He said, "No, Mandy. I believe that's your job." I thanked him and said that we would get back to him.

As soon as I walked into Margerie's tent, she said, "I know why you're here, Mandy." I looked at her in bewilderment and sat down on her bed. "Dr. Miller told you I was pregnant." I was shocked. "You knew you were pregnant?" She replied, "Of course. It's my body. My bosoms are growing bigger every day. Haven't you noticed that I just nibble at brunch?" "Yes, I've noticed," I told her, "but I thought it was your eating style."

After talking for at least an hour, there was still no solution to the problem. Margerie's not sure how she'd feel about destroying the child that's growing inside her. She thinks maybe this profession isn't for her and the baby is a sign she needs to leave this town while she still has some life in her. On the other hand, she doesn't know how she would support and raise a baby on her own. She finally asked me to leave her alone so she could think about the situation.

I see now it's a blessing that I can't get pregnant. I will never have to endure the torment of making a choice like that myself. It astonishes me how different experiences can vary one's perspective on life.

June 5, 1900   **3:00 p.m.**

The Inuit family I saw the other day was still on my mind and
that prompted me to ask Kuduk some questions about his people.
I found out the reason we don't see very many in the wintertime is
because most of them return to their home on King Island. I also
learned that igloos are only used in a winter emergency or during
hunting trips. The people of this cold region build their homes
using everything that is available: hides, driftwood, chunks of the
earth, grasses of all types, and mud.

I learned something else from Kuduk today. He told me he
believes Nome got its name from the Inuit words "Kn-no-me",
which means, "I don't know." The Inuit used this phrase a lot
because they can't answer the many questions of the white people.
Now I'm not sure whether to believe J.J.'s theory or Kuduk's.

June 6, 1900   **3:20 p.m.**

Earlier in the spring I was happy to have the mud boots but
now, once again, I'm frustrated with the skirts the ladies have to
wear. It's not logical. We need to be wearing pants. These skirts
we wear are like mops. Everywhere we go, we drag mud around.
We try picking up our skirt, but then we almost loose our balance
when we walk. It's ridiculous, but I don't think there's anything
we can do about it. Women can't even buy pants. I know I'm just
complaining. Hopefully the mud will dry up soon and then we will
have the dust to look forward to. I guess if it's not one aspect of
Mother Nature we have to endure, it's another.

Speaking of Mother Nature, her little tiny creatures that love
to suck our blood are back. I surely didn't miss them over the long
winter.

June 7, 1900   **2:45 p.m.**

This place never seems to be quiet. Every ship announces its
arrival with several whistle blasts, and each ship in the harbor
answers in return. On my walk today, I counted over 22 ships
floating in the water south of town. I didn't even bother to count
the little boats. This creates so much excitement in town that at

times I feel like a little girl again. At other times, I feel like an old lady and I just want some peace and quiet. If it's not the sounds of those busy hammers again or whistles blowing, I can hear dogs howling, drunken voices yelling, rinky-dink pianos playing the same songs, and sporting girls bellowing as they flash their upper charms to potential customers.

Not only is this place loud, but it also stinks. Every where I go, whether I'm indoors or outdoors, it smells of beer, whiskey, urine, unwashed bodies, and cheap perfume. Sometimes it is enough to make me sick, but I've got to remember this is where I'm making my money. I will just have to keep tolerating it and prepare myself to put up with more.

June 8, 1900 3:35 a.m.

I can't believe how foolish some men are. Take for example Oliver Hubbard, who is one of my customers. He's an ambitious lawyer who works for a Nome law firm with two other men. Their firm is set up in such a way that they represent miners with jumper titles and then if they win the case they become partners with their clients, thus getting half of the gold.

Today while he was visiting me, he just went on and on, talking about this plan of his to control Nome. He said in January of this year, he met a man in New York named Alexander McKenzie. McKenzie was the first person Oliver had met who was also willing to gamble that the claims of foreigners in Nome could be invalidated. If this happened, Oliver could stand a chance to become wealthy off other people's discoveries. He continued that McKenzie was a North Dakota political boss, who was very influential in Washington D.C. and knew several key senators quite well. It was McKenzie's plan to use these senators to attach an amendment to the Alaska Code that would void any mining claims in Alaska that had been staked by people not born in the United States. They figured if they wiped the slate clean of alien locators, the jumper's titles would be priceless.

Oliver said that he and McKenzie quickly agreed that their strategy would be to form the Alaska Mining Company, which

would be a phony partnership. Oliver figured if their company
could gain control of the richest mines in Nome for just one
summer, they could take out millions of dollars worth of gold.
By the fall, before anyone knew what had happened, McKenzie
would unload millions of dollars of worthless stock on Wall Street,
leaving the oblivious public paying the price.

When I heard all of this, I thought Oliver must be making it
up. How could anything like this really happen? I also thought, it's
pretty reckless of Oliver to be telling me all of it, especially if it
is true. I bet he thinks I am some mindless fallen woman, and his
secrets are safe with me. What a fool!

Oliver's biggest problem is he's a small, insecure man who
can't get an erection. Because he can't control his own body, he
tries to control other people and manipulate them with his wicked
ways. I pity men like him.

June 9, 1900   3:50 a.m.

It never ceases to astound me how some people's illusions can
get them in trouble. It was about midnight, which always seems to
be our busiest time in The Belmont, when a man tried to provoke
a fight with J.J. Once the man took the first swing, J.J. didn't
have any choice but to fight back. And fight he did! In less than a
minute, J.J. had the man in a hold that rendered him completely
helpless. It was obvious to all that if J.J. continued, he would
damage the man's kidneys. Being the soft heart that J.J. is, he let
the man go and told him to get out and never come back. Why
would a man smaller than J.J. start a fight? Did he really think he
had a chance of winning? I guess we all live in a world of make
believe that helps us survive. But every once in awhile, reality
reminds us, like it reminded that man, the way we see ourselves is
not always the way we really are.

Am I really a successful businesswoman, or is that an illusion?
When I die, will anybody notice my absence, or will I be like
the falling tree in the forest that no one hears? I'm a madam, the
lowest creature on earth, who arranges for other women to have
their bodies used to satisfy the lusty creatures who dominate this

planet. I need to stop writing now and go to sleep. I get depressed thinking about the control men have over women. Sometimes I think women will never get the chance to be anything more than subservient to men.

June 10, 1900   3:15 a.m.

Hearing the birds chirping so loudly on my walk today influenced my escaping ritual. Tonight as I swung back and forth over the imaginary water I pretended I was a bird flying. I heard birds of all types singing in diverse volumes and pitches. I made it a game to pretend I knew what they were saying to one another. Being able to focus on the bird's performance made it that much easier to forget about the moaning and groaning that was taking place above my body. I will have to share my new trick with my flock.

June 11, 1900   3:20 a.m.

I spent my free time today down on the shore watching four ships arrive that had all left Seattle on May 20th. It was fascinating to watch the hustle and bustle and to hear the many stories. People say that among the freight that was shipped in today, there was over $10,000 worth of the finest wood bars, bar fixtures, and liquor. It is also rumored that a printing press arrived, as well as a complete banking outfit, including $200,000 in coin and currency for the newly established "Bank of Cape Nome." I even saw silver canned goods without the labels scattered all over the shore. I'm sure they will be on sale next week in some mercantile.

I can't believe all the money that has been spent to bring up painted and assembled theaters, gambling halls, hotels, restaurants, and everything else needed to create an instant city. I tried to keep my eyes open for the rails and equipment for a seven-mile long narrow gauge railroad that Jafet's mining company will utilize for quick transportation from Nome to Anvil, but in all the chaos, I never saw it. I did see shiny buggies, new and used mining equipment, brown lumber, black coal, white 50 pound bags of grain, green hay, and tons of tan crates with general merchandise that had been unloaded on the sand just beyond the water's edge. I'm glad we arrived last year and are already settled. I can't imagine trying to find our freight among the possessions of the masses.

As I watched the commotion, I imagined what the new city of Nome will look like. One version had elegant hotels, saloons, and restaurants and everyone walked around with beautiful clothes and no worries. The other version was dark and grimy. Thousands of people arrived in Nome daily with no means of dealing with all the sanitation. Soon all the people were incapable of moving, surrounded by garbage and feces. They literally buried themselves in their own waste. It was a horrifying image. It scares me to think about it. I hope the city officials are planning wisely so that doesn't happen.

June 13, 1900   3:10 a.m.

This evening while I was in The Belmont soliciting for the ladies, I had the pleasure of Jafet's company. He was in very high spirits as he introduced me to his new business associates. There was Walter Patrick Butler of Minnesota, eight other men, and one woman. Together they make up the Los Angeles Mining Company. The two mining companies decided to merge and become even stronger. Jafet said he and his partners had made a few mistakes since reaching these shores, like when they recorded their first claim here in Alaska Territory. He went on to say they were mistaken in several areas. They had the wrong size, the wrong markings, no recorder, and no miner's district meeting. Later, with the correct knowledge and a new partnership, they returned and followed every needed step correctly. He bragged that all the hard work is finally paying off and now his alliance is more equipped and organized than ever.

Then he mentioned that Butler is keeping a diary of his experiences in Nome. To my great surprise, he announced that I kept a diary. I couldn't help but get all tingly inside knowing he knew something about my personal life. Everyone joked about how much more exciting my diary would be to read than Butler's.

June 14, 1900   4:05 a.m.

Tonight Margerie began bleeding while servicing a customer. She became hysterical. I heard her screaming and crying and ran as fast as I could to her tent. When I saw what was happening I thought she must be having a miscarriage and I asked Natalie to run and get Dr. Miller. In about ten minutes Natalie returned with him, but he was so inebriated he wasn't sure where or who he was. He just kept saying, "Whhhy don't we have a little drrrink and talk abooout it, thennn we will see what to do." I was so frustrated; Dr. Miller was totally useless. I guess when I think about it, why would any successful doctor leave a thriving practice to come this far north. Only the dregs would travel this far in hopes of becoming wealthy. The only other person I could think of to help us was Ryan. Natalie ran to get him and Alex and J.J. had to step behind the bar to make up for his absence.

Ryan suggested we give her some whiskey to calm her down. She continued to scream for several minutes, then suddenly she stopped and investigated that between her legs was a mass of spongy tissue. The top of it looked like a tiny baby's body, the bottom was unrecognizable. When we finally got the bleeding controlled and knew she would be alright, I had to go back to work. No matter how hard I tried, I just could not concentrate. I wanted to stay and nurture her. I felt like she needed the attention more than I needed the money, but we already had a dozen men on our waiting list and more potentials walking in the door. I was forced to be a businesswoman instead of a mother.

To make matters worse, three horrifying fights broke out in The Belmont. Several tables and chairs got broken. I guess people were taking advantage of J.J. being behind the bar and not so easily within their reach. It became clear tonight that Ryan is a big key to the success of our establishment. I, for one, never realized how valuable Ryan was. I always thought J.J. was the key player because he is the one with the money to invest, but Ryan is also very important in keeping everything flowing smoothly on a daily basis.

June 15, 1900   **3:15 p.m.**

Each day more ships arrive to the same lack of harbor as they did a year ago. With more ships come more whistles. The sound of the whistles takes me back to Durango and the sound the train made when it came home. I remember my father observing that throughout my whole life whenever I heard the train, I would go into a trance. He said he could put his hands right in front of my face and I would not even blink. He would tell my mom that it must have to do with the different pitches the train whistle would create. I remember when I heard those sounds; it was like I traveled in time for a little bit. I would see other places in my mind. I liked it. Sometimes I didn't want to come back into my own time.

Hearing whistles makes me think of my father. I hate anything that reminds me of him. I hear those whistles all day long. There is no escaping his memory and the pain it causes me.

June 16, 1900   **2:30 p.m.**

I must express the frustration I feel about myself. Several times after returning from a walk I have tried to draw a picture of the exceptional scenery I have witnessed. Each time I try, I end up wadding up the paper and throwing it away, embarrassed by my lack of ability. My talks with Rawslin have helped me understand why I have a strong desire to represent my adventures. I was hoping that someday someone would pick up my diary and be intrigued by its contents just by looking at the pictures, like I was every time I picked up a Twain book that had drawings in it. I want people to understand without reading my diary that I have a love affair with the extraordinary land I have encountered here. Some of my attempted pictures included the day I was first leaving the ship, the growing town, the flowers on the tundra, the chaos on the beach, the fog, the winter sunsets, the frozen ocean, the ice in the river, the ocean ice breaking up in spring time and, my favorite, the midnight sun behind the northern mountains.

With practice I hope to get better, but so far I see no evidence of my skills increasing.

June 17, 1900   **1:20 p.m.**

Alex and I were up to our usual games last night, exchanging stories and touching ourselves. Once again her top story for the evening was one of great bewilderment. She had a client who paid for her to carve his initials into his enlarged manhood. Alex said at first she was afraid to do it, but he kept giving her good-sized nuggets. After about the twelfth one she decided, "What the hell, it's his organ, it's not going to hurt me and if that's what he wants, I'll try it." Alex said she used his knife, which was extremely sharp, and as she started to carve in the A she was surprised because it didn't bleed very much. Alex continued by saying that the whole time she held his manhood in her hand and carved with the knife, the man was groaning in ecstasy. After she finished carving the A, reality hit of what she was doing and she wanted to stop, but when she told her client, he became furious and bellowed, "No, you can't stop. I haven't released my load. You have to keep doing it. Please, I'll do anything," and he dumped out the rest of the nuggets that were in his little leather pouch. "They're all yours. Please, please just finish." As soon as she had finished the last cut, he ejaculated all over her hand and went on and on saying he had never felt anything so incredible in his life and he would cherish that moment forever.

When I heard that, I started laughing. Then Alex joined in. I don't know what it is about her, but Alex always attracts those eccentric ones.

The tender way we joked about the day set the stage for another wonderful night of slowly bringing pleasure to one another's bodies. We fell asleep in each other's arms, but of course she left before I woke so J.J. will never know of our rendezvous.

June 18, 1900   **3:25 p.m.**

The building materials for our cribs arrived today! All the girls are anxious to have a structure of their own. I wonder how long it will be before we can move in. Alex and I will share a tent and Margerie and Natalie will share the other to make room for the cribs to be built. The way things go around here, it could be fall

196

before we get those cribs built. Hopefully it won't be that long because I think we'd all go a little crazy having to share tents for such an extended time. Though it will be nice to finally get to share a tent with Alex and to help keep those crazy clients away from her.

June 19, 1900   **3:40 p.m.**

On a walk today down by the shore, I saw a small group of women calmly camped against a pile of freight. They were surrounded by pieces of hand luggage and partially covered by a tarp. I heard a lady say that she had been sleeping in a goods box. I think the willingness of these women to adapt themselves to such conditions indicates they have retained the spirit of the frontier. Up here, people either adapt or they die. I'm happy to see other strong women.

June 20, 1900   **3:45 a.m.**

Margerie was back at work this evening and already the operation went smoother. Not having her work for the last seven days has put a tremendous load on all the other ladies, but there was nothing we could do. Dr. Miller got around to visiting the next day and said it was imperative that Margerie not have anything inside her for at least a week to prevent infection. There was no way that Margerie was going to stay down for seven days. She just didn't think that was necessary, so she has been helping out Dorothy as much as she can. She's given Dorothy a needed break from cooking and nobody in the alliance has had to suffer from the change. As it turns out Margerie is quite talented when it comes to cooking.

I'm very impressed with the way Margerie is handling her loss. She had told me earlier she still wasn't sure what to do about the child, but she knew that things would take care of themselves. She's happy the situation has been taken care of without her taking a life. I admire her resilience. She gave me a big hug tonight and said, "Thanks for sharing your love and treatin' me like family."

June 21, 1900   **2:10 p.m.**

Happy midnight sun! After enduring a long, dark winter, I am more fascinated by the never-ending light than I was last year. It fills my heart with more joy than I have ever known to see the sun in the sky throughout the whole day. I guess I can't say whole day because for about four hours in the morning it does sneak behind those northern mountains, but the sky is never dark. In the past five days I have not seen a cloud in the sky. This has an energizing affect on my mind, body, and soul.

The warmth brings with it more birds to hear and more flowers to feel, smell, and see. I saw more varieties of flowers today than I have ever seen before. The ones that really stand out in my mind are tiny purple flowers with cream-colored fuzz growing on them. It's as if they've learned from the arctic animals to grow fur to help them adapt to the harsh weather.

I find myself falling in love with the hidden beauty of the tundra. A surprise awaits me each time I walk to the top of a knoll. Whether it's a new species of flower, a unique arctic creature, or simply the breathtaking view, I'm captivated by the loveliness. It's so quiet and peaceful that I get the chance to listen to the voice inside myself. I believe all answers are inside us if we just ask the right question. Walking on the tundra is like going to church. It gives me the chance to visit the God within me.

Sometimes I wish I could stay away from the ugly town of Nome forever. Then the wind stops blowing on the tundra and the buzzing of the mosquitoes annoys me so damn much that I must flee. As much as I try to keep my mouth closed, I always end up swallowing at least one. I must remember to buy a mosquito net to protect my head. I always think about getting one when I'm on the tundra, but when I'm at the store, I never seem to remember.

When I'm back in my tent, I'm always thankful to be away from those blood-sucking insects. Speaking of blood sucking, each day I see hundreds of new faces. I call these greenhorns blood-sucking humans because it is obvious they are out to get something for themselves and they don't care whose blood gets spilled in the fight. Already major battles are occurring between miners who have claims and miners wishing to have claims. With so many people here, how can everybody expect to have a claim, let alone more than one? Some old and new miners need to get out and explore the peninsula more if we're all going to survive.

Talking to Kuduk today was very enlightening. He had a different perspective, one I had never thought of. He said, "The longest day of summer is also the first day of winter. When you depend on the land for your food, you must always think in those terms." I admire his foresight but I don't even want to think of the cold winter when the warm summer is here and now.

June 22, 1900   3:45 a.m.

The Belmont is changing as rapidly as Nome. Thanks to the barge shipments, new, elegant equipment has arrived to enhance the appearance of our saloon. Now that J.J. is sure this is a good investment, he went all out in assuring that he will have one of the finest drinking establishments in the Alaska Territory. Last night was the first night our new piano player, also known as Professor Henry, played in The Belmont. I am not sure how many of the gentlemen we served even noticed. The ladies and I agreed we liked listening to the faint music in the background as we worked in our tents. It was a welcome distraction. We now have a string of lights above the bar that will illuminate the area so people can see what they are drinking. In the middle of the room, we have three glass chandeliers that sparkle with an exquisiteness I never knew glass could possess. J.J. is so driven to have the finest establishment that he ordered six marble columns to be placed behind the bar. He also ordered more crystal mirrors and beautiful ornate pear-shaped light globes to be dispersed throughout the saloon.

Kuduk spent over two hours putting a rail up that hangs from the bar that we will put white towels on. This way the customers can wash their hands before they enjoy our free sardine appetizers. Jeremy reminded me nothing is ever free. His real motive for serving salty appetizers is so the customers drink more. He's not giving anything away. It just appears that way.

As The Belmont changes, Ryan has had to change as well. Ryan is now wearing a clean white shirt everyday with a black bow tie, diamond cuffs and several rings upon his fingers. Ryan reassured me that even though the outside is changing, he still expects rowdy clientele. He will keep his revolver cocked at all times just as he did when The Belmont looked a little shabbier.

J.J. is in high spirits these days. He said it is very exciting to see his projects unfold before his eyes. He spent a lot of time last fall planning the changes and it gives him much pride seeing it coming to completion. As soon as he said completion he had to correct himself, "I probably will never be done with what I want to do here. I still need to advertise more in the newspaper to help lure the customers as well as create a back room for high stake poker games. Then I'll be content. Of course eventually, I'd like to get pool tables and private hot tubs for the wealthiest customers. I suppose I'll never be finished."

June 23, 1900   3:15 a.m.

Tonight the main topic of conversation in The Belmont was the numerous vessels in the ocean. Hundreds of people left their footprints in the wet golden beaches as they disembarked and walked right into history. Everyone agreed there was no place else where you had thousands of people waiting to go ashore. The newspaper even said the scene was "worthy of the brush of an artist of renown." I must admit the fleet of ships anchored in the midnight sun was a beautiful sight. I counted over 25 vessels of varying sizes.

The people arriving today don't know how lucky they are. This is one of the calmest days I have ever experienced. There isn't even a trace of a breeze. Strange for a land where the wind is a very common sound. No air movement means no waves to battle as one approaches the shores. With such warm temperature, the water may even be refreshing. The ocean looks like a smooth sheet of royal blue glass making the sky pale in comparison. The only noticeable feature in the giant body of water today is Sledge Island several miles south of Nome. It looks like it grows straight out of the water, with a steep incline on the east side and completely flat on top.

No wind also means lots of mosquitoes. That is another reason I think the new arrivals are lucky. With their first steps on the golden beaches of Nome, the blood-sucking insects will welcome them. That way they know right away how annoying these damn suckers can be. If their constant buzzing is too intense for the ears, then one can just swim back to the barge. That would just save a lot of time and money. On a day like today, the thought of leaving this land of mosquitoes is very tempting. If it wasn't for the gold I sure wouldn't be here, nor would the masses that surround me. I remember writing when I was on the ship before we first arrived. I said it had been worth the trip just to see that outstanding mountain range. Deep down inside I still believe that if something bad should come of this adventure, the travel to this "Great Land", which is what Kuduk says Alaska means, would have been worth the effort. It's much easier to enjoy summer when the wind blows.

June 24, 1900   **3:00 p.m.**

As I predicted, the men who make up the city government were too overwhelmed by the masses to solve the sanitation problem. As a result, today the Chamber of Commerce requested General George Randall, the commander of all military forces in Alaska, to take control of the city of Nome. They have asked him not only to police the town, but also to enforce sanitation and quarantine regulations, and "to provide for the general welfare and protection of life and property." I for one am delighted to see something like this happen. We can't keep living in this filth. I hear more people are getting sick. The city has lost the sanitation battle. Hopefully the Army can win the war against the human debris.

June 25, 1900   **3:25 p.m.**

I just got back from walking west of the tents and I saw the saddest thing of my life. There on the beach was a whale taking his last breath. I guess it had become stranded in the sand. I don't understand how. It was humbling to see this massive animal die right before my eyes. No telling how long he had been suffering. If a creature of his size has so little control over his life, what little control does a person of my size have over hers?

June 26, 1900 3:30 p.m.

Natalie was in another unpleasant state of mind today after receiving a letter from Seattle. The letter was written by the head mistress of the baby farm where her children are staying. The letter informed Natalie that there had been an unfortunate accident to her daughter. While the attendants were out for the evening, the cook took advantage of the situation and raped the young girl several times. It was rumored that he left the city minutes later, but it was several hours before Natalie's daughter was found in the cellar, bleeding badly. The letter went on to say that since that day she hasn't spoken a word to anyone, not even her younger brother. The mistress closed by saying she would write if anything changed. After reading the letter to me, Natalie starting throwing all of her belongings around her tent. I stepped out of her way and let her release her anger.

By work time this evening it was like nothing had happened earlier to upset her. She was even cheerful, like how she used to be after her monthly beating. Now I'm worried about her. She has got to be hurting inside and sooner or later she is going to blow. I sure hope she doesn't kill anyone.

June 27, 1900 4:15 a.m.

This evening while walking on the tundra, questions flowed through my mind. Why does the tundra look like it has dents in it? Is it because animals bed down in it at night, or is it the heat from the earth creating the collapse? Why do rocks protrude randomly throughout the tundra? What has broken and shattered the pieces of shale at the top of the knolls? Why does nature create flowers with perfect heart-shaped petals? I was in awe when I saw that each of the five yellow petals of the flower were tiny hearts. What is it that smells so good growing on the tundra? I know it's not the flowers—they don't seem to have that much aroma. Why does the earth smell so good after the sunset? Why does an eagle lose one feather at a time? I found a large one tonight and I will consider it a lucky charm. What causes a bird's wing to get broken? Why is the wind perfectly still right before a storm? Why is the weather so dismal for such long periods of time? Why is it that the more man-made filth and destruction I witness, the more connected I am to the earth?

I wonder why I never hear thunder? Why do I have a faint memory of my father holding me in his big arms, making me feel safe and secure during a thunderstorm?

My last wonderment of the evening is why men need to be so demeaning. On my return this evening, I was confronted by that intoxicated simpleton who likes to heckle me. He repeated questions that had to do with his horse's cock. Would it fit inside me? Would I like it? Would his horse like it? Why does that man have to be such an ass?

June 28, 1900   4:05 a.m.

Lucius Golden and Frank Simons opened a no-limit Faro game at the Hub Saloon for the day. Everything was going great until Jimmie the Goat raked in $14,000. Then a free-for-all broke out. Someone fired a gun then fled out the back door. Nobody knows for sure who was shooting or why. After that, the crowd grew so large, the game had to be moved into The Northern Saloon. That couldn't have made J.J.'s friend Tex Rickard happier. It was proof that he did indeed have the biggest saloon this far north. That evening after closing I could tell by J.J.'s demeanor he was indeed jealous of Tex. He kept boasting that by next winter he would have the longest bar in Nome, made from the finest hand carved walnut.

June 29, 1900   2:30 p.m.

New arrivals swear that from the deck of their ship, Nome looked like it was covered with snow. Only after getting closer did they realize that the snow banks were actually thousands of tents, which gold seekers have staked for miles along the shore. General Randall told me he has estimated there are 16,000 people in Nome as of today. I hear that Nome is the busiest seaport in the world without a deep-water harbor. From my understanding, ferrying thousands of people and tons of freight ashore to Nome has become a complex operation. I also hear that it costs almost as much to carry a load of freight the last mile through the surf to the shore as it costs to transport it over 2,000 miles from Seattle. If it weren't for gold fever, no one would pay for such a crazy ordeal.

With the town hectic, the ladies have had an average of 30 men a night, which explains why we've already gone through much of our butter supply. It is great to be a part of this gold rush. It is also great to be a madam and have more overnights, less men, more profit!

June 30, 1900   3:30 a.m.

Tonight I received another visit from Oliver, the lawyer with the big mouth. Right away he started talking about his plan to rule Nome. He said they had run into some trouble because McKenzie's senator friend, Thomas Carter of Montana, could not get the amendment to the Alaska Civil Code passed to prevent aliens from holding claims. He said they have a new place to use the backup plan, which is to control the judicial appointments in Nome. This plan sounds like it might work. It's starting to scare me. I'm worried that it might affect Jafet and his partners. What worries me more is why Oliver is telling me all this.

June 30, 1900   3:20 p.m.

Today General Randall ordered everyone in Nome to clean up their own property. His soldiers watched to make sure this was enforced. He ordered that at least six public closets be built over the water "far enough out to allow the tide to do the cleansing work." Starting today, soldiers will routinely patrol the streets to ensure regulations are met. He appointed several health inspectors to create pest houses so contagious people living and arriving in Nome remained quarantined. Given the unsanitary conditions here, both civilian and military leaders fear that an epidemic of typhoid fever or pneumonia might sweep through the town, killing thousands of people. The filthiest part of the community is behind the large saloons and false-front buildings on Main Street, right where our new cribs are being built. Straw, paper, and packing materials have been piled across pools of stagnant water and urine to create pathways just to give us a place to walk.

July 1900

July 1, 1900   **3:15 p.m.**

At times I feel rather sorry for the new gold seekers. The first sight they see as they come ashore are the heaps of freight that have been thrown randomly onto the sand. Finding their luggage is a chore in itself, assuming it hasn't been looted or destroyed in the surf. With the ocean on one side, and the high piles of merchandise on the other, it's not an easy matter to maneuver along the crowded beach. Luckily for the newcomers, there are teamsters with horses and carts or dog sleds for hire.

Nome has such a short mining season, every day counts. The miners don't have time to waste on shopping. So, to help out the busy miners and ensure a steady business, several butchers, grocers and bakers are selling their goods right along the 30-mile stretch of beach. I've even heard some of the madams are taking their girls down to the beach. We won't have to be moving to the shore since our business is overflowing with affluent clientele, thanks to our page in the Nome entertainment directory. Jeremy believes the more money the customer has the more you can charge him.

July 2, 1900   **2:25 p.m.**

Right now it is the warmest I have ever felt it here. The wind has been blowing from the north all day. Thanks to a make shift slaughterhouse at Dexter Creek that butchers cattle and sheep brought in from Seattle, the whole town reeks of dead animals. I guess I shouldn't complain. At least there is fresh meat in town, unlike last winter when food was scarce.

July 3, 1900   **3:45 p.m.**

Nowadays, the city of Nome is two blocks wide and about five miles long. Front Street is the main access through the city, and in places it is less than 15 feet wide. We now have a First and Second street, which are about eight feet wide. To utilize every available inch of space, several businesses down by the shore have built on top of pilings. J.J. has recently invested in another laundry business. He believes any business on wooden logs close to the water is a worthwhile investment.

The heart of the city contains the biggest saloons, hotels and restaurants. The city is so crowded that people are actually jammed elbow to elbow along the storefronts. Shopping has turned into a nightmare. Simply walking through the streets is a hassle; between holding my dress and carrying parcels, it's almost impossible. I have no idea how Natalie finds such an activity enjoyable.

July 5, 1900   **5:10 a.m.**

In comparing last year's Fourth of July to this year's, I only see one similarity. Both are holidays, which is a formal excuse to carouse. In contrast, I see numerous differences. Last year, there was only spoken prejudice for the aliens, but this year, if what Oliver says is true, the hatred and greed has expanded to the lower states and McKenzie will be their star performer.

There are now more than 13,000 to 17,000 people in Nome depending on whom one believes. Newspapers, census agents, common folk, and the Army all have different opinions. It's estimated that last year the population was made up of mostly miners and business-minded people. Now there are a good portion

of sporting girls, gamblers, and criminals. It's rumored this is
the wickedest place on the continent—even worse than Butte,
Montana.

Last year I could see the tiny island off to the south of Nome
from my tent. This year all I see as I look in any direction is
dust. We have had a dry summer compared to last year. Last year
Front Street consisted of mostly tents with a path in between.
Today when I was standing on the boardwalk all I could see were
permanent structures housing some type of commerce. Most every
building proudly flew the American flag on a pole attached close
to the front door. None are as beautiful as the Strater Hotel back in
Durango. With the many hours I spent watching it being built as a
child, its tall brick walls are still vivid in my mind.

Lumber is expensive and scarce, and there are more people
here than there are accommodations. To take advantage of the
situation, several owners have tied up their vessels inside the
mouth of the Snake River and turned them into floating booty-
makers, whether it is a hotel, restaurant, boarding house, or a
private hospital. I heard they got the idea from the forty-niners in
the San Francisco Bay.

T.J. Nester has created the first floating hotel, "The City
of Chicago." It is also one of the nicest hotels in Nome. His
remodeled ship is big enough to accommodate 175 people with
private quarters going for $1 a night. His beer gardens and Key
West cigars are already competition for the other fine saloons in
town.

Of the hundred plus watering holes on land, the classiest ones
are: Wyatt Earp's Dexter, Charles Cobb's Horseshoe, William
Robertson's Eldorado, Tex Rickard's Northern, and of course
Jeremy James' very own Belmont. All those saloons are in a
class of their own, but by far the finest I have ever seen is Lucky
Baldwin's Saloon. The Baldwin is unique in many ways. It has the
finest piano in town, admirable mahogany bar fixtures, a beautiful
mirror behind the bar, and stained glass windows throughout the
establishment. I love being in there because it is so elegant.

I can't forget to mention the most unusual saloon in Nome—Dick Dawson and Charles Suter's Second Class Saloon. The reason it is so unusual is it has a large sewer that extends from the rear of the building to the low tide line. The two of them are always bragging that every 24 hours, their sewer gets flushed out. Of course, all of the Saloon names, plus more, can be found on the banners hung across Front Street.

Jafet has confided in me that his company has sold four claims to Charles D. Lane, a millionaire out of San Francisco. Now Lane has plans to create a pipe water system out to Anvil so he can upscale his mining operation. He's the one who is going to use the narrow gauge tracks for his train to transport him back and forth. Because of my connection to Jafet, I hope to ride the train to Anvil so I can begin my walking journey from there. This tent city has swelled to such a point it literally takes me half of an hour to escape from all the commotion.

Last year, we thought there would be a sanitation problem. This year we are engulfed in it. People descended on the shores of the Bering Sea so quickly, how could anything realistically have been done to prevent this ruination? Last Fourth of July, the fine gold on the beach was abundant. This year it appears depleted. The majority of miners are wishing for a huge storm. They believe the rough wave action could replenish the golden beaches.

In this last year, the alliance has seen some changes as well. We have lost two—Ria and Jime. And we have gained two—Margerie and Kuduk, both real assets. I have stopped worrying about Dorothy not grieving. Instead, I admire her strength more each day.

Last year on the Fourth, the alliance was busy working; there was no time for personal pleasure, just recuperation. This year was different.

After all of us took a bath and dressed in our finest clothes, we posed for a photograph in front of The Belmont. With some convincing, Kuduk joined us. The image will be forever planted in my mind. Jeremy James is standing in back of me with Ryan and Kuduk on his right. Alex and Natalie are to my right and Margerie and Dorothy are to the left. I don't like it that the photographer asked us not to smile. He said a smile uses more muscles, therefore, more chances of a blur. In his black hat, white coat, with his hands in his black vest pockets, I think J.J. appropriately dominates the picture. After all, none of us would be working out of these structures if it wasn't for him. I believe my physical arrangement in the picture shows respect for my position within the alliance.

I wore a low cut, light pink dress with black trim. My large hat with a perfect balance of feathers, flowers, and lace complimented my face. Even though we weren't suppose to smile, Alex still radiated with happiness. I think it was more her growing relationship with J.J. than the light green dress and matching hat she was wearing. I hate to say it, but Natalie looks heavier in the photo than she does in real life. I wonder if it was the black dress she was wearing. Her dark skin and her dark dress blend together, and none of her facial features stand out. Ryan's happiness can still be seen, even without him smiling. He wore a white working shirt with a small, white towel resting on his arm. His long red beard was neatly groomed; he looks honest and trustworthy. Margerie's long wavy hair and her serious eyes grab a person's attention. Her light blue dress helps create a perfect balance between the blacks and the whites in the photo. Dorothy's long braids hang on her large bosoms as usual. Her happiness is also apparent. Kuduk looks like a very wise, old man. In real life, he is a very wise man, but he is young. It is funny how a photograph can catch a moment and reveal a wealth of information about its prisoners in time.

As soon as the group photograph was taken J.J. surprised me with a request to have a picture taken with his business partner. The next surprise came when he insisted I sit for an individual photograph. He said, "Mandy, you deserve a picture of yourself. Something to always remind you of what a successful Madam you have become, and to help remind you of the prospects ahead." There was no time to explain to J.J. that I was very uncomfortable just looking in a mirror and the last thing I wanted was a picture reminding me of what I had become. J.J. must not feel any guilt for his profit. I guess I carry enough for the both of us.

The last thing the beloved alliance did was agree that when we get the photograph in a few days it will be hung behind the bar, next to the Nome Cash Register—one of the many products coming out of Seattle, designed especially for this gold rush. Others include the Nome Rocker and the Nome Medicine Chest.

July 6, 1900   2:50 a.m.

This place is ridiculous. When the weather is dry as it has been throughout the early part of this summer, Front Street is like a dust storm. When the winds really pick up, the sand is as bad as the piercing snow. It's been raining since yesterday and already the sandy roadways have turned into rivers of mud. People and horses alike nearly drown in the muck just trying to get from one side to the other. The talk in The Belmont this evening was that to avoid endangering one's life a wise person must plan his or her activities so as to stay on one side of the street.

July 7, 1900   3:40 a.m.

This evening I was privileged to have an overnight visit from General Randall. He said he was forced to take over Nome because the sanitation had reached the critical stage. He also stated quite firmly that he intended to keep Nome under military rule until the newly appointed District Judge Arthur Noyes arrives in a few weeks. I was happy to hear somebody finally had authority in Nome and was concerned about the sanitation and other problems facing this area.

July 8, 1900   4:50 a.m.

Just as we were closing this evening, Jafet came up to me and slipped a nugget into my hand and asked me if I would go on a walk with him. I couldn't resist because it was one of those rare evenings when there was not a cloud in the sky and the midnight sun was shinning. As we walked, he told me how he had come to Alaska Territory. He reminded me he was brought here to herd reindeer. While he was at Golovin Bay, John Brynteson confided to Jafet and his other friend Eric Lindblom his hunch that there was gold around Cape Nome. Eric was a Swedish sailor who had jumped ship to follow his dream of wealth.

As he talked I enjoyed the scenery around me. I saw five whales swimming in the water all coming up for air at the same time. The blue sky sparkled against the brilliant glistening water as the massive black and white creatures gracefully moved in and out of the water. It was a sight to behold. I got so excited that I wanted to show Jafet but he didn't seem to care. He came for the gold and he doesn't have time to enjoy the wildlife here. It saddened my heart that he was so narrowly focused on his greed he couldn't see the priceless splendor surrounding us.

July 9, 1900   2:55 p.m.

I hear stories that everything here in Nome costs two to five times more than it does in Seattle or San Francisco. It is rumored miners average $20 to $100 a day: cigars sell for $.25. A package of Durham tobacco, which costs $.20 in the states, is going for $.75. I can't believe how expensive everything is. A person can spend $.50 to take a bath and $.10 to $.25 just to use a public outhouse. I have heard real estate prices are as high here as they are in New York City. I'm told the high cost of lumber and construction material has made it impossible for most gold seekers to build their own shacks. As a result, people are once again using anything they can find to sleep in. Today I saw a man sleeping in a dug out hole with an animal hide on top for his roof. I also saw someone sleeping in a kayak that had been turned on its side, as well as people sleeping in abandoned packing crates. I hear those people are the lucky ones. It reminds me of last summer, only now there are four times as many people.

July 10, 1900   2:50 a.m.

Before the shift started, it stopped raining and the sun peeked out from behind the clouds. I took advantage and went on a swift walk on the tundra. I have no fear because there are no snakes.

I've always been afraid of them. In Colorado, that kept me from walking very far by myself. In Seattle, I was too busy learning the trade to explore nature. Up here I feel like I'm transformed when I go out walking by myself. Not only am I escaping from the filth of the populace, I'm escaping from the filth that grows within me with each day's profit. In Nome and in this profession, one deals with numerous human snakes. At least when I walk on the tundra I never have to worry that a real snake is going to be touching my feet or crawling up my gumboots. This knowledge helps me relax and enjoy my time with nature.

July 11, 1900   **3:45 a.m.**

Margerie came to my tent after work very depressed. This evening a man wanted to get his pleasure by shitting on her naked body. She couldn't degrade herself that low and she refused. Then her client slapped her across the face and said, "Whore, I own you until I'm done. I'll do whatever I want." Margerie saw no way out of the situation so she let the man do what he had paid for. I reminded her she sets the limits of what she will tolerate, and if there was a problem to call out and someone from the alliance will be there to help her.

As Margerie left my tent, I was in a stupor. I thought about the advice I had given her. "You have to get used to men demeaning you, it's part of selling your body. You can always say no if it is something out of the ordinary." What is ordinary and what isn't? It all seems so disgusting. Looking outside my tent, all I see is filth and disgust everywhere. I begin to wonder, is what I do worth it? Are all those nuggets and fine gold that I stash away really worth the humiliation I put myself through? How can I encourage other ladies to put themselves through this? I don't know. I guess there is no turning back, but I wish I had never chosen this path. I strive so hard not to have shame, but each day it wears me down a little more. When it all comes down to it, I put up with this every day because someday I will retire wealthy.

I just remembered another dream I had about the dark skinned girl dressed in beautiful furs. She was giving me feathers with intricate designs. Each time she gave me one she repeated, "If it wasn't for the animals you wouldn't survive." With each feather my body felt noticeably stronger.

July 12, 1900   **3:40 p.m.**

Lately the talk in town is of the large percentage of penniless people here. The situation is really getting pathetic and unless steps are taken to provide for these people hardship will prevail. The huge number of unemployed men is steadily driving wages down. The ease of getting here has lured many unsuspecting gold hunters north with only a few hundred dollars. They came expecting gold to be showered upon them, but the only shower they find is the rain day after day. Of course, the conversation always comes back to the wisdom Canada showed by requiring miners to have a year's worth of supplies before entering their country. Oh, the advantages of thinking ahead!

July 13, 1900   **3:45 p.m.**

I heard today that on June 6, 1900, president William McKinley signed the code of "civil procedure." This act will permit cities in Alaska Territory of more than 3,000 people to incorporate and to collect taxes for local improvements. This is marvelous! Maybe now Nome will have the opportunity to become an elegant city.

July 14, 1900   **2:50 p.m.**

Last night after work Alex came to my tent. We didn't explore the passions we have for one another as usual. Instead, we exchanged ideas and asked questions that we had no answers for. For example, why are humans the only species of this earth to crave lust other than for procreation? Are there prostitutes among any of God's other creatures? Are there similarities in the way men treat lewd women and nature? Aren't they both used for gratification with little regard for the consequences? Will mankind ever see that it is our own ignorance that kills us?

July 15, 1900   **3:05 a.m.**

I went to the post office after brunch and I had to wait several hours to pick up a few letters. I passed some time looking into the windows of The Alaska Chicago Commercial Company. They sell so many different items. The line to pick up mail was so long that it wound around the block. I hear tell that since there are so many people without an address or a permanent shelter, Nome has the largest general delivery service in the United States. A 30-by-35 foot shack serves as the Nome post office. Twenty-four clerks work three eight-hour shifts. Even with all those workers, mail is still several months late in being delivered. One of those postal clerks is a client of mine and he disclosed there are five boxes for people named Johnson alone. He also said that Tony, the postmaster, is planning on hiring two mail carriers to help eliminate the time-consuming task of waiting to pick up mail. They will deliver to people with permanent addresses. Having the mail delivered to The Belmont will ensure our profits continue instead of someone from the alliance having to waste time waiting in line.

J.J. and I both received a letter today from his mother in Durango. In J.J.'s letter, she asked him several questions about how he was doing. In mine, she updated me on her busy social life. She said she was very involved in the paperwork of last May's land rush. It was such a grand day in Durango that the children even got out of school to watch. She ended that topic by stating that, of course, the Ute Indians kept the best land for themselves. That comment made me sad for her prejudice. Why shouldn't they keep the best land? It was their land first.

She went on to say that the family had a wonderful Christmas dinner at The Strater Hotel and it was the highlight of the old year. This New Year finds her very active with the Durango Reading Club. In fact, her turn for hosting the weekly meeting was quickly approaching. She said she was looking forward to summer and her membership in the Durango Wheel Club, and she had already purchased a complete set of riding clothes, including a long skirt, leggings, and bloomers. She concluded by telling me there was a new beer garden on an island in the middle of the Animas River, where several of her women friends get together in the afternoon to have a cold draft.

I wonder if Geneva knows what type of service I provide for J.J.'s business? I noticed she didn't ask me any questions about myself. I take it as her way of telling me she doesn't want to know.

As usual Ryan received the most letters and parcels. He said it is because he comes from a large family. Then he confessed that the real reason is he takes the time each morning to write to a least one member of his family. He said, "How can you expect a loved one to write to you if you don't write to them?" He also explained his ritual of a quick walk before brunch was always to mail a letter. There is a lot I don't know about Ryan. Hopefully I will learn more each day.

July 16, 1900   12:30 a.m.

The long awaited day finally arrived! The Bantam Belmont did not open up for business today. Instead we spent our time and energy moving into our new cribs. Some people are already calling this part of town "The Blockade" while others are calling it "The Stockade." I finally got to hang the wooden signs Ryan made for each lady's crib door so clients will know where to go for his desired dove. The gentlemen we serve know the ladies by their working names. Out of respect, when we are not working I always call my ladies by the names they were given—the ones they are trying to protect. That respect goes so far that I have never even written our "working names" in my diary. These are the names the ladies in the kinship use to protect their blood families back home. In the business I am known as, "Rosie May." I got my name from Rosa who loved to give all the ladies she started in the business a name that had the word rose in it. Alex is "Baby Blue Nut" because of her walnut shaped eyes. Natalie is "Big Nasty Nat" (she likes her name) and Margerie is referred to as "Flaming Red." Ryan gave her that name.

I'm happy to say my crib is far cleaner than my tent with its dirt floor ever was. Still, no matter how expsensive my consumer guide rugs are, they get stained. I decided to put my bed on the north wall next to the coal stove. On the south side as I enter my small space, I have my desk and a small chair. In the corner is a room divider with my washbasin in back. I have created a small space so if a man wants to wash up, he can have a little privacy.

I spent several minutes today deciding exactly where I want to hang each one of my ten calendar pictures. Alex and I each gave Natalie two of our pictures to replace what she had lost in the blizzard. Margerie doesn't have any calendars yet. Being new to the business she hasn't learned how important they are to us. Given time, she will learn lots of things. I'm overwhelmed with joy to be in my own crib. A wooden shelter brings so much security. Now that we are living in our cabins, I need to start paying J.J. back for the wood. If it was not for his money we would still be living in tents until next summer.

July 17, 1900   2:10 p.m.

Waking up this morning in my own crib was very comforting. For the first time in a long while I woke up when I was ready and not when someone was conversing outside of my tent. I can already tell that I will cherish this new found silence that surrounds me, but at the same time I will miss walking around the other ladies' tents after working hours, and eavesdropping on whatever gratifying activity is occurring inside.

I was in such high spirits that I walked down to the California Bakery Café and bought several yummy pastries. They smelled delicious, and I couldn't wait to share them with the alliance. I ran back on the boardwalk as fast as I could. It wasn't really to keep the goodies warm as much as a strong desire from within that said, "Run, feel the warm breeze in your face." I hope that every day I awake in my new crib will be as wonderful as this one.

July 18, 1900   2:40 p.m.

I had the pleasure and the pain of another overnight from Milroy. I was ecstatic to see him again, having missed the way he brings out the animal spirit in me. I also missed hearing his mining stories. His deep, resonating voice is the most hypnotic quality he possesses. I was experiencing much pleasure being in his company, but as soon as we were alone the pain began. He seems to enjoy hurting me. My whole relationship with him is deranged. It continuously moves from love to hate, pain to pleasure.

This time as we were making merry bout he went into great detail about the moans Alex makes when he is inside of her. He said she makes so much noise a man can't help but think she is enjoying herself. As he says those things to me, as much as I hate it, I can't help but get aroused. Then I become irate at myself so I continuously move from ecstasy to guilt. After about ten minutes, he exploded inside of me and I couldn't help reaching satisfaction just from feeling his electricity throughout my whole body.

Afterwards I lay in his arms, which is something I had never done before. In the comfort of the moment he revealed some of his past. He used to run with an outlaw gang. They were very tight, and he liked it that way. There was nothing the others wouldn't do for a gang member. He said, "Those were my wild days when I could just take whatever I wanted. It didn't matter if I hurt anyone in the process. We had the power to do it." I started getting real intimidated thinking, "Here I am with this outlaw, who hurts people for amusement." I suppose if he planned on hurting me, he probably would have done it already. I had better be extra cautious now that he is starting to share some of his experiences with me.

The biggest surprise came when he said, "Mandy, I have plans for us. I'm working on a little plan that's going to make me rich and when it does, I'm taking you and we're leaving this rainy gold rush town. We are going some place where it's warm." He continued, "It doesn't matter what you want. You're coming with me and that's that."

As he drifted into sleep, I grew furious. What makes him think I would want to go with him? He didn't even ask. He just assumes because that's what he wants, he can have it. Oh, that man makes me fume. At the same time, a part of me loves the idea of getting out of this business and having a man to take care of me. I guess sometimes I want that but I'm not sure. I don't know what I want. It's all too confusing. I did ask him how Rawslin and Clark are doing. He replied, "I'm not wasting my time talking about them, I'm here to see you. Clark will be here next month to get supplies. I'm sure you'll find out then."

July 19, 1900   3:20 p.m.

The steamship *Senator* pulled into port today with the long awaited Judge Noyes. Ever since the word reached Nome about the passage of the Alaska Civil Code, the citizens have eagerly awaited the court to arrive so military control can once again be replaced by civil law.

There were a lot of people down by the beach to welcome the judge. Of course I didn't want to miss all the excitement so I was there also. After about five minutes, a burly man walked off the ship. The voice in my head told me right away this must be Alexander McKenzie and everything Oliver had said about their plan was true. Once I knew it was him, I had to get closer. McKenzie looked like an evil sorcerer. One look and I grasped what a powerful and dangerous man he was. I could see it in his eyes.

After McKenzie left, I remained on the beach with a group of onlookers, still waiting to get a glimpse of the judge. By the time I left, he still hadn't exited the ship. Maybe he is McKenzie's puppet. I began to grow concerned that the reality of their devious plan of stealing from the miners was taking form. Should I tell somebody? Would they believe me?

July 20, 1900   3:00 p.m.

I just returned from a quick walk around the town. The lack of wind prevented me from going further. I must make note that for the first time since the ships began arriving in May, I hear more piano music in the background than hammers. That could mean two things. Either the number of saloons is increasing daily or Nome has expanded at such a rate that the only building going on now is at the edges of the town site and too far away for the tools to be heard.

Maybe I'm just focusing more on the piano music. I find myself able to tell the time of day by it. One knows it is noon when the tunes begin. One can also count the fourteen hours of trade by the fifteen minute breaks the player is allow to have each hour. Then finally the silence returns, informing all residents the working day is over.

July 21, 1900   3:30 p.m.

I woke up in the middle of the night to relieve myself and when I walked outside to put my pee bucket beside my crib, I was captivated by the crispness in the air and the sun that already felt warm. I quickly went back into my crib, packed some jerky, water, and my gun, then I left a note on my bed telling J.J. and Alex that it was 6:30 a.m. and I was headed north.

Because I started my journey so early this morning, I was able to walk further than ever before. I walked to the top of the knoll beside Anvil Creek. My heart was spellbound by the spectacular sight, which caused my breathing to change in a way I have never known. With each breath my body seemed to keep the air in my lungs for as long as it could. I was deeply relaxed. The crispness of the morning created clarity that surpassed all my past experiences. The more I observed, the more detail I saw in each separate mountain. The rugged range farthest away was very light blue, the exact hue as the sky. The closer the set of peaks, the darker shade of blue that defined its grandeur. The rolling hills with their mix of jade and brown appeared to move slowly as it blended mosses, rocks, grasses and shrubs in the landscape. The smells of the intoxicating long-stemmed flowers swaying gently in the wind were a constant reminder that they surrounded me. I have learned those pinkish-purple flowers are called fireweed, because they do make the scenery look as if it were on fire.

I spent some time sitting on a large piece of broken shale admiring the show that nature presented today. When it was time to leave, "Thank you" slipped off my tongue. I must have been talking to the creator of the earth.

I believe this day has been a highlight of my exploration in nature. I'm already anticipating walking to the same spot when the sun is behind the mountains.

July 23, 1900   **2:30 a.m.**

The weather today was even better than yesterday so I couldn't resist asking everyone in the alliance to cover for me while I escaped for the whole day, and not just a few hours as usual. My family was more than happy to do that for me because they all know what a passion I have for the land. We know each other pretty well after more than a year of hearing each other's stories at brunch. J.J. is always talking about his investments, Ryan the saloon, Kuduk hunting, Alex her cards, and Natalie her facts of science. Margerie always has a story to tell about meeting someone new. We all have something we love to do and we do it well.

After my experience this evening I have to correct myself. I thought yesterday was the ultimate day, but now I would have to say my walk this evening holds first place. The sun behind the mountain range to the north was more magnificent than I would have ever imagined anything to be. It was the most tranquil encounter with the earth I have ever known.

The tips of the mountain peaks were aglow with brilliant white light, the last of the day's warmth. Directly above the peaks was a thick white line of drifting clouds. Above was a sky unlike any I had ever seen. Instead of any hint of blue or charcoal the sky was alive with bright shades of rose, violet and tangerine. Directly above was a much thicker set of huge puffy clouds lazily floating higher into the heavens.

I sat there staring for what seemed hours. I felt like a queen overlooking my majestic kingdom. The three peaks closest together resembled three fingers sticking up in the air. This was my castle. I decided I love not having my view distracted by trees. Maybe the fact I can see the horizon in every direction is why the tundra has such a hypnotic effect on me.

July 25, 1900   3:05 a.m.

Well, it happened! McKenzie and Noyes put their plan into
action. As I write, it is already prosperous for them. McKenzie is
now in control of a half a dozen valuable mining claims, each of
which is worth about $5,000. I know this because I had another
visit from Oliver this evening. This time he didn't even attempt to
get aroused. Instead he just paced back and forth in my room and
told me the last few days since McKenzie arrived has been hell.
He said McKenzie is now the secretary of the Alaska Gold Mining
Co. and that he has made threats against Oliver and his partners,
Beeman and Hume. If they didn't agree to go along with the plan,
McKenzie would ruin them and they would never win a suit again
in Alaska Territory.

Oliver said McKenzie went on to openly boast that he owned
and controlled the court. It had cost him $60,000 to have the
judge appointed and brought here. He also boasted he had paid
off Noyes' mortgage in Minnesota. Oliver almost cried when he
said that he and his secretaries worked all day and night for two
days straight turning out the flood of necessary documents. Oliver
said while he worked, McKenzie paced the floor of the office,
repeating, "I am worried the judge might lose his nerve, so speed is
essential." In the late afternoon when all the legal paperwork was
ready for the judge's approval, Oliver took the documents to Judge
Noyes' room in the Golden Gate Hotel, and he signed the papers
without even reading them. As soon as McKenzie knew the papers
had been signed, he and a deputy U.S. Marshal took two horse-
drawn wagons out to Anvil Creek. They began serving the papers,
which ordered the defendants to give him immediate possession of
their claims.

I can't believe this is happening and I didn't do anything. I'm
not sure what I could have done to stop it. I had put it in the back
of my mind. There was so much going on, and now Jafet and his
partners will suffer greatly. It's not fair! Jafet rightfully owns those
claims. Greed wears many ugly faces but I think this is the ugliest I
have seen since arriving on these golden beaches.

July 25, 1900   **3:15 p.m.**

My heart goes out to Jafet and his partners in the Pioneer
Mining Company and the Wild Goose Mining and Trading
Company. Their claims have been taken away from them and they
have no effective opposition. McKenzie, who is now the receiver
and is supposed to protect the interest of both the plaintiff and the
defendant, is working the richest claims in Nome as if he owned
them. The military force here in Nome is on McKenzie's side and
is prepared to back up his authority and the orders of the district
court. McKenzie even has the town's people fooled. I read in the
paper today in reference to McKenzie, "The gentleman possesses
excellent executive ability and has experience which will fit him
admirably for the responsible position to which Judge Noyes has
appointed him." He has lots of people fooled, but not me. I have
started telling people what I know about McKenzie, but they all
look at me like I'm stupid. How would a lady of the night know
something like that? Little do they know that some men enjoy
talking as much as they do receiving pleasure. I'm a daughter of
sin and my opinion doesn't count for anything.

July 26, 1900   **3:30 a.m.**

Jafet was in The Belmont this evening for a drink. Things
have gone from bad to worse. He said the attorneys for the Pioneer
Mining Company and the Wild Goose Mining and Trading
Company protested the appointment of McKenzie as the receiver.
Noyes heard their argument but refused to make a decision on
the motion. In the meantime, Jafet said his men were "allegedly
interfering with the work of the receiver at the Discovery claim."
Yesterday Noyes signed an order, which increased McKenzie's
power. Jafet cursed loudly, "Now that crook has the right to
confiscate everything on my claim. He can even rightfully take the
gold and moneyboxes, and there's absolutely nothing we can do
about it."

Before Jafet hurried off, I quickly told him what I knew of
McKenzie's plot and that he is a very powerful man in Washington.
I could tell Jafet wasn't sure of the truth in my information, but

he thanked me for it and gave me a quick kiss on the cheek before leaving.

July 27, 1900   2:50 p.m.

Walking has become a ritual in my life. Unless it is pouring rain, I tolerate the drizzle. Today I had the pleasure of becoming acquainted with five older Inuit women on the tundra picking greens and berries. We did not speak the same language but that didn't stop us from communicating. Through their smiles and their magnetic brown eyes, I know they were all gentle spirits. Their whole beings radiated of peace, harmony and tranquility. Through their hand gestures and their giggling, I learned about the needles of a plant I could pick to make what I will call Inuit tea. They were all so warm and friendly to me it touched my heart in a way I had never known before from strangers. After meeting these people, I have a desire to learn their language so I can converse with them. I'm intrigued with what brings them the happiness they possess. I would also like to know what the tattoos on their faces represent.

July 28, 1900   3:20 p.m.

Once again I must admit the more time I spend getting to know Ryan, the more I respect him. When I complimented him on his efficiency in running the saloon he said, "You know, Mandy, a mixoligist is kind of like the captain of a ship. There is nothing I wouldn't do for this saloon. I'd go down with it if I had to. If there was a fire I would do anything I could to save the building, even if it meant my life. There is just a certain code that we live by and there is nothing we wouldn't do for a person once they enter our saloon. I have pulled teeth, and even sawed off crushed legs of miners in my time behind the bar. I've delivered babies and warned my town of three fires. Of course, you were there for the birth of baby Ryan." I asked if he had seen baby Ryan lately and he said, "Yes, and he is growing faster than the mining town." Before leaving, he thanked me for the compliment and for listening to him. What a thoughtful, caring person.

July 29, 1900   **4:35 a.m.**

While on a stroll this afternoon, I was joined by the fog. I could see it coming in from the south. Within a half hour I was completely surrounded by it. At first I was scared, not knowing what animal might cross my path. As the fear left my body, I began to enjoy the tranquility of the immense silence that had accompanied the low moist clouds.

I could see the fog was driven by the wind at a forever-changing pace. One minute I couldn't see what I was standing next to and tiny droplets of water were upon my face. The next minute the mist had retreated. Secretly I wished it would return and never leave.

The flowers reacted to the moisture by drooping over from the weight. I observed that silver droplets would cling to the leaves of some plants but not others. From my experiment of touching, I deducted that it was the shape or the texture of the leaves that determined when drops fell and when they stayed on the leaf.

The low clouds brought so much peacefulness into my existence it was as if my soul had been cleansed. When they started to lift and I could once again hear the sounds of civilization, I felt like running wildly to find the next patch of fog, hoping to keep that feeling of bliss inside me forever.

July 31, 1900   **10:40 a.m.**

Last night I had a request from three mining partners. They wanted the same woman all at the same time. I told them Natalie would be more than happy to oblige, but after seeing the picture of Alex, they insisted on having her for their evening pleasure. Alex wasn't excited about the idea, even though they were all quite attractive. But after they each agreed to pay her double, she said, "What the hell!" I was anxiously waiting to hear her exotic tales, but instead, I heard her saddest story.

It was the first time I had ever seen Alex melancholy. She said she had been emotional all day and just wanted to cry. While holding each other in bed, she started talking about her past. I don't like to ask people about themselves. I find it best not to ask too many questions so I have never pried into her business. She said that growing up she had four brothers and was the youngest in her family of five siblings. Her Mom had died giving birth to her and she never knew what it was like to have another female around. Alex said she was about sixteen years old when she figured out that other families were not like hers. Up until that time, she thought it was normal for the female of the house to do all the laundry, cooking, and cleaning. She also thought it was expected of her to be intimate whenever any of the males in the house had the desire (whether it was in the bed she shared with them, outside in the middle of the day, or in the evening after dinner for everyone to watch).

After much crying and silence, Alex giggled and said, "Maybe that's why I like being so full of healthy vigor. During that time I felt that my father and my brothers cared for me and were just giving me their love. After hearing from other young girls that things like that didn't happen at their house, a part of me wanted them to stop touching me. It was too late. I already learned of all the pleasure they bestowed on my body. There was no reason to think of it as a pain. There was nothing I could do to stop it. So why not enjoy it? They never once hurt me." From the giggles and the laughter came more tears and she softly said, "The only thing I regret is not ever getting to know my mother. What about your mom? Did you know her well?" I told her that if it wasn't for my mom, I don't know that I would be alive and that I pray to her every night. Alex then asked if she could start praying to my mom also. I replied, "Sure, I think my mom would like that." Then we said a little prayer to my mother and curled up in each other's arms. I told her how my mother cried on the day Aunt Flow visited me for the first time. My mother never said a word on that day; she just cried until my father came home. As soon has he walked in the door, she pretended everything was just as it should be. We never spoke on that subject, but she knew we would both have to be worried about getting pregnant with my father thinking he had the right to "educate his girls."

August 1900

August 1, 1900   **2:20 p.m.**

Upon entering The Belmont today, I noticed there was something different. There just didn't seem to be as many people hanging around, leaning on the walls, or slouching on the chairs. As I started inquiring, I discovered that McKenzie has hired all the idle miners available and is now working his claims at full force, taking out thousands of dollars of gold each day. Because McKenzie is keeping the records, the plaintiffs have no way of knowing how much gold the receiver is taking from their property. Since McKenzie's bond for each claim is only $5,000, which is equal to about one day's production, the miners whose claims he is milking will have no protection or legal resource if McKenzie depletes their mine. I wish now I had tried harder to do something or tell someone about McKenzie's plan before he arrived. I still don't know who I could have told that would make a difference. No one believes me now, so why would they have believed me then? I need to get my mind off the idea of helping the situation because there's nothing I can do. I wish Oliver had never told me any of this.

August 2, 1900   4:30 a.m.

The last few days have felt strange, like something heavy floating in the air is making Nome residents go berserk. The activities of Monday evening, July 30, were astounding. It started when a woman's tent was cut into while she was sleeping. She awoke screaming. Then in another tent Mr. Lindsay was jumped by two men and robbed of the medicine he was carrying. Two fires were reported that evening but were quickly extinguished and no one was hurt. The top story was soldiers breaking up a fight between a lady of evil repute and an unidentified man in front of the Columbia Theater. After being hit in the head with a hammer, the man grew very angry and tried to shoot the girl.

I'm thankful for the newspapers. They confirm that it's not just the members of The Belmont alliance that are affected by this strange energy in the air. Maybe it's the full moon.

The best part of the day was eating the baked fish Dorothy had prepared for us! What would we do without her?

August 3, 1900   2:50 a.m.

This evening while in The Belmont, I overheard a conversation between J.J. and Wyatt. Wyatt appeared to be more intoxicated than usual and he was saying he used to be a deputy marshal back in Tombstone, Arizona in 1881. He rumbled something about how one day his brothers and he got into a gunfight with the Clayton brothers. He said he would never forget his good friend, Doc Holiday, the dentist, who was by his side. I guess I was a little surprised to find out Wyatt used to be a marshal. I always thought of people in law enforcement as being real upstanding citizens, not woman beaters. Every madam in Nome has let it be known that Wyatt has beaten at least one of their ladies. If he ever tries that again on one of my flock, I will kill that man. Even if he was a deputy—if that is even the truth and not the booze talking. I'm sure he's a pretty good shot; I would still have to try. I couldn't live with myself if I didn't do something to help my ladies. The more I think about it the more I really believe I saw Wyatt in a gambling house on South Second in Seattle. I would ask him right out, but I strive to avoid the man.

August 4, 1900   4:00 a.m.

I love hearing the sound of raindrops landing on my tin roof. Each time it rains real hard, it seems to wash away the fifth and disgust growing in my body. The harder it rains the cleaner I feel. Oh, no! It is already letting up. I never imagined that I would want it to keep raining, but I want it to keep washing away the fifth.

August 5, 1900   2:40 p.m.

My gold collection has grown so much that now I have to keep it in large bags in J.J.'s vault, except for the seven nuggets that Jafet gave me for Christmas. Before going to bed most nights, I hold them in the palm of my hand. I love the way they feel so heavy. Holding the tiny beauties always elevates my spirits. It is as if a blissful sensation is coming off of them and going into my body.

I think when I leave Nome I will exchange my gold for some land back in Colorado. I sure miss the beautiful summers and the hot sunshine that warmed my body. I can already feel a hint of cold in the wind and it is just early August. It can't be time to start getting ready for winter! The browning tundra reminds me that it is.

August 6, 1900   3:00 p.m.

One of the main topics of discussion at our bathing time today was the opening of the first church in Nome. The Episcopalian Church is located on upper Stedman St. and is run by Reverend Blair. Already the influence of the church has changed the town. Natalie was the most excited about the opening. She really wishes she could go, but everyone knows women of easy virtue aren't allowed in churches.

The other topic concerned the new resolution that the Grand
Jury passed saying that women are no longer allowed in the
saloons. It was said women break the law too often and cause
all kinds of trouble. I was furious when I heard that. McKenzie
is causing all this anarchy in town and it is the women who will
have to pay the price. Of course, madams will still be allowed to
work the men in the saloons and cater to their needs, but women in
general will not be granted permission to drink in public.

The way I see it, those people who passed such a law are
frustrated by what McKenzie is doing to them but they can't do
anything to him to stop this madness. Instead, they exert their
power on the one thing they can still control—women. Will this
oppression of the female species ever end?

McKenzie's operation is a perfect example of how influential
men dominate the society. Will there ever come a time when
women will have a share in decision making?

August 7, 1900   2:30 p.m.

As much as I enjoy living in my own crib and being close
to other working ladies in the kinship, I am frustrated. We are
surrounded with rubbish and living in the most contaminated
area in the community. Each time I walk out of my door I am
overwhelmed with the stench of rotting human waste. It is a
reminder that my spirit is rotting as well.

August 8, 1900   3:20 p.m.

I had a wicked dream last night. It wasn't about my father,
but it made me feel so disgusted with myself that I vomited when
I recalled it. I was part cat and part human. I had extremely long
claws. With my claws, I would reach out and grab women and
throw them down into a huge pit. I had several females down
there scratching and digging to get out but it was too deep. As they
screamed in agony, I would snatch up another young girl and drop
her into the pit. I couldn't get that dream off my mind today. I feel
such hate for myself sometimes.

August 11, 1900   **2:30 p.m.**

With McKenzie holding the best claims, and those with prosperous claims afraid of working them, the main businesses in Nome are now gambling and drinking, not mining. It's obvious to the men the saloon is a place of refuge because of the human companionship they find there. Whenever I am in a saloon and look around, all the men look the same. They're all wearing the same type of clothes. All of them are talking alike and drinking the same whiskey. They all smell alike and it's not appealing. Except men with money—they will always stand out in a crowd. The poor men remind me of fish in a school, all trying desperately to stay together, afraid of having to spend time alone. When men are together one of them has to prove who is the best right away. As soon as that is established, they can get along because they know they can't beat each other, so they might as well join each other. McKenzie is trying to prove that he is the smartest son-of-a-bitch around. He can rob everybody blind and get away with it.

August 12, 1900   **3:05 p.m.**

The population of Nome is decreasing since it reached its peak early this summer. Many smart people are returning to Seattle. All it took was seeing the actual living conditions in Nome for them to realize the gold, what little there is, was not worth enduring all this hardship. I wish I could say the same. Sometimes I wish I could return to Seattle, but that can't happen. There is still more money to be made here. I know from seeing the first car here today. I'm told it was brought up to establish a service between Solomon and Nome. This place isn't going to turn into a ghost town. It's just going to keep growing and making history. I can feel it in my bones.

August 13, 1900   **2:45 p.m.**

The loss of the sun a little each day is an excellent reminder that it is time to start preparing for the winter ahead. Of course, our barge order will include all the same staples as last year. I'm happy we have the resources to afford a plentiful supply of everything

231

needed to survive. I'm even more delighted I have some money
saved up for the sole purpose of spending on my loved ones and
myself.

After hours looking through several consumer guides, I have
finally decided I will be ordering two new pair of lace boots,
two mink hand muffs, and three hats with lace covering the back
instead of the front. I have always wanted a coat and hat rack as
well as a large kerosene lamp with purple irises painted on both
the front and the back. Now they will be mine. The purchase I'm
looking forward to receiving the most is "Dr. Sanden's Electric
Belt" designed especially for Cape Nome. He claims that it can
help fortify oneself against weakness, as well as kidney and
stomach troubles. Dr. Sanden claims "Electricity is Life" and if
a person properly applies the belt it will invigorate, nourish, and
vitalize the body.

For each one of the ladies, including Dorothy, I'm ordering up
a large floor rug, a hand pumped vacuum cleaner and a window
for their cabin. Dorothy moved into her permanent living quarters
last week and loves the new arrangement as much as all the other
females do. Whenever I think about a window in each ladies cabin,
I envision them sitting next to it watching the mesmerizing snow
during a storm.

I can't believe I'm already thinking about the snow. I guess it's
because the snow has a magical way of making things disappear.
I'm looking forward to it covering up all this filth that surrounds
me. At least when I don't see it, I don't think about it as much.

August 14, 1900   **3:00 p.m.**

I'm beginning to see some changes in Nome that are making it
into a respectable civilization instead of just a wild mining camp.
Each day I encounter more and more proper ladies. I make note of
this because they have a way of making me feel worthless. Today
while doing some shopping in the Northern Commercial Company,
I encountered two such ladies. They gave me a condescending look
as they put their noses up in the air. I could tell they were trying
to let me know they believed I was less of a human than them

because of my occupation. They spoke so loud it was obvious they wanted me to hear their wordy opinion. "A woman with a good reputation can go anywhere in the territory with no fear of any harm coming to her. If any man dare touch a good woman, they would be hung instantly. On the other hand, if a woman is of easy virtue, God help her if the men take a notion to get brutal with her." Hearing this almost made me cry. I tried to hold back my tears and not let them see that they got to me, but as I left my heart was crying inside.

My mother used to be one of those proper ladies. She made sure my sister and I were in attendance everyday that Longfellow School was open. She would sit around the parlors with the other ladies in her clubs drinking tea, reciting poetry, playing Beethoven on upright pianos, and complaining about the low income housing area, the opium dens, and the red light district, all on the south side of Durango.

Today would have been my mother's birthday. She really was the strong foundation that kept the family going. I am glad she is not alive. I wouldn't want her to see what has happened to my sister and me. I sometimes think it would have been different had she lived longer. But who knows, maybe this was my destiny, regardless of my mother's life span.

August 16, 1900   3:20 a.m.

Again Jafet briefly stopped by The Belmont to have a drink and gave me the news of his troubling ordeal. His attorneys for the Wild Goose Mining and Trading Company and the Pioneer Mining Company spoke formally with Judge Noyes, asking to appeal their cases before the circuit courts in San Francisco. Of course, the Judge denied their motion. Now they don't have any other choice but to take their appeals nearly three thousand miles by steamship to Judge William Morrow of the ninth circuit of appeals in San Francisco. Finally people are taking action against McKenzie. It's about time someone has the courage to battle him.

August 17, 1900   **2:05 p.m.**

Last night to my surprise and amusement, I got a visit from
Clark. He approached me in The Belmont by putting his hands
over my eyes and saying in a deep voice, "Guess who?" I knew it
was Clark and I turned around and hugged him while exclaiming,
"Oh Clark, it's so good to see you!" He announced to Dorothy he
had just hired me and we went over into a corner of The Belmont
and visited for hours.

As usual, he did most of the talking. I was thrilled to hear
about their new mining camp. He said he thought they had found
the mother lode; the amount of gold that they were pulling out
every day was incredible. He took out his leather pouch and
showed me by dumping a handful into his palm. He said, "Mandy,
these nuggets are just some of the small stuff." When I saw all that
gold sparkling in his hands, I got a chill down my spine. "Mandy,
there is much, much more of this. But remember, this is hush-hush.
Don't be telling anybody about this. I'll know if you let our secret
out because you are the only person in this town that I have told." I
kissed him on the forehead and told him that my lips were sealed.

We spent the rest of the evening together. He told me more
about the mining camp and his growing distrust of Milroy. As he
drank more his conversation focused on his wife, who is waiting
for him back in Seattle. He said that he didn't trust her either and at
times actually hated her. He stressed the fact that he only married
her for her money. After ordering a new bottle of fine whiskey,
he made a toast in the air to himself and spending her money. He
ended that subject by sharing the reason he travels so much is just
to stay away from her.

When he allowed me time to talk, I updated him on all the
news that had happened since he had left. By the time The Belmont
closed, he said he was ready to come see my crib. I asked him
about Milroy's threat regarding us being together. His reply was,
"He's miles away and we're both here." As soon as we were alone,
he acted just like any other man, a quick unzip and didn't even
bother to take off his boots. A couple pumps and he was satisfied.
Then he passed out on the bed.

As I lay there and watched him, I got the visions again. This time the there was a beginning and an end. It started with me calling for the child and looking across golden wheat blowing softly in the wind. I saw him face down in the field. I picked the child up and held his lifeless body, while I carried him back to the cabin. I sat in the rocking chair rocking myself back and forth as I cried with such hurt and sorrow. My heart felt like it had left my body. I continued to rock my child, never getting up to start a fire. Soon the day grew into the cold evening and I still rocked back and forth. I just clutched onto my child and I rocked back and forth sighing deeply. I felt my body become colder and colder and then there was no pain. A white light surrounded the child and me and carried us up into the heavens. When I was up in the clouds, I snapped out of the trance and once again I was looking at Clark lying on the bed snoring. I wanted nothing more than to lie down next to him and curl up into his arms, even if he wasn't conscious of me. That spirit who lost her child so many lives ago was ecstatic to be reunited with him once again.

August 18, 1900   **1:20 p.m.**

It was great to get up this morning while the sun was shining. I went on a hike to Gold Hill. After walking for an hour, I was exhausted and I lay down on top of the hill. I don't know how long I was asleep, but when I woke up there was an owl flying about a foot above me. It was so close that I could see all the intricate, exquisite colors on its feathers. I wasn't afraid because he was just as curious about me as I was about him. I knew I would probably never be so close to an owl again. I just laid there and enjoyed his beauty as he flew in circles above me.

On my way back to town I startled a family of ptarmigans. They were obviously not very happy to see me. The male ptarmigans started attacking me while the females and the babies ran into the bushes. I will always remember this as the bird day. Maybe it's a sign of good luck. I'll have to ask Kuduk.

August 19, 1900   **3:22 p.m.**

I find myself thinking more and more about Milroy when I am
serving other men. I pretend he is enjoying my body and I think in
detail of each and every step he takes to give me a wild release that
appears to come so easy for him. Later, while a different client is
using my vessel I let myself think about spending life with Jafet.
Going somewhere new together and starting all over again. I would
be a proper lady. Maybe we could even have children. No one
would know me and I could just be Jafet's loving wife. I almost
wrote Galen's name instead of Jafet's. Does that mean I would still
rather be married to Galen living back in Durango? It is hard to
know sometimes what to think.

August 20, 1900   **3:30 p.m.**

When I asked Kuduk about owls he told me his people believe
an owl is a sign of death.

The last few days I feel myself getting weaker. I don't have the
energy or the stamina to make it through the day like I did just a
week ago. I don't know what is happening to me. I hope when my
Dr. Sanden's Electric Belt arrives it will help with my fatigue. I
probably should have an exam from Dr. Miller, but it seems every
time I see him he is so tipsy. I can't really trust him getting close to
me. If my headache and general pain don't go away in a few days I
will try to find another doctor to care for me.

August 21, 1900   **3:10 p.m.**

I know now it was stupid of me to go on an outing when I was
not feeling my best. I'm sure that is why my mind was playing
tricks on me again. I had walked far enough down the shore line
toward the cape to be away from most any signs of civilization and
for the first time it became a problem.

The vastness of the churning, dark, gray ocean water and the
pale sky frightened me. It was as if the crashing waves were the
breath of a creature before me. The sea foam covering the starfish
was the creature's froth. The rocks of various shapes, sizes, and
colors were a reminder that the same waves that change them

over time change humans as well. With each crash of a wave time slips away! If the sun is the creator, then maybe the oceans are our timekeepers.

It must be the approaching storm that made me feel so unnerved this afternoon. What a tiny speck of sand I am compared to the big picture of life. I don't have control of my destiny. That is an illusion! Nature controls everything.

August 23, 1900   **4:10 a.m.**

Mother Nature showed me once again who was in control. While strolling across the brownish green tundra this afternoon, I crossed paths with a massive brown bear. I may have missed seeing him if it wasn't for a voice in my head telling me to turn around. The bear was on the left side of me. He was lumbering toward the north. I was walking to the south and the wind was blowing from the east. I was about one hundred yards from him and he didn't notice me. I held back a tremendous urge to call out and get his attention, just so I could get a better look at him. I stood still for the longest time watching him eat his share of blueberries. From this encounter I learned how much a bear depends on his sense of smell. I'm grateful the wind was blowing from the east.

I panicked a little, but I would like to think that if the bear had confronted me, I would have remained calm enough to fire my gun and shoot him right between his eyes. I know that is my only target if I plan on stopping him. Truthfully, I was shaking badly, not from fear but from excitement. The bear had done nothing to make me fearful, but his presence was enough. I'm not sure how accurately I could have shot. After seeing the size of that bear, I pray I never have to find out.

I'm now more grateful than ever that J.J. insists I wear a gun when I go walking. Thank God he is one of the rare men who has the foresight to think ahead, even when there is no wealth in it for him to gain. After being so close to that beautiful brown bear I'm not sure if I can even go walking in the fog, at least not alone. Ignorance truly is blissful.

August 25, 1900   3:35 a.m.

The situation here with McKenzie is showing no signs of
letting up. Each day the miners become more frustrated because
they can't do anything to prevent McKenzie from ruling. The
miners sit in the saloons and fuss like angry children. At least the
miners can talk about it. When someone is harming a child he
or she must remain silent. McKenzie is nothing more than a big
strong father who is doing exactly what he wants with no care of
the hurt he causes for others.

Last night he wanted to pay for my company and I refused.
There was no way I could put myself in that situation with him:
being intimate and having him touch me when I know how devious
he is. I'm thankful J.J. backed me on the decision and told him
to leave. I noticed J.J. dealt with him tactfully because rumor has
it McKenzie has the reputation of being the quickest draw in the
Dakotas, even though he is left handed. Nobody here is willing
to find out if it is true or not. I'm glad J.J. knows how to handle
people without them getting defensive. It is also rumored that
McKenzie has avoided writing any type of records concerning how
much gold he is taking from each claim. If there was no written
record does that mean there was no crime?

August 27, 1900   8:45 p.m.

A man with an intimidating piece of equipment paid for my
company last night. His name was Albert and he made all the
former manhoods I have known seem small in comparison. After
seeing the size of his organ, I asked if he could please be gentle.
That must have been the wrong thing to say because he instantly
became violent. He knocked me to the floor and ripped off my
dress. I wanted to scream, but he had just given me the going price
in fine gold dust so I lay there quietly and told myself to just give
him what he had come for.

I tried going into the numbness, that safe place in my mind that
I know so well, but he was penetrating me so hard that I couldn't
pretend it wasn't happening. With each pump his gigantic horn was

reaching further into the depths of my womanhood, causing a pain that had never been known before.

While most men can accomplish their deed in minutes, the giant on top of me seemed to take hours to reach his conquest. I could tell by his smell of frustration that his seed was stuck, not wanting to end its journey. When this man finally did reach his destiny he quickly crawled off and apologized several times for being so crude. He kept repeating, "I'm sorry madam, it's just that it has been so long since I was inside of a woman. I forgot how to behave."

As strange as it sounds, I'm glad that man chose me for his pleasure, otherwise I wouldn't have much empathy for whatever lady had to deal with his abuse. Never in my nightmares have I imagined that a man's solid equipment could cause such damage to the inside of a female. I had to remain in bed the rest of last night and all of today because it feels like I have been punched hard in the stomach. Any type of movement involving my mid-section is extremely painful.

I've got to be sure to warn the other madams in town about the abusive giant. He has already cost me a day in wages. The ladies in the sisterhood must all stick together even if we are in competition. No one else in our community will raise a hand to help us sporting kind.

I can't wait until Alex gets off of work. I'm looking forward to lying in her arms. I know it will make me feel safe and loved. It is indeed a wonderful feeling to know someone loves me and will take care of me when I need it most. I know I can always count on Alex to be kind and gentle with me.

August 28, 1900   2:30 p.m.

With so many current events, I haven't had much time to write about the ladies. Margerie has completely put her dead baby in the back of her mind. She's so exuberant. I can't believe she has recovered so easily. I guess she is much stronger and healthier than I thought. Instead of walking around town on her free time, she now ventures into the tundra to draw beautiful flowers. She is quite an artist and each of the ladies, including myself, has one of her drawings on our wall. She let me pick which flower I wanted to have a picture of back in July. She used red berry juice for the bright red middles of the long stemmed, white-petaled flowers I love.

Natalie seems to get heavier with each passing day. She spends most of her free time knitting or reading. As far as I know she still hasn't received any more news of her daughter since the letter that came on June 25th. She just doesn't seem as happy as she used to be. She must always be thinking of her daughter. The last time I saw her smile was at brunch weeks ago when was she talking about the beautiful countryside in Italy, where she lived until she was ten.

Alex, as usual, has been using all her free time to play cards. Whenever I peek in her crib to see if she would like to join me on a tundra adventure, she always refuses, saying she has to continue counting the cards. She actually writes down how often a pair of aces, three of a kind, a full house, etc. shows up when she is playing poker, pretending there are four other players. Her favorite saying is, "It's not luck that makes you win at cards, it is how well you know the odds." The exercise classes are turning into another time of day where the ladies and I get to enjoy one another's company. There always seems to be something that gets one of us laughing.

August 31, 1900   **3:05 a.m.**

The situation here is really getting pathetic, and the constant drizzle doesn't help with the atmosphere. All the saloons have removed their chairs so that the unemployed and needy men will not sit around in them all day and night. They are forced to stand and won't stay in one place too long. Otherwise these former miners fall asleep in the chairs so they don't have to sleep outside on the cold ground. When they are awake, all they talk about is how McKenzie is still having claims turned over for him to operate. Everybody knows what he's doing. The situation is so critical that miners are no longer filing claims or working the claims they have. There is too much fear that the property will be contested and turned over to McKenzie. The only mining that is going on is what McKenzie is illegally profiting from. It's absurd! When is this going to end?

Wyatt, Jeremy's friend, is surely not helping the situation. He was arrested yet another time this summer for starting a barroom brawl. Now more than ever I am sure he started the fight with Natalie. He seems to love to fight male or female, it doesn't matter. I have no respect for that man.

September 1900

September 1, 1900   **3:25 p.m.**

I just finished reading a letter I received from Ria's mother.
She thanked me for letting her know about Ria's chosen profession
and her death. It wasn't a long letter but it meant so much to me.
I'm glad I listened to the voice in my head, the ghost of Ria, or
whatever it was, and wrote to her in the spring. I have helped an
old woman feel at peace.

September 3, 1900   **2:45 p.m.**

As predicted, the mining equipment is abundant on the
beach even though the population is decreasing. There are many
machines on the beach designed to dredge the sand beneath the
sea. I've heard the most uneconomical dredge is the one people
call the "red elephant." It costs about $30,000 to build. According
to one story, a fifteen-man crew operated the red elephant in the
shallow water off the beach for three days and recovered $.90
worth of gold. Someone, somewhere, made a poor investment.

September 4, 1900   **2:50 p.m.**

Today I read in the paper that McKenzie is being blamed for
depriving hundreds of men from their only source of income. The
unemployed miners are spreading their gloom throughout the town,
and the general mood of the people is becoming more desperate.
Each day we get closer to winter and being locked into the frozen
land, the thought of McKenzie in power during the most difficult
season scares everyone. I think every person in this town fears that
if McKenzie can take from the miners, he could take from any of
us.

September 5, 1900   **5:30 a.m.**

Tonight I had an unexpected incident. It was just about closing
time and into The Belmont walked Rawslin. I hadn't expected
to see any of my miner trio until the rivers froze over. I was so
ecstatic I went up and gave him a great big kiss. I think that made
him a little embarrassed.

As usual, he paid for companionship instead of the act. For
something different I wanted to walk on the beach. The tide was
real low so we walked as close to the water's edge as possible
without getting our boots wet. Walking on the sandy surface was
very easy compared to the tundra so we were able to walk a few
miles in a short time.

The full moon laid low in the southern sky, reflecting on the
tiny waves as they met the land. Intricate ice patterns formed in
scattered puddles on the beach. As beautiful as the moonlit walk
was, I would have to say the conversation, or lack of it, was even
better. I felt like Rawslin was just as connected to the land as I
was. There were several times we both stopped and stared at the
sparkling ocean for minutes without saying a word to one another.
That never seems to happen if I'm walking with one of the ladies. I
guess we like to share gossip more than silence.

On our walk, he informed me that lately when he is outside
panning he can see different colored lights drifting above certain
plants. Then he said, "I know this sounds strange, but I believe the
plants have that kind of magical light above them because below

them is a gold vein." I didn't know what to say at the time. I have never heard anything like that.

Before leaving he confided in me that their mining company was doing quite well, but the more gold they took out of the ground, the less he trusted Milroy. He had never caught him doing anything except cheating at cards, but he felt Milroy was up to something. Then he handed me some papers and said, "Mandy, I want you to have these. They are poems I have been writing. I hope you enjoy them. Please don't read them now. Wait until I am gone. I can't wait to hear what you think about them. We should all be coming in as soon as the ice freezes so we can get our wagons back to town." He left without even giving me a kiss on the cheek. I was delighted that he brought me something and I sat down right away to read his poems. I was touched by the romance in some and the humor in others. My favorite one was about gold and greed. I'm impressed with his writing skills.

September 7, 1900   10:50 a.m.

Last night was the worst night since arriving in Nome. After my walk last night with Rawslin I wanted to venture further on the beach than I ever had. I took off as soon as I woke up without telling anyone where I was walking. I just didn't think there was a need to. That was my first mistake. My second mistake was crossing the little creeks. That is to say, they were little at the time I crossed them. I was so caught up in the beauty of the land I must have lost track of time. That was my third mistake. I turned around and started walking back as fast as I could. Not conserving my energy was my fourth mistake. I came to the first creek and saw it had grown twice its size. I tried walking up the tundra a little, but saw no welcoming paths, so I decided to swim across. I made it with some struggle against the current, but my real problem was that I got wet, fifth mistake! The depth of my situation was terribly frightening.

I tried not to panic. I had to walk slowly to conserve what energy the first creek didn't take out of me. As soon as I saw how big the second creek was I started to cry. I tried the tundra again with no success. My only choice was to wait until the tide changed the water back to the way it had been.

From the other side of the creek, I heard J.J. He yelled, "I knew you were in danger and needed my help. I could feel it!" As soon as he got the feeling he started asking if anyone had seen me. He ran into Rawslin, who mentioned our walk last night. Knowing time might be important he borrowed a horse. He took a chance and headed west. He got lucky and was right. By the time he reached me I was very cold and very hungry. I felt weak and was not thinking clearly. J.J. was prepared with blankets, food, and fresh water. With both of us on the horse he quickly got me home and in Dorothy's warm bed, so she could keep a good eye on me for the evening.

I made so many bad choices, one right after another. I could have hurt myself or lost my life, all from not thinking ahead and preparing for my journey. I was just in so much of a hurry to get outside and explore nature. I forgot to respect the power she has. Once again I felt that sheer helplessness I felt when I saw the whale die. All I could think while waiting for time to pass and water to change the earth was how we as humans really have little control over our lives. We make choices, some good and some bad, but nature has the ultimate control.

September 8, 1900   3:20 a.m.

There was some celebrating going on this evening in Nome. General Randall heard from the Secretary of War today that his request to send all desperate people out of Nome has been granted. I had heard that the government was very reluctant to come to the rescue of the foolish gold hunters, but they saw they had no other alternative; otherwise the miners would just perish during the winter. Sometime before the ocean freezes, the Army will transport at least seven hundred and seventy-five people from Nome to the lower west coast. Although the people leaving did not have money to spend for drinks, their attitudes were so joyous they spread good cheer throughout every saloon they descended upon. From what I witnessed, plenty of beer was bestowed upon them regardless of their income.

September 10, 1900   4:10 a.m.

Reading back on the last few months of my diary, I noticed I haven't mentioned unruly behavior very much. (Except for Milroy, but he's more personal than business, even though he still pays.) I see that as a sign of my abounding numbness. I'm saturated in lust every day, yet I can find other aspects of my life that I choose to write about. I always think about the positive and don't dwell on the negative. It that denial or is it survival?

September 12, 1900   1:35 p.m.

Tonight in The Belmont, I heard a very interesting conversation. A man said now days, the average age of the people in this community is about thirty-five. He said that the population consists mainly of white people, but there are a few dozens Inuit here, eight blacks, four Japanese, and three Chinese. He said that of the people who arrived during the height of the rush, only about sixteen percent had ever mined before. I guess this man has nothing better to do than sit around and count people. Many people came hoping to end their life of drudgery by striking it rich, but instead they have endured more toil than they ever thought possible. Life can be ironic.

September 13, 1900   2:10 p.m.

I have seen a lot of storms since I have been here, but yesterday the worst storm I have ever seen reached its peak. Some buildings were tied down with ropes to keep them from being washed away. Several that were not tied down were tossed in the air by the waves and crushed to pieces. I heard the strong winds destroyed or washed away everything on the beach as well as a good part of Nome's business district. Much of the sand spit was also washed away. Front Street was once a thriving, prosperous throughway but now it is mass of wreckage. The surging breakers have moved some houses several blocks and pounded them against the banks of the tundra.

The Belmont is several yards from the shore, and since it was still standing, it was used as an emergency shelter for those who had lost what they called home. Instead of working on our backs, the ladies and I spent the day bandaging injured people and getting warm liquids in them.

As I helped the people yesterday, I counted my blessings, realizing that our tents wouldn't have survived the storm, but our wooden cribs withstood all damage—a good sign for the upcoming winter. The only real inconvenience for the alliance is we no longer have a fresh water supply but for hundreds of people there has been a great redistribution of property. Some people have lost all they have, while others have acquired large stockpiles of food and building supplies. The soldiers have been striving to patrol the beach and have made several arrests, but with so many baffled people, there is just chaos with no signs of justice.

September 14, 1900   2:50 p.m.

I have heard the storm destroyed about twenty-five buildings in the center of town and about three hundred tents were washed away. The huge waves tossed twenty barges up on the shore and nearly two hundred small vessels were stranded along the beach. People are estimating that there is over $750,000 worth of damage done by the storm. It is still not known how many people have been killed. Already I see several surviving miners back at work on the beach and I hear rumors people think the storm has replenished the gold. But there are other miners who have lost everything they own. A large majority of them are preparing to leave as quickly as they can.

September 16, 1900   3:30 p m.

Before starting work this afternoon I went on an eerie journey down the beach. The wrath of the storm had relocated many small floating items, but it literally buried the large abandoned mining equipment.

Now it all seems like the gold stampede was just a dream. Not much evidence remains except McKenzie's greed; even the hoards of people are gone. Ships today have been departing the shores of Nome at about the same rate as they arrived. I wonder what the winter will bring.

September 17, 1900   **2:45 p.m.**

The talk around town today was that two days ago, McKenzie received orders from Judge Morrow to return any and all property which he had taken into his possession. Judge Noyes was to stop proceedings relating to the contested mining claims. I heard this hit McKenzie's camp like an explosion. McKenzie did not expect the higher courts to interfere so quickly. People are repeating McKenzie's already famous words, "To hell with them all! Nobody can hurt me. I am too strong in Washington D.C." I sure hope someone can stop him. As each day grows colder, I fear it may not happen.

September 18, 1900   **4:15 a.m.**

The people of Nome were ready for some type of celebration, thinking McKenzie's reign had been broken. No one thought McKenzie would just ignore the orders from the circuit court, but that's just what he is doing. He claims they are not valid and now Judge Noyes is maintaining that he is powerless to make McKenzie stop. The talk in the saloons is that McKenzie's decision to openly defy the orders of the circuit court is everybody's last straw. Miners such as Jafet and Lane have hired detectives to watch every move McKenzie and his men make. Now everyone is armed and prepared for the bloodshed they are sure will happen any day.

September 19, 1900   **9:45 a.m.**

I dreamed about Galen last night. He was watching my father force himself upon me in the predictable position of me laying stomach down on the bed. Galen walked over to my father, touched his back, but barely got his attention because he was absorbed in his pleasure. Galen looked right into my father's eyes and said, "It is time for you to stop." Without getting angry or questioning, my father withdrew himself from my body and his presence from the dream. Then Galen looked at me with disappointment and said, "I have been watching you for a long time and I never once heard you say, 'No, stop it.' I knew the first time I entered you that you weren't a virgin. I could tell by the way you weren't afraid of the pain because you had already known the pleasure." He continued with more insults, "Your father turned you into a whore because he could tell how much you loved him being inside you. You were probably happy when I died. You didn't waste any time taking my sister, Rosa, up on her offer to work on your back. Isn't that because you were broke in early for your years?"

Dammit, why do I have to experience such an unwelcome dream? I sure as hell don't need a dream reminding me I'm an insignificant common woman. I get disheartened just thinking about it. I must stop feeling sorry for myself. I'm a successful madam in a man's business world. Only a handful of women can say that. It is something to be proud of. I'm a businesswoman!

September 21, 1900   3:30 p.m.

Even though today is my birthday, I haven't had a chance to think about it much because there is so much excitement. I have had no time to write about anyone's birthday. Early in the morning, a group of Jafet's men drove McKenzie's men off several of the claims out at Anvil Creek. When McKenzie heard of this violence, he complained to Major Van Orsdale who is the head of the military force and also a North Dakotan. To help resolve this conflict, Orsdale arranged a conference between McKenzie and Metson, the leading attorney for Pioneer Mining Company. Rumor has it that McKenzie offered Metson $1 million as a bribe, but he refused it. After trading insults, I heard that if it hadn't been for the soldiers, they would have killed each other. Everybody can feel it in the air. Any day now something is going to explode.

We did have a little celebration for my birthday. We had the hotcakes this morning and afterwards, I was delighted to find that all the ladies, including Dorothy, had put their money together and bought me a beautiful dark purple velvet dress. It is low cut on the top with black lace around the waist and the bottom. It is exquisite and I cried when they gave it to me. I will wear it proudly tonight.

J.J. and Ryan went in together on a large wooden dresser. The intricate designs engraved in the wood are magnificent. I am so pleased with my presents. I love the gratitude I receive from the alliance.

September 23, 1900   11:20 a.m.

I was visited once again by the horrifying memory of my father. In this dream I'm about ten years old and I am laying in bed watching him put himself in my baby sister's mouth to keep her from crying. Instead of doing anything to stop that monster from hurting her, I softly cry myself to sleep. In the dream, my helplessness is intensified and I feel about an inch tall. He looks enormous and it is beyond my means to try to stop his wickedness.

I feel more frustrated than ever after one of these dreams. McKenzie reminds me of my father—abusing people with no concerns. I almost wish McKenzie would come in and get rough with one of my girls. That would give me a reason to shoot him. I know I could do it.

September 24, 1900   3:00 p.m.

I heard that three days ago, two prostitutes drew a large crowd as they fought in the street on Second Avenue. They clawed, bit, pounded, and rolled around for about ten minutes before police intervened. I find it frustrating that no one tried to break up the fight. Everybody just thought it was entertaining. I wish I could have been there. I think I would have had the courage to try to break up a fight between the ladies. I'm learning I can't show my fear. I just have to get in there and let them know who is in charge. Hearing about this made me thankful that all my ladies and I have a caring relationship.

September 25, 1900   **8:24 a.m.**

It was an illusion to think my crib provided more sercurity than my tent. Last night while sleeping two men entered my cottage. They were standing above me when I awoke. I was intuitively aware of their presence. I was helpless and they knew it. They both did what they wanted to my body and there was nothing I could do. It was the most terrifying experience of my life. At least with my father there was only one person and he never held me down.

I can clearly see I have nothing to gain by sharing this information with any one. When Alex got raped at least she saw them, she knew who they were. I didn't see anything with clarity. It was too dark. Society at large thinks women of the kinship are fair game and J.J.'s system of justice wouldn't work because I have no idea who to blame. I am scared! Will my teeth start to fall out? Come to think of it, I haven't noticed a change in Alex's teeth since those men had their way with her. As I try to imitate Alex and endeavor to see the best of each situation, I can say, "at least 98% of the men pay." Besides, with everything else that is going on in Nome, why would anyone care what happened to me? Oh, I know Alex would care, but it would just remind her of her own ordeal. I wouldn't want to cause her any pain by reminding her of something she had no control over.

September 27, 1900   **3:40 p.m.**

The situation in Nome has gotten so bad there are now soldiers standing guard at the Alaska Banking and Safe Deposit Company to ensure that neither McKenzie, Jafet, or Lane help themselves to the quarter of a million dollars worth of gold in the safe. Every man in this town is carrying arms and prepared for battle. There should be no bloodshed unless someone is foolish enough to try to take out the gold. I hope Jafet isn't one of those fools.

September 30, 1900   **11:25 a.m.**

I feel exhausted. All I want to do is sleep, but I can't because I ache all over. I'm sure I'm running a fever. I don't feel like eating and I keep having nosebleeds. If I don't feel better in a few days,

I will be forced to visit a doctor. I know there are other doctors in Nome, but I hear a person has to wait for hours just to talk to them. Before the storm I could have paid high dollars and gone to the private hospital that was floating on Snake River, but now it is gone. I just don't have the time or the energy to wait that long at the other hospital, especially since the storm. I hear they are still trying to recover from it. I'm going right now to tell J.J. I'm not feeling well enough to work and would like to spend the night sleeping. Maybe then I will feel better.

October 1900

October 10, 1900   2:30 p.m.

It has been such a long time since I have written because as
soon as I am done with the night's work, I come to bed and sleep
until J.J. wakes me in the morning. I'm so tired after brunch, our
baths, and our exercises, that I lay down before I go to work. I
think I better tell somebody about the rose colored spots. They are
all over my body now and I'm starting to see them on my face.
Somebody is bound to notice them sooner or later.

October 16, 1900   3:10 a.m.

I heard today was an exciting day in Nome and yet I missed it
all, not having the energy to travel outside The Belmont. Instead I
just waited till the news arrived here. The miners were all boasting
loudly it is a fact, not a rumor, that two U.S. deputy marshals
arrived in Nome from California aboard the steamship *Oregon* to
enforce orders from the Circuit Court. They have a warrant for the
arrest of Alexander McKenzie. They said he is being charged with
contempt of court for refusing to return the property he has taken

as a receiver. I also hear that the marshals are taking him back to
San Francisco on October 21st to stand trial. The marshals found
McKenzie eating breakfast in the Golden Gate Hotel, and I heard
at first he said, "No so and so is going to arrest me," but later on
the advice of his lawyer, he surrendered. The marshals ordered
McKenzie to open the safe but he refused. So the marshals pried
the vault open with crowbars and returned the gold to its rightful
owners.

Tonight, shots could be heard from out at Anvil Creek, but this
time everyone is sure that they heard guns fired in celebration, not
in hatred. Once again the city of Nome has something to celebrate
and as I write, I can still hear lots of merry-making.

October 17, 1900   2:50 p.m.

It is snowing outside but I wouldn't call it a blizzard, just a
sign of the season ahead. Things are starting to settle down and
people are beginning to concentrate on getting ready for the winter.
There is still lingering talk about McKenzie and what is being
called the Cape Nome Conspiracy. I would presume that will be
our main topic of discussion throughout the winter. I guess I should
get used to it. Unfortunately for all, Judge Noyes is still with us.
From what I hear, all he does is sit in his room and drink. What
a weak and pathetic soul he appears to be. I hope he gets what is
coming to him.

October 18, 1900   4:10 a.m.

Jafet's laughter is a sign things are getting back to normal.
When he is joyous, the other people around him can't help but
become elated as well. Tonight while in The Belmont, Jafet, his
partners, and several other men got into a conversation about the
difference between caribou and reindeer.

Jafet is quite an expert from his days as a government reindeer
herder. The government had two ideas in mind for the reindeer.
The first was to use them as a source of meat, and the other as
a pack animal that could haul supplies into the gold fields. He
enlightened everyone within listening distance that caribou and

reindeer are of the same species. The way to tell them apart is by looking at their legs. Reindeer have shorter ones and tend to be stockier. When caribou and reindeer mix, the reindeer usually join caribou herds and leave the region in the spring. He finished this speech by saying that both male and female reindeer and caribou have antlers.

I think because the tension surrounding the community has disappeared, we were all looking for something humorous. Reindeer and caribou became the topic of many jokes this evening. It was wonderful to hear laughter in our town once again.

October 19, 1900   9:45 p.m.

My spots have disappeared but now I have diarrhea and I'm coughing all the time. I decided not to work today because I felt too sick, so I decided to spend the six hours it took waiting in line just to hear from the wise physician. Right away he diagnosed me as having typhoid fever. He announced there was no doubt I had got it from drinking the infected water after the storm or contracted it from one of the infected customers. He said it was definitely a risk in my profession. He told me to stop selling my body or he would see to it that I was locked up in the pest house. He said the typhoid wouldn't kill me, but the pneumonia growing in my lungs would. I'm dying and there is nothing Dr. Drake can do about it, except recommend drinking as much fresh milk as I can afford.

After hearing such devastating news, I would have loved to have taken a solitary walk into the tundra, but it was so bitter cold I had no choice but to return to my crib. I think the temperature has already reached ten below and it's just October. Of course, that is with the wind blowing, but it feels like it's still too early to get that cold.

I wasn't strong enough today to share my news with anybody, so instead I laid in bed and thought about my life here in Nome and wondered if all the gold I now possess was really worth the risks I put my body through. I have worked so hard for this gold, but I will never have the chance to spend any of it. I'll never get to travel and see all the places in the world I so wanted to see. I will never get to see a reindeer or ride the train to Jafet's gold camp. I will never live to see another spring here or anywhere, and I will never get to find if what Natalie said about the river ice was true or not. I will miss Alex's scent and watching her walk around naked. I will miss J.J. and all the members of the alliance. I'm grateful I was given another opportunity to have a family to love.

October 20, 1900   7:30 p.m.

Today Alex asked if I was feeling all right. She said I didn't look very good. I broke down crying and told her the doctor's diagnosis. I don't believe I am dying of that. I have lived a life where my body and my emotions have not been connected with each other. My spirit has never known harmony and now I must pay the price. She held me in her arms for the longest time, but she didn't cry. I know she wanted to be strong for me.

Together we told Jeremy James. He actually cried, which made me cry even harder. Soon everybody in The Belmont knew what the tears were for. It was the quietest evening I have ever heard in there. Maybe I did gain some respect and friendship after all. Tonight it was made official that I would never work again and it's strange to say, but I'm going to miss everyone. I wonder if they will miss me.

October 21, 1900   11:20 a.m.

Natalie came to my cabin just a little while ago. By the sad look in her eyes, I could tell this must be serious. Without hesitating, she told me she planned on leaving today on the *Oregon*. She put her arms around me and said, "I love you and it has been wonderful to have you as a madam and a friend. I will always think of you as family. After what happened to my daughter, I don't want to be here anymore. I want to be with my children. I had a dream last night and I saw myself running my very own baby farm. The last ship is leaving today. I know it is my destiny to leave with it."

I didn't waste my time trying to talk her out of it because I could see in her eyes she was already gone. She sat in my cabin and we talked for several minutes. She said that with the money she made since arriving on the golden beaches of Nome, she really can afford to buy a decent house, fill it with children and spend her time caring for them. We were forced to say our last goodbye when the ship blew its whistle. She jumped off my bed, gave me a tight hug, told me once again she loved me, and then ran from my crib. I had never seen her glowing the way she was. I'm truly happy for her and wish her the best for her future.

She gave me a rainbow scarf before she left, just like what she had knitted for her daughter so many months ago. As much as I love her thoughtfulness, it struck me as odd that she would give me a gift when I only have weeks or months to live. She never spoke of me dying. If she's not here to see me die, maybe I'll stay alive in her mind forever.

In memory of Natalie, I will ask Alex to ensure I'm wearing the scarf when they bury me, or when they leave me in the snow pit with the rest of the dead who have to wait to be buried. What a morbid thought. If I die quickly, I might have a chance of being put to rest in the ground before next spring. In memory of everyone else, I will also request I be dressed in the gorgeous purple velvet gown the ladies got me for my birthday.

October 22, 1900   6:45 p.m.

The predominant thought in my mind today as I lay in bed, in and out of sleep, is my wonderful talk with Natalie yesterday. She said she knew that one day she would be telling me goodbye because men are always looking for the young and fresh chippies. She had learned from her first madam that it was just good business to change location at least once every two years, so the profits don't decrease.

The only comfort in knowing that I'm dying is knowing that I will never grow old and completely worthless. It is apparent that women have less worth than men in this world, especially as they grow older. Maybe in Heaven women will at least be equal to men.

October 23, 1900   10:30 a.m.

The closer I get to the end of my life I more desire to be outside in nature. I want to smell the fresh air, hear the vibrations of the earth, and see the many shades the sky can produce. I want to feel the different textures of the tundra, and to taste the sweet juicy blueberries. I used to believe each time I went out on a walk I returned healthier and cleaner than when I began. I thought that somehow the earth had a way of healing me, but I don't know if I believe that now. I always found such tranquility in nature but now there seems no place to even look for it, especially not within myself.

October 25, 1900   8:35 a.m.

I just awoke from the worst of all dreams. Of course it was about my father. He was living in hell and he said to me, "I'll see you here soon, you filthy scum of the earth." When I looked surprised he replied, "Where else did you think you would be going? Even before you started selling your body you were a harlot. Why do you think I always chose you more than your sister? You loved it and I could tell."

I woke up screaming, "No, I don't want to go!" I began to cry harder than I ever have. Am I really going to have to live in hell with my father after I die? Wasn't living with him on earth punishment enough? Will I have to be punished for all my sins, as well as the sins I have helped the ladies commit and profit from?

October 27, 1900   11:33 a. m.

My body hurts. I have been running a 104-degree temperature for days now. When I'm not sleeping, I'm coughing. Last night I had one of those dark moods where I ask myself questions. Did I contract the disease because of the fear I had of living in all of this filth? Maybe it was Mother Nature's way of keeping me forever connected to this spectacular Alaskan Territory since I'll be buried here. Or was it the hatred I carried for my father? If I had forgiven him, would I still have carried his crime with me all of these years?

October 29, 1900   **4:00 p.m.**

While laying half asleep in Alex's arms, I had a vision of what I believe must be another life we shared. In this vision we are both men who have a strong love for one another. We are in a palace garden surrounded by massive vine growth and statues. There are several couples with us engaged in intercourse of all types. All the men on the giving end were older and on the receiving end were the younger men, in some cases, boys. Alex was the older man and I was the younger man.

I believe this vision is telling me that I have loved Alex under many varied circumstances. That confirms my devotion for her.

October 31, 1900   **6:20 p.m.**

My client who pays to wear my dresses came to my crib with an unusual request. He heard I was dying and he wanted to buy some of my dresses, since I wouldn't be needing them. At first I was offended, but then I found the humor in it and couldn't help but chuckle. He spent an hour trying on all the clothes and left with four of his favorite dresses. He wanted the purple velvet one that I got for my birthday and I had to convince him it wasn't for sale. After the bartering was done for the dresses and my mirror, he crept out of my crib so as to avoid being seen. I'm sure if someone sees him, he'll just lie and say they're for a girlfriend. I hope that strange man enjoys my clothes.

November 1900

November 1, 1900   2:30 p.m.

Every once in a while, one person in the alliance will bring a
chair and their plate, as well as fresh milk, into my crib to eat their
brunch. It reminds me of how everyone helped nurture Natalie
back to health. But no matter how much attention they shower on
me, I'm not going to be healed.

The ladies took turns today reading aloud for me, but I can't
even remember what book it was. All my abilities seem to slowly
be leaving my body. I do recall what Kuduk said to me. "Don't be
afraid of the darkness. Your soul isn't dying, just your shell is."

November 4, 1900   3:40 a.m.

Tonight I had a surprise visit from Milroy. I said I didn't expect
him to return so soon. He replied the cold spell came in and froze
everything up, so they decided to get out of there earlier. When I
asked where Rawslin and Clark were he said, "Mandy, there was a
bad accident. Everyone's dead. I'm the only one that survived."

I was shocked. I couldn't believe what I was hearing. After

what seemed like an eternity of staring blankly at Milroy, I finally uttered, "What are you talking about? Rawslin and Clark, they're dead? What happened?" He told me they were traveling over the frozen river back into town when he had to shit. When he was gone, he heard a loud cracking noise and he came back just in time to see the last of the wagon go under the water. The ice over the river had collapsed under the tremendous weight of the wagon. The struggling horses tried to swim out of the freezing river water but did not succeed. Milroy said he ran over to where the men and supplies had gone under, but saw nothing except for a jagged circle of water in the middle of the frozen river. He continued saying he looked for Rawslin and Clark but they were nowhere.

I could not believe my ears! This news brought such immense sorrow to my heart I lost all composure. I sat down on my bed with tears streaming down my face. Milroy sat next to me and wrapped his arms around my shoulders. As he held me he said in a soft devilish whisper, "It's O.K. Mandy, it's all part of my plan. I'm finally going to be able to take you out of here because all the money will be mine. Now it's time for celebrating. Get me some whiskey, woman. I'm ready for some pleasure."

I tried to explain that I was contagious and that was why I was alone in my crib instead of soliciting in The Belmont, but Milroy was unaware of my condition. He was wrapped up in his own thoughts. He drank almost two bottles of rye whiskey as I sat on my bed watching him prance around my crib. I was stunned as to how he could be so indifferent to the death of his partners, even exuberant. Milroy was more intoxicated than I had ever seen him. When he was finally ready for the act he threw me onto all fours and forcefully sodomized me. As soon as he reached his satisfaction, he collapsed on my bed. In his drunken stupor he mumbled, "My plan worked, my plan worked! Now I own all that gold. Nobody will ever know how I plotted this infallible crime, throughout the winter down to every last detail." I presumed he must have been talking in his sleep. He started snoring and didn't say any more.

As I write, Milroy is laying on my bed and I'm not sure what to think. Was he just delirious from drinking or was he speaking the truth? I want to shake him and demand he tell me more, but I know if I did I would be endangering my life. For now I will just try to get some sleep. I think that would be safest.

November 4, 1900   11:10 a.m.

Milroy awoke suddenly this morning. He realized he told some of his secrets in his drunken slumber. Without hesitation he grabbed my throat with a deathly grip and declared, "Woman, if you tell anyone about my plan, I will kill you. It's a perfect plan and I don't want some dumb whore blowing it for me. When the time is right next summer, I'll hire men to divert the river until it dries up and recover that gold. Then I'm taking you and we are leaving this town. You better not tell anyone that I caused the accident that made Rawslin and Clark's wagon go down. It was only my two partners. The rest of the men had come into town two days before that. I planned it that way. I didn't want to kill too many people, just the key ones. Now all that gold is mine, and it's legal. Nothing is going to stop me from getting it, especially not you. You just keep your mouth shut, woman." He let go of my neck, got dressed and walked out of my crib without looking back.

What a situation I am in! Milroy could easily kill me because of the information he revealed to me. I am slowly dying of pneumonia, yet I am afraid of this man murdering me. I know I'm going to die, but I need to die on my own terms. That heartless son-of-a-bitch does not deserve to live. I need to kill him before he does away with me.

I will be prepared to shoot him the next time he comes back. I'll make sure my gun is loaded and I will defend myself. I wish I could share this secret with Alex and J.J., but I would be jeopardizing their lives. No, I have to handle this myself. I can do it. After what I have been through in the last year and four months in the Alaska Territory, I can do it. I can do anything.

November 7, 1900   **5:30 a.m.**

Tonight Milroy stumbled into my crib and woke me up right when closing time would be if I were working. I remembered him doing that once before and taking me to my tent and tying me up. I was worried he would do that again rendering me helpless and unable to defend myself. Even though I was still dazed from the abrupt awakening and my deficient health, I knew I had to make my move quickly.

The rain was pouring against my wooden structure. The outcome could have been different had it been drizzles as usual. As the rain turned to sleet I felt my courage grow. I knew my only chance was the element of surprise. I prepared myself by thinking of all his possible reactions. When Milroy went behind the room divider, I grabbed my gun from my desk. My heart was pounding louder than the force of nature outside. Without the slightest hesitation I walked close to the divider. When he reappeared I was standing with my gun cocked, pointing straight at his face, ready to fire. He was startled and bellowed, "What the hell are you doing, you dense ill-repute woman!" I replied steadily without a quiver in my voice, "I'm going to kill you before you kill me." "What do you mean?" he asked, not moving a muscle. "I'm not going to kill you. I'm taking you with me." I told him, "I don't want to go with you, Milroy. Clark was a good friend of mine, and so was Rawslin. You killed those people and you deserve to die." Before he could draw his gun, I fired three rounds into his chest. I saw the look of defeat in his eyes the moment he knew I would survive him. Watching the blood drain from his body brought an eerie feeling of completion over me. Instead of being frightened I was intrigued. I came close enough to hear him take his last breath. I touched the warm liquid of life flowing onto my floor. I felt no remorse. I only wanted proof that he was dead.

Alex ran into my crib. I was having trouble focusing on her voice—the memories of a plot to kill my father flowed into my mind quickly and without reserve. It was a cold winter night when the rage had built up inside me so much that I exploded. I know now that I could never finish that dream because I had pushed those memories so far in the back of my mind that I made myself forget them. I had so much hate for my father that I planned his murder to perfection. I had already put the hemlock in his whiskey bottle. I knew he would drink as soon as he got home. I planned on dragging his corpse into the river in back of our house, and pushing his body into the current to make sure it would go down stream. The only problem was he never came home, that night or any other night. I was grateful that he never came home again, and I never had to endure the horrors of his brutality again. I can't believe that I forgot these events for all these years. I guess I had to in order to survive. It took something as powerful as killing a horrible man to bring those memories back.

Once I recalled every detail of that night I proceeded to tell Alex what Milroy had done and why I reacted the way I did. After listening to what had happened and what I remembered Alex said, "I'm going to get someone and tell them that you killed Milroy in self defense. We have to stick with that story." Alex took control of the whole situation.

I sat on my bed and strived to comprehend what had just happened. I killed Milroy, but I knew I had to in order to survive. Even though he said he wouldn't, I knew that he could have easily killed me at any time. Why am I trying so hard to survive when I am dying? I guess I just had to rid the world of a man with so much venom flowing in his blood. I killed him for the sake of all the people in Nome. Or did I think that killing him would somehow kill the disease that is growing within me? Either way, he got what he deserved.

As a teenager I harbored the illusion that killing my father would end the torture, but instead I have carried his sins and mine everyday of my life. I hope I have suffered enough to leave behind the anguish and shame that those two men brought me. When I leave this body, perhaps my next lifetime will be free from their savage memories.

November 9, 1900   **11:45 a.m.**

Last night I dreamed about Rawslin's books. They were just
lying at the bottom of the river while his poems floated away with
the current. I clearly saw some of the titles: *Huck Finn, Gilded
Age, Pudd'nhead Wilson,* and *On The Origin of Species.* In the
dream he told me the reason he never touched me was because he
really enjoyed touching little boys and in my heart I know that was
true of him. I'm sorrowful for Rawslin because he will never get to
read all his books. I'm sorrowful for me because we will never get
to walk on the moonlit beach again or sit in my crib drinking tea,
watching the snow swirling around outside my new window.

I wonder if Clark's mining adventure was as exciting as he
thought it would be. As much as he loved the thrill of life, I wonder
if he loved the thrill of death. He had such great courage. How will
Clark's wife find out about his death? I wish I had the strength to
write and tell her the sad news.

Each time I write it gets more exhausting. I'm afraid I will not
be able to write much longer. I can't do much of anything now but
sleep. I hope I dream of Clark as the little boy. We could go run
and play in the sunny wheat field. I could hold him in my arms and
give him all my love.

November 10, 1900   **10:40 a.m.**

Last night I dreamed of both Rawslin and Clark. It had
nothing to do with Clark being a little boy like I had wished, but
it was even better. Both of them hugged me and thanked me for
killing Milroy. Then the three of us went for a walk on the beach.
The waves were tiny and slowly changing the earth. The noise it
created as it moved to the rhythm of the planet was one of peace
and serenity. The moon was full and its bright reflection on the
water stands out in my mind. Before parting company, they each
gave me another hug and said, "We'll see you when you get here."
It was a wondrous dream and it brought much joy into my painful
and frightful existence.

J.J. spent some time with me today. He knows that we don't
have much time left so he is trying to recall all the wonderful

experiences we have enjoyed. J.J. has already put Alex in charge of everything. That will be a sound business relationship for the both of them, as well as a loving one. Instead of going to New York next summer with Tex Rickard to start a boxing garden, he decided to stick around and get married to Alex sometime this winter when things settle down. He confided how his priorities have changed. He now knows that the love of a good woman is the most important commodity a man can possess, far more important than what legal tender can buy. Knowing how much I love Alex, J.J. asked for my blessing in their future together. I could tell when I gave him my congratulations he was truly touched by my sincerity. I'm genuinely happy for both of them.

November 11, 1900   1:00 p.m.

I had a wonderful visit with Ryan today while I rested in my bed. He said, "It has been an honor working along side of you and your ladies. I will never forget you or our time together." He gave me a long embrace before leaving. Usually he avoids touching too much of my body but this time he held on tight. I have a feeling it was his way of saying goodbye.

I'm not ready to say my goodbyes yet.

November 12, 1900   11:30 a.m.

After my father disappeared, my mother never spoke of him again. Not even once. One winter night Galen out right asked her, "What ever happened to your husband? People don't just disappear." Without saying a word she got up from her chair and walked away, as if she had never heard the question. She acted like he was never alive, so how could he have died? We didn't have any clues or evidence of his disappearance so it became easy to pretend his whole existence never happened. Since no one in the family saw my father die, does that mean he lives?

No matter how my mother handled the situation she encountered with my father I can't judge her. She did what she thought was best at the time. If anything I need to thank her for my life. It has been a struggle at times and at other times I have experienced many pleasures. Without her none of it would be possible. I guess I should thank my father, but I don't have the strength within me to forgive.

November 13, 1900   4:20 p.m.

Alex spent the whole afternoon with me and I loved every second of her company. I informed her that I wanted her to keep half of my gold when I die and to please see to it that the other half goes to my sister Lizzy. She brought up a very good point—what would Lizzy really use gold for? Someone would just steal it from her. I had to admit she was correct. Now, thanks to Alex and her great questions, I have decided to leave what gold I have collected to the Botton's Circulating Library. I agree with Alex that it would be an excellent use of my profits since she refused to keep any of my nuggets for herself after my decision was made.

I told her again about Milroy's crime and how there was now a wagon with boxes of gold sitting at the bottom of a river, but I don't know where the incident happened. If someone could travel back into the tundra before winter hit hard, there may still be some clues as to the exact location of the tragedy. She didn't seem to be interested in that news.

The last thing I remember about our conversation today was her telling me that she never got to share one of her earliest memories. "I think another reason I really enjoy mounting is because when I was living with all those brothers of mine, if I won poker for the evening, I got to choose the position. I really thought that's where the game got its name." When I heard that I laughed from my belly. I can't remember the last time that had happened.

November 14, 1900   7:25 p.m.

My days on this earth are now limited. I went to see Dr. Drake today and he told me my gall bladder is now inflamed and my coughing has gotten worse. He informed me that I was lucky to have people to care for me in these last days because the pest house is more crowded than it ever has been. Was that his way of making me feel better?

November 15, 1900   2:15 p.m.

I was beginning to wonder why I hadn't seen Dorothy lately, so I gathered up my strength and went looking for her in the cooking cabin. When I entered she was heating up the water for baths. I asked her bluntly why she hadn't come by to visit. She said, "Mandy, I love you too much to watch you die. If I do, I will think of Jime and I might fall apart with pain. That is the last thing the alliance needs now. So I will just pretend that you are fine and when you die I will pretend that you just went away on a trip."

I asked if I could at least have a hug before I left. I'm ready to start saying my goodbyes. We embraced for a long time. Her last words ring in my mind, "Mandy you have been a very caring and supporting madam to your ladies. You have done a wonderful job of making them feel loved. I'm proud of you for that."

November 16, 1900   10:20 a.m.

Margerie has been bringing me hot soup and fresh milk first thing every morning. Each day before leaving my bedside she gives me a big kiss on the cheek and says, "Thanks for everything you have done for me, Mandy. I will never forget your kindness." I love her thoughtfulness. I don't think I could ever grow tried of her gratitude.

November 16, 1900   3:50 p.m.

As I lay in bed, the pain increases each day, and so do my doses of laudanum. I have more time to think than ever before. Today I was thinking, "Why did I really come this far north?" Was it all in the name of greed? Or did I have other motives for making this trip? Was I hoping I would find a husband who would take care of me? Was I hoping I could make enough money to support Alex and me as we got older? If Alex and I had the perfect situation working above our very own brothel and being able to openly show our affection, would our relationship flourish? If by some chance a man like Jafet did want to make me his wife, would I be content having one lover in my life, or would I always miss Alex's touch and the delightful way she smells?

My thoughts wandered from myself to my extended family. What drives them to do the things they do and what does the future hold for them? Does J.J. strive for success for the profit, the adventure, or simply to increase his knowledge and his followers seeking his wisdom? Will he make Alex a good husband? If Alex's wishes could really come true, would she wish that people would cry less and smile more, or would she wish herself a life of luxury? Is happiness all that really matters to her? Can one man keep Alex satisfied?

Would Ryan really die for the saloon, or is that just the famous words of a mixologist? Will he ever have his own saloon? Or will he continue sending most of his money to his large family?

Is Dorothy a happy person, or does her smile hide the pain and loneliness she must endure everyday because she lost the love of her life? Will she ever find someone to replace Jime? Will she ever make enough money to buy the home in Idaho she always wanted?

Will Margerie remain a prostitute, or will she find the courage and resources to escape this wicked way of life? Will Natalie be successful in her baby farm and will she cherish every moment with her children?

Will Kuduk continue to work for the alliance and share his knowledge in exchange for theirs?

November 17, 1900   **11:30 a.m.**

I have a lot of time for thinking these days, but it is getting harder to record my thoughts. I saved pounds of gold in Nome. I taught my ladies how to defend themselves. I have turned into a great listener, as well as a great planner. I would even call myself organized. I had to get that way to be efficient. I have in all aspects become a successful madam. I am proud of myself. Jeremy says Mattie Silks, the successful madam he met in Dawson, would be proud of me, too.

November 17, 1900   2:40 p.m.

A young man came to my tent a little while ago with a letter from Jafet. It read:

> *Greetings my love,*
>
> *I have heard that your health is failing. This news breaks my heart. I will not come to see you because I wish to remember you as the beautiful woman I fell in love with. I regret that I never expressed my love for you.*
>
> *Since the first time we laughed together, I wanted to make you my wife. I wanted to wait until I had enough money so we could leave this cold country and start a new life together in California.*
>
> *I sincerely apologize. I will always regret that I didn't share my feelings with you sooner.*
>
> *With all my love always,*
>
> *Jafet*
>
> *P.S. It was very brave of you to tell me about McKenzie.*

All I could do was cry. I'm glad he's not coming to say his goodbyes in person. I like the idea of always being beautiful in his mind. To think I could have been Mrs. Jafet Lindeberg! I would have made him a wonderful wife. I don't know if I'm crying out of sadness or happiness. To know that Jafet dreamed of me being his wife brings a happiness I have never known. To know that dream will never come true breaks what heart I have left.

November 17, 1900   8:00 p.m.

I wonder if *Ben Hur* became my favorite book because I could relate to being a slave from another lifetime? Sometimes I get angry with myself for choosing the easiest path. I could have tried other things. I didn't have to go with Rosa, but at the time I didn't know what else to do. I feel that by choosing this profession, I have become a slave to society and all the ideas it has about a madam.

November 18, 1900   **6:15 p.m.**

Since I first set foot on the golden beaches of Nome I have seen this mining camp grow into a highly populated city. I have seen it destroyed by the wrath of nature. I came here not knowing much about the business and I leave a very knowledgeable woman. This place really isn't so bad. In the whole time I have been here there have only been six murders (including the one I committed). There have been at least five drownings and four suicides. More people have died, and will die, of typhoid fever than from anger. Is that something for a community to be proud of?

I regret I will never get to see what will become of this place. I will never get to see who leaves Nome as millionaires.

I wonder in all of Jeremy's foresight, did he ever think that some of the people in the alliance would not leave Nome?

November 19, 1900   **5:20 a.m.**

As I drift in and out of sleep, I've been thinking about Jafet coming to visit. It brings me much peace to know I will forever remain beautiful in his eyes. I imagine myself as a large cottonwood in mid summer. My green leaves bask in the hot daytime sun while at night they enjoy a cool breeze that whispers them to sleep. I am dying in the summer of my life. I will never know what it's like to have my leaves lose color and wrinkle, or to endure the harsh winter without leaves to protect me. At least this way, I can die with my beauty and family to share the pain.

November 20, 1900   **9:45 a.m.**

I just awoke from a vivid dream. Ria and Jime were both standing in water up to their heads. From the looks on their faces they both seemed very comfortable. Neither one of them spoke a word—they both just looked at me. Jime tipped his head, then turned and walked away, still surrounded in water. Ria mesmerized me with her eyes. As I looked deeper I thought I heard her say,

"Don't be afraid, it is......"

A fight between two chippies right outside my crib interrupted my dream.

November 21, 1900   11:45 p.m.

Yesterday all the members of the alliance brought their brunch plates and chairs into my crib. I was reminded of our first working days in Nome and how we were all just getting to know each other. Unfortunately, I had such a bad coughing spell that everyone was forced to leave before they were done eating. Alex gave me my cough medicine and spoke softly to me. She said since she's taken over the establishment, she doesn't have much time for cards, but she doesn't feel the need for them anymore. Running the business is enough to keep her mind challenged. She spent most of the time talking about J.J. and how he told her just the other night she was indeed the best poker player he had ever met. He said, "A man doesn't stand a chance winning when he is playing cards with you. Between your quick counting, your poker face and your sweet body, a man has trouble staying focused. Even if it wasn't for your distracting looks, you are one damn good card player." Alex no longer feels she needs to compete with men in order to feel respected by them because she has won the heart of the finest one. She cried when she suggested, "I hope you're not dying so that J.J. and I can be together. My heart is big enough for the both of you." We cried for hours in each other's embrace, drowning in sorrow of the loss to come.

We ended the afternoon reassuring each other that this was not goodbye, for we will meet again in another lifetime. Alex says she knew about the Greek and Roman structures and history before she ever read about it. She also believes her soul has experienced the world in that era. She also said, "Mandy, when we meet again in our other lives I will recognize you by your smile." In the last few weeks, she has turned into such a motherly figure. Maybe she will be my mother in my next life.

"When I die, please don't let the grief consume you," I told her. "I know I did, in the life I lived as the mother of a little boy who died in my arms. Hours after my loss I died because I couldn't take care of my own needs. I know that will not happen to you. You are too strong to be consumed by anything other than life itself." Alex encouraged me not to worry about her as tears fell from her eyes. This started both of us crying once again. All I remember after that is falling asleep in her arms. I already miss her gentle touch and precious smell.

November 22, 1900   5:20 p.m.

My whole body hurts and I am very weak. I have the desire to continue recording my thoughts. I feel like it is all I have left. As I lay here slowly dying, I'm thinking that if I'm still alive by the time the ice forms over the Bering Sea, I will walk out to the ice and throw myself in the water. Kuduk says that is what his elders have done for generations so they will not become a burden to their families. It would be nice to choose a day to die. On the other hand, a part of me wants to keep living so I can once again see the magical northern lights dance in the sky to their hidden symphony.

Of all of the memories I hold of this great land, the summer night out by Anvil with the midnight sun behind the northern mountains is still my favorite serene expedition. I have seen many wonders of nature in this Arctic desert, but nothing compares to the grandeur of that evening. I feel like I had to come to this turn-of-the-century gold rush so I could see what my eyes got to behold on the evening of July 22, 1900. If my life is what I must pay in return for that visual gift, I would gladly do it all over again. Thank you, Earth, for the gifts you have given me.

When Alex came to see me after her busy evening I asked her if she would do one last favor for me. I asked her if she could make a point of appreciating the beauty of this unique Northern land. I told her I was afraid the magnificent view might vanish if no one admired it. I don't think Alex really understood what I was talking about but she reassured me she would go out walking as often as I did. I tried to explain that it was more than just walking but I think once she gets out there the land will speak to her just like it did to me. I'm sure Alex has the wisdom within to listen to the land.

November 23, 1900   **12:45 p.m.**

This isolated community fueled by greed seems to bring out
the worst in a person. In reflection, I must admit that each one of
us in the alliance have had at least one breakdown that lasted for
hours or days. J.J. got really drunk one night and accused people
of stealing his gold. Ryan lost his patience and took it out on the
drunks, yelling and cursing. Alex verbally abused the ignorant
asses at the poker table, expressing in detail her opinion of their
woeful lack of skills. Marjerie went into a depression and cried all
day long. Dorothy threw every pot, pan and cooking utensil in the
tent without saying a word. Of course, Natalie showed the worst
side of herself on a regular basis.

I guess the typhoid fever is my breakdown.

November 24, 1900   **4:30 p.m.**

Seeing Rawslin's book *Joan of Arc* on my trunk, a book I will
never return, made me realize how much Mark Twain's literature
has inspired me over my lifetime. His female characters have
helped me learn to have the courage to take risks and not to be
afraid of anything, not even dying.

November 25, 1900   **10:30 a.m.**

I dreamed of birds last night. The birds were small with exotic
feathers and strange shaped feet. They were on the beach and the
sky was painting a picturesque sunset. A white owl swooped down
and they all flew away at the same time. As the birds rose from
the sandy beach, I felt peace and contentment enter my body. I
remembered the day I spread my wings in Seattle and took flight.
I never dreamed I would be gambling with my life. I always
believed the birds were a sign of good luck.

The last thing I remember about this dream was Alex moving a
feather over my naked body, not touching me with the feather, just
gently moving the feather all around me. Then the girl from the
animal dream I had in the winter walked up to me and presented
me her fur coat. She said, "Take this. You will need it. Always
remember if it wasn't for the animals whose lives I took to make

this coat, I couldn't have survived." I wanted to ask her several questions but when I looked up both she and Alex were gone.

November 25, 1900   **2:30 p.m.**

Memories help lessen the pain in my body. My mind is a kinetoscope, like the one in The Belmont, and it keeps playing the same pictures over and over. Instead of dancers I have the pleasure of recalling several experiences I have had with Mother Nature since arriving in the Great Land: the intriguing tundra with its delicate flowers; the beach on a bright sunny day with tiny waves coming ashore; the mighty fall storms that transform the land; the multicolored winter sunrises and sunsets; the dancing northern lights; the magnificent frozen ocean with its varied structures; the beauty of a blizzard and the brightness of the winter sun reflecting on the crusty snow.

Then I see the many unique aspects of springtime in the North: ice rushing to the river's mouth, watercolor hues painted on the ice (or so it appears), the smell of fresh sea water, ice floe hopping, and the many strange sounds ice makes. In my mind, as the tundra awakes from its winter nap, I recall the musk oxen, whale, moose, bear, and the many, many birds.

I see my encounter with the older native women who taught me about picking blueberries. They each, in turn, hug me, leaving my body at peace with itself for the first time in my life. Then I walk into a fog that is so dense I can't see my hand in front of my face. My whole body feels clean and pure when I feel the moisture on my face and hands. It is as if the fog has the power to cleanse my very soul. After minutes of this bliss the wind blows slightly and the thick fog is replaced with light patches of clouds dancing close to the tundra. As I begin to see glimpses of the greenish-brown land surrounding me, I notice there are no birds singing. The only sound I hear is the sound of my heart and soul slowly dying.

I have lived through each of the seasons in this extraordinary northern land and I would be hard pressed to name my favorite. Each has its own unique beauty. I have loved them all and through them I have learned that Sun is indeed the creator of Earth. Without it the earth would be a frozen mass. Therefore I'm thanking the sun, our creator, for the enchanting experiences I have had since coming to Alaska Territory.

Alex has been like the sun to me, for without her I don't know how I could have survived. Each of her seasons has a unique beauty and I still couldn't name my favorite. Thanks Alex for being the greatest love I have ever known.

I am not going to survive. I am not the fittest. Was I a prisoner in my own body because I never had the courage to spread my wings and fly to the heavens? I know now that gambling, mining, and serving the appetite of lust are all very similar. You risk your life for the chance to strike it rich.

November 27, 1900   12:35 p.m.

Each day as I grow weaker and weaker, my last wish is if I am ever born again into another life, I will be lucky enough to be born into a society where women are allowed to use their minds to survive instead of their bodies. I know now that indeed the choices we make for nature and ourselves come full circle. Whoever is out there passing judgment, please forgive me. I did what I had to do to survive.

In Memory of Mandy

A week ago I walked into Mandy's crib. Her diary was lying open on the bed. Right away I knew the "someday" Mandy had talked about finally arrived. She must have followed in the Eskimo tradition of walking out on the ice in search of open water and an end to her suffering.

During the last seven nightcaps we have taken turns reading aloud from Mandy's diary. The bond she spoke of between the alliance grew with each entry. Reliving the last eighteen months of our adventures through Mandy's eyes were the ropes that cinched us together.

Ryan read the last entry with tears in his eyes. After a respectable silence had passed J.J. swore all of us to secrecy about Milroy's wicked scheme. We drew up paperwork making us equal partners in the Belmont Mining Company. We all feel we owe it to Mandy. She left us with clues to where a treasure awaits. Why not profit from her story? Come next summer we will do whatever it takes to recover the gold.

~Alex

Historic Photos with Journal Entries

All photos courtesy of The Carrie M. McLain Memorial Museum, Nome, Alaska

July 3, 1899   **3:15 a.m.**

   It was exciting listening to Jafet Lindeberg tell me how he and his partners
Erik Lindblom and John Bryneston started staking their claims on Anvil Creek
on September 22, 1898. Now they are refered to as the "Lucky Swedes" because
of their Scandinavian backgrounds. With the Lucky Swedes having already
staked the best ground out at Anvil Creek, there has been a lot of resentment and
anger among American miners who feel that only citizens of the United States
should be able to stake mining claims here in Alaska Territory.

June 22, 1899   **5:55 p.m.**

As I write, I am watching the first passengers leave. It is total chaos as people push and shove to get off the ship. I can't believe the remaining water that needs to be crossed to reach the sandy shores. Men too anxious with gold fever to worry about their clothes getting wet are wading the last few yards to the beach, hoping to discover gold before others. Their prospecting is already impeded since the first ship arrived two days ago. No one told me there wasn't a harbor here, but then what did I expect? There has never been a need for one until this gold rush.

June 29, 1899   **4:45 a.m.**

I walked about two miles north this evening, away from the tents and all the people. As I looked back over the speck of civilization, I saw tents spread from the shoreline to the tundra for about two miles along the water. It is as if the people are trying to see how close they can exist next to each other. Of course the real reason is that no one wants to be very far from the establishments.

June 11, 1900   **3:20 a.m.**

Today I spent my free time down on the shore watching four new ships arrive that had all left Seattle on May 12th. I found it fascinating to watch all the hustle and bustle and to hear all the many stories. People say that among the freight that was shipped in today, there was over $10,000 worth of the finest wood bars, bar fixtures, and liquor. It is also rumored that a printing press, a complete banking outfit, including $20,000 in coin and currency for the newly established "Bank of Cape Nome" has arrived. I even saw silver canned goods, without labels scattered all over the shore. I'm sure they will be on sale next week in some mercantile.

July 5, 1900   **5:10 a.m.**

In comparing last year's Fourth of July to this year's, I only see one similarity. Both are holidays, which is a formal excuse to carouse. In contrast, I see numerous differences. Last year, there was only spoken prejudice for the aliens, but this year, if what Oliver says is true, the hatred and greed has expanded to the lower states and McKenzie will be their star performer.

Nome has grown by more than 13,000 to 17,000, depending on who one believes. Newspapers, census agents, common folk, and the Army all have different opinions. It's estimated that last year the population was made up of mostly miners and business-minded people. Now there are a good portion of sporting girls, gamblers, and criminals. It's rumored that this is the wickedest place on the continent, worse that Butte, Montana.

July 6, 1900   **2:50 a.m.**

This place is ridiculous. When the weather is dry as it has been throughout the early part of summer, Front Street is like a dust storm. When the winds really picks up, the sand is as bad as the piercing snow. But it's been raining since yesterday and already the once sandy roadways have turned into rivers of mud. People and horses alike almost drown in the muck just trying to get from one side to the other. The talk in the Belmont this evening was that to be wise, a person must plan their activities so they stay on one side of the street to avoid endangering their lives.

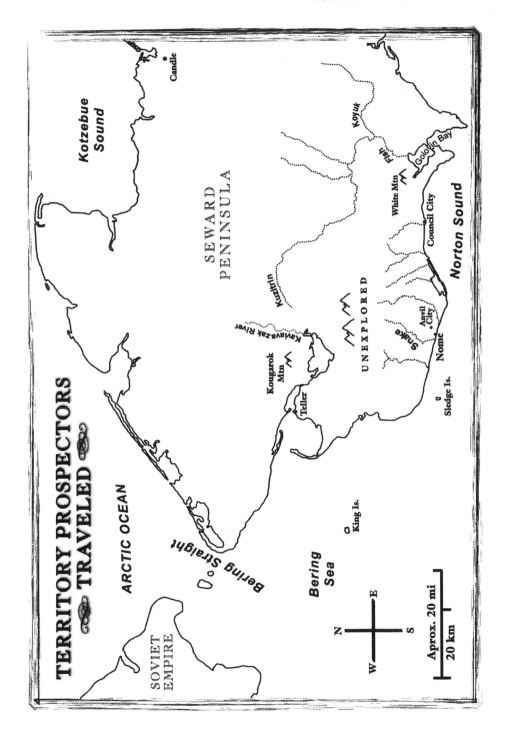

285

Following are the books used in my research:

Blair, Kay Reynolds. *Ladies of the Lamplight*.
Chronicle Publication. *Chronicle of America*.
Cobb, Edward H., *Placer Deposits of Alaska*.
Cole, Terrance. *The History of Gold Rush Nome*.
Cole, Terrance. *Nome: City of the Golden Beaches*.
Erdoes, Richard. *Saloons of the Old West*.
Gruening, Ernest. *An Alaska Reader*.
Hunt, William. *North of 53: Alaska - Yukon Mining Frontier 1870-1914*.
Lillo, Engvald. *The Alaska Gold Mining Company and the Cape Nome Conspiracy*.
McLain, Carrie M. *Gold Rush Nome*.
Martin, Cy. *Whiskey and Wild Women*.
Rutter, Michael. *Upstairs Girls*.
Seagraves, Anne. *Soiled Doves*.
Smith, Duane. *A Colorado History*.
Sprague, William F. *American Women Images and Realities*.
Time-Life Books. *The Old West: The Alaskans*.
Wharton, David. *The Alaska Gold Rush*.